The third book of
THE GUARDIANS SERIES

CHER UBIM

THERESA POCOCK

IMMORTAL WORKS
SALT LAKE CITY

Immortal Works LLC
1505 Glenrose Drive
Salt Lake City, Utah 84104
Tel: (385) 202-0116

Cover Art by Rebecca Barney
barneydesign.com

This book is a work of fiction. Names, characters, businesses, organizations, places, events and incidents either are the product of the author's imagination or are used fictitiously. Any resemblance to actual persons, living or dead, events, or locales is entirely coincidental.

ISBN 978-1-953491-77-0 (Paperback)
ASIN B0CW19S38Z (Kindle)

For Him

CHAPTER 1

SUNDAY
Peter

The sun shone on Peter Miller's face, its magical warmth soaking into him. He stretched, yawned, and splayed himself on the bed like a cat with a belly full of cream; however, at the thought of all that had happened over the last few days and all that he knew was ahead today, that metaphorical cream curdled.

A list intruded upon his mind. He had to help get the Travelers settled. Deal with the tent people, and the influx of their friends heading toward Edenia. Worry about the world in chaos affecting Edenia. The Joneses—his family's enemy of hundreds of years—attacking en masse at this vulnerable time because of the whole Miriam stealing all their men debacle. These were only a few of the weightiest issues.

There was so much more to do than he had time for. Plus, it all seemed precarious. He had allied himself and his family with the soldier part of the Jones team, and he hoped he could trust them. And then there was the matter of Seth, the guy who had betrayed them all by kidnapping his sister Miriam and revealing many secrets to the Joneses. These things were enough to sour any stomach, but Peter had also figured out that Seth's Nature was super important. He was the Revelator of these end times. That Nature was one that could not be dismissed. Even his pa acquiesced to Seth's visions.

Peter's Nature of seeing time and relationships was also important but, in a way, redundant. He hoped having two Guardians that could tell the future might somehow be an advantage.

Pulling his feet from under the blankets, he sniffed and rolled out of bed. He could smell pancakes or rolls or something delicious and was about to open one eye when his Nature took him. It was a violent transfer. One where his mind was yanked from semi-consciousness into darkness, through the ribbon room of time forward, and toward the tapestry of life until all the threads that were human spirits went from a thread to a pillar before him. He saw the Travelers. Their pillars did not precisely lack light, only they were all clustered around one bright white pillar of light: Miriam. Having them grouped helped Peter see something he'd never noticed before.

Miriam's pillar looked like it had hair.

Like tiny splinters of light and darkness that, as he zoomed in close, were thin silken threads sprouting out of Miriam in all directions. They came from elsewhere. He touched one, and his mind pulled him to Gerald's pillar. He touched another and saw Josie, another Karl, another Ben, another Seth, another, another. They made a tangle and pulled all those threads/people closer to Miriam than they should be.

He intuitively knew what it signified—the memories Miriam had taken from these men forced a tentacle to sprout between their pillars. It was the connection they had with one another. Miriam's Nature literally took something from her victims. But if that were so, Miriam's pillar did not have hairs. The other pillars had a tentacle that reached out and connected to Miriam, meaning they did not originate with Miriam. They were just connected to her. That made him shiver. Poor Miriam. No wonder she hated this part of her Nature. It was practically strangleholding her on a deep level—a level she couldn't see but felt.

A difference between the pillars drew his attention. How luminescent Miriam was in comparison to the Travelers. It was not a new thing. All the Guardians were brighter than those mortals around them. As he thought this, his vision pulled back, so the pillars shrank to threads, and Peter saw the point of the weave.

It was here that he understood why the comparison mattered. Just ahead in the weave, those Travelers changed from being different from Miriam in brightness to being the same. This was not a week away. This was hours away. It was their immediate future.

Peter's eyes popped open, and he jumped from his bed. The Jones warriors somehow had to become Guardians, and they had to do it today. It took him only moments to get dressed and race to the kitchen.

"Mama, where is Pa?" he asked his mother, who was up to her elbows in dough.

The woman jumped. "What in heaven's name, Peter Christopher Miller! If I were not covered in flour, I would take a switch to your bottom for scaring me half to death."

"Sorry, Mother. Where is Papa? It is important."

She stopped then and looked at him closely. His demeanor must have convinced her to speak. "He was heading to the barn with Seth Johnson on account of Seth needing to talk to him, and Miriam being here." She whispered the last bit so that Miriam, whose room was not fifteen feet down the hall, would not hear her.

He nodded, said "Thank you," and raced for the door.

As he ran to the barn, he wondered if Seth had beaten him to telling his pa the crazy news. As the Revelator, Seth always had sister-visions to his own, and Peter's competitive Nature did not like having someone tell his secrets before he could.

He saw his papa inside the North barn, sitting on a hay bale, chatting away with Seth. Peter gritted his teeth and slowed his jog.

They watched him approach. Pa rose and took half a dozen steps in his direction, probably concerned that something was wrong.

Peter slowed further so he would have the breath to speak.

"What is it, Peter? Is something wrong?"

"No, Pa," he answered and took the last few steps to his father's side. "Can I speak with you privately?"

"Of course."

Seth took the hint. Turning, his shoulder-length black hair swung back and forth as his long legs carried him in the direction of the orchard.

They watched him get ten yards away, and then Peter started. "I just had the craziest uhm...dream." Peter looked down at the ground, knowing he had not discussed his Nature with his father in detail. He quickly said, "I saw the Joneses become Guardians today."

The blood drained from his father's face. "Miriam's Joneses, the Traveler Joneses?"

"Yes. Though I still like calling them Miriam's warriors better." He said the last of this under his breath.

"Peter, we need to talk about this more particularly. I am the leader here; how am I supposed to utilize you as a tool to protect the Garden if I do not know what you are capable of?"

Anger and fear rose in Peter's belly. He'd already told his pa he could see time. Why wasn't that good enough for the man? He said, "Papa, can we talk about it later? I just told you that I think a bunch of Joneses will become Guardians today. What in the world are we going to do about that, and how in the world are we going to make it happen? I mean, they must do a week's worth of committing in one day. They are hardened, worldly men. How will they change everything about themselves in one day?"

Hirum Miller, his pa and Head of Edenia, massaged his massive jaw as his crystalline blue eyes squinted into the distance, seemingly distracted by the questions.

Thank goodness. Peter didn't want the subject to be turned on him again.

However, his papa spoke. "Peter, you saw them become Guardians? Like in a vision? Like the way Seth does?"

"No!" Peter whined out slowly.

Implacable, his father ignored his wail and moved forward. "Well, explain, my son, because I don't understand what all this means."

Peter sighed, knowing there was no way around this. His gut might be clenching, and his hands might be sweaty, but he had to tell his papa this, or he would keep running into this same problem: he knowing what the Master needed him to know and not being able to tell the man in charge. Peter's eyes glanced up to the sky. It was bright blue. The clouds were thick but scattered in huge pillowy mounds. His mind conjured the memory of three years ago of his ma and pa talking about Miriam and her strange new Nature. He saw how they disliked it, how they were embarrassed by the invasive way Miriam's Nature worked. How they worried about what the Nature meant. He did not want that visual display of his pa's disapproval. Not right now, with so much to do. He would rather have a whipping than be a disappointment as a Guardian.

He looked back at his papa, who was waiting with a penetrating glance and a patient set to his jaw. This was as good a place and time as any. He had his papa all to himself. It wasn't like he had to tell his mama.

It came down to this: would he change his Nature if he could? Peter thought about that as he looked into his papa's eyes, and the answer was instant. No! His Nature, the way it felt, it was like his left arm or his teeth. They were a seamless part of him, and he loved them—well, appreciated them—it was the same with being invisible and seeing time. The only reason he was hesitant was the mutant thing.

He was just going to have to trust his pa.

Peter looked deeply into the man's face and knew right away that his papa would get over it.

Growling and throwing his hands up, he decided to rip the Band-Aid off. With a considerable breath, he began, "It means that I have a huge black room that is almost like my own private universe, where I can see time or something. In this big black room is a ribbon of light and color and energy. I see the tapestry that is life on this Earth; I see pillars of light that ARE us, Guardians, mortals, humans. But Guardians are the brightest of them all. Today I saw Gerald and his friends go from looking like dull human pillars to bright Guardian pillars, and I saw it at the weave of the tapestry." He exhaled the remaining air in his lungs and blinked. Spitting it all out felt like a relief. Then he looked at his father.

The man's eyes bulged, the bright blue irises sweeping from side to side as if he were attempting to access the part of his brain that would allow him to understand Peter's words.

Finally, he breathed out, "You used a lot of comparisons there, my boy; ribbon, tapestry, pillars, light, weave? What does this all mean?"

Peter's impatience at his father's obtuseness tightened the muscles around his eyes.

"Don't you glare at me, young man. You are the one who has kept this to yourself. Now spit it out."

Taking an exaggeratedly deep inhale, Peter explained, "When I fall asleep, instead of being pulled into a dream, I am pulled into a gigantic black chasm, like what you would imagine the blackness and grandness of the universe is. But in this place, the main feature is a ribbon of light and incredibly diverse color that goes on forever in both directions." He lifted his hands, pulling them apart as if he were holding an actual ribbon and was showing the single weave side or the thin side. "When I first saw it, it appeared to be a single thread of light in a sea of black, as it would be if you only saw the skinny side of a ribbon.

"But I can change my perspective. By moving around the thread through the darkness, I can see the colorful, decorative side of the ribbon. From this angle—the multi-thread side—I see a beautiful, intricate pattern of light, dark, and color that is as wide and tall as your mind can imagine. And I guess this is where it might get confusing, because with the change of perspective comes a change of description. It no longer resembles a ribbon but a tapestry, a gigantic tapestry. One so large it holds the history of the world memorialized in threads of color and light. It is wondrous and glorious to behold.

"At the top, just as one can with a tapestry, I can watch as the Gods of the universe blend and mix colors and light, weaving a never-ending display of soul and agency. I can see free will and how it moves people from one place to another on the weft and how it can disrupt the pattern."

His pa's eyes were wide. "Peter, what an incredible gift." His father exclaimed to him with bouncing eyebrows and a trembling grin. "I cannot imagine seeing something so vast."

"It is overwhelming."

"So, you see all you have seen on such a grand scale?"

Peter exhaled again and hung his head, not wanting to go further but knowing he must. "No, not exactly. Well, this next part gets a little complicated." He paused.

"Go on, son. I think I can handle it."

"Okay, well, when I am looking at the tapestry side, I can move my mind closer to the tapestry. Because it's so huge, the closer I get, I understand how small I am in relation. Closer, I can see individual threads. I zoom closer, till not only can I separate the threads one from another, but at that point I'm like a little louse or mite, and the threads are enormous pillars of light all around me. If I concentrate on the pillars, they become individuals. One thread for each person alive. At this point, I exist inside the weave. Is this making sense?"

His father again rubbed away at his jawline, only saying, "Continue."

"If I look in what we would think of as up toward the place of weaving, the pillars go from being solid to being ethereal, and without color, their light dim and almost scattered. They still reach into space in a way I don't understand, like they exist but have no real substance. This is the place of creation, I think. This is the moment before free will. This is the future."

His pa took another deep breath, closed his eyes tight, gnawed on the inside of his cheek, and then looked down at him. "So, you have the tapestry, which is the past. You can look at the pillars. Is that like the present, and the ethereal part, the future?"

"Yes! Wow, Pa, great summarization. But one correction, I call the part where the threads are physically getting weaved the present. When I pull my vision tight, I am at the weave, so 'in' the present."

"So, like when you saw me die?" His father asked and left that hanging.

"Okay, that was in the future. I saw the ethereal part of your thread end. Time cut your thread, and you stopped being part of the weave."

"Were you watching my weave? How did you know to look into the future?"

"The Master, I suppose." Peter frowned and shook his head. "I really have very little say about which part of the weave I'm attracted to, or which pulls my attention."

"Fascinating, Peter." His father smiled a tight smile at him. "That isn't what I thought I would hear, but it is fascinating." His father further questioned, "So, with the Travelers?"

Peter bit his cheek. "Well, with the Jones warriors, it seemed obvious. I saw them change. They were one thing..." Peter recalled the Jones warrior's pillar's dimness of countenance and how they changed to light in the future portion of the weave. "...but I can see they have become something different at the tapestry's weave."

"Which means today."

"Today!"

"Do you get impressions with the vision?"

"Yes. So, when the Joneses kidnapped Miriam, I saw her thread get pulled from the Edenia grouping of threads to a place of darkness. And it was almost as if I heard her screaming. I knew she was in trouble, in pain. I knew things had not gone in the optimal direction, but the weave took it in stride. Then all of us swooped in and fixed it."

His papa looked at Seth. "Unfortunately, I don't know if anything can fully fix that. Once someone has betrayed themselves..." Hirum sniffed and looked down at his son. "Let it be a lesson. There are some things you can't take back. You can receive forgiveness, but sometimes the damage is done, and that can last forever."

"What are you saying, Papa?"

"I'm saying..." He shook his head and pushed his fingertips into the corners of his eyes, then shook his head again. "I don't know what I'm saying, Peter."

Peter didn't know what his pa was fretting about, but he did know they needed to get back on task. "Papa, if you're done questioning me, can we please focus? There are twenty-plus scary warrior men out there who need to become Guardians. We need a battle plan."

His papa pulled off his hat and scrubbed his fingers through his hair, glancing around the barnyard. Peter watched him anxiously and saw the moment the man's eyes landed on Seth. "We do, don't we? I hate to say it, but I'm fresh out of plans, so let's just ask our Revelator." He nodded and plopped his hat back on. "Yes, that is exactly what we will do. Seth!" his pa called out. "Seth, come here, son."

"Pa, why are you fraternizing with the enemy? I mean, I know he's one of us now and all, but he kidnapped Miriam, drugged her, and gave her over to the Joneses. Do you have to be so nice to him, call him son, et cetera?" As many emotions crossed the man's face, Peter kept his eyes on his father. However, he didn't respond to Peter's question, and then Seth was there.

The dark-haired, dark-eyed boy caught Peter's glance. His face was full of contrite wrinkles, which made Peter instantly annoyed. He wanted to hate Seth when he was away from the guy, but Seth was so miserable and penitent, and Peter knew precisely how real those emotions and regrets were. He'd touched Seth's pillar, been pulled into it where he saw the plethora of memories and emotions that were Seth's soul. His mind had condensed that knowledge now, but it did not matter. He could not hate Seth; he understood and empathized with him too well.

Peter sighed.

"Seth," his pa said, side-eyeing Peter with displeasure, "why is it that you call the Joneses warriors Travelers?"

This question surprised Peter. That was not what they were talking about.

Seth kicked at the dirt. "I have no idea, really. It's the name that came to me when I saw them all together on the hill last night."

Peter wanted to butt into the conversation with his questions, but his papa went on, "So you don't know why they are here? Or really anything about them?"

Seth shook his head. "Not yet."

And again, even though Seth knew nothing about Peter's gift, Peter wanted to butt in and tell him what he'd seen. It was a strange urge.

He looked at his father sheepishly. "Before this morning, the only thing I have seen regarding the Travelers was about that meeting on the hill." Seth ran his hands through his hair, his face once again doing that pathetic you-should-feel-sorry-for-me thing. "I am new at this. I have no clue if I am doing it right."

"We all feel that way at the beginning, don't we, Peter?" His papa said, and took Seth by the shoulder.

Peter did not answer. It took quite a bit of willpower not to blurt out everything, all his secrets to Seth, and the feeling was highly uncomfortable.

"Well, Seth, Peter, you boys have brought me different perspectives of the same event, I think. So, it seems we need to discuss it in more detail. But can we please do it over a plate of hotcakes? I'm famished."

CHAPTER 2

The sound of her mother calling her name and the smell of freshly baked bread opened Miriam's eyes. She pushed the loosened strands of blonde hair out of her face and turned toward the door. Her mother stood there waiting for Miriam's reply.

She blinked her eyes and said, "Yes, mother?"

"My dear, you need to get up and ready for the day. You have thirty burly men waiting to see you, and they need to be fed."

Miriam shot up, smacking her lips and brushing her braid out of the way. She made fast work of her morning essentials and found herself in the kitchen in no time. Five other women were in her mother's kitchen, each wrist deep in some kind of food item.

"What can I do to help?" Miriam asked no one in particular.

Her mother found her, "Nothing at the moment except go out to the front and calm all the men waiting to see you."

The kitchen went silent as the women looked at Miriam, uncertain of what this all meant.

Miriam blinked into the silence and felt the necklace of scars she'd received at the hand of Willis Jones, and which she'd covered with a button-up blouse of ivory. Her life had taken a drastic turn for the worse only a day ago when she had been kidnapped by the boy she was falling for, and she was tortured all because her Nature was to take memories. Now, she had an army of Jones defectors she had stolen memories from waiting on her.

She turned away from her mother and headed toward the front door. After carefully closing the screen door, Miriam turned at the sound of talking going quiet. Off her porch, filling her small front lawn, were thirty gnarly, tattooed, unshaven, bemuscled warriors, all previously employed by Willis Jones. As one, they left chairs behind and surged toward her.

"Miriam." The name out of many mouths came at her like a flood. Many girls would be frightened at the sight, but this was a good flood. It was a flood that swept away the debris in her life. She could no longer deny that she had a piece of these men inside her. A bit of their soul. A portion of their memories. Their life.

She could no longer be ashamed about what her Nature did, that she was a thief. Everyone would know before this day was over anyhow.

She went to them as eagerly as they moved toward her.

The first to her side was a de facto leader and her favorite Jones, Gerald. He'd saved her on two separate occasions. He was a huge, bald man with small flag tattoos on his knuckles. She touched his arm and smiled up at him; the intimacy of the conversation they'd had the night before—where she admitted to having pieces of all the people she'd taken memories from inside her—thrummed between them. Miriam hadn't told a single other person that she carried soul slivers. Only Gerald.

"This is really weird," she whispered and felt her cheeks warm.

Gerald answered. "It is weird for us as well. We can talk more about it after you meet all the men. They are on edge." He emphasized the last few words, and it helped Miriam understand his meaning. She owed these men many things, and first of all, an explanation. She swallowed her fear of exposing herself, but knew she had to.

As Gerald introduced the men, Miriam looked each man in the face, repeated each name, and touched each man on the arm or shoulder.

Once things settled down, Miriam took a deep breath and returned to Gerald, who helped her move to the porch. All the Joneses stood before her. She cleared her throat and began.

"First, thank you so much for your role in freeing me from

Willis." She paused and touched her scars. "I do not know what I would have done without your help." She smiled at them, and they smiled back. Swallowing back her fear, she said, "Something has happened between us—you and me. I did something to you. I took something from you."

Eyebrows crinkled and glanced around. She hoped this would not end badly. She was defenseless here, in front of all these brutal men.

Gerald must have sensed her emotions, for he took her hand and nodded for her to go on.

Encouraged, she blurted out the truth. "In this place, we all have powers. We use them to protect something sacred. My power is one of the mind. With it, I took a memory from you, one where you saw something you should not see. I do not exactly know how, but those memories, those pieces of your soul, are inside of me. Because of them, I can feel each of you, and you can feel me. I'm sorry. At the time, I thought it was the right thing to do. I do not know if I can return them to you, but I will try."

The group was silent. Many mouths were hanging open. Many unasked questions caused squinting eyes.

Gerald spoke. "Men, we all know what these people are protecting. That secret cannot get into the world; it would cause mayhem. I think Miriam was doing her job to keep us from finding those secrets out."

She nodded. "Yes, that is exactly it."

Gerald looked over at her and continued. "We all know what lengths we have gone to on the job to keep secrets," Gerald said, and Miriam could tell he was attempting to sway those who might be upset by the information.

Finally, someone from the crowd called out. Miriam found his face. It was Karl. "But why? Why do we feel this protectiveness toward you? So, you have a bit of my soul in you." He finger-quoted 'soul.' "What does that have to do with the price of rice?"

"I do not know, exactly."

"Can I answer that?" Gerald asked the group, surprising everyone.

Miriam nodded, as curious as Karl.

"I think it might be self-preservation. Inside our bodies, we do extreme things to protect our own cells. Perhaps the soul is the same way. We need to protect what is ours, and as of now, part of us lies within Miriam."

Karl and many others nodded, placated.

"How do we get it back?" A man with a very raspy voice asked. It was Ben.

Miriam smiled. "I do not know. But please trust me that I am going to find out."

"So, what do we do now?"

"Yeah, Willis ain't going to take this little desertion kindly."

Miriam looked toward Gerald. The man stepped up beside her. "That is a personal choice. But I myself am going to stay next to Miriam. I am going to respect the rules they have here. And"—he paused, looked down at the ground, swallowed, then looked up into the eyes of his men—"and then, I'm going to become a Guardian."

That caused all the men to shift in their boots. Several called out. "What do you mean?" "A guardian?"

Miriam turned wide eyes toward Gerald.

He glared down at the men. "You saw! The vision we got when we were called here by that girl with swirling eyes. Don't stand there and pretend you don't know what's happening here and that you didn't see what you saw. That you haven't felt and known this comes next. I had the same vision you did. Whatever power is out there in the universe wants us here with Miriam, with these people, helping them in their work, and by coming here, even though a tornado tried to stop you, you acknowledged your part in all this."

The men settled down instantly.

There was something about Gerald. There was something about his way of speaking, of laying out the truth, of verbal bravery that

Miriam admired. Right then and there, she knew she needed him; he would be an example of how she needed to act.

Richard, a man with a tattoo of an eagle covering the front of his neck, including his Adam's apple, said loud enough for all to hear. "I personally have seen some extra crazy goings on, and I have determined that only God or aliens could make this kind of thing happen. I'm staying. Whatever comes. I'm staying."

"Me too." Miriam heard from the back of the group. It was Remy.

"I'm staying," Ben said.

"And me," Nate commented.

"That means you'll have to stop looking at porn, Nate," Richard jeered.

Nate was quick on the comeback as Miriam's cheeks flushed. "And Ben will have to stop smoking, and you'll have to stop cussing, and Gerald will have to stop snorting. We all have our vices and can't do them here."

Trent stepped forward. "But why? Why are you doing this? I mean, I saw the vision; it didn't make me forget that I'm a human with wants, needs, and plans. I feel Miriam, but that doesn't mean I don't feel other things. Why are we doing this?"

Sam said from the back, "Not to mention Willis. You know he won't let us go without a fight. He still has twenty or so men with him."

"And one of them is Frank."

"And Les."

There was a physical shiver that went through the crowd. Miriam felt it too. Les had branded her. He was heartless. He was evil.

Gerald let them marinate. Miriam watched as he eyed his men. Finally, he took a deep breath. "You're right. This will be hard. It is a huge sacrifice, but aren't we used to sacrifice? Don't you remember how you felt in training? Like that feeling of having a purpose. Of saving people. Of being the guardian of freedom. Do you remember?"

He waited and was rewarded. The men all nodded, a look of bygone purpose in their eyes.

"Well, I traded my country—that let me down—for Willis, who turned out to be a monster. Now I can forsake my pledge to protect and serve, or I can become a new guardian of this place." He looked around Edenia, past the faces of his men. "Can you feel it?" He whispered to them. "This place is different. It's sacred. Can you feel that?" He pounded on his chest to emphasize. "I can tell you one thing for sure; I know good when I see it. I have been around every kind of bad, so when I see good, I know it. And this place, these people...are good."

"Besides being supernatural in power," Karl added with wonder.

"Yes, and so if I can be a part of something good and magical, how could I say no, especially when the getting here was so personal?" He looked over at Miriam and touched her. "We individually were chosen. We were the ones who were called. We were the ones who had our memories taken. We were meant to be here. So, choose."

At that moment, Miriam's mother and many other ladies exited the home, hands full of plates of food. "Your breakfast is served, gentlemen," she stated as she walked through the crowd of Joneses, the smell of sweet cream and pancakes following behind her.

Miriam asked her Aunt Sarah if anything was left inside that she could bring out. The woman shook her head and said, "You look pale. Why don't you just sit down and eat with the men?"

Her stomach growled loudly at that exact minute. So she nodded. Turning, she searched the wooden tables someone had set up in her front yard for a place to sit when her eye fell upon three men coming up the road.

Before her mind fully acknowledged she was seeing Seth, her gut twisted, her heart sped up, and that inside sense, the one she now knew was connected to the soul slivers she had inside her, those pieces of her knew it was him.

Once her mind caught up, her eyes were immobilized by him, her gaze locked. Cold grief and hot anger raged within her heart, like two hurricanes with opposing winds battering at one another.

The men continued walking, chatting, unaware of her. They moved closer and closer to her home as Miriam remained frozen on the spot. She did not know what to do, or if she could do anything.

She sank down to the porch steps, her hands clinging to the porch spindles, her breath stopping, her heart thundering. He was close now, just outside her gate. Seth looked up. Tears sprang to her eyes as her heart clenched in her chest. Why, oh, why did he have to be so beautiful? He saw her. Their eyes met.

Miriam grasped the railing and somehow pulled herself upright. She stumbled backward, still unable to look away. Seth's face crumpled, and that was it. Clutching at her chest, she ripped her gaze from his, then turned and fled into the house.

CHAPTER 3

Seth's mind went back to the vision he'd had of seeing Miriam face to face. How she'd shrank from him. How she'd held onto her papa. Meeting Miriam's eyes in that vision felt more like a dagger to both their hearts but for different reasons. But this...

The reality of her eyes, her hurt, her terror, ripped at him so much more than he imagined. If he could hide under a rock, he would.

He could get lost in the guilt, but he remembered the feelings in his bed this morning. The sense of forgiveness, of peace. He knew he could do nothing about Miriam's pain on his own.

Still, he saw the hurt in her eyes. He would have to stay away from her.

Seth stopped walking, and Peter and his father looked back at him questioningly. "Hirum, I can't come in." He touched the fence surrounding the Miller's yard and glanced around at the faces of the Travelers eating their breakfast. "I am going to have to stay away from Miriam."

Peter gave him a sardonic look. "Scared you'll have to pay for what you've done?"

"Peter!" Hirum chided.

"What? The truth hurts, and Miriam is scary." Peter said to the side.

"I know you don't want to hear this, but I can't hurt her any more than I already have. I never wanted to hurt her in the first place." He could not meet Hirum's eyes. "Let's just talk later."

"But we need to know what to do about the Joneses," Hirum said with a lowered voice to not be heard by said Joneses sitting not five feet away shoveling in pancakes.

Seth nodded. "I will let you know the moment I know anything."

"But do you not think that being here, with the Joneses near you and us talking about it, might help with that?"

"Papa, you are hungry; go eat. I'll stay with Seth."

"No," Seth stated. "You both go eat. I will..." Seth blinked, and between one heartbeat and the next, he was taken from his current reality into a new reality, a future reality.

Seth was on the bank of the Eden river. So was everyone else. This was the same vision from this morning. It was frightening. Still, the vision continued. He looked into the water and saw the Travelers. He saw Edenians standing over them in the water. He saw the Travelers struggle. He saw them kick. He saw them being held down by an Edenian. He knew inside himself that the Travelers died there in the water. He saw the Edenians murder them.

Seth shook and violently pulled himself out of the vision. His exit was rough enough that Hirum's hand shot out to steady him.

"Seth! Are you okay?" Hirum stepped closer, putting both hands on Seth's shoulders.

He shook his head, hoping to shake the violence of the vision from him, and then nodded. "Yes. I'm fine."

Peter butted in, "You had a vision."

Seth found Peter's eyes. "Yes," he whispered.

Peter's brow wrinkled, his intuitive yellow eyes seeing more than Seth wanted him to see. "It was not a good vision."

"No." Seth bit his lip and spoke. "I take it back. I will stay. We need to talk. But can we sit somewhere private, with a low chance of seeing your daughter?"

Hirum nodded and led Seth and Peter into the yard toward a table with empty seats. They pulled these to the side yard away from everyone, returned for food, and sat in relative solitude. The two Millers filled their mouths with breaded goodness. Hirum looked at

Seth, his eyebrows asking the question his mouth had not gotten to yet.

Seth inhaled and whispered what he saw. Before Peter interrupted, he'd already told Hirum some of this, but he emphasized the violence of this second vision.

With each word, Hirum's face drained of blood, but it was Peter who spoke. "Papa." He looked sheepishly at Seth as if he did not want to say what he was going to say in front of him. "What we talked about earlier." His eyebrows went up in expectation.

Hirum squeezed his jaw in a thoughtful gesture. "I suppose it could happen that way."

"It would require a lot of trust."

"Way more trust than most people gain in a week."

Peter countered quickly, "Yes, but perhaps they have a special mission that takes more trust than normal."

Seth butted in. "What is happening here?"

Hirum looked over at his son, who shook his head slightly. The man turned back to Seth. "We have some information that indicates the Joneses must be made into Guardians on a very accelerated timeline."

Seth thought about this information in light of what he had just heard, "And you think that..." he whispered, "drowning them is how it is to be accomplished?"

"I don't think that, Seth, you just revealed it to us."

"As per your job as a Guardian," Peter added with a touch of condescension.

"So, we just are going to kill a bunch of men?" Seth asked in a disgusted whisper.

"No, we're going to turn them into Guardians," Peter said with a smile. Like he was looking forward to murder. He took a massive bite of his toast and asked, "So, who's going to tell them?"

CHAPTER 4

Miriam watched through the window. Her father and Peter talked to Seth as if he had done nothing wrong, as if he were just another Guardian. She could not stop the tears or control her breath. Lightheaded, she turned to sit on the couch, then noticed Josie and Todd standing in the doorway of her living room, watching her.

The moment she saw them, they both came to her, Josie with a big hug. Todd squeezed her hand. It melted her. She'd forgotten how this felt, to have people who cared. To have friends.

She heard Josie whisper, "I'm so sorry, Miri. This is my fault."

"This is our fault," Todd added, and he pushed the hair out of Miriam's face so he could look into her eyes as she cried on Josie's shoulder.

Miriam didn't know what they were talking about, but she didn't care. Feeling the comfort of arms around her after so long being denied felt wonderful. She looked into Todd's amazing turquoise-green eyes and let the tears roll down her nose.

Finally, she pulled away. Todd still had her hand in his, but it was Josie who spoke. "I have to say something, Miriam." She sniffed, and Miriam looked at her friend. Her face was just as tear-soaked as Miriam's was. "I can't help but feel responsible for this. If I had been there for you as a best friend should, you never would have gotten close to Seth. This would have never happened if I had been eating lunch with you and hanging out with you after school."

Miriam was shocked by this admission. "No. No, this isn't your fault. It was mine. I know now that I separated myself from you as much as you separated yourself from me. I was ashamed about what had happened"—Miriam added stiltedly, not wanting to bring up a difficult subject—"when my Nature took me."

"It wasn't your fault. You didn't know what was happening. It was out of your control, the same way my wind Nature is out of mine. I just..." Josie grew uncomfortable. She let go of Miriam and sat on the couch.

"Just tell her," Todd said in an impatient tone.

Miriam looked between the siblings. "Tell me what?"

Josie wrestled with herself for a few more moments before she found a way to say what she needed. "I heard what you were saying to the Joneses out there."

Miriam considered confused, and then she froze. With huge eyes, she looked at Josie and said, "Oh my gosh. You..."

"Yes. I thought I was some kind of mutant at first. I thought I was obsessed with you. I thought... I don't know what I thought. All I knew was I knew where you were, always. I could point to you with my eyes closed."

"We made a game of it, actually," Todd smiled.

Blood drained from Miriam's face. "Who's we?"

Josie reassuringly touched her arm, "No, just Todd and me. Do you think I'd tell anyone else I had a Miriam radar in my head? They would think I was a mutant."

Miriam wiped the residue of tears off her cheeks and sniffed. "So, you feel the same way about me as the Joneses do?"

"I think so," Josie said her tone rising with uncertainty. "I sort of think about you all the time, not in a weird way, in like a worried way. Like you're my kid or something, and I always know where you are. It's been hard on me. I sort of hated you and my own head for a while."

"Well, that would make me really weirded out and angry as well, especially since we didn't know what was happening."

Josie looked down at her hands and dry-washed them before looking back up at Miriam, her bottom lip in her mouth. "I keep thinking that. What if I had said something? What if I had told you? There are a million what-ifs in my head."

Miriam considered this and acknowledged that this piece of information could very well have made an enormous difference. If they knew that whoever Miriam used her Nature on would know where she was, they probably would never have done it to the Jones men.

Josie interrupted her thoughts. "Do you think you can make it go away?"

Todd jumped in, "We just heard you talking to the Joneses out there. It never occurred to us that it could go away, but now that we heard you say that, we've been talking about it, and it seems like..."

"It would just be nice to not have you in my head." Josie smiled as kindly as she could. "Not that I couldn't live with it if I had to, but..."

Miriam smiled and rose, "No, I get it. You don't have to explain." She turned away from them and walked back over to the window. Seth was gone. Only her pa and Peter remained, downing pancakes like it was the end of the world.

Todd come up behind her. She turned around and was practically nose-to-nose with him. He stepped back, smiled, and said, "Sorry."

She stepped back as well and looked up at the handsome boy who had been her crush for practically her whole life. His messy strawberry blond hair, angular bright green eyes, and smattering of freckles across his nose made her lick her lips nervously.

"Miri, I wanted to admit something as well. I think your Nature was super cool. I mean, I wanted to think that. What would it be like to have a friend capable of erasing all my mistakes?" He gave her a huge smile. "Like that time I spilled milk down the front of my clothes, and I hadn't done my chores the night before, so I didn't have any extra pants, and my Ma said I could wear the milk all day as a lesson to always do my washing. I would LOVE to not have that day in the old noggin anymore."

"Or like the day I told Greyson I was in love with him." Josie stood and came over to them with a big smile. Her hands went to her cheeks as they flamed red at the memory. "I would love to not remember that." She laughed.

"We used to play the game of what we wish we didn't remember."

Again Miriam asked, "Who's we?"

The siblings looked at one another. "All of us," they said together.

Todd added. "I think many of us were jealous of your Nature."

Miriam thought for ten seconds before asking, "Then why?"

She left the question open. Knowing they wouldn't have an answer if they didn't understand her question.

"Why did we not let it go and talk to you about it?" Todd asked.

Josie took her hands. "At first, we were all a little scared."

"The way we are with Peter," Todd added.

"Yes, but Miriam, you didn't make it any easier for us. Please don't be mad. I have to tell you the truth while I can. You know that is how we do it in my family."

It was true. Miriam loved that about Josie's family; they were open with one another and talked about everything honestly. Still, her words shook Miriam to the core.

Todd sidled up even closer to her. "You were so sad. So standoffish. You wouldn't look at us. You wouldn't come over unannounced. You wouldn't plop yourself down at our usual lunch table like normal."

"You stopped answering questions in school. And arguing with our teachers."

"You quit hanging out. And coordinating our chore schedules."

"You just sort of disappeared. I thought it would go away, that you would get over it. But you didn't."

Miriam felt a sinking in her stomach. They hadn't chased her. But she hadn't chased them either.

The tears welled up again. Had her lonesomeness over the last three years been self-inflicted? Had she hated herself that much?

This time it was Todd who wrapped her in his arms. He included

Josie, so it wasn't entirely inappropriate. But the feel of his arms, his, around her felt so wonderful that she had a hard time focusing her mind on what she had just figured out about herself.

If she hated herself for her Nature, no wonder other people felt like they did. Peter, her mother, and her friends took their cue from her actions. That was quite a bit to take in.

Todd interrupted her quiet ponderings. "There is another reason I would gladly let you take my memories." He pulled away from the embrace, gazed at her, and smiled.

"Oh?" Miriam asked, a bit dazzled by his expression.

"Yes, I feel like you've always been in my mind as it is. It might be nice to have a legitimate connection. One I can understand."

"You understand this?" Miriam asked and waved her hand between Josie and herself, indicating their connection.

He gave an amused humph. "Yes, I suppose I do. At least I understand it better than what I have always felt here"—he put his hand over his heart—"where you are concerned."

Miriam felt her cheeks burn. She looked at Josie, who smiled knowingly, warming Miriam down to the soles of her feet. The girl squeezed Miriam's hands and moved to the window, where she studiously proceeded to ignore them.

"Miriam." Todd drew her attention back. "I have to..." He licked his lips and took in a deep breath. "I need to know why your parents chose Foster to be your..." He paused yet again and glanced at his sister before whispering, "intended."

Miriam blinked at him. Was this really happening? She shook her head and looked into his eyes. "I...

Looking back into his eyes, finished, "...I don't know. Probably because they knew I had a history with you, and that Josie and your family hated me."

Josie burst in, "We never hated you."

Todd confirmed, "We never hated you!"

"We were just a bit nervous. And you cut us off instead of talking to us." Todd sliced a hand through the air at his sister and gave her a shake of his head.

He looked back at Miriam, and his forehead wrinkled with concern. "We just didn't understand."

"But you understand now?" Miriam asked, trying to understand herself.

"We have for a while. We all know that it is just your Nature."

"Your standing up to the Elders was like the first time we saw signs of the old Miriam. We hoped that meant you had stopped feeling sorry for yourself." Josie blurted out, then returned to examining the window curtains.

Todd took her shoulder and turned her toward him. "We thought it was the excuse we needed to prove we were still your friends if you would let us in. But that is not the point. The point is, I want to still be considered. I talked to Foster, and he is fine with it. He even said, 'may the best man win.'" Todd rolled his eyes. "You know Foster. Competitive. I also talked to your father and asked to be reconsidered. I hope that is okay."

Miriam felt her brain about to swirl out of control. What in the world was happening here? Was she in some alternate universe? A universe where the boy of her dreams wanted her. Where more than one boy wanted her and was competing for her. Where her friends actually had been her friends the whole time, but they were waiting for her to get over herself. She shook her head as an entirely different life passed before her eyes. A life where she acted utterly differently and had a totally different present.

"Miriam?" Todd asked and attempted to capture her glance.

She shook her head again, "What did he say?" she asked unsteadily.

"That it was up to you."

Miriam nodded. "I'm really stunned right now. I don't know what to say." She smiled, and at that moment, her father, Gerald, and Peter entered the living room.

Her pa assessed the situation very quickly. "Ah, I see Todd has told you the good news."

Miriam smiled at her father. A raising of the corners of her mouth. She knew the smile did not touch her eyes. "Yes, Papa," Miriam recalled the look her pa had given her the afternoon she'd taken Seth's memories. How he had beguiled her by promising Seth would be considered in the list of her suitors if they both wanted that. She shivered. Her pa allowed Todd back on the list as a Band-Aid for losing Seth.

An exciting thought occurred to her: if she did not use her Nature that way, did she need a babysitter? Were all her parents' reasons for marrying her off at sixteen moot now? The prospect excited her.

Her pa's voice interrupted her ponderings. "Good, good. Well, Josie and Todd, we have some business to discuss. Would you mind helping with putting away the chairs and tables outside? Also, Josie, you are on interference duty in what...?"

"Thirty minutes," Josie answered.

"Take that job seriously, my dear. The Joneses, I am sure, are not taking kindly to us having so many of their employees here."

"Of course," Josie answered.

As they moved to leave, Todd gave Miriam a beautiful smile, a smile that showed just how much he really cared. Josie hugged Miriam, kissed her cheek, and whispered in her ear. "I would love us to be sisters." It shocked Miriam to the core.

A warm sensation grew in her middle. What would it be like to be connected to people who were so forthright with their feelings? They were so open with their honesty. As the duo left the room, she smiled back at them and tried to let it display all she felt.

Then her father spoke. "We need to talk."

"Okay, Papa. But will it take long? Breakfast cleanup is happening, and I didn't help prepare. Mama has been working hard, and I would hate to not do my part."

Her pa cleared his throat. "Uhm, no, I don't think it will take too long." He gestured toward the couch. They all sat except her pa, who was rubbing his hands together and would not meet Gerald's eye.

Peter had a similar demeanor.

She looked over at Gerald, and he looked at her. She gave him an I-have-no-idea-what-this-is expression and lifted a shoulder. After a full five seconds of no words, she exploded. "Papa, what is it?"

He must have been scared into speaking by her tone because he immediately began to talk.

"Gerald. As you know, we have a few new members to the Guardians, the Johnson family."

"Yes," Gerald said with ascending decibels and a sideways glance in Miriam's direction. "And?"

"And, well, we always do a bit of an initiation for those people. It's the story of our origins, followed by those people taking an oath."

"Sounds interesting."

"Yes, it's a wonderful tradition and important for all young Guardians. To feel included, you understand."

"Well, wonderful." Gerald's chin went down, and he leveled Hirum with his very intimidating gaze, waiting.

Miriam was astonished at her father. She had never seen him act this way. What on Earth could be wrong?

When Hirum did not go on, Gerald looked at Peter. "Li'l Boss, what's going on here?"

Peter scratched his cheek and said, "Gerald, you need to be sure you and your men want to be here. I mean, like be here permanently, be on our side, help us out, be committed and willing to live the life expected. Because tonight we will tell you everything, and then you are getting initiated into our club. But because of your particular circumstances, that initiation will be atypical."

"Atypical?"

"Yes."

"How so?"

Peter licked his lips and leaned forward, eyeing the man. Then he nodded and blurted out. "It's going to be violent and scary and test you to the very ends of your strength."

Gerald blinked at Peter as if he wanted to say, Excuse me? To his credit, he did not. He only tongued his teeth and glanced at Miriam. Then he swooshed his lips to the side as he looked out the window at his men. Finally, he said, "Okay. Thanks for the warning."

Peter smiled at him. "No problem."

Hirum shook his head at his son, and Miriam knew what the man was thinking. Peter wouldn't live past fifteen; someone would kill him for his stupid, brave mouth.

Gerald stood. Nodded and then exited the house without another word.

"Peter! How could you just blurt it out like that?"

Peter looked aghast. "Well, you weren't saying anything! Besides, Gerald and I have an understanding. There's trust between us. I had to. And it's not like I told them the details." He sat back into the couch and crossed his leg. "I couldn't repeat what Seth saw. It is too graphic." The boy shivered.

Miriam wondered what they were talking about but was distracted by the feeling of imaginary sewing needles piercing her heart.

Seth.

Her hand went to her chest, and she ignored the conversation between Peter and her papa. It was a real possibility that she could never talk about or see him without having a negative, painful reaction.

It confused her because people had said the "Joneses" around her plenty of times, and it did nothing. Yet they were the ones who'd actually tortured her. She squeezed her eyes shut at the memory.

They had hurt her physically and psychologically. She hated them, and she would probably melt into a puddle of fear if she ever saw her tormentors again. But Seth—even her mind stumbled over the name—he had lied to her. He told her he loved her after he drugged her, which was a manipulation of the acutest kind. He pretended to take her on a date and then handed her over to the Joneses to be tortured, which was the ultimate betrayal.

He might as well have held the branding instrument himself.

Her face flushed as anger and hurt boiled inside her. Her eyes clouded, and her nose ran.

She turned away from her pa and Peter to clear up the mess of her emotions before they saw.

"Miriam, are you okay?" her pa asked the moment she moved.

Miriam took a deep breath that ended with a sniffle and said the first thing that came to her mind. "Sounds like the two of you need to coordinate so that you can stop causing contention." She wiped at her eyes, turned to them, and continued, "You don't need me in this conversation. I'm going to go clean something."

As she walked away, she heard her father say, "That is not a bad idea, Peter. You and Seth should work together. It seems that when you do, we get things figured out. Besides, two witnesses are better than one."

Miriam felt as if she'd been kicked in the solar plexus.

CHAPTER 5

The slightly musty fragrance of the chapel, or "Divided Hall," pulled at Seth's thoughts, his mood full of self-loathing and impatience. As he sat on a pew, leaned forward with elbows on his knees, fists holding up his chin. The huge latticed panel that divided the Divided Hall brought his mind to Miriam.

He could still see the violet of her eyes and the blonde of her hair through the tiny holes of the patterned wood. The way woodsy familiarness filled the space made him ache. The very first time he'd met her, or noticed her actually, Miriam had organized his chaos in two seconds flat. He recalled how the very spirit within her showed through the vast partition and sprinkled a little fairy dust on his burdened heart. He felt indebted to her before he even knew who she was.

Then he thought about the look in her eyes when she'd seen him today. He moved his head so that his fists dug into his eye sockets. He pressed hard, wishing he could unsee what he'd seen. He wanted so much to take back the last two days. He thought of when he'd dumped the drugs into her soup. The feelings he'd had before. The peace. The surety that he could trust Edenia, his parents...Miriam.

His chest felt tight.

He'd screwed everything up.

Just as he thought he might lose it and cry like a baby, someone sat beside him. He looked over to see Peter.

"Hey," Peter said.

"Hi," Seth answered, reining in his emotions.

Silence for about thirty seconds.

"So, I'm just gonna say something."

"I figured."

Peter took a deep breath. "My Nature, uhm, I need to talk about it with someone, and I get the feeling you are the person who needs to hear about it."

Crinkling his eyebrows at the younger boy, Seth asked, "Why in the world would I need to hear about that?" He blinked and, in that in-between moment, Seth was transported to that other sight where he saw Peter telling Hirum that he'd had a dream as Seth stood by his future self, eager with anticipation over this dream of Peter's. Seth was perplexed. Was Peter also having visions, only they came in the form of a dream?

He blinked the vision away and focused on Peter, who stared at him, watching him with an expression of understanding.

"So, it just happens like that, huh? Man, I wish it were that way with me."

Seth needed clarification. "Sorry, what?"

Peter smiled, "Miriam said something extraordinary today, and it got me thinking..."

Seth interrupted. "Did your dad tell her what I saw?"

"That's my point, Seth. Yes. He did. But I was already on my way to tell them the same thing." He added to the side, "Well, basically."

"You? What?" Seth examined the boy's eyes. "Okay, I'm lost. What is going on here?"

"You tell me yours, and I'll tell you mine." He raised his eyebrows up and down.

This kid was incorrigible.

Seth had no idea what they were talking about, but he wasn't about to disagree with Peter. He would just agree to the kid's terms and see where things led. "Sure, okay, but you have to go first since you brought it up."

"Yeah, fine. So,"—Peter squirmed around a bit—"besides being awesomely invisible on demand, I sort of can see time in my head. It's like a huge colorful ribbon. I can go to certain parts of that ribbon of time and see like what's about to happen, sort of; not as clearly as you can, not in a way that I can change it but more like a warning; but I can see the past too, and like the sentience of like, life, I guess. Like sort of 'what' a person is." These sentences went up in pitch like a question, and his face and body language showed his vulnerability. This was hard for him to talk about. Probably because he felt like a freak.

Seth connected with that, making him want to be vulnerable.

Knowing it would be his turn soon enough, Seth spoke carefully. "So, you see time, and it's like a big ribbon."

"In a sea of blackness."

"In a sea of blackness," Seth repeated slowly.

"And each of the ribbon threads are the people in this world."

"You can see eight and a half billion threads?" Seth said, impressed.

Peter squinted. "Yes and no. The ribbon is massive, and I 'know' everyone is there, but I haven't, like, 'walked around the block,' so to say. I've kinda been focused on, well, Miriam."

"She does seem somehow to be at the heart of all that is happening. Do you know why that is?"

Peter shrugged. "But I wish I did. Miriam and I are at an impasse. She is my sister and all, and I love her, but she is not my friend, not really. It is just weird and a little disturbing that my Nature is so focused on her."

Seth palmed his chin. "I see. So what do you mean you can see 'what' a person is?" He looked back at Peter, waiting for him to go on.

"Uhm, well, that is hard to explain. It's sort of about light and refraction and the by-product of that."

"You mean color?"

"Yes and no. All the colors are there, but it's about light. It's hard to explain."

"But what does that have to do with the price of rice?"

Peter quirked an eyebrow at him and wrinkled his nose, "I do not know that saying, but I'm going to assume that it means 'what's your point.'"

Seth smiled at Peter, licked his lips, and nodded.

"The point is, I have no idea what it means, only that when people start heading down the wrong path, their light changes." He squirmed in his chair, and when their eyes met, Seth felt like Peter could see right through Seth with his mustard yellow eyes. Like he knew everything Seth had ever done and was still here talking to him. The moment between them got uncomfortable. Peter cut the tension with, "Look, I don't get it. All I know is if I go toward the ribbon, the threads become people; they are light and the absence of light. When I touch or focus on them, I know things about them, their immediate choices, and where their head is."

"Okay," Seth said, realizing that Peter could see through him. He averted his gaze and tried to picture this thread thing, and failed. "I have a hard time picturing it, Peter. But I'm glad it's you, not me. That seems like too much for my little brain to handle."

"Sure, I would have been happy with just earth Nature. Believe me."

"But you get both."

"Yeah, I do, don't I?" The boy wiped a strand of hair and dust off the bench beside him. "So now to the reason I just stripped my soul naked before you. I want to contrast what I do with what you do."

It was Seth's turn to squirm. "Uhm, well, I see visions. Like just a second ago, I saw you telling your father about a dream you had. That's it. I don't understand why I saw it, except that it makes what you just told me more manageable in my head."

"So, you just see visions. Like you blink and see a vision."

"Yes."

"Okay, well, let's compare the whole Dad lightning scenario. I saw the future part of my father's thread cut that day. Meaning I saw him die. Except the thread was not gone, only not there..." He narrowed his eyes at Seth as he thought about what he'd just said.

Seth narrowed his eyes back in confusion at his contradictory statement. "Just go with it; it's too hard to explain."

"Okay."

"By my understanding, his death was what it was. I did not see a way out of it. I knew I had to be there. The lightning would strike. But then you came along, and my father did not die." His face turned grave. "How did you do that?"

Seth was happy he was talking to Peter. These last few words answered a big question that had begun to form about his Nature. He took a deep breath, ready to spill his secrets. "Actually, what happens to me is way easier than what happens to you. I see a picture of something that will happen. Sometimes I'm a part of it; sometimes, I'm not. So, like with your dad. I saw you get hit by lightning, but the 'in-focus' or the important part of my vision was you letting go of your father's ankle. And then I just knew it was happening now. I had to hurry. In that instant, I not only saw what I needed to do, but I also had the speed and strength to do it."

"Whoa!" Peter exclaimed with eyes as round as the moon. "So, of all the Natures, that is so amazing. Watching you help Doc with that tent city guy is on my top ten awesome things list."

"His name is Westley."

"Yeah. Don't care. It's the Natures I care about."

Seth nodded and smiled. "It was pretty awesome, wasn't it?" And he meant it. Like to the tips of his toes meant it. His heart warmed over it, and gratitude for his transformation over the last day tightened his throat. Again.

Peter's voice pulled him out of his emotions. "So, what, you didn't see the future per se, you saw a...correction of the future?" Peter pulled the word out slowly, and Seth thought how perfect it was.

"I like your word, and it may be accurate; I'm not sure." He sniffed and considered. "At first, I got the information and skill I needed to get out of a sticky situation. The second time it was just the information I didn't know what to do with until after the fact. Then, with Westley and the tornado, it was more like I saw my future self do something, and then I did it exactly how I saw myself do it. But with your dad and the lightning..." Seth paused, pondering the moment and his vision. "...it was what you said. Like I was correcting something."

"What about with the Travelers today?"

"So, when something is going to happen a bit in the future, like this Travelers one, it's like..." He paused to think it through. "Okay, it's like seeing a movie you've never seen before, but you've read the book, and because of that, you know what to look at to follow the action."

"Uhm, never watched a movie, Seth."

"Oh yeah. Sorry. But you get what I mean, right?"

"Sure." His tone was not convincing.

"So I saw the Travelers in the river simultaneously and Guardians holding them under the water..." When these words were out of Seth's mouth, he was again taken by the same vision. Again, it was expanded. He saw all the Guardians on the bank of the river, including Westley, who was standing on his own two feet and was dripping wet. The man looked at him, and his eyes were all white. No color in his iris. Yet he smiled at Seth and nodded. Seth's perspective changed. He was above the water and saw the Travelers go under it, almost as if they were being baptized. He saw many of them struggle. He saw them still. But then there was a flash of light, and...the vision ended.

Just as quickly, he was again with Peter in the Divided Hall.

"What did you see?" Peter asked.

Seth shook the vision off and looked over at the other boy. "First, tell me again what you saw would happen to the Travelers."

"I saw them become Guardians. Today."

"And Westley too?"

Peter's brow knotted as he shook his head. "I did not see anything about Westley. In fact, I haven't paid any attention to him. I will try to remember to do that."

"Something is missing." Seth palmed his face, his mind moving quickly, and as if a gift of understanding were placed into his brain, he connected the dots. "It's like you see the hidden parts of things, you know, like the internal consequences on a spiritual level..."

Peter interrupted, "Yes, and you see what happens next here in the physical world, and if we do something wrong, you can act like some great cosmic corrector."

Seth smiled. The boy was zealous and made him feel good about the part he played in all of this. "But we don't understand how the two work together."

"And as Miriam said, I do think they are supposed to work together."

"Two witnesses are better than one."

"That's what my pa said," Peter added and clapped Seth on the shoulder, "But I think the quote is actually 'out of the mouths of two or three witnesses shall truth be established.'"

They sat quietly for a moment.

Seth said, "I think talking things out between the two of us helps us struggle together to get to the truth of it all. Do you think that is the purpose?"

Peter shrugged. "Well, if the Gods of the universe are anything like the Master of the Garden, they love it when we struggle as long as it brings us to the truth."

"The Gods of the universe and the Master of the Garden?" Seth asked with emphasis and raised eyebrows.

Peter shook his head and made a sweeping gesture with his hands, "Forget it. We have more pertinent things to talk about."

"Like?" Seth could not think of anything more pertinent than God.

"Like, how are we going to get the twenty-something Joneses to let us drown them?"

Seth shook his head, "I have no idea. But I know that if that is what is supposed to happen, it will."

Peter leaned back and gave him an impressed nod. "Where did this Seth come from?"

Seth looked down at his feet, "This Seth ruined his life, and he learned from it. That's where." He scrubbed at his palms and then glanced over at Peter.

Peter returned the serious gaze. "Give it some time." He patted him on the shoulder. "In the meantime, you get to take the Guardian oath, you get to protect the Garden, and you get to have the coolest Nature I've ever seen."

"Guardian oath?"

"Yes; remember, it's my Papa's plan for getting the whole drowning thing done. I personally don't like it, but it might work. You Johnsons get to take that same oath tonight. Unfortunately, we don't get to drown you, though." Peter smiled wryly.

"Hilarious," Seth answered, deadpan.

"And just so you know, I'm pretty impressed. You are, like, really chill about this. I got the impression that getting a Nature would not be on your top-ten-favorite-pastimes list."

"You got me there. But I don't know; I somehow don't feel any different. I know that sounds crazy, but it's true. And P.S,. you have uncommonly good lingo for a country bumpkin."

"Thanks, it's a gift. And that is crazy. You can see the future and have all the Natures; how could you possibly not feel different?"

"Don't ask me. But I really hope it has nothing to do with the fact that my eyes didn't change color. Please tell me I am not that vain." Seth raised his eyes to the heavens for emphasis.

Peter smiled. "You know it's called a Nature for a reason. You have led a pretty incredible life, from what I've gathered; perhaps it doesn't feel strange to you because you are a chameleon in your real life."

He wagged his eyebrows up and down at Seth. "Ya know, someone who can adapt to whatever situation he is put in. So it fits that you adapt, if you get my comparison."

Seth laughed. "Maybe." But he still had questions. "So, what is up with that, anyhow? The Travelers and Miriam?"

"I hate to break it to you, but all the Travelers have the same problem. Miriam took a memory from them. For some reason, Miriam leaves a mark of sorts when she does her thing. This mark, this taking of memories, it forces the one taken from to feel, how shall I say it...drawn to her. That might be the best way to put it. Like you need to be near her. Does this sound familiar?"

Seth reluctantly nodded and considered that knot of emotion in his heart and head that had Miriam's name all over it. He'd heard people talking about something that had happened between Miriam and the Travelers. Still, Seth had not put two and two together.

"Well, then, those feelings are not real."

"What?"

"So, you probably don't actually 'really like her.' You probably just think she's pretty or something; I mean, come on, you've known her for a week, and you were planning on betraying her the whole time you knew her. Not a very sturdy foundation for...anything, really."

Seth sat there, reeling and stung.

He cleared his throat, "Are you telling me everything I've felt since the day she took my memories...all the crazy, over-the-top emotions toward Miriam have been a manipulation? Something she did to me?" By the last words, he was whispering fiercely.

"Yes," Peter stated without hesitation, but then he added, "And no. She did not know that's what happened when she took memories. No one did."

"And all those Travelers feel the same as I do?"

"Yes. Well, they don't know Miriam, so you've got a leg up there, and they don't think they are in love, they just think they need to be near her. I think calling them Miriam's warriors would be better because it's almost like they need to protect her."

Seth's hands were in his hair, and he bent over himself in almost visceral pain to his chest. Miriam. Manipulate his emotions? Was he manipulated? Honestly, it would serve him right.

His mind raced back, wondering what was real and what was not real. When had he begun to have feelings for her? Again he was drawn back to their conversation in this very chapel. Her words and very heart showed through in how she talked to and helped him. How he opened up to her. When they'd first shared lunch together, he recalled her serious demeanor and honest admittance of dissatisfaction with her life. He liked her.

He liked how she phrased things. How she listened and made sense of the mess he made when trying to express himself. He liked how innocent and funny she was. He thought of the first time he had made her smile, and his toes tingled. Besides being intelligent and genuine, she was the most beautiful girl he had ever seen. He couldn't like her more. He couldn't want her more. He even fought all his feelings, uncertain of the whole cousin thing, but even thinking they were cousins did not cause his affection for her to slow.

They clicked, and the attraction was overwhelming; it was as simple as that. No, he knew the truth. Whether it took three days or three years, Seth was well on his way to falling for Miriam before she ever took his memories. For that matter, who was Peter to quantify his feelings for Miriam?

He lifted his head, a new bit of confidence entering his countenance. Yes, he identified a weird craziness, borderline obsessive feeling that he had, which started for certain when he'd found her lying on the road three days ago. He couldn't stop touching her and looking at her. He thought he was going crazy because he was falling in love so quickly. That was the manipulation. He knew it from the organic maturation of their relationship. And even within that timeframe, even after he knew what she'd done to him, he thought about playing soccer with her, about teaching her about the world. There was "real" in those circumstances too. And Peter was right; he had always held back.

"You know we are not related, right?" Seth added randomly.

"Yeah, I've known from the first day you guys got here," Peter said nonchalantly.

"Why didn't you say something?" Seth almost yelled into the cavernous room.

"Why would I?" Peter answered defensively. "Everyone older than forty knows."

"You guys have problems."

"No, we just operate on a need-to-know basis."

"Yes, well, that need-to-know basis being breached could have changed...everything."

"Yes, like you telling the Joneses everything. Miriam knew you were working for Joneses from the day I got my Nature, so there was no way we would have opened up to you. We were trying to get your phone every second we could."

"Wait a minute. She knew? Since Sunday?" Seth thought about it. That meant the only conversation they had had where neither knew anything was the one in this very chapel. "Oh, my gosh. She knew the whole time but still treated me with love and respect." Seth whispered this to himself.

"She knew you had a choice. She hoped she could help you. That's what we do here. We attempt to rescue people from themselves. Look at the Joneses. Do you know how easy it would be for us to 'take care' of them? That's not what this is about. It is about saving them."

Seth's head was spinning. "They are definitely not very appreciative."

"Nope." Peter's lips popped with the word. They sat in silence for a while.

Seth's mind flitted over the information he had gathered here. He needed more time to sort it out. Unfortunately, he did not have time. "Well, I better go tell your father what I just saw."

"And I want to go visit your sisters. I haven't really spoken to them since they became Guardians."

Seth smiled, thinking of Abigail and Lillian. They had huddled in their room, not letting anyone in, just wanting time together. "I think they would like that."

CHAPTER 6

Westley

Esther sat next to him. He could sense the weight of her frame on the bed. She smelled like cinnamon and apple cider. Her eyelashes fluttered like the wing of a dove every time she blinked at him. Her hand was in his, he knew it was, but he couldn't really feel it. He blinked and told his brain to wake up.

As soon as he felt alive, Esther's papa entered the room after a quiet knock. Esther quickly pulled herself free from all touch.

"How are you feeling today, Westley?" The large man asked.

"Good, thank you. But I have the best nurse a man could hope for."

Esther's father smiled and blinked down at the ground. He looked embarrassed, or as if he were trying to decide on what to say, "I uh spoke with Noah. They are happy to come to get you at any time and bring you back to the tent city. Doc says you can be moved in the next few hours, the Master willing."

Now it was Westley's turn to be rendered speechless.

"Papa?" Esther asked. "Why can't he just stay here while he is healing?"

"Well, Esther, you know why." A significant look passed between them.

Esther's marvelous green eyes found his. She looked frightened.

Westley closed his eyes. His heart pounded in his chest. He did not want to be away from Esther, but there were a few things he had to reconcile in his mind. Things he had not brought up to Esther, afraid they would make her go away. His mind moved backward in time to what he saw after his accident. What he knew. What he heard. He knew these people had some sort of strange power.

Esther had moved him and his horse with her mind or something. The Doc had made plants and other things grow out of thin air. The boy Seth had told them a tornado was coming when there was nary a sign of one and told them that Westley needed to be here, in Edenia, like he knew, like he was a prophet. And...he could feel his wrists. He was paralyzed. Completely. However, these people talked as if that was not a problem. And with the treatment he'd received over the last day, he went from no feeling whatsoever to being able to feel his shoulder to his arm and now his wrists.

And then there was Esther. She was an angel. He just knew it. She was one of those prophesied to come to prepare the Earth for the second coming of Christ. There was not a doubt in his mind. And if she were an angel, that meant that they all were.

Plus, why else had Westley been attracted to this place from the beginning? He knew he would be here. Noah knew as well. He all but told him. This was the will of God, and who was Westley to deny God? Perhaps there was a work he could perform here. If there was, he would gladly do it.

Westley opened his eyes and looked at Hirum Miller. "Sir, I have seen plenty of miracles in my lifetime; shucks, through God's power, I've performed a few on his behalf. As a believer, I want to be of use. I want to prepare the world for Christ's coming. I think I am called to do that here, in Edenia. Besides, I know what you are. I am with you. I want to stay."

Hirum smiled, nodded, and glanced at Esther. "Well, then, you are called. And I am glad you are so willing and faithful, for you must perform a hard task today. You and you alone can do it."

Westley blinked and tilted his chin down to indicate his broken body, "How can I help tonight? I am still—"

"Westley, do you truly have faith?"

"Yes, Sir, I do."

"Well then, if your god needs you to accomplish a task, do you not believe he will give you the *legs* to do so?" He emphasized legs in a way Westley understood what he meant.

"Yes, Sir, I do."

Hirum nodded. "Good. I will see you tonight. I will send some men to help you. We will need you down at the river at six."

Westley nodded, and Hirum turned to leave.

"Sir, there is one more matter."

Hirum turned, an unmistakable twinkle in his eye, as he glanced between Esther and himself. "Yes?"

"I know I have been here but a very short time, but in that time," —he swallowed hard—"I have come to feel some very passionate feelings for your daughter," he stated in a hurry. "I cannot in good conscience remain here without gaining permission to pursue her, for that is my intention."

Hirum folded his arms and raised an eyebrow at him, but the twinkle still played over his mouth and glance. "Well. I see. And Esther, how do you feel about this?"

She moved to his side, her smile as wide as the Mississippi. "Yes, Papa. I would very much like to be pursued by this man."

Hirum eyed his daughter for a count of five before nodding. "Good. We will see you both this evening. I will talk to your mother and give you my answer at that time." He glanced at Esther. "Since these feelings have developed, I will ask that you keep a chaperone with you from now on; it is our way," Hirum said with the first stern look Westley had seen on the man.

"Papa, Westley cannot even move. How could anything untoward happen between us?" Her cheeks flushed a beautiful pink.

Her father laughed, "I suppose you are right, Esther..." He gave Westley's legs a discerning smile and added, "...for now." Then he turned and made for the door.

"Thank you, Sir," Westley called.

The man harrumphed, and Esther closed the door behind him. She turned and placed her back against the door, a blushing smile filling her face. She was so beautiful.

"I am twenty-one years old, and I have never had a man interested enough in me to ask my father what you just did." Her cheeks went a darker shade of pink. "I've never really wanted that. I have been too invested in my studies and my students." She wrapped her arms around her waist and used her bottom to push herself off the door. There was something in her eyes. Something magical, something hypnotizing. Westley felt utterly smitten as he watched her sway toward him. "Thank you."

"For what?" he asked, almost in a trance.

"For wanting me," she replied as she sat on his bed. Scooping his hand into hers, she brought it to her mouth, planting a gentle kiss over his knuckles.

"Thank you for returning the feeling," he answered as her plump lips rolled off his skin, leaving a burning softness behind. His eyes went big. "I felt that."

Her eyes left him and went to his hand. "You did?"

He nodded.

"You did!" She smiled, and his heart exploded with love for the beautiful, smart, kind angel before him.

CHAPTER 7

Peter stayed at the Johnsons' home until it was time for initiation, talking with the girls about everything. Lillian was the dream of his life with her blue-green eyes, and Abigail was like a nightmare he loved with her exotic amber eyes. He could not decide which girl was more beautiful or more wonderful. He just liked them both. They talked a lot about what it was like living with cancer and about their life in so many countries. It was like they were different people now. No holding back. No more lies. It was awesome.

He spent a lot of time helping them with their Natures, telling them what they could and couldn't do and how they could be helpful. And the girls were suddenly no longer selfish beings; they wanted to give and fight. They were one hundred percent in.

Peter reveled in it.

As they walked to the river, Peter discovered that Zeke had already told the family the history of Edenia. Though it was his right to do so, he told the girls, "I hope you will at least pay attention to how my Papa tells it. I literally have listened to him tell it fifty times, and I never get sick of it."

The girls laughed. Lillian said, "Of course, we will listen. It is a pretty cool story. But why don't you get tired of it?"

Peter thought about this for a moment and came up with, "I think it's because I know that every time it is told, it's because we have a new Guardian, and I have always just put myself in their shoes. That feeling of knowing that I was finally a part of something so cool...it just never goes away."

Abby smiled, "That's really deep, Peter."

Zeke commented from behind them, "And pretty dedicated."

"I think he just lacks creativity," Seth snarked from the same direction, but added injury to insult by whacking the back of Peter's head.

"What the..." Peter was startled as Seth ran past him, laughing and giving him a challenging beckon.

Peter kicked up dirt as he raced to take Seth down.

HALF THE WORLD was there by the time they got to the river. His papa was standing on the bridge, ready to start but waiting for the other half of the Guardians to arrive.

Peter noted that the Travelers were up front and center and said, "I think you guys need to take your place of honor up front by my father."

They nodded, and Peter watched them go.

Not two minutes later, Miriam's voice spoke from behind him. "Hey, Peter."

He turned to look at his sister and was surprised to see Josie linking arms with her. Elle, Jonathan, Todd, Foster, and the whole old gang followed behind the two girls.

Miriam smiled at him, a refreshingly happy smile, and said, "I'm so glad things worked out with Lilly." And she meant it.

Miriam had a massive heart when she wasn't lording it over him and feeling sorry for herself.

He smiled back at her. "Looks like the whole gang is back together. That's great." This was an impasse. They would be friendly, for now, and he was glad for the reprieve.

The older kids moved on, and Peter watched them go. He noticed that off to the side of the road, a parade of people moved his way. They were carrying a substantial something.

It must be Westley.

Since he had no idea what would happen with that, he decided that where Westley landed would be his home as well. It didn't take long for Westley, on his makeshift cot, to be settled near the bank of the river close to the bridge. Peter maneuvered around the many people. Everyone was present.

And sure enough, his papa began.

"Long ago, here in this grove of trees, the Creators spoke with our first father, Adam, and his wife, Eve. God the Father and God the Creator had to turn Adam and Eve out of the beautiful Garden they had created for them. As he did this, the Creator gave them one last gift. 'I will set Cherubim and a flaming sword to guard the tree of life lest you eat of the fruit and forever be sealed to your ignorance, damned to this estate and left behind.' The word was spoken, and the cherubim came together. Formed from four powerful Natures; earth, water, fire, air...'"

Abby turned around and found his gaze; she pointed to her raised arm, then shivered and smiled.

Peter wondered what she was trying to say, but didn't have to wait long. "She has goosebumps." Miriam's voice whispered confidently behind him.

He didn't turn in response to his sister, just nodded. Peter listened with attention, but he also watched the faces of the Joneses and Westley. He wished he could tell what they were thinking.

Before he wanted it to, the story came to a close.

"...Our ancestors chose to hide the very existence of the Cherubim and the garden, thus protecting other like-minded treasure hunters from the Joneses' fate, and they did this with a covenant." His father motioned those new ones to rise. "It is the same covenant you will take tonight. And cursed will be those who break this covenant."

Gerald looked back at Peter, or maybe it was at Miriam, who was directly behind him. His eyes were terrified. Peter smiled reassuringly at him. And that was when Peter noticed that many of the Joneses were looking back at them. But it was time for the covenant.

As the words were spoken, that place in his mind, his Nature, beckoned to him. He didn't understand it but allowed it to pull him in. As he was standing at the river, his mind was in his ribbon room.

He was pulled right into the midst of his family and instantly noticed the change. The Joneses became light, and a sense of fulfilled balance encompassed him. He moved back, pushed his vision wide, and was surprised at what he saw.

Suddenly the future of the tapestry was not a random yet beautiful smattering of light and color but a balance of shape, color, and light. It was just about to be woven into the pattern of time. The almost harmony, the promised harmony, exploded in his soul.

And then he was on the riverbank again, tears pouring from his eyes. He was uncertain what it all meant, but he knew that this evening would set to right many years of imbalance, and he could not help but weep for joy.

CHAPTER 8

Westley had heard this story before. It was as familiar as the Christmas story or the story of Jesus getting baptized by the hands of John the Baptist. He had made this covenant before, and it filled him with gratitude that the Lord did things in the same manner the whole world over. It might look different, but the promise was the same.

So when it was his turn to say the words, he knew them by heart and spoke them with fervor and devotion. He was already at one with these people.

The moment the prayer was done and the hands of the Guardians were pulled away from him, he saw what must happen next. He must go into the water.

He looked up at Hirum. The man looked at him and into him. And so Westley spoke.

"Garren, Jai, will you help me rise? I must go into the water and be baptized into this new life."

Garren and Jai looked at one another, confused by his words, but they did as he asked.

"Aunt Betsy, will you still the water?" Garren spoke to an older woman to his left.

The woman nodded, and the three of them plunged into the water.

It was not cold; if it was, he could not feel it. "Let me go," he commanded the men.

"Are you sure?" Jai's kind voice asked.

"Yes, please do it now."

They complied.

Westley did feel the water on his upper body as he sank below the surface. The two men stepped away from him, and Westley saw their legs stir up current and bubbles as they moved.

Calm filled him. He used the power he regained in the last day to raise his arms slowly. They floated up until they reached toward the surface of the water. He felt the words he said in his mind, all the way into his heart.

"Lord, I know you can do all things. If it be thy will to heal me, do so."

And just like that, Westley felt a power, not unknown to him, but certainly more potent and more forceful than he had ever felt, start in his center and build so quickly that when it burst from him, it felt as if light were leaving all his limbs.

With only faith, he concentrated on his legs and willed them to move. And move they did. He placed one foot down, then another, and then his head was above the water. He shot out of it as he pushed off the bottom, and kicked until he was at the bank, which he crawled up.

Esther was there. Her eyes were full of tears, and only for him. She pulled him up and into an embrace, and there he stayed.

CHAPTER 9

Whispers about Westley's eyes began when he came out of the water. But Seth was not surprised. Of course. He only wished he knew what it meant. His own eyes were black, which was the sum of all colors. Westley's were white, which was the absence of all color. What did it mean?

More importantly, would what needed to happen, happen?

All eyes were on Westley, including the Travelers. Would they do it? Seth searched for Hirum, who looked at him. Tears were rolling down the man's face. Seth raised his eyebrows and chin and glanced at the Travelers.

Hirum nodded and looked upward. The man was leaving it in God's hands.

At that precise moment, Gerald turned to his men. "Okay, men. This is it. We go in, and come out Guardians. Are you ready?" And just like that, the lot of them moved into the river. Hirum must have set this up because twenty Edenians moved behind the Travelers and followed them into the water, which was as still as a pond.

He heard one of them tell the Travelers, "Relax, we are only here to help you." They took a moment to get all lined up, just as he had seen in his vision.

Westley called out to them, "Believe it will happen and don't come up until it does."

Then he looked at Seth. That look was the one from Seth's vision, and though he knew it was coming, it was eerie.

Gerald called out, "Together! Three, two, one." And they all went down. Seth wanted to look away, but he could not.

It only took a minute before the Guardians, who Seth noticed all had hazel eyes or strength Nature, began to hold down the Travelers, which began to struggle. Another minute passed. The anticipation of the crowd and Seth himself ratcheted up. He wondered what kind of struggle the Travelers were having down in the cold depths of the water. What kind of conversation was happening in their head? Seth waited and watched for the light. The one that would…

There it was. A flash, and Gerald bobbed to the top.

Déjà vu to the max. Dizziness overcame Seth.

Gerald stood in the water, panting and crying like a newborn baby. Seth watched in fascination because he had seen none of the other Travelers come up. He wondered if Gerald would be the only one. He asked if the Edenians would really have to drown them all.

He didn't have to wait too long. There was another flash of light, and then the man next to Gerald popped up, and suddenly it was like popped corn. Travelers popped up out of the water, preceded by their light exploding out of them. Seth vaguely wondered if that had happened to him. If it had, no wonder the security guards at the hospital had flipped out.

However, three minutes later, four of the Travelers had not popped. Miriam was standing now. Her hands were over her mouth. Suddenly she screamed, "Pray for them!"

And the Guardians did. They pulled together, touching one another, focusing their attention on the men still under the water, and Seth felt the power of it like a wave on the beach or like a rolling gust of wind. And just like magic—

Pop.

Pop.

Pop.

Only one left. Seth got that terrible sensation, the same one he had during his vision. This last Traveler wouldn't make it. He was going to be killed. Right now. Seth took two steps forward, wanting to stop the murder.

Sure enough, Hannah, the Guardian holding the last man down, pulled him up without the light hitting him. He was blue-faced, his body heavy and floppy. "Karl!" Gerald screamed.

And then Seth was in that place where he went between blinks, and he saw what he must do. Hannah already had Karl's body waist-high out of the river, her hazel irises swirling with the power of her strength Nature.

Seth ran to the man. "Keep praying!" he yelled to the Guardians around them, and it was like he'd given orders to a band of disciplined soldiers. Hands were grasped, heads were bowed, and the power was there.

Splashing through the water, Seth balled his hand into a fist and rubbed his knuckles onto Karl's breastbone as hard as he could. And suddenly, Seth had the strength he needed. "Brace yourself," he said to Hannah. Then he used his other hand to punch Karl upward like a standing Heimlich maneuver. Then Seth looked at the crowd, "Hirum, I need lightning. Now."

Seth punched Karl again in the abdomen, and then the wind came up.

"Seth!" Hirum called in an escalating scale, which meant the man had what he needed.

Seth knew he needed this water cleared, or he would kill the other people in the river, so he reached for that part of him that knew water Nature and said, "Clear this water." It was so. Like the Red Sea, the water flew away from Hannah, Karl, and himself. The strange bottom of the river was revealed in all its rocky, muddy, and slimy glory. Seth yelled, "Hannah, let go of him." It was done as quickly as the words left his mouth.

"Now, Hirum!"

And the lightning came. Seth knew the moment it was there, and so he pulled his wind Nature to him and controlled the power as it entered Karl's chest. Instantly the man heaved; water and vomit flooded his mouth and nose, and the air was sucked in. Seth let the water go, and it was at that time he realized he had held three Natures at once; strength, water, and wind.

As if Hannah were reading his thoughts, she looked at Seth with awe. "Your eyes were incredible. All swirly and multi-colored."

Seth shook his head as he held Karl up. "What?" and he wondered at these people. She saw a guy use wind, water, and strength to save a man's life without a blink, but was impressed by the colors in his eyes.

Seth shook his head. He turned to the man he was helping up the bank of the river. "Karl, are you okay?"

Karl looked at him, and Seth almost dropped the man. Karl's facial tattoos were gone, but even more disturbing, he had one red eye, one brown.

Then Gerald was there. Taking Karl out of Seth's grasp, Seth almost screamed like a little girl when he saw that Gerald's eyes were red like vampires.

One of the Travelers said, "Hey, all my tattoos are gone."

Another one said, "All my scars are gone."

Someone else said, "The pins in my ankle are gone."

"I don't have a bullet hole in my lat."

Then Hirum was there. "Betsy, will you dry these drowned rats out? They are Guardians now."

Seth heard from behind him the old woman's voice say, "Of course." But he didn't turn to her, unable to take his eyes off the Traveler's eyes. Red. He shivered, and the water soaking him ran from his body as if a giant magnet had pulled it from him.

Again Hirum's jovial voice rose above the crowd. "Oh my, Master preserve us. Red eyes." He laughed out loud.

"What could that mean?" the crowd was murmuring, though.

And in that second, Seth saw something that made him forget everything else. *He was in the most beautiful, shining, glowing place possible, and an Angel, a literal angel, stood before him and said, "Now, Traveler, this is what you need to do."*

CHAPTER 10

Miriam watched Seth as he worked. His eyes, his glorious eyes, flickered from one color to the next. Like Moses from her book, he pushed the water out of his way, just like how he controlled lightning, and ultimately how he saved Karl.

She couldn't take it. She wanted to go to them both, to touch them both. Grateful for all that had transpired, but she could not. She turned and walked away, her mind buzzing, tears flowing.

Her men were Guardians now. That was something to celebrate. Right? Maybe, she didn't know. Perhaps the stupid Revelator could tell her. Ugh. Seth was in the middle of everything. He hurt her. Just looking at him made the inside of her burn and freeze at the same time.

She wiped violently at the tears pouring down her face. She hurt. Her arms wrapped around her middle. She hurt. Her throat seized in a silenced cry of anguish. She HURT!

Why did she care so much? If you ignored the one who hurt you, couldn't the hurt get better? Even if you had to be around them, ignoring them could be like they don't exist, right? And if they don't exist, then they don't remind you of the pain they put you through, and if you aren't reminded every second, then you can heal.

But this pain.

Miriam touched her chest and felt her whole body wince.

She took a deep breath wondering why Seth hurt her so much. The idea that struck her felt like she'd been hit with a lightning bolt herself. Was this about the betrayal, or was it about rejection? She wanted it to be about betrayal, but what had Seth really betrayed? A girl he had known for a week? A connection they had? Both things were so infantile, especially compared to Seth's bond with his sister, that her logical mind could not begin to compare them.

So her pain had to be coming from rejection. Was it the rejection of a possible future together?

Her mind pondered this, and instantly her soul bucked at the idea. Her hand went to the neck of her shirt as the emotions inside her built. She ripped at her blouse until her scars were in the open, until they were exposed, and she could feel them under her fingertips. This was not only about rejection.

Her legs moved, pushing her faster as her hand clutched at her chest, and tears poured down her face. She would never get over this. She would never be whole again. This went so much deeper than a petty rejection of a crush. What was in her heart for Seth was not of her own making. She had decided that. It was the only thing that made sense. It was a gift. They both knew it. And he threw it away. Like it was garbage.

Miriam thought back to the night before their date, when she'd found Seth's phone in Eve's pocket. She'd stood on her back porch, gazed up at the moon, and promised herself that Seth would be hers, that she would have no other. She'd realized she loved him and wanted him and dreamed of how they would be so good for each other.

As these memories filled her mind, the tears flowing down her face became a monsoon. Her shoulders convulsed with the pain and the loss of her hopes. Her stomach ached. Her head throbbed, and then the sorrow took a turn.

Her feet stomped into the hard dirt. Her fists clenched at her side. Her jaw tightened, and she wanted to scream. The intensity of the tears morphed into rage. She flung herself against the side of a building and punched the wooden slats so hard it broke the skin over her knuckles.

She didn't care.

She punched it again and left blood on the whitewash. Then she kicked the building, with sounds coming from her mouth reminding her of a cow in the throes of birth.

The anger burned hot and fast, and as she gazed at her bleeding knuckles, the anger was snuffed out, leaving room for her brain to kick back into gear. That brain of hers led her from the ball of emotion back into the logical world. The tears of sorrow flowed once again.

Seth was backed into a corner by her, by his family, by the timing of this all. His sister was almost dead. He had no other choice as far as he knew. And he didn't know the Joneses would hurt her. Her logical mind understood all of this.

But her heart.

She hyperventilated, making her lightheaded. She wiped at her tears and cleared her vision.

And that was when she saw him.

Todd.

He was watching her. He had sadness and helplessness in the downturn of his features. He neared and said, "I came after you. I knew you would need someone. I saw the way you looked as you watched..." He looked away and pursed his lips; he swallowed down whatever he was going to say and turned his face back toward her.

She shut her eyes. And put her head down.

Before she could count to five, Todd's worn shoes were in her sight. His hands were on her back rubbing. "I'm so sorry this happened to you. You are the strongest person I know, Miriam, and I love you for it."

The words stopped her breath. Her head slowly came up, and she looked the beautiful boy in the eyes.

She sniffed as her heart, and her mind fluttered and fumbled over his words. "You love me"—she pushed her hair back—"For my strength?"

"Yes, and your smarts and your wit and your beauty and your goodness. I pretty much love everything about you and have since you were, like, ten and I was twelve." He said the words slowly and blushed as red as Miriam had ever seen.

She wiped her nose. "How is that possible?"

He snorted. "Uhm, it's really easy." He spoke the words gently and pushed a strand of hair out of her eyes, his thumb brushing her cheek in the process. It was the first time he'd touched her like that, and it sent a wild shiver down her back. Their eyes locked, and the whiplash of her emotions weakened her knees. Agony and rage, to sadness and the beginnings of understanding to...this...revelation. This incredible shock, astonishment, and then rush of validation and heart-thumping remembrance of first love.

Todd's face seemed huge and close, and moving in quickly. His gigantic blue eyes focused on her. His lips were no farther than five inches away as he whispered, "I am here. I want to carry this burden with you. It would be my absolute pleasure to do you any benefit at all regarding this problem." His eyes left hers to glance down at her open shirt and the scars that lay there. She could see the pain of her scars on his face. Then his emotions changed to display confidence. "Though I know you can handle it yourself." He pulled away from his intense posture and shook his head in amazement. "In fact, I don't know of a single person in all of Edenia that could go through what you have been through and still be walking around. You are a force, Miriam." His smile softened, and so did his glance. "A force that has pulled me along like a lodestone since we were children."

Again, as if he could not help it, Todd's hand rose and touched Miriam's cheek. It remained there carefully, tentatively caressing. "I can't tell you how painful it has been to be separated from you in the last three years. Waiting for the moment you came back to us."

His words rang true, and it took a second for her to figure out why. He was the same age as Gabe. She blinked at this because, where Gabe was a courting machine, always out with this girl or that, trying to decide who he liked the best, Todd had not courted a single girl.

Miriam also recalled all the times she had caught Todd looking at her. Sure, they were not often in the same room together, but when they were, his eyes were on her. The old Miriam felt his glance was filled with pity, but could it have been longing?

And one more thing. Despite the circumstance with Miriam taking her first memory from Josie and scaring the tarnation out of her in the process, Todd was on her parents' short list of suitors for Miriam. And everyone knew what was at the end of that process—a marriage. Todd's parents would not have agreed to put Todd on that list if he was not good with it. His parents were not the force-your-child-to-marry-someone type. Todd wanted to be on that list. And when she'd reminded her mother that she felt uncomfortable with Todd because of the Josie thing, Todd had been removed. He had not removed himself.

How could she be so stupid? How could she have wasted so much time?

Miriam couldn't take it anymore. She took Todd around the waist and pulled him to her. She pressed her face into his shoulder hard and squeezed him. All the feelings for him barreled back into her heart. He was practically perfect; she remembered thinking that. He was so handsome, intelligent, and kind. She had loved him for years. She had pushed him away, ashamed of herself, hating herself for what happened with Josie, and treated him like a stranger instead of one of her best friends.

"I'm sorry, Todd, for being so stupid," she whispered into his shoulder. After regaining her control, she pulled away from him and looked into his eyes. "I pushed you all away. Wasting so much time." She stepped away from him and shook her head, "I'm very sorry. I didn't treat you like the...friend you were to me." She stumbled over the word friend, not knowing exactly what to call him. "I was crazy! Things were complicated, yes, but very silly; I see that now."

There was a pregnant pause, and finally, Todd quietly asked,

"Friend?" His eyes whipped back and forth between hers, his brows scrunched.

Miriam bit her lip and closed her eyes. There she saw Seth's face. And she knew down to the soles of her feet that things between her and Seth were not over. "I have to be honest, Todd. I care for you deeply and even loved you at one point, but there is something between Seth and me. Something powerful, obviously"—she looked down at her bloody knuckles, which had started to hurt—"has happened between Seth and me. I don't understand it, but I have to figure it out before I can move on with life." She looked away from her hand to Todd's eyes.

Again, that boy stepped closer, never looking away. He gently took Miriam by the hurt hand, pulled a handkerchief out of his pants pocket, and gently wrapped it around her knuckles. "I know that you have a calling grander than my own, but I want you to know I am here for you now and from now on." And then he did something that sent Miriam into shocked bliss. He leaned down and kissed her cheek. It was a slow kiss. A long-time-coming sort of kiss. A please-last-forever kiss, a just-in-case kiss.

A slight, sad grin crept onto his face when he pulled back as a blush raced up his cheeks. "Can I walk you home?"

Miriam nodded dumbly.

And that grin of his became a smile.

He turned and started walking. After a minute, he said jokingly, "I am way too happy to hear you say I haven't been pining after you for six years for no reason to even worry about the competition."

Miriam smiled back at him and shook her head. She felt so much better inside. Almost refreshed. She'd let go of some of the hurt. She'd worked through some of the anger. She'd gotten the surprise of a lifetime and had been kissed on the cheek by the nicest, best-looking guy in Edenia. A guy who was in love with her.

Without the hesitation propriety demanded—Todd had just kissed her, so propriety was out the window—Miriam took Todd's hand in hers and softly squeezed. He'd really comforted (or distracted) her the way Gerald had. "Thank you," she said, keeping one of his hands as they walked. "Can I introduce you to the Jones men that helped rescue me?"

He smiled and said, "Sure, but only if I can help you clean up those knuckles. You look like a prizefighter."

CHAPTER 11

Peter

The day had been a busy one, and Peter fell into sleep quickly with thoughts of red-eyed warriors filling his mind. Once sleep came, the other work Peter did for the Master began.

His consciousness pulled him into the ribbon room, and he randomly wondered if his irises behind his closed eyelids were rotating as all Edenians did when their Nature was upon them.

But his mind became quickly alert. The dark chasm of the time room felt different. The darkness wasn't as dark, and it didn't feel like the immensity of space or time any longer.

It felt like the way light looked, influential, purposeful, enlightening, and straightforward.

This difference, whatever it was, had order. It had always had that, but now it was like, suddenly, Peter could feel it. Like The Weaver had arrived, and all the threads were making their best weave because of it.

He liked it. It had energy.

Excited to find out what had changed, Peter quickly oriented himself. He recalled he wanted to look at Westley's thread but also to be open to whatever time had to show him.

This mental openness did what it always did; his attention was drawn instantly to a thread far away from where he knew his family in Edenia was. Oddly it was not the present he was attracted to; it was something in the future of this soul.

Like a full day in the future.

Typically, there would be nothing he could see about a life thread at this height. They were no longer even ethereal tubes of speckled matter, splattered and indiscernible. However, this thread reached upward into the imminent as a golden tube, as solid looking as the threads below.

Up in the reaches of foresight, he noticed that this thread was not alone. Without a conscious will, he moved to the nearest one. He pulled up close to the bright thread and examined what he could. The line had a silvery golden glow to it. Then he was attracted to another thread just like this one. He moved to it. Again, the same solid future, the same golden light.

He wondered how many there were.

His eyes raced along the space where the future of these souls lay and saw all the threads that stood out. With ten billion people on the Earth, he thought he would not be able to see all. Still, his sight seemed perfected here, and he could discern many threads the same as this one along the whole of the tapestry's future.

He moved horizontally with the weave and counted how many odd threads there were. It was a strange feeling to be so far away from Edenia. He'd never traveled the width of the tapestry before. He wondered why.

He was uncertain how long it took him, but he finally came to the tapestry's end and counted forty strange threads. Once he reached that last one, he moved down into the presence of this soul, pulled his vision tight so the unique thread, and watched as it became a pillar before him. Then he moved closer still so he could touch it.

Instantly the face of a wizened man with skin as dark as an avocado peel came to his mind, and the force of the man pulled at Peter until he had a deep understanding. *This man was the clan chief of his tribe; he had seen much war and bloodshed, yet he had fought for peace in his land. It was a place he loved.* Peter felt the sum of the man's being, the bend of his mind, the path of his heart. And Peter thought he would burst with love and understanding of the man.

Knowing he was getting drawn in too deeply, the way he had with Seth that once, he told himself to wake up!

Peter sat up in bed sweating and shaking, his head about to explode and his stomach about to empty. Throwing the covers off, he raced for the back door and barely made it outside before he dumped the contents of his stomach on the grass.

CHAPTER 12

MONDAY
Seth

Seth woke up again, dreading what he had to do this day. He practiced saying it: "Hirum, the Travelers must go into the garden and get training for what they need to do from the angels that live there." He smiled his most winning smile too.

It was no use. There was no way to prepare. He rose, got dressed, and moved into the kitchen. Sitting at the table were his father and mother.

His father looked up from his bowl to say, "Good morning, Seth."

"Morning, my darling," his mother repeated and smiled at him. "I've made some oatmeal with apples and raisins if you are hungry."

"Morning. And thank you." He spooned some into a bowl and took a seat across from his mother.

When the man looked up with grey eyes, Seth smiled and blinked away the shock. His mother, with her blue eyes as bright as the sky, just looked beautiful and exotic. Still, his father's new eyes made him look even more formidable.

His father smiled back at him, and there it was. Joy. This new development of peace and joy in his father's eyes and countenance caused Seth to shake his head in wonder.

"What?" his father asked.

Seth shook his head more.

"What?" The word was touched by humor this time.

"It's nothing—just, it's so weird to see you not only with grey eyes but happy. At peace." Seth answered and looked away from his father and down to his oats.

"Yes. It is good to be at peace. This is nothing like my previous Nature..." He let the sentence taper off.

"Oh, yeah. You had my Nature before. Tell me more about that," Seth answered.

Ezekiel Miller swallowed hard, glanced over at Seth's mother, down at his food, and finally up at Seth.

It did not take a rocket scientist to know whatever his father was about to tell him was a big deal. So, Seth put his spoon down and turned to fully face his father.

He cleared his throat before saying, "The first thing that happened to me was that I could see the future. Not far into the future, but enough so I could know what would happen seconds before it did."

Stunned, Seth's mouth opened to respond, but his mind didn't seem connected to his mouth any longer.

"Next, I saw things differently. Like I would see it one way in my head, and it wasn't the same when I got to that place in actual time. That's how I knew when I needed to change something."

That was it. Seth whispered, "Oh my gosh, you were me!" He looked at his mother, then back again. "You were the Revelator! I guess I assumed you had the same Nature as me, not the same...I don't know, position as me."

"Yes."

Seth looked down at his hands, a creepy feeling swirling around in his stomach. He pressed his thumbnail into his palm and finally knew what he wanted to ask. "Was it so bad? Is that why you left?"

His father took a deep breath. "Seth, I am trying to be more open. I really am. But..." He looked away, and Seth swore he saw a tear glistening in his father's eye. "But I'm just not ready to tell that story. Can you respect that?"

He nodded, understanding that it didn't matter that Seth needed to know. If Ezekiel Miller wasn't ready, it wasn't going to happen.

Sniffing, his father asked, "So, has what I described been your experience so far?"

Seth nodded. "Yes, exactly. I saw Westley get hurt but didn't know what I was supposed to do about it, and I was able to change what happened to Hirum during the tornado."

"You mean, you changed what you saw? Because Hirum is not dead," his mother questioned.

"Yes, sort of." Seth bent his head to the side in thought. "It was actually more like I saw what I had to do without knowing Hirum would die. Or maybe I sort of knew. I don't know. Honestly, I don't know what is happening half the time."

"Yes." His father's raised eyebrows and pensive face told Seth he recalled how that 'not-knowing' felt for him.

His mother touched his father's arm. "I can imagine that being difficult for you, my dear."

"Chaos every moment? Yes, it drove me mad."

Seth could see that. His father had a schedule he kept every day. He was militant about it.

The man looked away, deep in thought. So Seth remained quiet. However, his mother asked, "What is it?"

"I just thought if I had stayed in Edenia instead of leaving, I would be the Revelator at this precarious time. I would be the one to lead everyone, to protect Edenia, and I would be the one they put their trust in. And I would have spent thirty years honing my abilities, making them perfect and succinct." He bit his lip, and Seth saw tears in his eyes this time. He finished, "Now, the whole future of this battle lies in Seth's hands. We are at the end of this all, and Seth, who has only been endowed for a single day, must take on the responsibility." He sniffed. "I'm ashamed, and I'm terribly sorry." He touched Seth's hand. "Not that I don't think you can do it. I do. I just know you shouldn't have to do it. And I'm sorry."

Seth didn't know what to say. He could only squeeze his dad's hand back and shake his head. "It's okay, Dad. I actually like my Nature and how I feel useful and connected to things. I'm good."

His mother added, "And you are here with him. You can help him. He is not alone."

"Yes, you can help. Tell me all about what you learned. It is all useful."

His father had to pull himself together openly, and Seth could not believe how much the man had changed. This was not his father, this crying, honest, earnest man. He liked it, though, and was encouraged by it. If his father could change that much this quickly, he could too.

"All right," he began. "Well, like I said, there were what I liked to call the bad ones. When I saw something bad happen that I wanted to stop."

"Like the lightning or the tree branch breaking and killing that little girl."

"Yes. But I also saw benign things in the future. Like things that I couldn't help with or wasn't even a part of."

"Yes, I have that too. Like I saw the Travelers get drowned. How does that have to do with me? But then I realized I was to say something to Hirum about it, and he was able to have people in place to ensure all went down as it should. I also saw Hirum talking with the tent people, but I had nothing to do with that. I don't know why it needed to happen. I'm actually pretty sure that I didn't need to be there. But it did happen, and I guess we will see."

He paused and noticed his father watching him intently; however, another thought popped into his head. "I also saw the tornado coming. I didn't need to see that, but it prompted my trust in the visions, and so did the Westley thing. And then there are brief moments where I see stuff before it happens, and when it does happen, I just know that things are on track. Do you know what I mean?"

At the end of this speech, his parents exchanged a look. His father said, "Ya know, I think you are going to be just fine on your own." And he smiled at him more confidently than Seth had ever experienced from his father.

"I think you are right."

He smiled back and thought about what he had to do next. "I

think half the time it's only a matter of bravery, like right now. I have to tell Hirum that the Travelers are supposed to go into the Garden. I don't think he's going to like it."

"Ooh, that's a biggie. Asking him to lead his age-old enemies into the Garden?"

"No, look how supportive Hirum's been up till now. It will be fine." His mother touched his cheek. "Go, my love, be brave."

"The Travelers have to go into the Garden," Seth blurted out the moment Hirum gave him a moment to speak. The man was busier than a one-armed paper hanger.

Luanne Miller was the first to speak. "Excuse me?"

Hirum glowered at his wife, "You heard what he said, Lu." Then he stood up from the kitchen table and walked to the back door window.

"I just knew it. Those men are going to be an issue," Luanne commented and bit her bottom lip.

"I thought I had some idea of what we could do with the Travelers, though we don't know what this red-eye Nature is..."

"Throw them off a cliff?" Luanne interrupted sarcastically.

"Luanne." Hirum rolled his eyes. "They are literally Guardians now."

Seth smiled. At that moment, Seth saw a little of where Peter's moxie came from.

She rose from her seat. "I can see I will not be helpful here. My prejudice is too strong. I suppose I should go and relieve Peter."

Hirum turned. "What is happening with Peter?"

Luanne's cheeks flushed, and she dry-washed her hands. "I've banished him to his room until he figures out what we are supposed to do with the Joneses. I will let him know he's off the hook. The Master is going to take care of them." And the woman left the room.

Hirum's eyes lingered on his wife, his face as enamored as a teenager. Finally, he turned to Seth severely. "Are you certain they need to go in?"

Seth nodded.

He moaned, "This is hard."

"Your wife might be on the right track." There was a pause where Hirum eyed Seth dubiously. Seth caught on. "Not with the cliff thing. Perhaps if we can ask Peter about it?"

"Two separate witnesses. Yes, Seth, that is a great idea, and not that I don't trust your visions, but it just would make me feel better." He moved toward the hall. "Let's go find out what a night of dreams has yielded, shall we?"

He nodded and followed the man into the hallway. Hirum entered his son's room, but Luanne was also in there, so Seth stayed in the hall.

A door behind him opened, and when he turned to see who it was, he ran headlong into Miriam. It was the moment from his vision.

He'd assumed Miriam was gone. He'd clarified that he did not want to be in the house when she was around. He did not want to hurt her.

But here they were, just like he knew they would be.

He watched as the reality of what was happening cleared in her vast, glorious eyes. They changed from shock to revulsion. Scuttling back from Seth's arms—which had jutted out as their bodies slammed together—Miriam pressed her back against the wall and gaped at him. Instantly she looked like a caged animal, eyes darting, blood draining from her face, and breathing loud.

He raised his hands. "Oh, no" Seth said but knew he needed to clarify. "I didn't know you were home. I wouldn't have come."

Her hands went to the collar of her shirt as if she were afraid he could see something there, and her face turned away from him.

There was nothing he could say. He knew it. He knew that "I'm sorry" was not what she could or would hear from him.

Then her father was there. He took her in his arms and pressed her head to his chest. She melted into him, closing her eyes and burying her face into his shoulder.

"I didn't mean to," Seth explained. "I just ran into her."

"I know. I know. But you best go. I will find you later."

"Of course," Seth said and hastily approached the door.

CHAPTER 13

Miriam

Miriam heard Seth leave the house. She held on to her father a bit more before moving away, head down.

"Thank you, Papa. I just…" She swallowed hard. "I cannot look at him. It hurts…" She put her hand to her chest and met his eyes.

He took her by the shoulders, his eyes gleaming with unshed tears. "I know." His hands went up and down her arms in a gentle, loving reassurance. "I know, my darling." He then pulled her to him, hugged her gently, and kissed her head.

She was so relieved to have his love that her residual anger and fear melted away.

Her mother made her way into the hallway and rubbed at Miriam's back. "This is a hard lot, my dear."

Her mother had been more understanding and so much less abrasive since their talk. It was enough to heal other weighty hurts Miriam had carried around like rocks in her pockets.

Her mother said, "I cannot imagine having to look at a person that kidnapped me." Blunt, as usual.

"Lu," her father's voice chided softly.

"What? I could not."

"No human in the world could kidnap you, mama; you would burn them to a crisp before they could say barbecue," Miriam commented, her voice muffled by her papa's chest.

There was silence for a good three seconds before her pa and ma began chuckling.

Her papa patted her back. "You have the right of it, Miriam. You most certainly have the right of it."

Miriam pulled away from her father's rumbling chest and looked at the pair of them, smiling at one another and at her. It was a good moment. A touch of joy came back to her.

But then her papa's expression faltered. And he looked at her with a seriousness that meant he had something hard to say.

"What, Papa?"

He took her back into his arms and squeezed before he let her step away.

Then he said, "Miriam, what will you do about Seth?" He asked slowly but then followed it with very quick assurances. "You can be mad and hurt. If that means crying for a week or a year, do it. If that means spending time on your knees, do it. If that means having Gerald kick Seth's butt, do it. Do what you need; I will support you in it all." He shuffled his feet and added, "But I will encourage you to do the thing that will heal you and not the thing that will make this worse."

Miriam wrinkled her forehead at him and narrowed her eyes.

"What I mean by that is, do what you must do to feel better. It's like when you fall off a horse or a ladder. If you turn your back on those things and allow yourself to think of them with trepidation, you will be scared and unable to use them the next time you need them. However, if when you fall off a ladder or a horse, if you get right back on them again, you will be hurt; the bruises don't go away, but the power to make you afraid does."

Miriam heard his words and knew what he was getting at. She also knew he was right.

He went on. "I saw you just now. I saw the fear and your body's reaction. You looked at him as if he were the one..." He paused and did not finish the thought, but she understood. The one who wielded the hot iron. "If that continues, your remedy to your trauma will be worse than the trauma itself and will last much longer because you let Seth have control over you when you act that way. I don't want that to happen, though he will not use that control falsely. He still has it. Find a way to take control back. You need not shrink in fear of any man."

Peter's voice came from his doorway, where he had obviously been eavesdropping on the conversation. "Pa's right, Miriam. Even more than all his reasons, though, I get the distinct feeling you need Seth. The Master has a plan for the two of you that has nothing to do with love or a relationship but does have to do with a partnership. Take control of that."

Miriam fell back against the wall and let herself sink to the floor. The words she heard, words she already knew.

Her mother squatted down next to her. Took her by the chin and raised her own chin. "You need not fear any man!" Then she brushed Miriam's hair back and whispered, "I don't know how to help you move forward in this mighty trial before you, but I challenge you to heed your father's counsel. Take control of how things proceed. See what happens. That, in and of itself, might be the thing that frees you."

Peter added, "Make a plan. Tell him what you expect. Then give him a good old one-two punch on the chin. I'm pretty sure it will make you feel better."

"Peter Christopher Miller!" his mother chided.

But she saw her father's eyes; they sparkled with the image of her punching Seth in the face. She smiled at him. And she realized just talking about it made her feel better. Why was Peter always right?

"Let's go have breakfast—it's over at the Tomco's this morning, and I am certain the Travelers are there waiting for you." Her papa reached for her hand. She took it, and he pulled her to her feet.

"Ooh, those red-eyed devils creep me out," her mother said, as she took Miriam's arm and looped it through her own. "But I know they are special to you, so I will say no more."

Miriam smiled at her mother and added, "It is super creepy. I hope they grow on me."

"Let's just hope they don't grow fangs," Peter said, using his claw-like hand to pinch her on the side of the neck as he hissed in her ear.

"Peter!" she said, exasperated. "Stop it."

He slid by them out the front door, laughing all the way.

They were met on the porch by Westley and Esther. The two were arm in arm. Speaking of spooky eyes, Westley's eyes were so ice-blue they looked white. The rest of the man's face was extremely handsome. White-blond hair, chiseled jaw, and broad shoulders. He was taller than Papa, but only just, and had the full, beautiful lips Esther always liked on men. He was a good balance of beauty and masculinity. And he gazed at Esther as if she ruled the world. Oh boy! Esther had a boy!

This made Miriam smile.

"Hey y'all." Esther greeted them in a very cheery voice. "Are you heading to breakfast?" Miriam nodded. "Can we join you?"

"Of course," Miriam's mother said, and when Miriam looked over, she saw that her mother had flushed cheeks. Mama thought Westley was handsome as well, Miriam figured out with a big grin.

But Papa said, "Now that Westley is healed and the two of you are courting, I thought I made it clear that you needed an escort at all times."

"Papa, Aunt Betsy was with us; we just dropped her at her house. You don't think we need an escort to walk a hundred yards from her house to ours, do you?"

Her pa cleared his throat and stuck his chin out. "No. Well, good then."

"How are you settling in, Westley?" Mama asked.

But Miriam ignored the answer. She thought about the conversation she'd just had in the house. Taking back control of her anger and her fear seemed like an idea worth consideration and action. How would she do it, though? Many scenarios came to mind. Many of them consisted of her making Seth her slave. Some had her handing him over to the Joneses, who gave him the same treatment. Then there was screaming at him. None of them seemed exactly right. However, the idea, in general, did seem right.

As they reached the Tomcos', she left thoughts of Seth behind and considered how she would act around Todd. He would be here. Certainly, she had invited him. Would he tell her he loved her again? Butterflies twirled through her stomach and brain.

Sitting at the tables in the Tomcos' cul-de-sac with a plate full of food, Miriam sprinkled walnuts on her flapjacks. Todd sat on one side of her, Gerald across from her, and Josie next to Gerald. After chewing, she took another bite of her food and asked Gerald, "I haven't gotten to talk to you since yesterday. How is it going?"

Gerald, a plate full of eggs, bread, and jam, pointed his fork at his eyes. "You mean since I drowned and turned into Dracula?" he said around a mouth full of food. Then he shrugged his shoulders, took another big bite, and concluded, "I've never felt better in my life."

Miriam smiled. Gerald had taken care of his body, but his old wounds had bothered him. Not anymore. He looked better, and it wasn't because the scars and the tattoos were gone. It was his countenance.

"Do you know what your Nature is yet?" Todd asked.

Todd. Oh my. He'd found her as soon as she arrived and had not left her side. And she admitted to herself that having him there made her feel far more comfortable in case Seth showed up. Besides, she liked being around him. She always had.

The table fell quiet while everyone was eating their food. And that was why she felt it. She paused with her fork halfway to her mouth. Her stomach flipped and swirled.

She scanned the area, arching her back to gaze at the monstrous men surrounding her. Following her instincts, it took her only a moment to see him.

Up the road, rounding the corner, were Seth and his family. Miriam bit her bottom lip, set down her fork, and closed her eyes. Breathe. She focused on her drumming heart, telling it to settle down.

Her mind went back to her conversation with her father and mother, and it was like her whole body took a left turn. Instead of going down the path of fear, terror, and hyperventilation, the road she took was rage.

Miriam gripped her skirt and looked down at her food. There was no way she would let Seth control her again. She was angry. She wanted to make him pay, even if it was just a little bit.

Before she knew what was happening, Miriam had risen from her seat and turned toward Seth. She thought of the first time she'd seen him, walking up the Edenia road, the swirl of trepidation he'd put in her stomach then. It had been a warning. And she'd ignored it. She'd followed him and snuck out to chase him down. She fostered their relationship, and she loved him. He made her love him.

She took a step, then another, then another. She maneuvered around the tables and stepped past them to the road. Seth saw her. Their eyes met, and a thrill race up her back. Her heart sped up. Her anger mounted. And her feet were moving fast now. A part of her mind registered that the Travelers men had gone quiet, but they did not follow her.

When she was about ten feet from Seth, beautiful Seth, he stopped walking; his face went blank, his eyes glazed over for an instant, and when his black irises again focused on her, he braced himself. She saw him.

Her hand rose without her conscious mind telling it to. When she was a mere two feet away, that hand swung backward and slapped Seth Johnson so squarely across the face that his head and shoulders followed her movement.

He huffed as if he'd been holding his breath, and then his face slowly swiveled back to her. Again, without complete cognition, her hand came back around, connecting her knuckles with his other cheek. And again, his head spun, his black hair in a ponytail fanned out as the elastic came loose.

This time Seth's hand came to his cheek, and when he turned back to her, his face flushed, his hair all clinging and messy, she thought she'd never seen a more beautiful person she hated so much.

The dark place inside her bubbled and roiled, and she felt

exhilarated. She smiled. But that was when Miriam heard some whoops and claps from the Travelers. She looked their way, and when she saw their approval, she instantly felt ashamed, and it snapped her out of her haze of rage.

She turned back to Seth, who had composed himself and looked ready for more abuse. In fact, he looked like he wanted it. Studying him, she saw that was exactly what he needed. He thought he could pay for his crimes this way. She narrowed her eyes at him and jutted her chin out as she shook her head.

"No. No," she said, and shook her head more. "You do not get absolution this way." Then she started yelling. "Do you even know what they did, Seth? They branded me. Here." She touched her collarbones. "They burned their name into my skin." Then she knew she had to show him. She undid the top button of her shirt and pulled it down just enough that the top of a branded letter "n" could be seen.

Seth looked. His countenance morphed from stoic martyr to absolute horror. He had no idea; she could see it.

She whispered, "They tied me to a chair, drugged me, tortured me, and branded me. Like an animal."

His chin had disappeared into his chest, and he had crumpled into himself more and more with every word. His hand balled into fists, his eyes on the ground.

She continued, "So, as deserved as they may be, a couple of slaps will not change anything between us. You are not absolved. But it will change my ability to move forward with power." Clearing her face of all anger, she blinked and took a deep breath. "Which I suppose I need because my father and Peter say you are the Revelator and that the Master is causing things to happen. That we might have a task to take care of together." She refused to look at the ground, keeping eye contact with him, though her insides swirled and tumbled like the river Eden. She firmed her voice. "So, I want you to understand that I will speak to you—when it is necessary—and work with you, if I must. But today is not the day for either of those things. Tomorrow, maybe. I will let you know. But for now, please, go, have your breakfast elsewhere, and if you need to talk to my Papa, do so when I am not home."

She turned on her heel and moved away from him. And as she walked, she felt something inside her; it was a strong, hopeful feeling. It was a powerful feeling. And more than anything, she was no longer a victim.

CHAPTER 14

Peter came running up to him, cream on his nose. "Well, that went better than I thought."

Seth rubbed at his cheek, "Yeah."

"She can be so scary with those eyes." Peter shivered.

Seth's eyes stayed on her retreating form. Her extra-long braid swung back and forth. "Yes..." Seth nodded, a tiny tendril of hope entering his heart. Even as terribly angry as she was with him, she had not said, 'you must bow and scrape to earn my forgiveness.' She had set boundaries. She was brave and exquisite, and Seth could not help it, his heart burst with love for her. "...She is amazing."

Peter sighed, "Oh boy. When a girl can slap you across the face twice, and you still look at her the way you are...you're lost, buddy." The kid patted Seth on the shoulder. "And may I add, yuck."

Seth spared a glance for Peter and smirked. "And your crush on Lillian is equally nauseating." Then he turned to obey Miriam's request to go elsewhere.

Peter blushed and moved to follow him. "I have no idea what you are talking about. Let's go get some breakfast." And the boy began walking quickly toward his home.

"Wait, no. I am never going to disobey her." Seth's eyes found Miriam again. She sat down next to a big bald man, Gerald, who turned to glare at Seth with scary red eyes. It occurred to Seth that Gerald was Jeremiah's bodyguard, the one from the diner they'd visited on the first day he'd come to Edenia. The man put a hand on Miriam in a comforting gesture.

Seth walked away, replaying the confrontation he'd just lived through. He smiled, happy that she had stood up for herself, finally. Miriam was fierce, beautiful, and powerful, and Seth knew he would do anything to make things right between them.

Seth grew up in a home full of love, trust, faith in one another, and discipline. The person Miriam had met, that person was in crisis and acting like it. Death of a sister. Trust between parent and child broken. The world breaking out into a dangerous war. Moving across the globe. But a crisis does not a person make. Yes, it could reveal one to oneself, but what did his situation reveal about him?

He cataloged these lessons in his mind as he'd been taught, so he knew himself and reminded himself that though Miriam met him in his worst hour, he was still worthy of her love. One day.

1. Seth had a hero complex, a desire to be like his fantastic father. And it could get out of hand if he didn't watch it.
2. Seth had a deep, loyal love for his family, which made him willing to betray other people if it meant protecting his family.
3. Seth needed connection, and it was his Achilles heel and thus what he needed to watch out for the most.
4. Seth was capable of doing really terrible things, like any man in a desperate position.
5. Seth distrusted people once he felt betrayed by them. Totally normal and understandable, but also something that could control him.
6. Seth could not put faith in things he did not understand, meaning he was faithless.

He knew, at the moment, by the tree, with the roofie Jeremiah had given him, that he did not need to hurt Miriam. That secret place inside him had told him, had warned him. He did not listen.

His hands clenched at his side, and he made a deep commitment to himself, a life-altering promise that he would listen to that voice from now on. That was the behavior he had to change.

Seth had always been a man of action. Showing people who he was with his choices, not his words. That quiet sense came to him, and he knew things would work out.

"Seth, Earth to Seth."

"I'm here."

"I overheard that you saw a vision of the Travelers going into the Garden."

Seth stopped. "You nosy little turd. We wanted to see if you could collaborate."

"Yeah, well, I can't. My dreams are super weird. I don't understand what they mean right now. I must have eaten something bad."

Seth started walking again. "Tell me what you saw, and I'll tell you if it makes sense to me."

Peter shrugged. "I saw a really old guy with saggy baggy skin, and I saw stuff about his life."

Seth wrinkled his forehead, "Stuff?"

"Yeah, like how he's the chief of his people, and he's seen war and like famine and stuff. I have no idea, dude. None."

"That is strange. Is it the first time you've seen someone random? Meaning no connection to Edenia?"

Peter nodded. "I think so."

"Well, maybe you are right. Perhaps it is a fluke."

"So, I have to sit this one out?" Peter asked.

"No, I think you need to figure out how to have visions when you are not asleep."

"How can I do that?"

Seth clapped his hands together. "I have a few ideas."

"Really? Let's do it!"

"Yeah?" Seth asked and slowed his pace.

"Yeah."

"There's no one at my house," Seth offered.

"Let's go."

CHAPTER 15

Peter

"Try again." Peter sat up to see Seth sitting elbows to knees, his black eyes intent. "We are going to have to figure this out," Seth muttered.

Peter lay back down and pulled the blankets close. Tucked them just so and closed his eyes.

"Have you heard of meditation?"

Peter blinked at him, then scrubbed his hands through his hair. "No. Enlighten me. Because my way is not working."

"So, you quiet your mind. You, like, concentrate on your breathing."

"What? Where are you getting this bull?"

"Try it."

Peter opened one eye and peeked at Seth. "You saw a foretelling about teaching me to breathe, didn't you?"

Seth smiled. "Maybe."

Peter fidgeted.

"Stop. Get comfortable, then stop moving."

Shaking his head and taking a deep breath, he skootched back and crossed his legs.

"Now close your eyes."

Peter complied.

"Try to clear your mind. Try to think about each part of your body and relax it and then think about your breathing. You can even count and focus on that counting."

Peter obeyed. He started at his feet, and he breathed deeply by the time he got to his neck with the relaxation exercise. His mind was completely relaxed, and then like magic, the darkroom of time surrounded him. Just to ensure he was awake and not sleeping again, he said, "I'm in, Seth. Can you hear me?"

"Yes!"

Peter felt himself pulling out of the room, so he relaxed again and breathed. The darkroom came back. But it did not come to him the way it did when he knew he needed to know something in a hurry. It just was there, and he could explore it at will.

He pulled himself into the weave. Then he pushed himself out. Then he let go.

He opened his eyes.

"Do it again."

WHAT SEEMED LIKE AN ETERNITY LATER, Peter entered his dark ribbon room as easily as pulling on a pair of trousers. He looked around and knew he'd accomplished what he and Seth had set out to do. A warmth entered his heart. He was beginning to love this place. It had that sense of completeness, of order. In his head, he decided he should check on a few threads. The Travelers', first. Nothing new was going on there except what he knew would be. They were Guardians now.

On to Westley's thread. But this one did not come to him as it did when he knew he needed to know something quickly. It did come, though, so he explored, and as he did, a rush of wonder filled him.

Wanting to tell Seth what he'd learned, he pulled himself out of his ribbon room and opened his eyes to ask, "Do you think we have done it enough?"

Seth answered, "Depends. Can you do it on demand?"

"I think so."

"Well then, I think so too. Now go in there and see if you see or feel anything about the Travelers."

"I already did. I got nothing. Except..."

"Except what?"

Peter wasn't sure he wanted to tell Seth everything he'd learned today in his ribbon room. Still, he decided the Revelator should know as much as possible. He began a little hesitantly. "So, some interesting things are going on in there."

"What kind of interesting," Seth asked, and leaned forward.

"Well, I wanted to go check up on that guy Westley. So, I went over to his thread, and it was sort of like your thread. In fact, your thread and his thread were doing some weird kind of resonance thing. Like vibrating off of one another and making sparks. Also, where you are in the tapestry matters. It's a subtle shift, but Westley's is suddenly in the middle of everything. Not because he became a Guardian, that is about light. So, as it is, his thread is right next to yours, like I said, and you are next to Miriam, which isn't surprising, but you three are surrounded by the Travelers. Like they are protecting you. I'm not sure what it means, but I instantly wanted to tell you about it, so that's something, right?"

Seth wrinkled his forehead at Peter. "That is strange. I have had the urge to talk to him all day, but I've been so busy..." He let that hang in the air.

Peter nodded his head as he watched Seth, deep in thought. He had to bite his lip to stop himself from telling Seth about the other strangeness.

Seth looked at him, cocked his head, and asked, "There's more, isn't there?"

That was all the excuse Peter needed. "Okay, so something different is happening to the tapestry." He pulled the covers off and got out of bed. Then he turned on the light and sat back on the bed, his mind working out how to say what he needed to say. "It's like it's organizing itself."

"Organizing?"

"Yes, like, it was just random shapes and colors before, but now it's like preparing to make a distinct pattern. All the threads are lining up as they should, and the whole thing has a feeling of purpose."

"Okay. Uhm, that sounds ominous. I guess it makes sense, though. It's the end of the world. I feel like whoever runs this joint has had some pretty specific plans for this time in history, i.e., the Apocalypse."

"I never thought of that."

"But what I don't get is how this is relevant to us here in Edenia. We are completely separated from the world. Why should we worry about what is happening out there?" Seth thought about that for a long moment before standing. "Okay, well, we will talk more about this later. For now, let's go see Westley."

CHAPTER 16

Westley

The house he had been given was cozier than the tent he'd lived in for the last three years. If only he had Buttercup in the backyard instead of far away in the community barn, life would be just about perfect.

Speaking of which, Esther made life practically perfect. At least with her by his side, it was hard to complain about anything.

He'd just begun eating a slice of homemade bread slathered thick with freshly churned butter, a gift from Luanne Miller, when there was a knock at the door. Hoping it was Esther, Westley rushed to the door, taking a bite of the delicious bread. It was decadent in a way he was no longer used to.

Pulling the door open, he smiled at the two young men before him. The native boy he recognized from the day of his accident and the other boy was Esther's kid brother, he was certain.

"Hello, how can I help you?"

"Westley. How are you?"

Westley looked down at his now working body and smiled. "I am right as rain. Thank ya for asking."

"Can we come in?" the native boy asked.

"Uhm, sure." Westley brushed at his pant legs with his free hand like he had to clean mud off them before he let guests into this house the Edenians were allowing him to use.

The boys stepped in, and they all moved to the sitting room. Once they all sat down, the boys stared at Westley like he had butter on his nose, or like they expected him to tell them the secrets of the universe.

After the silence progressed into awkwardness, Westley cleared his throat and asked, "So, how can I help you?" This time the pitch of his voice rose with uncertainty instead of falling as typical verbal niceties did.

The boys looked at one another. The native boy answered slowly, "We aren't really sure. You see, uhm, now that you're a Guardian..." he started, but the other boy butted in.

"We need to know about your Nature, Westley. Do you know what it is?"

He shifted in his chair, set his bread down on the side table, and then looked back at the boys. "Well, you know how to get to the point." He licked his lips. "Hirum told me that it was called divining. Some here call it prophecy, I guess. Which is so weird." Westley shook his head and sighed when he considered his faith outside of Edenia. He looked back at the boys, who were a mess of crunched foreheads and knotted eyebrows. "What?"

Esther's brother spoke first, "That's real interesting, Westley. Real interesting. Seth, what do you think?"

Seth, the native kid, shook his head and worried his bottom lip with his teeth.

They both stared at him like he was the winner of the barrel races.

Then Seth asked, "So has your Nature done anything yet?" He drew out the word 'anything' and rolled his hands with the word. The whole thing implied quite a bit, none of which Westley understood.

"Anything?" Westley asked.

Peter sighed. "Has your Nature taken you? Like burst out of you so that you feel a power of some sort?"

"Oh," Westley said. "No. Is it going to do that?"

The two boys deflated and didn't answer his question.

"May I ask what this is all about?" Westley asked as politely as he could, though his curiosity was at an all-time high.

It was Esther's brother who spoke. "Well, Westley, you're a

prophet, Seth here is a revelator, and I can see time. So, we are just wondering why in the world the Master needs so many people who can do almost the same thing."

"We don't do the same thing at all, Peter," Seth broke in.

"True, but it's just weird. Right? They all feel like the same thing, but we have different eye colors."

"I am confused about it, for sure."

Westley added, "That makes three of us." In his mind, prophets and revelators were a real thing. They were the leaders of his church. They were the men that helped God's purposes come to pass in the scriptures.

He must have whispered part of this idea aloud because both boys asked, "What was that?"

Westley looked down at them, "Oh, nothing. I was just thinking about how in my church, the leaders are called prophets, seers, and revelators."

Peter took this up the fastest. "A triad." He pointed at Seth. "Revelator." He pointed at Westley. "Prophet."

Then Seth pointed at Peter. "Seer."

That silenced the room for a good thirty seconds.

Peter broke the quiet, though. "But what do those words mean?"

Westley knew this one. "Well, a prophet is a teacher of truth, a seer is a perceiver of hidden truth, and a revelator is a bearer of new truth. I learn that in Sunday school. We actually sing a song about it." Westley shrugged his shoulders.

"Oh my," Peter exclaimed.

"That is exactly right."

The boys exchanged a glance.

Westley waited, confused. Once the strangely colored irises turned back his way, he asked, "Are you boys going to let me in on the secret, or what?"

Peter looked away, almost as if he were embarrassed. Seth cleared his throat and started, "Well, I, as the revelator see the future or new truth. I see things in vision form, things that will happen. So, you know how you were brought down to the water and told you needed to participate in the ceremony there?"

Westley felt the hairs on his arms rise as he warily responded. "Yes."

"Well, that was because I saw you standing on the bank of the river, soaking wet, with your white eyes, and I told Hirum."

Westley thought about his conversation with Hirum about the ceremony and felt his heart start beating faster.

"And Peter here, he can see time. It's complicated, but let me tell you, he sees hidden truths for certain, things that none of us can comprehend. Which sounds like it makes him a seer."

"Which leaves me as the prophet. But what does that even mean?" Westley shook his head, "I mean, I know what it means to my people, but here?"

Peter looked over at him. "I guess it means you are a teacher of truth, just like you said. And with my Nature, I saw that the three of us are supposed to accomplish something together."

Suddenly Westley felt something in his middle. It was a swirling of his inner parts, a circular motion inside his chest, and then it encompassed his entire body. It was power, which built and built, and then it exploded out of him, and with it came words. "But if you return to Me and keep My strictures and do them, though they who have been scattered into the most remote parts of the Earth or the heavens, I will have my vessel, my travelers, my triad gather them from there, and I bring them to the place that I have chosen to be taken into the heavens that all might start anew." The words were out, and the powerful swirling dissipated as quickly as it had formed.

Silence.

Westley reeled from the occurrence. He shook his head, hoping to alleviate the out-of-body feeling.

Finally, Peter whispered a stilted question. "What. Was. That."

Seth answered, "That my friend, that, was a prophet. Quick, let's write it down."

Westley shook his head. "No need, I remember it. That was very strange."

"So you get the grand privilege of speaking in riddles. I get to see riddles. And Seth never gets to know what he will be asked to do from one second to the next." The way Peter said this made Westley wonder if the boy was complaining, but he continued. "I love this, don't you? It's like a puzzle we get to figure out." And he grinned from ear to ear.

"Sure, it's great, but what does Westley's...little speech..."

"Foretelling," Peter supplied.

"Okay, what does his foretelling mean?"

"I have no idea, but it was super cool."

Both boys looked up at Westley, clearly anticipating an explanation. Westley thought back over his words. "I said that if we do as we should, God will use us to gather people that need to be gathered, even though they are from the four corners of the Earth."

"Gather them?"

"Like bring them here?" Peter asked.

Westley thought about it, reevaluating his words, but his thoughts were interrupted.

"Wait, wait, wait..." Peter exclaimed and reached out for Seth's arm. "The old man I saw. All the golden threads that reached beyond the weave into space." Then the boy cut his words short and became very still as he watched Seth, who looked like he'd entered a trance.

After a moment, Seth drew a quick deep breath, and Westley looked his way.

Peter asked quickly, "What did you see?"

"I saw us. Doing this."

Westley felt a prickle in his shoulders. Then he had that bursting feeling again, and it was as if a voice, not his own, exited his mouth. "Seth, that was not true. You must speak the truth. Remember the admonition."

Peter's eyes, the color of turmeric, found his. "What are you, a lie detector as well?"

"Uhm…" Westley answered brilliantly.

"The only problem is that is what I saw," Seth interjected, but his cheeks were pink.

The feeling came over Westley again, and words were in his mouth. "No. Focus. Tell the truth."

"I did," Seth complained.

Peter blurted, "Perhaps he doesn't mean truth like the opposite of a lie. He means truth like in discernment, like the point of the vision, what you were meant to learn from it."

Seth thought, "Okay. Well, we were together…" His voice trailed off as his mind moved. His eyes widened. "We were putting our minds together and using our Natures in concert."

Westley spoke up. "We are the triad I spoke of in my prophecy. The vessel, the travelers, and the triad. That's what God listed."

"It isn't God, Westley. It's the Master." The boy practically rolled his eyes with the comment. Westley did not understand what Peter meant by calling God something different. Still, he was smart enough to realize that perhaps Peter thought the cherubim from the Edenian legend were running the show here. Westley decided not to correct the boy.

"The travelers are the Jones defectors; we are the triad. Who is the vessel?" Peter asked, but it only took two shakes of a horse's tail for both boys to speak a name simultaneously. "Miriam."

And Westley felt the words and power exploding out of him again. "And then the cherubim with their flaming sword, which protect the tree of life, will, in the last days, bring a mighty end to pass. They will counsel the travelers and fill the vessel and bring the Father's work to conclusion and prepare the Garden for the Mother world and a new beginning."

Westley pulled himself out of the powerful experience with a gasp, blinking. He looked at the two boys, who seemed to have their jaws on the floor.

Peter snapped his shut as he said, "Well, Seth, there's your second witness. I guess we better go tell my Pa."

CHAPTER 17

Miriam

She could not figure out what to do with all the brawny men. They joked and teased each other ruthlessly. She had already had to talk to them about their language and jokes, but regardless of it, she liked them. Especially Gerald. He was a teddy bear with claws. She smiled and watched Gerald steal the soccer ball from Ben and run it to the goal faster than she thought possible. Clapping, she thought of the only other time she'd played soccer and felt her happiness fade.

As if she'd called him to her with her thoughts, Miriam saw Seth, Peter, Westley, along with her parents, and her Uncle Ezekiel walking down the Edenia road toward the ball field. Miriam's heart skipped over the vision of Seth. He was coming here to the place of the crime. She licked her lips and looked at the men in the field. Chiding herself and her fool heart, she told herself she would not let Seth have a moment more of control.

She looked back, and Seth, Peter, and Westley had stopped at the edge of the field. Seth was talking and gesturing at them, and then he turned away. Miriam sucked in a deep breath, not knowing she'd been holding it, and looked at her mother. Luanne Miller had her business face on. Finally, it dawned on Miriam that this group—coming out here toward them—was undoubtedly a bad omen.

Once they arrived, her father called the Joneses to gather up. It took them no time to do so, and Uncle Zeke raised an impressed eyebrow at them.

"Guardians," he began, but there were snickers all around at the title. "Yes, well, you hate that, so what should we call you?"

Karl called from the back of the group, "Li'l Boss calls us Travelers. It seems to work, though we have no idea what he means by it."

"Who's Li'l Boss?" Zeke asked.

Miriam answered, "Who else? Peter, of course." Her parents shared a look that held a thousand words in it.

"We have some news..." Miriam felt her heart thump hard in her chest. Her father continued, "The Master needs you to enter the Garden. You will learn about your Nature in there."

The men went utterly silent.

Miriam felt like her heart had beat one thousand times before Gerald spoke up. "Did I hear you correctly? You want us to go into the Garden of Eden?"

Miriam's mother spoke up. "I would rather die a thousand deaths. But it seems it is what the Master wants."

Gerald swept his hand over his bald head, looked around at his men, and nodded. "All right. Let's do it."

The walk to the bridge felt like it only took one minute. The ten steps through the Eden wood, a moment. And then the light. Then the peace. Serenity. Joy.

Her eyes were down. She knew from her one experience before in the Garden that blindness from the extreme light happened, but if she kept her eyes on her feet, she could keep her balance.

The extreme light filled everything in the Garden. The moss under Miriam's boots was an intense green, but it almost looked as if it had golden blood pulsing inside its thin hair-like tendrils. The leaves and thickets were somehow green, gold, and misty at the same time.

Her ears were enchanted by the sound of a trickling rill, the smell of magic and dirt and life, which delightfully reminded her of a garden of sun-warmed honeysuckle. Even the air tasted sweet, like a drop of nectar in her mouth.

The feel of power and pure electricity lifted the hair off her arms and the back of her neck.

Finally, she looked up just as the shock of it all wore off for the Travelers, and they began oohing and ahing. She did not take the time to look behind her at them, but she did smile. The rills turned to rivulets gathering and heading forward as if they were leading her to her destination. Her eyes followed them only briefly to acknowledge the beautiful and bounteous diversity of vegetation. All led to a slight incline of ground that acted as a plateau for two incredible trees.

One was a willowy, golden, radiant-filled arch of limbs and leaf. The other was a small, leafless, silver- and copper-veined thing with dark shedding bark like a strange grandparent to a sycamore. The plateau on which these incredible trees found root gushed water out and over in a thousand little waterfalls, but they did so in an oddly quiet way.

Miriam moved toward the trees in a trance. Her life force was pulled onward by this place's exotic peace and magic.

One moment, not a single creature existed besides Miriam and her company, but suddenly out of nowhere, the Master materialized before her.

They were light, beautiful, and deadly. A being that took up the space and capacity of four immortal, all-powerful entities of luminosity, knowledge, and experience. A unity of four human-like bodies that had somehow agreed to be one. A lethal yet peaceful joining.

Instantly, a voice filled the entirety of her insides. "Welcome Guardians, Travelers, and Miriam, our Vessel." She felt the power of these words and the eyes of a being upon her burn through her like fire.

Her knees hit the moss as her head and heart thumped with the magnificence of the voice of the Master filling her. Had the Master just addressed her personally and then called her a vessel? Like it was a title the same as Guardian. And then the Master was talking directly to her again.

"Miriam, you have done well. All has been done for your good. Do not allow the destroyer to take you. You are so near the fulfillment of all things. Be faithful. Use the tools I have prepared for you. Trust them. They will protect you, guide you. Your path is not easy, but know it was created for you with love and understanding of who you are. You are treasured."

Tears filled Miriam's eyes, and as she looked up, she saw that the Cherubim was not before her but before the Travelers. She rose and looked behind her, and though the Master seemed engrossed, slicing an arm in front of Gerald and the others, one of the faces of the Master was turned toward her. It was distinctly female, and when she met its eye, it smiled a love-filled brilliant split of light, lips, and teeth.

She moved sideways toward and around the Travelers. As she got closer, she noticed that many red-eyed men had their irises swirling with power. They, too, were moving their arms in the manner of the Cherubim.

Miriam found her father's face, who also seemed to be having an experience with the Master separate and distinct from what the Travelers were having. Her Uncle Zeke—the only other person who came—looked around at everything happening around him. He met Miriam's eyes and, circling around, moved toward her.

"What is happening to them?" he whispered.

Miriam blinked at him and could not look into his eyes. They were Seth's eyes. She whispered back, "I assume they are getting the training Seth saw they must have." She stumbled a bit over his name.

Zeke turned to her. He bent down, putting his face in her sight path. Capturing her glance, he held onto it as he stood, pulling her eyes upward. He held so much emotion in his face, his eyes. Vulnerability—an attitude he was unaccustomed to, she was sure—and he also looked sorrowful.

"Miriam, can I just say...please let me say, if I could take your suffering, I would, and deservedly so. The whole thing is my fault for not being more open with my family. I am truly sorry for all you suffered at the hands of the Joneses."

Her eyes narrowed at him, confident that this was neither the time nor the place for this conversation. However, it did bring up a thought; she'd spoken to Seth twice, and he had not apologized. She would not have heard it if he had, but still. Then her mind recalled what the Master had just said; all was done for her good, all meaning her kidnapping and torture—all? Or all the torment she'd experienced as a Guardian?

She guessed all meant ALL.

Biting her lip, she blinked at the man who would not allow her to look away. "My mind understands all that happened. I know this was an impossible situation." She narrowed her eyes again. "All except being drugged. All except being lured away from my family and those who would protect me. All except being betrayed directly after being told I was loved." She swallowed hard. "You are not responsible for those things." Finally, she looked away, tears gathering in her eyes, and her hand unconsciously clutched her chest.

"You are right. And you have my permission to use corporal punishment on my son for these transgressions. I have no defense for him where you are concerned."

She glanced at him. He was not looking at her. His arms were crossed, and his jaw was pulsing with contained rage.

After moments, he leaned in and whispered, "Did he really tell you he loved you?"

She sucked in a breath and nodded. "He told me right before the drugs took me. As if it were a deathbed confession." Tears streamed down her face. "He told me after giving me one the most wonderful nights of my life."

Zeke's jaw dropped a full inch. His eyes bulged. Then he looked away and shook his head in disgust. "Well, I will leave that up to him to fix if that is possible. But I hope you know that I am so sorry for my part."

Miriam's heart trembled, but she knew how she felt and what she had to say. "I forgive you." The words were whispered so softly that only in the peacefulness of the Garden could they have been heard.

And in her soul, she felt something. A lightness, a freedom, an exhilaration. Like a broken thing mending. The lighting of understanding struck her mind. She knew, just knew, that forgiveness was not for Zeke but for her. Sure, it might make him feel better, but it was her soul that healed.

A different kind of tear fell from her cheek this time.

"What do we use this for?" Miriam heard Gerald say aloud.

She turned toward him and watched him do the thing with his hand again. What were they doing? Seeing them all waving their hands in such a weird manner was such a strange sight.

Gerald's answer must have happened in his mind, for he nodded at the Master and moved forward, and the strangest thing of all happened; Gerald disappeared. Then, within the space of five heartbeats, all the Travelers disappeared.

CHAPTER 18

Seth walked away from the ball field with a knot in his throat. Seeing the Travelers playing soccer in the same field he'd played with Miriam, to see the swath of white-blonde hair blowing in the breeze...

He wiped at his nose, the regret and anguish for his role in what happened to Miriam so bone-deep he wished he could cut the pain out of him. He was about to turn the corner, heading to his house, when he heard running feet behind him.

He turned and saw Peter. "Wait up, Seth."

Seth turned away from the boy and attempted to clear up his countenance. He told himself he couldn't do anything about how Miriam felt. He could only be as sorry as possible and change.

"So, Pa says I can't go into the Garden with the Travelers. He says that, if we want, he will take me in with your family later tonight or tomorrow." Seth stumbled at the thought. "What do you think?"

"I, uhm, I'm not sure. That seems pretty big," Seth stammered.

He had no desire to go into the Garden of Eden. His stomach trembled with excited swirls. Or maybe he did.

"Don't be afraid. It's awesome."

Seth looked at the precocious boy and smirked, "How do you know?"

"I just know, okay?"

"This coming from the boy who thought it was cool to drown Travelers."

"I did not think it was cool. I just knew it would end up cool."

"How did you know that?"

"Because I know the Master. I know how They work. I know that They do only those things that are good and purposeful."

Seth blinked at the boy. If there was ever an example of pure trust, it was this boy. He had utter unadulterated faith in this place and this person they called the Master. Seth would give his left hand for an ounce of that faith.

At that moment, a warm, quiet something whispered to his mind and heart that he did have faith. It was just a tiny seed, but it was there. Seth smiled to himself. "I guess I would like to go. Let's go see if Abby and Lilly feel the same way." Seth moved his hand to cuff Peter on the back of the neck in a chummy manner when time slowed. His hand moved toward his friend as if moving through water or zero gravity.

Finally, after an eternity, his hand clapped down on Peter's skin, and the moment it did so, a vision, bright and huge, formed before his eyes. It was long and powerful, and what Seth saw felt more like a movie than real life.

⁂

"The second your hand touched my neck...bam!" Peter yelled as if he had won the lottery. "I was in my ribbon room."

"Mine felt like a movie, and it happened when I touched Peter," Seth said to Westley and felt like the guy was not even paying attention.

Westley nodded at the two of them. "Well, that's great, but what does it have to do with me?" The cowboy pulled on his collar., "Not to be rude, but I was just about to take my lady out on a walk."

Peter walked up to the man and slapped him squarely across the face. "You are a Guardian now. You do not have time to moon over my sister. We have work to do."

And Seth couldn't agree more.

The man touched his cheek and glared at Peter, but then he was taken up in a vision. "And the Lord God says, He will have a righteous people. If he has to burn their homes and fields and cattle, if he must torment them with plague and death and famine, a righteous people will he have." Finally, Westley took a deep breath and quivered himself out of the vision.

Peter smiled and said, "Got ya!"

Westley finished the excellent glare he'd started and wagged his head at the boy. "Fine, let's figure this thing out! But I have to go tell Esther that I can't come. Let's walk and talk." The tall man stalked to the door and pulled it open.

Peter grinned.

Seth shook his head at Peter and followed Westley out. The afternoon was getting on, and Seth felt the day's heat on his back as they walked.

Westley kept a quick pace with his long legs as they walked toward the middle of town. He stated in a surly tone, "Will you please start over? I wasn't listening to anything you all said back there." His accent made the words you and all sound like one word, y'all, which made Seth smile. "Though I do get the gist of it." His hand rubbed at his cheek once again.

Peter, who was jogging to keep up, looked at Seth and shucked his chin. Seth began speaking. "First, there's the whole touching thing. I want to talk about that in detail, but I have got to tell you what I saw. In my vision, a huge volcano erupted. I mean, this thing was massive. I saw ash, and lava and earthquakes and..."

Westley stopped walking, his pale blue irises moving in a creepy spiral. Seth thought it looked like seeing a hurricane from space. A pale corkscrew with his black pupil as the center. "The Lord God will cause a great destruction upon the land, earthquakes, and famine, all to chasten his people so that they might choose Him as their true God and forsake all their idols." Westley shook his head as if he had to rid himself of the power of his Nature.

Peter threw his fist into the air like he had just won some kind of contest and said, "Ooo, Ooo, my turn. I was pulled into my ribbon room and instantly pulled toward one of the strange golden threads; I saw Miriam and Travelers move as one unit from the light of Edenia and toward one of the golden threads."

Westley once again stopped. "And it shall come to pass that a work and a wonder will come among all the peoples of the world. The Vessel will travel to every corner and gather from those with knowledge of good and evil the spark for the fruit." Again, Westley shook off the power. But this time, he did not continue walking. He turned slowly toward Peter and Seth, his pale blue eyes as round as saucers.

A volcano destroying a fourth of the country did not faze him, but this did. Seth was confused. What had he said? Seth reached his hand to shake Westley, and that slow-moving sensation returned. Seth was pulled into a vision as his hand contacted Westley's sleeveless forearm.

It was of Peter telling Seth about the golden thread with people and Seth using a terribly old computer to look up the people. Then his mind spun like he was on a roller coaster, and the room also turned. He stood in front of Miriam, Gerald, and Westley. He was relaying the information from the computer. Westley did his thing to confirm it, and then Gerald and a team of armed Travelers took Miriam by the hand and disappeared.

Seth stumbled out of the vision as if he'd been pushed. He landed on his butt, the dust from the road puffing up into his face and causing him to sneeze.

"Whoa, did it just happen again?" Peter said as Westley held out a hand to help Seth up. "What did you see?"

Seth closed his eyes and hung his head, attempting to organize what he'd seen. "I saw something I don't understand at all. I was in front of a terribly old computer. You told me about your golden thread and people, and then I told Miriam about it. Then she and the

Travelers disappeared." Once done, he pulled on Westley's proffered hand and stood.

Instantly Westley did his thing, "The Vessel will travel to every corner and gather from those with knowledge of good and evil the spark for the fruit."

The three boys look at one another, stunned into silence.

Peter broke the silence. "I think we better go talk to my papa."

CHAPTER 19

Miriam

Walking out of the Garden, Uncle Zeke and Pa questioned the Travelers on what they had done, what they had learned, and what they said seemed impossible.

"It was like we just ripped a hole in the fabric of time and space and stepped into a different part of the world," Gerald said.

"Incredible!" Zeke exclaimed.

"What on Earth could you use that Nature for?" Her pa wondered. "We don't go around the world. There is no need for that. We Guard Eden, which is here."

And that was when she noticed Peter, Westley, and Seth running toward them.

Once they got close enough, Seth looked at her, and his face fell. He stopped running, and Peter looked back at him. Seth said something to Peter and then turned around and moved in the other direction down the road. Miriam was instantly able to breathe again.

The two guys reached their group a moment later, and Pa asked Peter, alarm in his voice, "What is it?"

"Seth, Westley, and I saw something, and it's big."

***

Once the boys finished spilling the beans, Miriam felt utter shock. The Master wanted her and the Travelers to rip holes in time and space and travel all around the world, gathering something from random people. What? Deep in the pit of her stomach, she knew from Westley's prophecy that she was to take memories. She was to gather soul slivers. And all of a sudden, the name Vessel made sense.

Peter, Seth, and Westley would work together to figure out where she and the Travelers needed to go, and then go they would. Miriam thought about all this implied concerning her and Seth, and they were working together. On the side of the road, she burst into tears in a fit of pure excitement and utter dread.

PAPA, the three amigos, and Gerald went into town where Edenia's only computer was housed. As Miriam washed the dinner radishes and handed them to her mama, her hand trembled. But then she saw the light above the table swinging, then a slightly unbalanced feeling and a shaking under her feet.

She turned to her mama, who had also stopped moving.

"What in the world?"

"It's an earthquake."

"Here?" Miriam asked.

Her mama's eyes were wide, "Yes, Miri, here."

CHAPTER 20

The computer was in the basement of his uncle Brian's house. Seth sat in the chair with everyone gathered around him.

"What else did you see, Peter? Was he wearing anything in particular? A symbol of some sort? Did he have a tattoo?"

"You're not listening to me. I did not really see him, or more. What I do see of him is different from me looking at you right now. It's strange to explain. I know him completely. More completely than any person should know another person, but I can't tell you how to find him. He is a tribe leader. His tribe has had many wars. He has led them through them with as little bloodshed as possible. He has power and respect among his and many other tribes because of this." Peter thought hard, closing his eyes and sifting through his memories.

"That's a great idea, Peter. Go back and touch the thread again."

Peter opened his eyes. "I wasn't doing that."

Suddenly, Westley piped up, in his way. "And the servants of the Lord obeyed his call by the laying on of hands and by the gifts of the spirit." Westley shook his head, his eyes returning to the boys. "I'm sorry, but I don't think I'm going to get used to you busting into conversations at awkward times like that."

Peter wanted to stay on task, but he could not help but ask, "What happens to you when you get taken by your Nature?"

Westley took a deep breath and looked upward. "It's sort of like that game telephone except the person whispering in my ear is so loud, the voice so soul-crushingly reverberating I am compelled to repeat the words it tells me out loud or else, I don't know, risk having my ears explode."

Seth nodded, "Sounds painful."

"I think it could be."

Peter pulled everyone back to the subject. "Okay, so what was meant by that, and why did it happen right at that moment?"

The trio went silent as they all thought of what it could mean.

Gerald spoke up from the corner. He'd insisted on coming with them since he would lead the Traveling. "You want an outsider's perspective?" He asked it as if he needed permission to speak but went on without anyone saying yes. "As a church boy myself, the laying on of hands seems a pretty obvious statement, somebody's gotta touch somebody. And gifts of the spirit, I think, could easily qualify as our Natures, don't you think?"

Peter smiled. Having this guy around was helpful as having ten regular men. Gerald was the bomb. He looked over at Seth and Westley. The two were thinking hard.

Seth spoke up. "Okay, well, I can see that when I touched Peter, and when I touched Westley, that 'laying on of hands' caused a vision to pop up."

"It also caused Westley to do his thing, and me to be pulled into my ribbon room," Peter added. "I saw Miriam and the Travelers move from Edenia to the first Golden thread."

"And I said, 'And the Lord God caused that his servants should search the land, that they use every means and tool.'" Westley quoted himself.

Seth said, "Westley's foretelling matches my vision, but Peter, your thread vision with the Travelers does not match my vision of a volcanic eruption."

Gerald stood and walked over to them. "Unless the eruption is the sign that it is time to go find the golden thread person."

Peter smiled and clapped Gerald on the arm. "Makes sense to me."

Westley shifted his weight and said, "So does that mean that God is telling us to touch one another while using our Natures?"

Peter rolled his eyes. "The Master"—he emphasized the two

words—"seems to like having us work together, or else he would give all of us black eyes like Seth."

"Working together has a refining effect. That is a fact," Gerald stated.

"Okay, so that means we gotta touch each other," Peter said, closing his eyes to pull his Nature to him. Once he had it, he said, "Ready?" He heard murmurs of agreement, and he reached out to Westley and Seth. He found their hands at the exact same moment and gasped as his ribbon room moved him to the ribbon of the tribal leader.

He could hear Westley speaking in the background but could not understand his words. He didn't really know what to do but be with the ribbon. He pulled tighter and reached toward the ribbon, though he knew the consequence. Suddenly everything about the man that was the thread pushed into his mind and overwhelmed all his senses.

CHAPTER 21

Seth saw a wild and lush valley with all sorts of life. Before him stood a man, wizened and old with black, painted skin. He wore a crown of feathers, flowers, and bones on his head. Surrounding Seth, Miriam, and the Travelers were warriors with spears, and knives pointed at him. Seth noticed in the background a group of men painted with white paint, making them look like skeletons.

The leader before them leveled the group with a wise stare. And that was when Miriam, who looked like a goddess with her long blonde hair and violet eyes, stood and held her hands up placatingly. She stepped near the chief and suddenly had a spear at her throat.

Those eyes shifted to the side and found Gerald, and that was when the man moved his hand in a peculiar way. Miriam disappeared only to reappear behind the chief, her hands on his head, her irises swirling. The Travelers, armed to the teeth, drew their weapons and used them on the tribesmen, not to kill but to disengage as they did so, so they surrounded the chief. Miriam and Gerald were there to catch Miriam as she fell backward, unconscious. And then they all disappeared.

Peter pulled Seth out of the vision by letting go of his hands. Seth opened his eyes to the world around him and saw Peter on the floor. Gerald was already at the boy's side, gently rolling his head and opening his eyelids. He lightly tapped his cheek. "Li'l Boss, you okay?"

Peter moaned and then opened his eyes. He immediately clutched his head and whined in pain.

"What is happening?" Gerald asked and looked up at Seth for

answers, but before Seth could say, he had no idea. Peter was quiet and trying to sit up.

Gerald helped him. "Easy now, bud."

"I'm good," Peter said. "It's just when I go that deep into someone…it hurts to come back here." He got to his feet and moved on. "So, what did we find out?"

"I did the usual and murmured some mumbo jumbo. Basically, we must not do violence, only adhere to the task."

Gerald confirmed, "Yep, that's about what he said."

Seth described what happened to him, from the setting to the strange painting on the faces of the men.

Gerald said, "I took my ex-wife on a backpacking trip to Indonesia ten years ago. We learned about native tribes in the eastern part of the country who painted themselves similarly to what you just described. If I remember correctly."

Seth's jaw dropped. Gerald was so useful not only with his skills as a soldier, but his life experience. He sat at the computer and searched for Indonesia + skeleton tribes + chief.

The Papua New Guinea tribe popped up with a few pictures of women and men painted extravagantly. Seth pushed the images tab and was inundated with the creepy visage of human skeletons. However, that was not what dropped his jaw; there, also on the screen, was a picture of the man he had seen in his vision. The chief.

There was a rumbling of earth and house under Seth's feet. It was slight at first, but then the pencil on the desk bounced and trembled. He looked at his companions. Gerald's hand was up on the ceiling of the cellar, his feet wide for balance as if he could hold up the house if it fell. The house shook harder.

Gerald said, "We gotta get out of here." He made a sweeping movement with this hand, and Seth noticed the rotation of his red irises. "Hang on to me," Gerald yelled as the wood creaked and the ground grumbled.

Seth knocked his chair over in his haste to take Gerald's arm. Once the others did as well, they took a single step forward. Seth could not see but could feel through something, and suddenly they were out of the house and in the middle of the street in front of Miriam's house.

Peter exclaimed, "That was so freaking cool!"

Gerald smiled but also searched the surroundings and planted his feet in case the earth still rolled.

Then Westley had a foretelling. "When the Lord God shall give his Vessel the sign, when the earth shall shake and roll, then will my servants know they are called to begin their work."

Peter looked up at Gerald. "Guess you were right. Once again."

"I guess so. Are you boys all right?"

They all nodded.

"Okay, well, I am going to round up the troops. We have a mission, and the Master just gave us the go. I trust the two of you to brief Miriam?" Gerald said as he walked backward away from them.

Peter piped up, "I'll do it."

"And your father?"

"I'll tell him too," Peter promised.

But then Gerald halted, "How many men did we bring, Seth?"

Seth closed his eyes and reimagined the scene. "I would say ten at least."

Gerald nodded to him, turned, and jogged up the road.

"Where do you think he will get the weapons?" Seth asked the air.

But Peter, of course, answered. "He brought a fairly large cache with him from the Joneses."

Nodding, "Of course he did. But does that mean it is all plastic and wood?"

"Gerald is worth ten regular men. Do you think he brought wooden and plastic weapons with him?"

"You have a point." Seth turned toward the house. Miriam was there watching them. Anxious to keep respecting her wishes, he looked at Peter. "You got this?" And patted him on the back, careful not to touch his skin.

"I do," Peter said and flattened his lips together in regret.

Nodding, Seth turned toward his own home and started walking.

However, he heard a sweet voice call, "Seth." He paused but did not turn around. She repeated, "Seth."

He did turn this time. She had come to the gate and looked at him. "You can stay."

Shocked Seth answered, "Are you certain?"

Her hand went to her chest at the sound of his voice, and her cheeks flushed, but she said, "Yes." Then she proved her utter sweetness. Her forgiving nature. Her incredible character by adding, "Thank you for trying so hard to respect my wishes."

Seth felt his heart drop into his shoes. She was the most amazing person he had ever met. He wanted to run to her and scream his apologies. To weep at her feet and beg forgiveness, and as the feeling built, another feeling came with it. A warning. A big fat stop sign. He remembered the vision or dream he'd had. He could not say those words to her yet. It was not the right time. She would not like it. So he listened to that wise voice inside him and only moved with Peter to the gate.

At that moment, Hirum, who had sort of disappeared after the Travelers entered the Garden, came thundering down the road on a beautiful white mare.

He hopped off the creature as if he were a cowboy in the middle of a hog-tying competition. "Is everyone all right?"

Peter spoke up, "Sure, Papa. Where have you been?"

"You think you are the only one the Master gave a job to?" His eyes fell on Seth and then Miriam, who just happened to be a few feet away. His eyebrows knotted up and raised. Concern and question.

"It's all right, Papa. I told him to come."

He nodded. "Well, all right then. I have the feeling we have much to discuss. Let's go in. I feel a nip in the air."

CHAPTER 22

Miriam

As soon as the four of them had settled inside—Westley had taken off to find Esther—Peter spilled the beans of everything.

Miriam was very clear that this was about her in a big way. Still, the fact that she was in the same room with Seth, that he sat two feet from her, and that the last time they had been in this room together was when he had picked her up for their date kept creeping into her brain. Her eyes moved to his face over and over again.

Her father exclaimed, "Miriam, you are going to Indonesia to take memories from a long-forgotten about chief." Her brain kicked into gear.

"Yes!" She breathed and looked over at Seth.

Peter chimed in, "And if the golden threads are any indication of what the future holds, Miriam will travel the globe, taking memories."

"It's almost as if this job were tailor-made for someone who wanted to see the world." The voice of Seth added to the conversation in a gentle, quiet way.

Miriam shuddered and commanded her heart to calm down. "But, how will I know what memories to take?" she finally spat out.

Her father answered, "I'd imagine the right thing will happen once you are there."

Miriam considered. "Yes, sometimes the memories are a product of my need. I suppose if I need to take what is necessary..."

"Knowledge of good and evil is what you're after," Peter clarified. "That is what Westley revealed."

"Okay, thank you, Peter. Then the knowledge of good and evil will emerge when I pull." Miriam answered and found that her hands could not be still. She wrung them continually in her lap. Was it Seth, or was it this adventure that lay before her? Indonesia.

Seth said her name, and it pulled her out of her thoughts. "Yes?"

"I saw something very specific. I have already told this to Gerald, but you need to know as well." He cleared his throat and shifted in his seat. "At some point, the warriors surrounding the chief may threaten you."

"What does that mean?" Hirum chimed in, concerned.

"It means they might put a weapon close to her and threaten her with it." He turned back to Miriam. "If they do, all you have to do is give Gerald or one of the other Travelers a look. They will move you from where you are to directly behind the chief, where you can easily reach his head and do your thing."

Miriam nodded stoically, but her father said, "That sounds like a complex maneuver. Perhaps we should have you all practice it before you leave."

Peter said, "I think that's a great idea, but, Papa, the Master said, through Westley, the earthquake was the sign they needed to leave. So..."

At that exact moment, Miriam heard the sound of clopping boots, a lot of them, on her porch. Then Butch opened the door, and Gerald, armed to the teeth, marched into the front room.

Seth stood and said, "Wow, that was fast."

Gerald smiled, the corners of his eyes wrinkling in such a way as to make him look even creepier with those red eyes.

"Traveling is actually the best." Gerald moved to stand before her. "Miriam. I need you to come outside with me."

Hirum said, "I hope you want to practice these maneuvers with her."

Gerald smiled again. "That is exactly what we are going to do. There is no chance whatsoever that she will be in danger."

Miriam took Gerald's arm and allowed him to lead her outside.

"So the men and I have been talking. We know how to capture a room and an area. You stand in the middle of us, and we will take care of you."

"Seth told me about getting into trouble. All I have to do is give you the eye, and you will move me." They stepped outside, and Miriam was surrounded by Travelers. She smiled at them as Gerald continued.

"I can't really move you. I will need you to take one step forward. That step will be into safety, but I can't pull the portal around you. You must walk through it. The boys have been practicing, and we got this down."

Remy said, "Let's move out into the street."

They did so.

"Peter, can you play the part of the malefactor?"

Peter whooped. "I thought you'd never ask."

Miriam rolled her eyes at her brother, but her eyes were again drawn to Seth, who was sitting on the stairs of the porch.

Gerald turned to him. "You coming?"

Seth looked around and then pointed to himself. "Me?"

"Yes, you are the only one who knows what the target looks like. You have to come."

Seth shook his head and looked at Miriam. "No. I showed you a picture of him."

Gerald argued, "You showed us a man in crazy makeup and a crazy outfit. If my life depended on it, I wouldn't know who the chief was. You have to come."

Seth looked at Miriam uncertainly. She took a deep breath and said, "You heard the man." Then she motioned him to come to the road.

"So this is how it's going to go down. We must be touching each other, so we go to the same spot," Remy explained. "We have been practicing drills where we are shoulder to shoulder, so our arms are free."

The men lined up in an awkward circular formation, where they were all touching. Good thing these men had massive muscled arms and shoulders. Miriam walked forward with Gerald and Seth.

"In there with you," he said to her and Seth. They looked at each other hesitantly. "Is there going to be an issue? Because we have to have both of you. So you might just have to set aside the baggage for a few minutes at least."

Miriam smashed her lips together and breathed deeply before saying, "I'm good." And she walked forward. Richard moved out of formation to let her and Seth in and allow Gerald his spot.

"Miriam, you hold on to me here," Gerald said, pointing to a strap on the back of his vest.

"You hold here," Remy said to Seth, pointing to a similar strap on his back.

"We move as one," Gerald said.

"You civilians, keep low and hold tight," Remy said and waited until both she and Seth nodded their understanding before saying, "Boys, same as before."

They began tightening the circle. They pulled their weapons out from their holsters and tucked them into place. They all crouched as one and began calling out weird things. Mark. On my signal. Portals up. Forward.

They moved as one. Seth brushed her. She felt his warmth. Then they went through the portal, which led to the soccer field. The moment they stepped into the field, the Travelers spread like a sideways diamond, Remy and Gerald remaining inside the formation.

Miriam couldn't describe the way the men moved as one but more as a cog in the mechanism of safety. Their eyes went everywhere. Their heads turned in a practiced way so that when one looked left, his buddies next to him looked forward and behind. It was incredible to watch, and Miriam felt so proud of these men and their hours of training.

It shocked her that if it hadn't been for the Joneses, these men would not be collected here. And if it hadn't been for Seth, she never would have known that they could do this for her. The words from the Master echoed in her mind. "All things have been done for your good."

How could you fight against the plans and schemes of the Master? No one could. Because she did not know the future, it gave her the illusion of freedom, but she was not free, not really. None of them was. The Gods and the Master molded them all to do and be what was needed. They were all being woven as threads in a tapestry.

Miriam looked over at Seth. He was just as much a victim as she was. Seth did precisely what the Master knew he would do and, in so doing, brought to pass this. Whatever THIS was. Yes, she got hurt along the way, but who was to say that all these ex-Joneses, trained, loyal soldiers, would have come to her aid and joined this cause without the harshness and injustice of her torture?

She tried not to get lost in her thoughts. She would have to play a part here. The men went through the same formation and moved through space and time back to her house, where Peter waited with a makeshift spear.

The second the men came through and spread out, Peter sneaked between the men and put the stick to Miriam's throat threateningly.

"What ya gonna do, little girl?" he asked in a menacing voice.

Miriam wanted to laugh and hit the stick away—he wasn't pushing it into her neck—but she remembered what Seth said. So she gave Gerald the side eye. He sliced his hand through the air and then nodded at her. She took a step forward, and instead of having the stick go farther into her neck, she stepped to freedom right behind Peter. She took him by the head and shook a little.

"What *you* gonna do, big meanie?"

The men laughed. But Gerald called them back to attention. "Miriam, you have to pretend to faint." Seth said, "'Cause that's what happens, right?"

"Oh yeah." She rolled her eyes in her head, put the back of her hand to her brow, and let herself fall dramatically. But she didn't fall. Gerald caught her, and just like that, they were back in the field. Just her and Gerald. But that was only for a moment. Then the other men arrived. Gerald sat her down on the ground.

"How long are you typically unconscious?" Remy asked as he stepped up to them.

"It depends on how much I have to take. Sometimes hours, sometimes minutes."

Gerald looked at Remy.

"Noted," the man responded.

"How did we do?" Seth asked.

"Good; let's practice it a few more times," Remy said, "and Seth, you get involved. You are not here for the ride. We need you to identify the chief. Pretend you see him. If you can't say anything, use this as a symbol." He took two fingers from his right hand, pointed them outward, and then tapped them in the air twice as if he were pointing at someone/thing but with emphasis.

"Got it."

THEY PRACTICED FOR AN HOUR, and then Mama called them in for dinner. As Miriam sat with Gerald, Remy, Ben, and Richard, she felt an overwhelming love for them and gratitude for their hard-won skills and moxie. Observing her family as well, she felt pride in the mission they all participated in, and love for them and the new closeness they had together.

As she looked at Seth, she had new eyes. Knowing that, in fact, him playing the tricky part the Master gave him was why they all sat together at this moment. Yes, there had been malevolence behind his betrayal—which she was not yet reconciled with—but also, she could feel and see the regret and know the impossibly hard choice he had to make.

Her mind went back to earlier. Was it a choice? Did he really have a fault in the situation? He had not been the one to hold the branding iron. It was a circular mess in her head. However, she was proud of herself because she had spent several hours with him and had not broken down into tears or panic once. She had come an impossible distance since breakfast. She'd taken control, and then found a place in her heart that held understanding. She smiled. It was a good day.

Uncle Brian entered their yard and pulled up a seat next to her papa. He whispered in the man's ear, and Hirum's eyes widened. She watched him mouth the word, "Wow."

She supposed she would have to wait to find out what was happening because they were leaving for their mission as soon as they ate, and the Travelers' plates were almost clean.

"Does anyone know what time it will be when we get there?" Ben asked.

"I looked it up," Remy stated. "They are twelve hours ahead. So if we leave now, it will be seven a.m. there."

"Your phone is still working?"

"No, I Traveled to my apartment in Yonkers and looked it up."

"You did what?" Gerald asked Remy.

"Don't worry, I only stayed for a moment."

Right then, Seth came up to them. "Hi, I don't mean to be a pest, but the thing happened again, and I am supposed to tell you not to eat anything while you are out of Edenia. If you do, you might not be able to Travel back."

Boaz called from the other side of the table, "You saw these people wanna stick a spear in our Miriam. I don't think there is any chance of us sitting down for a meal together." Many of the men laughed, but all murmured agreement.

Miriam's heart warmed at the protectiveness of these hardened men. They were the absolute best. Rocks on the outside, pudding inside.

Gerald turned to Remy with raised I-told-you-so eyebrows. "Let's keep the extra jaunts around the world to a minimum, please. They have a computer here. We can use it if we need it."

"How was I to know?"

"You ask."

"Well, I didn't eat anything," Remy said, and his cheeks went pink. It was an odd look for a warrior such as him.

Seth's eyes found Miriam, and he said, "Don't worry, they don't eat anything good in Indonesia." Then he smiled a reassuring little smile and returned to his seat.

What he didn't know was that her present worry was about taking memories. Though Seth, Peter, and everyone reassured her that this was what her Nature was intended for, she wondered how she would feel about it when it happened. Would it still feel like a violation when she was asked by the Master to do it?

Still, he was trying to make her feel better because he knew how much she wanted to experience the outside. A weird, warm feeling came to her then, and she wanted to throw her arms around Seth. He was like the Travelers, always thinking of her, remembering her hope and disappointments, and trying to make them better.

A tear came to her eye, and she squashed the warm feelings for him instantly.

"Well..." Gerald started. "Ya'll ready to do this thing?"

The men cleared their throats and pushed back their chairs, and then there was a flurry of getting things snapped and strapped back on.

Before Miriam could count to fifteen, the Travelers were ready and lining up in the street. She and Seth in the center of the staggered diamond-shaped circle. She looked at Seth, and he looked at her.

"Are you ready?" he asked.

"Not even remotely," she answered.

Seth smiled. "These guys know exactly what they are doing. They are pros; they will keep us all safe." He reassuringly reached for her but stopped himself before he touched her. He looked down at his hand that moved of its own volition and pulled it back. Then he looked straight ahead.

This gesture made Miriam cringe. Why did he think he could not touch her? But then her stomach lurched, and she shuddered. Because he couldn't. No matter what her heart was getting over, her body struggled with all things Seth.

Gerald said, "Remember, men. Violence is the very last resort. These natives have only spears and stone knives, but they are skilled warriors, so be on your guard."

Seth interrupted. "Gerald, I hope you don't even have real bullets in those guns."

Gerald looked over at him. "In this"—he patted the gun he held—"are rubber bullets." Then his hand went to the gun at his belt. "But all of us have the real thing, just in case."

"Okay, fair enough. But Westley's foretelling was completely clear. We are not to hurt anyone."

"Copy," Gerald said. "Men?"

The nine others repeated Gerald's word. "Copy."

Miriam took a deep breath and closed her eyes. When she opened them, she grabbed Gerald's strap and prepared to do this.

One last look at Seth. He smiled. "Don't worry. I've seen this whole exchange. You might be threatened, but you will not be harmed. It will be over in a few moments, and we will be successful."

Seth's words penetrated her fear, and she nodded calmly.

Gerald added. "Don't let Seth's confidence affect your watchfulness. The very reason he saw success could be because of our watchfulness. We must keep Miriam safe. Remember what the Master said."

The men grunted.

Remy yelled. "Ready?"

As one, the men pulled their weapons to their shoulders and bent in a defensive posture.

"Mark. On my signal. Portals up. Forward."

Miriam took a step forward into a wild jungle.

IT HURT Miriam's brain to think about how Gerald and Remy knew where they were going. But the men navigated around the tiny huts made of some sort of green log, large leaves, and straw. The heat and humidity blasted Miriam's skin, bringing instant perspiration to her brow and underarms. Green and brown was the color of the earth here. Everything looked dusty, used, sickly, almost diseased, like the people here used the vegetation almost to death and did not bother to protect the life-sustaining plants and trees for the future. It felt like an alien planet compared to her people's respectful and preservative way of using the land.

Above all of this, though, she noticed the way things smelled. There was dirt. Yes. Clay-like ground that had its own aroma. There was plant life. Yes, with its smell of rot and chlorophyll. But there was also something foul. She couldn't decide what it was. Human. Death. Sewage.

Miriam looked over at Seth, who kept low and aware as she remembered what Seth described as how Cairo smelled. It made her smile and consider how much she wanted this exposure.

Remy rounded a hut and paused his advance. With the thought of this in her mind, Miriam reached across Gerald and touched the leafy, muddy wall of the hut. It was like bamboo or banana tree trunk. When he narrowed his eyes, she whispered into Gerald's ear, "I need to touch the places we go, or else it is like I was not here."

It was only a moment before they were moving again. Miriam looked at Seth, who looked back at her, and she brought her fingers up to her nose and pinched the end. A signal to tell him what she thought of the smell of this place.

His eyes went wide, but he instantly saw what she was saying and took it for the very small olive branch it was. He nodded and smiled. Then mouthed silently. "Told you." Then he pinched his own nose.

The progression stopped again, and that was when Miriam heard voices. People jabbered in a language Miriam did not know.

Remy heard it too and froze except for his clenched fist flying up in the air. The men stopped instantly. Remy turned to them, slouching even lower than before. His eyes wide, his face pale, his ear cocked into the air.

He looked at Gerald and tapped one of his ears, his eyebrows raised as if he were asking a silent question.

Miriam looked at Gerald, who had a similar expression. He nodded slowly at Remy, and Miriam's eyes flashed to all the Travelers. It seemed the shock and surprise were a plague, for they all looked the same.

She tried to get Gerald's attention to ask what was happening, but he brushed her away and put a finger over his lips. His ear was cocked up the same as Remy's.

Seth moved next to her and tapped her on the shoulder.

He was only a foot away, and her heart thundered. His mouth started to move silently. She watched his lips but was far too distracted by this opportunity to gape at the beautiful line of flesh to discern what he said. His mouth stopped moving, so she looked into his eyes. The question of did-you-get-that was there.

She shook her head. She hadn't gotten a word. He bit his bottom lip in frustration and contemplation. Then he pointed to her ear and leaned a little toward her, the other hand cupped at the side of his mouth. He wanted to whisper in her ear.

She blinked at him. Her hands began to tremble. Their eyes caught. She looked into Seth's soul through those black eyes, and all she wanted at that moment was to forget everything that had happened between them. To never think of it again. To take him by the shoulders and pull his lips to hers. She wanted him. She wanted all of him, even the malevolent part. There was no way of denying it. Her body tingled with desire for him, for possessing him. It was overwhelming and frightening, and not really appropriate to be feeling this way at this moment.

Seth raised an eyebrow at her, and she moved into action. Of course, he could whisper in her ear. She would have to control herself to not pull him into her arms and tell him all was forgiven. She nodded and turned her ear toward his face.

He moved in close, his cupped hand touching her cheek. "I think the Travelers have more than the gift of portaling us around. I think they can understand the natives' language."

He pulled away. And Miriam shivered a good shiver. She smiled at him and nodded. "Cool," she mouthed.

When she looked back at Gerald, he gestured to Ben. She had no idea what the complex mix of hand and expression told Ben, but he immediately broke away from the group, slid behind the other side of the hut, moved to the ground, and pulled a scope from his vest. He didn't use it, though. His head ducked a quick peek around the hut, then slid his head out for a more extended glance. He watched for a full minute.

As he kept his eyes forward, his hand reached back and made gestures again. After communicating whatever it was, he pulled his head back, turned, pointed to Seth, and motioned Seth to come to his side. Seth did. The man whispered in Seth's ear.

Seth nodded and promptly turned invisible.

The men stayed in formation and kept their eyes roving the woods and the buildings around them.

At one point, Miriam saw two women and several children walking together in the trees. They were chatting and did not even look toward the group. The funny thing was that they were all wearing modern clothes. They did not look the way Miriam pictured natives.

And then Seth was back. He moved back into the circle and gestured to have the men move in tight. He whispered, "The chief is eating his breakfast in the shade of his hut about fifty paces that way. We passed right by his hut a few moments ago. There are seven young men shooting their bows at a target twenty yards past him. They are who we need to watch out for."

Gerald's mind analyzed the information and said, "Let's circle back to that hut and see if we can get Miriam in and out without anyone the wiser."

They nodded and formed up, then moved.

However, before they could get ten paces, several young men in cutoff jeans with long, very simple bows and arrows came out of the trees and right into their path.

The Travelers were on sudden alert, and so were the young men. Before Miriam could say Bob's your uncle, bows were drawn, arrows nocked, and guns were aimed.

Miriam stepped forward, hands up. "No, no, no, we mean you..."

And that was how she found a spearhead at her throat. The spear that had Miriam by the throat crossed over Boaz's shoulder. Miriam knew as clear as day the man could disarm the native in a moment, but a look between him and Remy had told him to hold off.

A man, old and in an elaborate feather, got up and moved to stand behind the group of warriors. He started speaking in their hiccupping language. Then suddenly, Remy was talking to the men in the same language.

Seth cleared his throat, but she could not look behind her to find him. In fact, the only person in her sight was Gerald, who listened to the conversation, but had his eyes on Seth. Once they were done communicating, his eyes moved to her. His mouth whispered, "Chief." And he chin gestured toward the older man. She looked back at the old man and nodded at Gerald.

The chief shouted. This was not going well.

So, she nodded and mouthed, "Do it." And she pulled her Nature to her.

Gerald sliced his hand in the air and then nodded. Miriam took a step forward and landed right behind the chief. Quickly she placed her hands on the man's head from behind. She settled in her mind the need to pull what was proper, and the moment she did so, the man in her hands relaxed into her grip, and she felt something like pride fill the bond that connected them. This man was anxious and almost excited to give her his memories. He had chosen them carefully; she knew this as clearly as she knew her own name. How he could know when she didn't even know astonished her.

Closing her eyes, she pulled what he'd prepared for her.

This pulling was the three-dimensional kind, like Seth's and Josie's. She could feel, smell, taste, and see it all. She was with this man as he was stabbing someone through the heart, and all the emotions and violence of the moment filled her. Then she was in a hut with many other men yelling and cursing, all fighting for their own opinion to be heard. Then she was with him as he signed a peace treaty in blood from his palm. She was with him as he pulled bananas from a tree and gave them to a lady with a suckling child on her breast. And then she was there when he took his son hunting in the wild for the first time. She saw white men come and show the natives gadgets and gizmos. She saw, felt, and breathed with him as he tasted chocolate for the first time.

The connection thinned. It was time to sever the memories. As the delicious sensation of collecting what she was *meant* to collect filled her, this was nothing like it had been before. However, her sight still went black.

CHAPTER 23

Peter

Was it possible to be so tired? Peter wanted to go see Abby and Lilly, but he could not keep his eyes open. It was only eight, but after telling his family good night, Peter found his bed, and no sooner had his head hit the pillow than he was in his ribbon room.

He was pulled instantly to the golden thread of the tribal leader, and as his perspective zoomed closer and closer, he noticed the tentacle the thread now had. He followed the ethereal arm, and it was no surprise that it led to Miriam, just as all the tentacles did.

They did it. They got the first memory. Inside this world where he was nothing but a mind, he could not jump for happiness, but he wanted to. However, he felt a tug. And soon, he zoomed down the tapestry. As he went, he counted the golden threads. As he neared twenty, he was pulled to a thread in the middle of a purple section of the tapestry.

The golden thread grew larger until he was before it, a pillar of light and dark. Peter prepared himself and reached out.

It was a woman this time. She felt like a mix of fear and terror, so entangled with rage. Peter could only stay briefly. The taint of her filled him with dread. He pulled away. He marked where she was on the thread and willed himself to move out of the room.

When his eyes flickered open, he felt as if he'd been asleep for five minutes, yet his body ached as if he'd slept hard for a long time. A knock at the door startled him, and just as he pushed the covers off, Seth popped his head in.

"Hey, buddy. Did you have another dream?" He asked it as if he knew the answer already.

"You obviously know I did." Peter hopped off the bed. "Get out. Let a man get dressed. I'll meet you..." He rubbed his eyes. "Where should we meet?"

"At the table?"

"But Miriam?"

Seth smiled so wide it might have been creepy if his eyes were not filled with utter joy. "I think we might be okay."

Peter raised his eyebrows and nodded. "Okay. See you at the table in five."

CHAPTER 24

TUESDAY

Seth

Between one step and the next, Seth blinked his eyes and entered a vision.

Seth saw himself with Hirum, Westley, and several people unfamiliar to Seth. They sat at a table inside a big white tent, eating and planning how Edenia could help Noah and the people coming to join the tent people.

Once back in his own mind, Seth altered his course for the kitchen and headed for the sitting room where he knew Hirum was having a meeting.

The several people that Seth did not recognize from his dream were sitting with Hirum. As Seth walked in, Brian and Westley came in the front door. Hirum paused speaking to look at the three newcomers.

Sighing, he said, "I take it we have news."

Brian spoke first, though Hirum looked at Seth. "Hirum, the United States has just been invaded by The United Countries of Communism. Not only did the UCC have several hundred thousand troops landing on the east and west coasts, they had over a million sleeper agents living in America. All these have put on the UCC uniform, taken up arms, and run around like the USA doesn't have a military."

Garren finished, "They claim they are here to help. With the emergencies following the plague, tornados, and the super-eruption... ya know, displaced persons, looting, and the like. But no one believes that. Also, by tomorrow this place will be covered in ash."

No sooner had Garren stopped talking than Westley was taken by a foretelling. "Death and destruction, plague and famine, all have I used to chasten my people, saith the Lord. The strong have been made weak, and the proud bent low, hewn down, and cast into the fire. Only those people who heed my warnings and prepare for this great and dreadful day, making their hearts right and their actions godly, shall be saved." Westley shuddered out of the speech and looked around the room. "I apologize. I cannot control when that happens. I did not mean to interrupt." His slow drawl delivered these words with humility.

Hirum stood up. "Please Westley, don't concern yourself, we are so privileged to have a prophet here to help us understand what is taking place."

Seth met Hiram's eyes and said, "I don't have anything quite so big to say. Only that this group of people, whoever you are..."

"This is the council of Edenia," Hirum informed him.

Seth nodded in the general direction of the group, then went on. "Well, all of you plus Westley must have a meal with Noah. We will have to aid the tent people with those arriving in a couple of days."

Whereas when the council heard the news of the USA being invaded they remained quiet, but with this news, they were out of their seats, protests on their lips in a moment.

Hirum shut them up with one word. "Please! You can't yell at the messenger." He turned back to Seth. "Thank you, Seth. Anything else?"

He shook his head.

"Okay."

"I'm going to be in the kitchen with Peter discussing the next memory that needs to be taken if you have any other questions. Westley, you best come," Seth said to the room.

The man nodded, and they left sounds of murmuring and anger rising behind them.

Peter came out of a room down the hall as Seth headed that way.

He was wiping his hands. "All washed up. Let's get some food," the boy said.

He did as instructed. There was a pile of what looked like French toast slices on a plate in the middle of the island. Peter immediately filled his plate and slathered the food with jam. Seth and Westley followed suit.

When Seth went to pour himself a glass of water, his other sight pulled him in and showed him to leave the water alone. It had almost been three days since he'd actually had water. His tongue felt parched his insides ached.

"Do you have milk?"

"Yes, in the ice box," Peter answered, his words garbled from the food he talked around.

Seth got himself a glass of that. Once he joined Peter and Westley at the dining table, he asked, "So I saw something really strange just now, and I've been seeing it for days."

Peter stuffed his mouth with egg-soaked bread, so it took him a minute to say, "Saw like with your eyes or saw like with your Nature?" Peter stopped chewing abruptly, his eyes wide. "Oh my gosh, I just realized another reason your eyes are black...so you can have visions all day long, and no one can tell that your Nature has taken you." He laughed and cut another huge bite of bread as he shook his head. "Man, the Master thinks of everything." He put it in his mouth and started chewing, but he looked at Seth expectantly.

"Uhm, well, I saw it with my Nature. I saw myself not drinking water. Like every time I go to drink, I see myself choosing to drink something else. I told my family to not drink it just in case."

Peter had his cup halfway to his mouth but stopped and put the cup down.

"I haven't seen it for anyone else but me. What do you think that is about?" Seth almost turned to Westley, knowing that this was when he usually spouted some foretelling.

Westley said around some food, "I got nothing."

Seth's stomach growled at him again, so he took a bite. It was a delicious blend of egg and cinnamon with fresh raspberry preserves. So, he took a few more bites, thinking.

Peter spoke up. "What's the deal with Miriam?"

Seth took another bite and raised his shoulders up and down in response.

"Has she forgiven you?"

Seth swallowed and tried really hard not to get excited. "I don't think so. In fact, I am pretty sure she hasn't, but she is not wilting when I come near her, and she is not slapping me, and she is sort of talking to me. So..."

"Well, that seems promising."

"Do you love her?" Westley asked and smiled.

Seth chewed slowly and swallowed. "I don't know how to answer that. I betrayed her, so I think that means that I don't love her. A person who loved another person would never do what I did."

"No, it just means you loved your sister more than a girl you'd only known for a week," Peter said seriously.

Seth rolled those words around in his head. "Yes. But before that happened, I was pretty sure I loved her. I have never felt anything as passionate and strong as my feelings for Miriam. I mean, within the space of two conversations, I was a goner. And then it just grew so fast."

Westley nodded. "I know exactly what you mean. It is super scary, but amazing. A gift."

"Yes, well, at least you are at the proper age to have feelings of forever with a girl. Miriam is sixteen. I'm seventeen. That's just plain crazy."

Westley laughed. "Who cares how old you are? When it happens, it happens."

"I think the world would disagree with you there."

"You're not wrong, Seth, but Edenia is not truly in the world. Plenty of people get married or engaged that young around here."

Seth said nothing. He just finished eating and drinking. He

couldn't even fathom that. He'd, in fact, laughed at Miriam when she mentioned things going that fast. He'd told her that wasn't how it worked. He wished he could take back those words. He wished he could take back so many things. However, he'd sought forgiveness for himself and gotten it. And soon, he would have the go-ahead to ask Miriam to forgive him. It hurt to wait, but he had learned to follow that voice.

When the plates were empty, he said, "Well, boys, let's get to it. I am eager to get all these memories collected. The world is falling apart, and I don't want it to be any more dangerous than it needs to be."

Peter nodded with cheeks full of milk he stole from Seth's cup.

"We probably should have a witness."

"Yes, Gerald was exceptionally helpful."

Luanne Miller came into the room carrying a bunch of plates. "Mama, are the Travelers outside?"

She looked over at him. "They are. What are you lazy boys doing in here? There is a mess to clean up." A freckled, strawberry blond-haired boy and a cute blonde girl came through the kitchen next, carrying an equally big pile of plates and cups.

The boy said, "Where is Miriam today?"

Luanne said, "I think she went down to the river, Todd. She will be back soon."

Peter got up and jogged to the door, and Seth gathered up his plate and the other two dishes and walked them to the sink.

Westley said, "Ma'am, we were going to do the whole Nature thing, but if you want, we can help clean up first, or we can do it real quick-like and then help out."

The blonde girl said, "Bree is bringing in the last of it, and the Travelers are actually helping out. They got the tables put away."

Sure enough, a woman his mother's age came into the kitchen with an arm full of dishes and said, "This is it. Now, Luanne, you step away from the sink. Josie and I will get these washed up."

"Thank you, Bree, Josie. I do believe my feet could use a rest."

Then Peter was back. "I got Gerald."

The big man made his way into the kitchen.

"You all scoot outside. It is too crowded in here," Luanne said.

Peter moved to the back door, and Seth and the others followed him. Once they were on the back porch, Peter said, "So I know which thread we are to find next. Are you all ready?"

There were nods all around, and Peter held up his hands. "Three, two, one."

Seth pulled his Nature to him as Peter's and Westley's hands touched his. Seth immediately found himself in a place he knew as well as his own face. Piccadilly Circus, London. Seth saw himself in this vision standing with Miriam. The Travelers were there, but in everyday clothing, eyes still roving, posture alert. But Seth noticed Miriam's face was all astonishment, her eyes drinking in the surroundings.

Suddenly a woman in rags and missing teeth walked straight up to Miriam and put her head in Miriam's hands, which surprised her. The magic happened, and then things went weird. The vision turned. It was like everything was suddenly in black and white. They were in the Tube. Then they were standing in front of Big Ben. A man in an electric blue three-piece suit ran from them, calling for an officer. However, Ben was as fast as a bullet and got the man by the collar. Miriam did her job.

Seth was pulled out of the scene. "What happened, Peter? I saw two people. Both in London."

Peter smiled, "Well, I saw another thread close by, so I just examined that one as well."

Seth frowned, "It did not work out well for us. The vision was off, and the guy set the officers on us."

"Did you get the memory from him, at least?" Peter asked.

"Yes, thanks to Ben being quick on his feet." Seth turned to Gerald as if to ask if this seemed in character. "But we aren't supposed to do it."

Gerald's eyes were huge, and when all three turned to him for confirmation about Ben, Gerald shook his head and nodded, "Uhm yeah, Ben was in track in college. He can outrun any of us. But you three..." He slid his hand down his face. "You three are something, you know that?"

Confused, Seth asked, "What do you mean?"

Gerald turned to Westley, "What do I mean, Westley?"

Sighing, Westley said, "My prophecy went a little something like this: 'I will gather my sheep one at a time. The work of the Lord must be done in the proper order and fashion.' Etc."

Gerald smiled. "So, it's a hard no on grabbing two memories at once. The big guy says so."

Peter shrugged. "It was worth a try. I counted, and we have like forty threads to do."

Seth exclaimed, "Forty." What in the world was the Master going to do with so many memories? It was taxing on them all to get one. But forty?

Westley said, "I think it would be appropriate to have all the Travelers and Miriam together for these little sessions so that we are more efficient."

"I agree about Miriam. I wonder if there is a divided area we could meet—the four of us and Miriam on one side, the boys on the other. So they don't interrupt the process you all do, but so that we can take off as soon as we know where to go."

"It would also be helpful to have the computer there so we can research," Seth added.

"Great idea," Gerald said. "Speaking of which, tell us about your vision so we can figure out where we are going."

"Oh, this one's easy. I know exactly where it is. And the target actually puts her head right in Miriam's hands."

Peter's eyebrows lifted. "Well, that's strange. Why...? Never mind. She was strange in my vision of her as a pillar, so I guess I understand. Okay, well, go tell the boys and Miriam, you two.

Westley and I will get a headquarters of sorts organized here." He patted the cowboy on the back. "Right, Wes?"

The man gave him a crooked smile. Peter was growing on him as he always did. Seth grinned. The boy was incorrigible.

CHAPTER 25

Miriam

Ben, Richard, and Karl surrounded her on the porch in the morning sun. The rest of the men kicked a ball around on the street. With breakfast still sweet on her tongue, Miriam listened to a brutal story about training as a Marine. It all sounded exciting, but very intense and challenging. She found that it called to her. Proving oneself. Living on the edge. It gave her butterflies.

All of a sudden, she noticed Seth and Gerald had joined them. Gerald waited until the story was done, but then he got the attention of all the Travelers. The men in the street jogged in to gather around the porch.

"What's up?" Karl asked once all the men were there.

Gerald folded his arms and looked at he., "These boys did their thing, and we have another mission."

Her eyes slid to Seth. Miriam's heart raced and her stomach knotted as she strove to calm her reaction to his face.

"We are off to London, but this time we go civilian." He cleared his throat. "Li'l Boss said we need to collect at least forty memories, one at a time."

The men shifted and murmured under their breath, but when she looked around at them, she saw that their concern was more for her than anything else. She did pass out every time she took a memory.

Gerald went on, "So we've decided to set up a camp of sorts. A place where we all can gather, have the computer, have a place for Miriam to rest, and we will work in shifts based on how quickly

Miriam recovers and how quickly the boys figure out where we need to go next."

"Does anyone know what we are doing this for?"

Gerald shook his head.

"To gather the spark of the knowledge of good and evil," Westley stated. "Whatever that means."

"Doesn't that feel wrong?" Ben asked. "I mean, I didn't like it very much. Until I met Miriam, of course." He looked sheepishly at her.

Miriam stood and brushed the dust of the porch off her bottom then said, "I have been pondering this. It is true that when I took memories from you all I wondered if my Nature was evil. Thankfully that got sorted out. But these memories, they are different. It feels right to gather them. Like it's my destiny. I felt like the chief actually chose the memories he gave me. I cannot imagine that the givers of these memories feel any differently about the process."

"Maybe we should ask first?" Remy said.

Gerald shook his head, "I don't want Miriam talking to these people. It's bad enough she has to get that close to them. Sounds like some people will know it's coming, maybe some will fight it. What does it matter how they feel about it, really? We have to do it."

There was a murmur of agreement between the soldiers. Still, it would be good if she felt that same sharing as with the chief. She made a decision. "But it does matter if they are not prepared. We will do what we can to help them understand. That's all I ask."

Gerald gave a reluctant nod.

Karl interrupted. "Not to change the subject, but if Noah and Zeke are right, we will have a huge group of religious zealots here in three-plus days."

"Karl's right, Gerald. Those refugees are bound to have that virus we heard about the day before we left the compound. Why are we taking so many risks with Miriam when we should be preparing for disease control?" Ben asked.

"And what about the volcano? I just know that the ash will be hitting us soon," Remy stated.

"Boys, chill," Gerald commanded. They settled into an uneasy quiet. "Now, I don't know about any of that, but I do know I trust Hirum; he's handling it."

"What we are doing is the most crucial thing we can do at this moment," Seth said.

That seemed to help these men. Seth was such a surprise in so many ways. She again felt her stomach twist, and she sank back down to the porch. Her eyes glanced over that the boy she hated and loved. He licked his lips and then bit them, the way someone would do when they knew they were being watched. She looked away. Taking a deep breath, she told her conflicted mind to settle down so she could listen to the men's plans.

Karl slid his hand over his head, completely wrecking his usually pristine hair, and cleared his throat as he stepped forward. "Just so I can get my mind set up here, if we do five missions a day—assuming that works out with Miriam and the boys—that means it will take us eight days to finish this up." He looked around as if he wanted someone to confirm that his simple math was correct.

Gerald did. "Sounds about right."

But she heard Seth whisper, "It can't take that long." She looked at him, her eyebrows telling him she didn't understand.

Seth stepped up. "This next memory will literally take less than five minutes."

Miriam felt herself deflate. "Oh no," she said out loud, in a whiney, childish voice. She promptly slapped her hand over her mouth.

All eyes fell on her. She looked down and felt her cheeks heat.

Gerald asked, "What is it?"

Miriam didn't want to say anything. It revealed her for what she was, selfish in her core.

Seth's knowing eyes saw her blush. "I think I understand."

She blushed even deeper and looked away.

"Do you want me to tell them?"

"Tell us what?" Gerald insisted.

Seth nudged her with his knee when she didn't speak and whispered, "Do you want me to tell them?"

She thought she'd given this up. She'd felt that she had moved past it. But here it was. The emotions were so on-the-surface that she couldn't even trust herself to discuss it. She had to have Seth do it for her. She rolled her eyes and nodded.

"Miriam has never left Edenia, though it has been her dream to do so. I've told her a lot about London. I think she really would love to"—he paused and looked down at her—"not hurry, if you get my meaning." His eyebrows raised in an am-I-right question.

Tears filled Miriam's eyes, and she turned away from everyone.

She felt the men's eyes on her back, and the pity radiating from them. She was about to clear this all up, telling them it was okay. It was not important. Then Richard said, "Well, are we Travelers or not?"

Karl butted in, "Yeah, I say if we are going to a cool and typically safe place, like London, let her see something she wants to see."

Then men were calling things out.

"Like Big Ben."

"Or Leeds Castle."

"The White Cliffs of Dover."

"Winsor."

"We could make an appearance at all those places and not take more than an hour total."

"If we don't have an hour for our Vessel to fulfill a dream, then I don't know what we are doing here," Gerald whispered in the air between them with a massive smile.

Miriam began crying in earnest. She looked up at Seth, but his eyes were unfocused, staring over her head. When he blinked, he looked down at her and bit his lip.

She wiped her eyes. He probably had a vision thing. The way he looked, unhappy about something, scared her. She sniffed.

"What?" she said to him.

Without taking his eyes from hers, he crouched down their faces only a foot apart.

"Miriam. Our mission, with the memories, is the most important thing the Master is doing right now."

Gerald stepped closer. "Did you just see that?"

Seth looked at him and nodded.

Miriam closed her eyes, knowing at once what he meant. The answer to a bit of sightseeing was no. She took a moment for that to hurt her. And then she nodded. "Thank you all for wanting to be so wonderful, but I am a Guardian, and the Master has a task for us that is far more important than any childish desires I might have." She sniffed again. "Besides, I still get to go to London. I might not get to go to the White Cliffs of Dover, but I am not stuck here in Edenia. It is all good. I am blessed."

She looked at the men reassuringly as their faces fell. But when she looked at Seth, he was absolutely beaming. He said nothing but stood up.

"Shall we go?"

Gerald said, "You are certain we will not need anything special?"

Seth looked at them with a different expression. "No, you were all wearing what you are wearing now. And I think only five will be necessary for this trip. I know several of you have been to London. We will need you to coordinate an incognito place to portal into."

"I thought of that. We can't just appear in the middle of Piccadilly Circus."

As the men hashed out what was to be their strategy, Miriam looked over at Seth. The way he looked at her a moment ago, as if the sun rose and set in her face, as if he had tested her and she had passed, as if he were proud of her, made her feel everything. And she was sure that feeling everything for a boy that betrayed her was not supposed to be desirable.

But it was. She desired him.

Her eyes swept over him as he added bits and pieces to the

conversation. He had taken to his role masterfully. Her mind went back to the river with Karl. Seth had used four different Natures in concert with one another to save Karl's life. Seth was twenty-four hours a day doing the bidding of the Master; how dedicated and effective of a Guardian he was.

She thought of Seth's roots and what sort of man Zeke was. The story of Ezekiel Johnson being born a Jones but raised a Guardian, leaving his outside job, skills, and cancer, and now coming back to Edenia, felt incredible. The admiration Miriam had for her Uncle Zeke grew by the day. Parts of his story even felt personal to her somehow. And not only had Seth come from that man, but the Master had chosen the son over the father to be his Revelator this time around.

It all made Miriam a bit dizzy and warm and squishy inside. He paid attention to the Travelers' conversation, and she couldn't help but feel mesmerized by his submission, his prowess, and his beauty.

She couldn't believe how much he had changed over the last week. Or was she seeing the real Seth now? The Seth that was not under the pressure of having to save his own sister's life? The guy with the weight of his own world on his shoulders had her in love with him within a week. That guy had betrayed her, yes, but he had also dazzled her right out of her duties as a Guardian. That person was capable of such incredible love and single-minded devotion to his sister. He had simultaneously saved said sister and made her, Miriam, feel like she was the most important thing to him.

What would this Seth do to her if she let her guard down? This Seth had no more secrets, fear, or betrayal in him. And he was proving to be more incredible than she could have imagined.

In the future moment when Miriam finally let go and forgave him —and she realized she was more than halfway down that road—she would be so in love with him she probably wouldn't be able to think straight. It was already starting to distract her.

Did she want to be in that condition? Did she want to be so entirely in the thrall of this boy?

She'd been staring at him, and so she'd drawn his eye to her. He smiled without showing his teeth and held her glance for a full five seconds before Gerald pulled him back into the conversation. Miriam blushed deeply, her heart racing.

Was she only halfway down the road to forgiveness...or was she further than that?

She had to remember all the reasons to be mad at him and the betrayal of not only her, but of everyone he loved. She tried to conjure up the anger she'd felt before, and it was there, somewhere. It just felt hollow.

"Are we ready, then?" Gerald asked, interrupting her attempts to protect her heart.

Miriam had not heard one single word. "Uhm, I was not listening. Can you repeat the parts I need to know?"

Peter rolled his eyes. "I won't even be there, and I was listening."

Miriam blushed. "Sorry." She flashed a glance in Seth's direction. It was confirmed that she would be worthless if she did not stay mad at Seth until they were done collecting the memories.

Gerald was formidable. He saw everything. She blushed again as he spoke. "There isn't much for you to do but take the memory, which Seth explained is a woman who will put her head in your hands. You pass out; I catch you and bring you back here. The end."

She nodded and forced herself to keep her eyes on Gerald.

"You good?" he asked. She nodded again. "Great. Men, form up."

Miriam stood and moved to the center of the Travelers' formation. The grouping was more casual this time, with no loaded and aimed weapons. No shoulder-to-shoulder configuration. They did touch each other but gathered casually.

Once settled, Seth reached over and touched her arm. "You okay?"

She shivered at his touch, but not in a bad way, and nodded. "I'm good."

"Well, you will be perfectly safe in London, so as we walk, take the time to look around. Piccadilly Circus is a great intersection of

London. Lots of lights and tall buildings and big red buses. Try to enjoy it and just wait for the homeless lady to approach you."

"Ready..." Ben started with his orders, and it was time to concentrate.

How could she do so with Seth talking to her?

"Just enjoy as much as you can." He squeezed her hand and smiled. Then he let her go, took Richard by the strap, and looked forward. She felt the loss of his touch and sighed to herself as Gerald eyed her with a raised eyebrow. The man nodded to his strap. She took it, and they jumped into a completely different existence.

The public washroom smelled, and paper covered the ground. The men filed out of the bathroom and onto a street, unlike anything Miriam had ever seen before save for in pictures.

First, the buildings were huge—white and grey stone with details, grandeur, and class, dazzling the eye and the mind. One building was covered in unique, brightly colorful pictures that moved. "Is that a movie?" Miriam asked with delight and awe.

"Those are advertisements, but yes, they are on movie screens," Seth answered.

"Incredible," Miriam stated, and hated to take her eyes off the screens but knew she had but a moment.

There were columns and flags and lamp posts. There were buses and cars and people. Not as many as Miriam thought there would be, but they were all dressed strangely. Some had pink hair, and others had metal in their faces. And at the center was a beautiful fountain with steps leading up to a marvelously carved sculpture, the image of a winged child holding a long bow at its top.

"Beautiful." She looked at Gerald. "Can I touch it?"

He smiled down at her, "Of course, go on."

"Why in the world are there so few people here? It's dinner time; this place should be hopping," Richard said.

She moved up the steps and reached out. The stone was cold and wet, but it felt to her that she was touching the history of something.

She closed her eyes in gratitude, so happy to be here, even if it was for only a moment.

However, at that moment of perfect felicity, a loud voice that hurt Miriam's ears filled the air around them.

"Attention, this is a public service announcement. The biological weapon Camazotz and the lab-released GSR virus have been in our beloved country for ten days. It infected seven thousand one hundred and thirty London citizens as of yesterday. Death count Camazotz: one hundred and twenty-five GSR: twenty. There is no cure or treatment for these diseases. They have a statistical death rate of one hundred percent. Please stay in your homes, no exceptions. If you are found on the streets, you will be arrested and taken to the Wembley Arena, where you will be presumed infected and cared for until you perish. Repeat: You will be arrested and taken to Wembley Arena. Check your local parish's website to schedule food drops and rubbish pickups."

The announcement shocked Miriam. The screens that held advertisements a moment before were now covered in pictures of death and sickness, arrest and imprisonment.

Gerald looked at Miriam and subconsciously reached for his gun. She moved to him as he moved toward her, and once they met, she stood behind him, her back to the fountain. Miriam looked around at the people this time instead of the surroundings and found that she had been blind before. First, none of the cars or the buses were moving, and they were empty of people. The few people who were out and about hurried around. Miriam now saw that their eyes were wary and their movements that of prey.

"What in the name of all that's good and holy has happened here?" Ben asked as he looked around. That was when she noticed that the Travelers were now surrounding her.

And then, out of nowhere, one of the humans walking by made a beeline for the group. Gerald tensed, but Seth put a hand out as if he could stop Gerald. "This is her," he said, never taking his eyes off the woman.

Miriam first noticed her hair. It was blonde, and in what looked like a ratted mess of thick matted plaits. Her face was filthy. Her hands and clothing were grungy, and once she was close, Miriam smelled the most putrescent odor.

But before Miriam knew it, the woman was in her face. Her eyes were the most transparent blue, a fringe of white-blonde lashes framing them. She was beautiful aside from the dirt and the smell, but those eyes told the story of hardship, of torment, of inner demons.

Without a preamble, the woman took Miriam's hands and put them on her head. Then her mouth opened to reveal terribly mismanaged teeth and rancid breath. "I've been waiting for you. Please take it away."

Blinking and thoroughly mystified by this woman, Miriam's Nature took her and began pulling. As she did, Miriam entered a three-dimensional world of horror and pain so depraved and violating that Miriam wanted to pull herself out of it. Just as she had with Seth, she pulled harder and harder so that the events sped by at a pace she could not recognize. However, she felt pity for this woman even as she did so. She wanted to pull as many of the horrid scenes as she could, knowing that the memories would no longer exist inside the woman and thus would torture her no longer.

Miriam pulled as hard as she could, but suddenly the pulling stopped. She stumbled back from the woman who stood with her eyes closed. Miriam felt her mind close around the rather large soul sliver, rendering her unconscious as she heard the woman whisper, "Thank you."

CHAPTER 26

Peter

This was not going to be easy. Westley could not stop gawking at Esther, and Peter had never had to calm his gagging reflex so much in his life. "Westley, concentrate." He and Westley were helping ten other Guardians clear out the Divided Hall to repurpose it as a workspace for the Travelers' mission.

Westley shook himself—he did that a lot—and found Peter's face. "Sorry, I really don't know what is wrong with me." He leaned forward and started connecting wires and cords hanging from the computer parts in a fashion that hurt Peter's head. Finally, he answered the question he was supposed to be pondering. "I plan on attending that dinner tonight with Noah and your parents. They all need to discuss what is goin' on with the group of people headin' this way, and I'm the man in the middle of these here camps. I am one hundred percent committed to this, but I've many friends in the tent city, and thus feel responsible."

Peter looked over at Esther, who was situating a bed in one corner of the room and smoothing the covers and pillows. All the benches had been moved and stacked against the west wall. The wind and strength Guardians had turned the partition in the middle of the room to separate the stage area from the rest of the room. This separate area offered privacy and would work for Seth, Westley, and Peter's process. The remainder of the open space was soon filled with couches, tables, chairs, and beds. The Travelers claimed their areas with their few possessions and the expectation that they would not be going out into Edenia much.

There was already a kitchen area on the east side of the building behind some large doors that opened up like a barn. Several Guardians stocked the ice box and the cupboards with food. In the center of the room, a large fire pit, usually covered with a large sheet of thinly milled wood, had been uncovered and had a big fire burning. A few amber-eyed Guardians stacked wood in there. A wind Nature told the air to pull the smoke rising directly up to the ceiling. where an ingeniously disguised hole and fan worked as a type of flue.

Seth walked in with purpose in his step. Miriam, Gerald, and the Travelers entered directly behind him.

Gerald spoke up. "So, this is the spot?"

"Do you approve?" Peter called back.

The man looked around carefully, then pointed to the stage area. "Is that where..."

Peter pointed to himself and Westley and nodded.

A moment later, "I am assuming there are toilets somewhere?"

"Toilets and two showers." Peter pointed toward the nondescript door.

"Well, that will be sufficient. Yes, this will work nicely. Good work, boys."

Peter smiled and looked over at his sister, who had joined Esther. "How did the memory retrieval go?"

"Successful and interesting."

"How is it that Miriam is walking around?"

Gerald shrugged his shoulders. "I caught her when she finished the retrieval just like last time. But by the time I'd traveled back to Edenia, she began to stir in my arms, and not a minute later, she could stand, totally awake."

Peter considered this. "Do you think that is because we have forty memories to collect?"

Seth, who had immediately begun helping Westley set up the computer, butted into the conversation. "Thirty-eight memories." He smiled the self-satisfied smile of a man who had a purpose and knew he was well on his way to getting it done.

That made them all smile. "Thirty-eight," they said together.

"So what made it interesting besides the Miriam thing?"

"The world is freaking out."

Ben started shaking his head as he relayed how London imprisoned anyone on the street. Peter's jaw dropped. "How can government do that? Aren't there way more civilians than authority?"

"Yes, many more. But over the last few years, the European governments have taken away the people's means of defense and conditioned them to obey. Also, this really is a scary virus from what I learned before I came here."

Westley pushed a button, and the computer started making some strange sounds. "Let's look it up."

"Speaking of which..." Richard asked a little sheepishly. "How much of that sickness stuff do we need to worry about? As Guardians traveling all around the world, I mean." His eyes floated to Miriam. These men were so protective of her; it was impressive.

Peter loved to answer this question. "We don't get sick here. You have nothing to fear."

Seth spoke up again, "As long as you don't eat anything outside of Edenia, you will be perfectly protected."

Gerald looked at Peter. "Really?" He was so impressed he couldn't hide it.

Peter smiled as big as a whale and nodded, his eyebrows bouncing with awesomeness. "Yup. I'm telling you. You might have had to drown yourself to get here, but it is totally worth it."

Gerald appreciated Peter's zealousness, and so he full-out laughed. "I guess so!" he exclaimed in the middle of his laughter.

Seth stood up from adjusting some wires. He made it so they were all organized and not hanging all over the place and said, "Hey, I, uhm, think we need to get busy. As long as Miriam is all right."

Miriam had just walked toward them. "I'm ready to go again if you guys are."

Peter smiled. This was the life. Serving. Fulfilling missions. Being epic. "Let's do this. Follow me." And he led them up to the stage.

CHAPTER 27

Miriam couldn't help watching the interaction between Seth and the world with admiration. The moment they were in the Divided Hall, Seth went to help. He was the one who wanted to get the mission moving along. He was protective of the Guardians and of Peter and of her.

Her heartbeat sped up as Seth mounted the steps of the stage. He was beautiful in the confidence that his true self showed. She was not looking forward to watching him use his Nature to find the next memory. She might just melt into a puddle and forget that he had betrayed her. The funny thing was she didn't feel betrayed any longer. She was more a casualty of fate. Events had to go the way they had. Seth played his role *then* just as well as he did now.

She had a responsibility as well. She hadn't told her parents. She hadn't taken his memories of that first day in the shed. She hadn't taken it the next day. But she had taken it the day she should not have. So, she was not innocent.

She blinked and was pulled out of her thoughts by Gerald, who whispered, "Are you ready to see something crazy?" He chinned toward the circle of three before them.

They all reached their hands out, and Seth said, "Ready?"

Westley and Peter nodded as they closed their eyes and grasped one another.

Seth and Peter went still as Westley started to foretell. "And the Lord God made a covenant with the house of Israel in the which if the people of God would keep the commandments of the Lord, repent, and offer him sacrifice, they would be blessed up to the tenth generation. So, the children of the Lord built him a house. A house of worship, a house of sacrifice, a house of prayer."

As Westley spoke and Peter and Seth concentrated their energies combined, they started to glow.

Gerald elbowed Miriam. When she looked at him, he raised his eyebrows, but did not turn away from the boys. "They are glowing," she said, and looked back at them.

"Yes," he whispered with a smile. "Like the Master." He let that settle for a moment.

They were glowing like the Master. It was a light that came from within. A light that was not about their surroundings, but entirely about the inside of them.

Gerald spoke again in a whisper. "They don't know this happens, so don't tell them."

"Okay. Why?"

"I don't want them to stop me from watching," he said with a smile of pure delight and gave her the world's quickest wink.

They were silent for a moment longer as Westley went on about the temple in Jerusalem.

Gerald again pulled her attention away when he said, "What do you think would happen if there were four instead of three?"

Completely stumped by the question and all that he was attempting to imply, Miriam turned to him and shook her head.

"Is not the Master a being composed of four beings?"

Miriam felt as if her mind had just exploded. It ran down several possibilities of what this all meant, of whom the fourth person was. Instantly, she knew it was her. And with that, her instincts led her. Without thinking or wondering what she should do, she ducked under Peter and Westley's joined hands and, at that exact moment, placed her hands on theirs.

The boys inhaled with her touch, and she pulled her Nature to her. And she saw the why of it all.

This was about collecting the full spectrum of the human experience. All that was good and bad. All that was light and darkness. All that was sickness and health. All that was pleasure and pain. All that was virtue and vice. All that was knowledge.

The information was not vital, but it was interesting to understand that the next memory would collect fanaticism and religiosity, piety, and humility. The calming part of her Nature that understood and pulled emotion fully comprehended the complexity of these seemingly opposite qualities and how they could be used for good and evil. And with this understanding, she felt whole. Complete. Like her life and herself and her Nature had come full circle. Like she was useful and valuable and talented all in one.

Suddenly the experience was over. Miriam opened her eyes. She stood in the middle of the group but was face to face with Seth, and somehow her hands ended up in his hands.

He smiled at her. He still glowed a little bit. "That was incredible. Is that what it feels like to be you? All those emotions; all that understanding?"

Tears burst into existence in Miriam's eyes. She nodded, and once again felt understood.

Peter's voice said, "I didn't feel anything."

But they ignored him.

"Can we please talk?" Seth asked her, his face as serious as she could imagine. But then he looked over at Peter and the others. "Alone. Just for a moment."

Peter backed away from them. "Say no more, brother."

"Miriam, are you okay with this?" Gerald asked.

Her hands were still in Seth's hands, and her eyes were still on Seth's eyes. She nodded. Gerald silently left them alone on the stage.

Seth's thumbs rubbed over her knuckles. He swallowed. He took a deep breath. Then he spoke. "I am going to say this as fast as I can. Not because I want it to be over with, but because I have been holding it inside for days. Waiting until it would not hurt you but would help you."

Miriam herself swallowed, her hands tingling.

"Miriam, I am so sorry. I know I could never say or do anything to make my actions right. But please know I am so terribly sorry for my part in it. Hate me until the day you die. I deserve it. But I want you to know that I am truly sorry. I hope all the pain I've caused you will heal. I hope..."

She interrupted him, her voice even, if a little breathless. "Do you know what's so sick and twisted about this whole thing?" She let go of his hands, which she had almost forgotten about holding. Her whole body tingled so. "If you just would have asked me to go with you... If you had told me the Joneses would trade an interview with me for your sister's life, I probably would have willingly helped. Because I've never been scared of them. I've always considered them sort of pathetic. And I was so desperate to get out of Edenia; who knows what I would have considered reasonable? You didn't give me a choice." Her pitch had risen with emotion, so she paused and turned away from him momentarily. After she calmed down, she added in a quiet, controlled voice, "If you had just asked. If you'd just trusted me." She looked down at her shoes and turned back toward him. "And you know what? Then you and Lillian could have taken off, and I would have told you to go because her life was in jeopardy." She paused again and gazed up at him.

His face looked utterly chastised. "You are right. I should have trusted you. I was very short on trust with a lot of people."

She clutched at her chest. "Yes, it is another kind of betrayal."

She saw his face change from sorrow to questioning.

"By distrusting everyone who loves you, people who've earned your trust time and time again, you throw all that history, all that connection away." He didn't argue, so it spurred her to push on. "And it goes deeper. If you had trusted me and included me when the Joneses tortured me, I couldn't have blamed you, because first, it would have been my choice to go and my choice to send you away. My choice. My fault. Don't you see?"

"I see it. Like an untraveled road behind me," he said, and his black eyes flared with anger, but not at her, at himself.

She went on, taking a step closer to him. "If you had trusted, you would have come back here when things didn't work out with the hospitals and the doctors...and you and I...we would have been okay. We probably would have picked up where we left off." She started crying, and then, she was yelling. "I would be in your arms right now, telling you how badly they hurt me, and you..."

Seth pulled her into his arms. He held her as tight as one human could hold another human. "And I would tell you that I would never let anyone hurt you again," he said into her hair.

She hugged him as tightly as possible, "And I would know in my heart that you would never betray me or leave me behind." She was sobbing. She shook and clung to him.

She knew they were acting out what would have happened if the Travelers had not been needed. What would have happened if Zeke had not lied his whole life? If Miriam had not kept Seth's deal with the Joneses from her parents? What would have happened if the past had not needed to go exactly as it went?

He said, "Then when I found out they had you, instead of knowing I had done it to you, I would have rescued you, and the trust between us would have grown." By the end of this conjecture, Seth was sobbing as hard as she was.

After that, they did not speak. They only lived within the moment filled with the imagined future they had conjured.

Miriam pulled back so she could look at him. "But that's not what happened, and I want to forget that we could have had a different past." She sniffed and wiped her face. "But my hopes are crushed. My heart is crushed. I am damaged. And I don't know if there is anything we can do about it."

"I want to try." He stepped closer. Their noses were only inches apart. "Can we try?" She pondered this as he kept his eyes on her. He spoke again, "I will understand if your opinion of me is ruined, and if my very face hurts you. I promise to leave you alone as much as I can. But..." Seth reached down and took her hands into his. He wove his fingers between hers and said, "But if there is even a glimmer of hope, even a chance that we have a chance..." He blinked and bit his lip.

"Then I will have to tell you that I see you. I know you. And I love you. I cannot give up on us." The words cut into all other sounds and emotions. "That love started from the first time I saw you smile. No, that was the moment I understood that I could live in Edenia forever just to see your smile. I loved you since I found out you were the girl in the church."

This admission, out loud, unreserved, to her face, his black eyes spilling tears, reached into her depths. It answered all her questions and told her what a strenuous battle he'd fought. His love for his sister and his helplessness must have been overwhelming to overthrow the feelings she now saw in his eyes.

No, she told herself, *he had as much control of this situation as I did. None.*

All the tiny pieces of anger and hurt melted away. She stepped closer to him and reached up to take his face. Her thumb trailed through the remnants of tears on his cheeks. Her eyes left his for the first time in what felt like days to look at his mouth. She wanted to kiss him. She wanted to end this conversation with a token of her forgiveness. But she couldn't, not yet.

She whispered. "Let's just keep talking, okay? Let's put it behind us. I feel like we've come a long way in just one conversation. Let's keep that going and see where it leads."

His eyes left her mouth as well. It seemed his mind went to the same place. His gaze found hers, and he nodded his assent. As he did, the need for him almost overwhelmed her. They moved closer, but at the last second, Miriam remembered her earlier reserve. If she let herself be undone entirely by Seth, she would never accomplish her mission.

She quickly placed a kiss on his cheek, then whispered, "Thank you for loving me."

She walked away from him, and it took every single shred of her strength to do so.

CHAPTER 28

Peter

Peter stayed near the Divided Hall all day, pushing himself into his ribbon room as soon as the travelers left with Miriam and Seth. It was so easy for him now to move in and out, to see what he needed to see and then pull himself out of his meditation.

He'd just sent the troops off, and needing to prepare himself for their next thread, he sat cross-legged on Miriam's cot, his breath easy, his heart rate paced slowly. The black room surrounded him.

As the threads moved toward him, his consciousness singled out the pillar of light he needed next. This person was a female and a gifted singer. She was surrounded by much good and beauty. He was momentarily mesmerized by how she pulled other lights toward her almost magnetically. Equally, he noticed how those pulled toward her shared their own light with her, providing strength, energy, and love. These things buoyed the singer up and enhanced the beauty of her gift. It was something to behold.

Peter basked in the exchange until someone else pulled him. Another light. Another soul. Another being. He allowed the feeling of consciousness to move to the place attracting him, and there, in the middle of much darkness and many colors of darker hues, Peter saw one full of light. He instantly saw that the man in the center was gifted as well. He was strong. He was large and faith-filled. He was an athlete, one of great renown.

Peter's mind did not allow him to linger on this one long before he was pulled to another pillar of light. This one was not as bright, but very colorful. It was another man. He was surrounded by many other colorful pillars and threads. This man had many exciting people and adventures in his life, all of whom were simultaneously dim yet full of color.

Peter felt pulled away again, but it was not by his own will this time. He felt the pull toward a part of the tapestry that was colorful and bright. The woman he saw there was a healer.

Again, he was pulled. He saw a man with a mind for facts and figures.

Pull. He saw a very good man, kind and gentle.

Pull. There was a small group of people, all happy and positive. All talented with musical instruments. A family that all played together, spreading happiness and joy.

Pull. He saw a woman surrounded by young children, laughing and patting their cheeks. They looked at her with love.

It went on and on and on. And now—thanks to Miriam joining the circle—he had the profound reason behind these memories. These memories represented the summation of the human experience. To know what being human meant. Pain and heartache, but also beauty and pleasure. It was very interesting for someone in Peter's position to be exposed to such a wide breadth of humanity.

It still left the question: What could these memories be used for?

CHAPTER 29

Westley

The day and evening were full of the same. Gather to get the mission location, and who to collect a memory from. The Travelers, Miriam, and Seth leaving to complete the task. Peter and Westley staying behind to finish cleaning up the meeting hall, and then helping Hirum, who was busy preparing Edenia for the expected ash, and also to prepare them for the invasion of his people, The Saints of God.

Westley felt weird; he hadn't seen Esther in several hours. Up to this afternoon, he'd been unable to get her off his mind, but ever since they moved into the meeting hall, those obsessive feelings had cooled to a more normal level, and he was grateful for it. Intensity of that sort of exhausted him, and he had a lot on his plate.

Westley washed behind his neck and pulled on his Edenian-made slacks. They were extremely comfortable and cut as if made for his body. The Travelers had been gone for a half hour. They were going to a very remote tribe in Africa, the Sentinelese, he thought was the name. Seth had seen some danger, so all twenty Travelers had gone. Today, they had gone to China, Belgium, Canada, Belize, London again, Samoa, Chile, and Florida. If they could get five more done today and twenty done the next day, they would only have a few left. Seth said they didn't have that long, though he wasn't sure why.

None of them felt tired, though. It was amazing. They were like stallions. Go, go, go. They planned on dinner a break after this next one, which is what Westley prepared for. Dinner with Noah.

He'd thought on and off all day long about why Noah needed to eat dinner with the Edenian council and why they needed to eat Edenian food, but it didn't matter how much he thought on it; no answers came.

He also found himself a bit nervous about seeing all his friends in his new condition. A Guardian. Would he look different to them? Would they think less of him because he had chosen a different path?

He hoped not.

There was a knock at the bathroom door. "Westley, are you in there?" the sweetest voice in all of creation called, though her voice was muffled from behind the thick door.

"I am, my dear," Westley answered.

"Well, come out. They are back and want to get the next one figured out before they eat. Mama isn't quite finished with supper."

Westley pulled a soft cotton shirt over his head and smoothed his hair before moving to the door and pulling it open.

Shining bright green eyes waited for him on the other side. He smiled and reached for his girl. She wiggled under his arm and moved them toward the center of the room where Westley could see the Travelers and Seth.

"I've missed you today," Esther said.

He lovingly squeezed her arm and replied, "Me too."

"Do you think after you have your dinner with Noah, and after you have settled things with the Travelers, we could go on a walk in the moonlight?"

"I would love nothing better," he said honestly, and kissed the top of her head.

Once they reached the group, Westley heard Miriam excitedly telling the story of their travels. It sounded like she'd gotten separated from them all in the jungle of Africa. It was the middle of the night there, obviously. But because the Travelers could feel her location, it did not take them long to find her, and a good thing too, because she was about to get squeezed to death by an anaconda that happened on her.

"I can see that you got the memory, though," Peter said, enraptured by the rescue story.

"Yes, but only just before the woman's husband took a bite out of Max."

"They were a cannibalistic tribe."

Westley said out loud, "I didn't know that was still a thing."

Max, a blond-haired bearded Traveler, spoke up. "Oh, it's still a thing."

And everyone busted up laughing.

Westley looked down at Esther and felt the spirit of this gathering, this family. They were united in purpose and in heart. It was beautiful and made him think of his family in the tent city. It would be good to see them.

"Well, shall we get to it?" Westley asked.

Seth looked at Peter and Miriam, then nodded and said, "Let's do it."

DINNER WAS SIMPLE, but it was wonderful. Though the conversation was serious, it felt like Westley was home because he was. Living in Edenia was also great, but being with the Elders felt like, well, home.

The Edenian council wanted to know what was expected of them. They also organized protocols for ushering the members of Westley's church around Edenia.

After the council left and it was just Hirum, Esther, Noah, and himself, Westley told Noah about all his duties as a Guardian, and what they were seeing out in the world. He also told him about his Nature and what that was like.

"Thank you for having us, Noah."

"Thank you for bringing us the food."

Esther asked, "Why *are* you gathering all these people here?"

"It is just another ark I am filling," Noah said without a hitch.

Westley cocked his head at his friend. "Another?"

The man's eyes and face instantly radiated light from the inside, "Yes, another. And this time, it will be even more violent and terrifying for those on the outside."

Westley felt the food stick in his throat. It was true then Noah was Noah, like the prophet. So many moments of his foresight, calm, and confidence returned to Westley's head. He swallowed and coughed and looked over at Esther. She smiled at him and then noticed his distress.

"Are you all right?" she asked, and patted his back.

She was not disconcerted in the slightest by this news; how was that possible? He said, "I'm fine. Just swallowed wrong."

Hirum spoke up. "So you said that there would be about thirty thousand of your followers coming. I'll be honest, I cannot imagine a group that large, but..." He shook his head and let the words hang in the air.

"Well, I'm happy to tell you that is only Joe's group. He is coming from the West and will settle on the Edenia side of our camp. We have another group coming from the East, but they will settle in the valley."

"How many people will that be?" Hirum asked, a bit weary.

"I hope around one hundred thousand."

Hirum's eyes bulged. "Really?" he asked slowly and contemplatively, "That is a lot of people."

"Yes, I wish it were more. But this is not the only gathering place. Every continent has one."

"Really?" Esther asked innocently. "And what is the purpose of these gathering places?"

Noah smiled at her. "Well, that is a big question, and I don't really have time to do it justice, but I will tell you that God protects his people, and gathering them here will keep them safe."

Esther's face became serious. "So, how does your God protect his people? And who are his people? How do you know them?"

"Esther." Hirum's voice held not censure, but seriousness. "I am glad that you are interested in Westley's religion, but can you not ask *him* about the particulars later? We have many plans to discuss at present."

"Yes, Papa. Sorry," Esther said, smiling at her father. She was so beautiful. Westley felt a tingle in his heart.

"So, how much food do you need?"

"Well, I have about a thousand here who will have a final trial of faith concerning their health. I am sure that number will be similar in percentage with the other two groups."

Hirum thought. "So, what, I need to feed five to six thousand people in one meal?"

"That sounds about right."

Hirum eyed the man carefully. "You know what I am."

"Yes."

He shook his head. "I will not be taking on any more of your members as Guardians. Are we clear?"

"Perfectly. If all goes well, those of my people eating your food will not need any other food from then on."

Westley narrowed his eyes at Noah. "Then what, they are translated?" he asked skeptically.

"You understand what it takes to ascend, Westley. If that is their last trial, why would you consider it unworthy?"

He rolled this around in his mind. "I don't, I guess. It just seems..."

"Easy?" Noah supplied.

Westley added the word to his understanding and nodded. "Yeah, maybe."

"Well, you have been healthy your whole life, with energy and vitality. You have lived without addiction or allergy. For those who have struggled with that, this will be their last trial, their biggest mountain to climb or cliff to jump. Essentially, their most dramatic change. And believe me, it will not be easy for them."

"Easy, like a paralytic hopping into a river and coming out whole," Esther said and eyed him knowingly with a little grin.

"About as easy as letting yourself be drowned," Hirum added, his face lost in memory.

"We all have our crosses to cast off," Noah said.

Hirum cleared his throat. "Well, will the victuals I brought tonight be enough for those ready now?"

Noah answered, "Yes. Westley saw the exact amount, and thus it will be enough. Thank you!"

"I will bring what Westley tells me to bring each day."

"That will be wonderful."

"Well, shall we get to the other reason you are here?"

Westley sighed. "Am I worthy?"

Noah shrugged. "Are you?"

Westley looked the man in the eyes and knew he was done considering this. He was as worthy as he could be. So he nodded.

Hirum spoke up, "What is happening?"

Esther smiled and said, "Westley is being made a High Priest and a Patriarch in his religion."

"What does that mean?" Hirum asked.

She shrugged. "I have no idea, but it's a big deal." She snuggled up to her father. "So, we gotta go. We can't stay and watch."

"Okay. Well, I will see you all tomorrow." He nodded.

Westley smiled at his girl and watched her leave.

"When will you ask her?" Noah said.

Westley smiled. "Is it that obvious?" The man smirked. "They have stringent rules about that, so I'm not sure. And have you seen her father's biceps?"

Noah laughed out loud. "Do not wait, my friend. You have very little time before the Christ comes. And after that..."

"I know. When will it be, Noah? With all we are doing in the Garden and the urgency the Cherubim have placed in my prophecies, I feel it could be weeks."

"Days," Noah stated flatly.

And he again had a flash of crazy knowledge that his friend, this man he'd known for three years, was Noah. The Noah. Not only that, but Noah was telling him that in days Christ would be here, on the Earth, doing his final work. Again, Westley's throat tightened. But he took a deep breath and nodded. "So why are we doing this now? I feel it is an awkward time."

"I cannot tell you all, but I will say this. It will be of great help to you in your next estate."

Westley considered that but no more understood it than he understood why the grass grew green. "Okay." And he shook his head. "Well, let's do it."

"Will you sit, my friend, and tell me your full name again?"

Smiling, he took a seat. "Westley Jostin Nelson."

CHAPTER 30

It had been one heck of a day. Miriam rubbed her arms and felt the goose flesh there. September was coming on nicely, and there was a bite in the air. Still, the fireflies were out thick tonight, and so were the stars. She sat on the Eden bridge, legs dangling over the edge, and thought back to the frightening and unforgettable moments of the day to pass the time.

Quebec was so beautiful; well, the cathedral they had found the memory person—a Catholic bishop—in had been. Notre Dame, or Our Lady in English, had sweeping cream arches, brightly colored stained-glass windows, and gold leaf and statues of Mary the mother of Jesus—the Lady they named the building after—everywhere. It was the most intricate space Miriam had ever seen in real life. She was awed by it. Though she did not understand the decadence, she did appreciate the feast for her eyes. Seth had placed her hand on the cool stone of one of the pillars. She smiled even now as she thought of it.

Touching it made it so much more real.

In London, they walked by Big Ben when they went to get the man from earlier, the one who would have gotten them arrested. They saw another church there—Westminster Abbey—and though they did not go inside either historic building, Miriam touched them.

China was practically empty. Of males, that is. Miriam learned that was because China was one of the countries in the UCC, and they were invading the United States with a million soldiers. Miriam couldn't even imagine what a million soldiers would look like. They found a tiny, wrinkled lady in an even tinier fishing village. She beckoned Miriam close, and they clasped hands. And as Miriam took her memories, the bedridden woman passed away with a sigh of relief as her last breath.

In Samoa, Miriam received her first mosquito bite. At the thought of it, she reached down and scratched her ankle. Boy, that was pesky. There, though, Miriam took a memory from the largest man she had ever seen in her life. He must have weighed five hundred pounds and was at least five inches taller than her papa. When she, Seth, and Gerald approached him, he offered them a meal. They had to refuse. Still, it was bizarre and yet wonderful. Miriam saw so many different types of flowers and birds, and was so sweaty by the time they left that she had to wipe her face on her skirt.

Africa, Belize, and actually Florida were the dangerous places. The giant snake was terrifying, but Gerald quickly took care of it once he found her. In Belize, she got grabbed by the hair and pulled ten feet across the pavement before Gerald and Karl had the guy flat on his stomach, his face smashed into the road. But in Florida, they had to go into what Gerald called a drug den. Miriam had never seen so many tattoos and guns in her life. Knowing this was not a place to ask permission, she used the trick of appearing behind a person, effectively ridding them of the issue of violence; what was scary was entering and exiting the drug den. The entire coast of Florida had been rocked by fifteen different hurricanes, and there was water everywhere. When they Traveled to the proper place but landed neck-deep in water, panic hit. Emergency swimming got them quickly spread out.

However, Gerald had a protocol for this. It only took five seconds for the men to remember their training. They returned to Edenia. It took Gerald a hot minute to figure out a travel portal away from himself for Miriam and Seth, but it worked out just fine once Seth took Miriam in his arms.

Seth freed them of all the water once they got back, and when they tried again, they portaled to the second story of the building they needed. The thugs were so astonished that when Miriam disappeared from before them to behind the one guy they needed and took his memory, the others sat there confused, not knowing if they should run or shoot Miriam and her group. However, the moment Miriam removed her hands, the man sank to the floor weeping and whispered, "Thank you. Thank you. It's gone. It's gone."

Miriam felt that woozy feeling of needing to pass out, but the man clawing at Miriam's dress distracted her. His crying continued, and she blinked and pulled herself out of the darkness to place a hand on his shoulder comfortingly.

Her hand left his shoulder and sprang to her ears as a terribly loud siren went off. One side of the building had large windows facing the city. The men freaked out, yelling, "Tsunami!" and scrabbled to gather up all their drugs and money, and weapons.

Miriam, however, went to the window and watched as a force of the Gods swept through the city. Gerald got them out in time, but Miriam had never seen anything so destructive in her life. It was frightening, even more so than the snake. She frowned to herself. Those poor people in Florida were already buried in water. She wondered how many survived.

The wood behind her creaked.

She turned just as Seth sat next to her. He did not put his feet over the edge. Her eyes were adjusted to the darkness, and so she saw the subtle smile on his face. "Hi," he whispered.

She bit her upper lip, effectively stopping her own smile. "Hey." She pulled her legs up and moved them to the side as she turned to face Seth. "I was just going over our amazing day today."

"It has been pretty incredible." He slowly reached over and took a piece of her hair between his fingertips. It made her giddy inside. "What was your favorite part?"

Again she bit her lips to stop the smile creeping up on her. "I really liked the Cathedral in Quebec and the flowers in Samoa."

"But those weren't your favorite part?" He asked, his eyebrows knotting.

"Nope."

He raised an eyebrow at her challenging her to speak.

"It was when you took my hand and put it on the pillar in the cathedral."

He wrinkled his forehead at her and tilted his head to the side, "Really? Why?"

"Because that's for me to know and you to find out." She took her hair out of his hand and used the railing to stand. Once up, she waited for Seth to follow suit. He did.

"Oh, really. A mystery. Well, I love a good mystery."

Miriam turned toward him, her eyes wanting to inspect him to see if he was telling the truth. "You do?"

He looked down at his feet. "Actually, no. I don't. I would much prefer a straightforward answer."

"Well, so would I," Miriam answered quickly. "Why did you come here tonight?"

His forehead wrinkled up. "Here, here, like the bridge here?" He pointed down.

"Yes," she said, and gave him a deadpan look.

He turned away from her and leaned over the bridge rail with crossed arms. "That is a mystery." He looked back at her and said, "I don't suppose you would believe that I just was on a walk and happened to pass by and thought, hey, now that I'm playing for the right team, I guess I'll go explore that bridge that almost killed me."

She shook her head that it would not do, but then she asked, "Almost killed you? This bridge?"

"Yeah, I was trying to sneak into the garden, but it did not work out."

Miriam smirked, "Met some resistance, did ya?"

"Yes, I did. Though I gotta tell you, it was so well done I just thought I had terrible luck." Seth turned around, leaned his back against the rail, and crossed his arms over his chest. "Ya know what's funny? In the process of almost drowning me, the Guardians saved me as well." He cleared his throat. "It never occurred to me before now how much power we have."

"That's just because you haven't fought any Joneses yet. Once you do, it is easy to understand how pathetic they are, with all their weapons and schemes. They have never even gotten close to the Garden." Miriam smiled.

"You guys save them from themselves every day, and what do you get in return?"

"It isn't about a return. I'm just glad they don't die. I am opposed to killing."

"They are evil, though. At least Willis, Jeremiah, and Tally are."

"That's the other thing. I don't want their blood on the ground of the Garden. It is a holy place." She crossed her arms over her chest and locked her face into that stony expression she used when talking about the Jones.

"Are you okay talking about them?"

Miriam blinked and looked down. She gathered her thoughts momentarily before saying, "Aside from our extremely cathartic conversation earlier, I've had a bit of an epiphany, and it has allowed me to see this whole situation differently. It has allowed me to not hate you so much and not feel so betrayed."

Seth moved toward her, and she held out her hand to stop him from getting closer.

"I'm working on it. *Working*." Seth moved back, so she continued. "It's like my head got the memo. I'm just still working on my reactions physically."

"What was your epiphany, if you don't mind my asking?"

She shook her head at him. "If you're a good boy, I might tell you someday."

"Fair enough," he said, and scrubbed his hands through his shoulder-length hair. Then he reached to the sky and arched his back. "Well, I better get to bed. We have so many memories to retrieve tomorrow. It's going to be a super-long day."

"And if it's even half as eventful as today..." Miriam added.

"Yes, I hope it's not. But if it is, we have the Travelers to help out."

"We do. Thank goodness." Miriam allowed her smile to reveal the depth behind that statement. Seth did not understand, but he caught the look and wanted to question her about it. So she moved the topic onward. "Do you want to walk me home?"

He put his hand in his pocket and said, "Sure. I would love to, but is that appropriate?" He began to move across the bridge toward town. "I mean, you told me we aren't allowed to be together and take walks and stuff unless..."

He left the words hanging there between them.

Miriam really appreciated the consideration, and it brought Todd to mind. He would for sure not like Seth walking her home. And just then, it was as if she had conjured Todd out of nowhere. He was suddenly there, across the street, walking toward her.

He eyed Seth. Miriam's heart jumped into her throat. Todd turned to her. "Your father said I could find you here. He asked me to walk you home if you were ready."

Miriam glanced quickly at Seth. "We were just heading there. I asked Seth to walk me home, but you can join us." She smiled at him and moved toward her house, effectively leaving it up to the boys to decide what happened from there.

Seth called to her, "Hey, Miriam. I think I will just head straight to my house since you are all taken care of. I'll see you tomorrow."

Now her heart was in her shoes. "Great," she said, and nodded noncommittally, then hurried down the road.

Todd moved beside her. "Hey. I didn't know he would be here. I'm sorry if I interrupted an important conversation."

"No. I wasn't expecting him, either. He found me. I think he is trying to apologize again." Miriam glanced over at Todd, and her eyes stuck. He was the boy next door, adorable. The guy who all the girls think is cute until he becomes a man, and then he turns into something more. Her middle fluttered. She adored Todd. At least the Todd she knew three years ago. And he'd told her he still loved her.

She longed to go back to the time when all she could think about was Todd. Maybe she could get there.

She threw herself into a conversation with him. "So what happened with you today? Tell me everything."

They walked and talked, and Miriam smiled and laughed and remembered Todd's great sense of humor and how he was so open, forthright, and honest.

When they reached her home, Gerald was waiting on the porch, his arms crossed, his expression serious. So they stopped at the fence instead of going to the door.

Todd took her arm just as she was about to open the gate. "Miriam."

She looked up into his eyes and smiled, "Yeah."

He let go of her and glanced at his feet as he gathered his thoughts or courage. "I don't know how to bring this up, but I have to." He paused again and then spit it all out. "I know Seth betrayed you, and that you cared for him. I completely get it. He was there for you in a time when no one else was. But that has changed. He is not the only choice, okay? Please don't close me out before we have a chance to reconnect. Promise me you won't." He took her hands in his. "Because I really care about you. We had such a good, easy, happy relationship before. If you let us have time..."

"Todd, stop." She placed a finger over his lips. The feel of those lips on her finger distracted her, and she lost her train of thought as she took in his flawless face. It was so symmetrical, so generous. His large bright green eyes lined with millions of eyelashes, full lips, chiseled cheekbones, and thick blond hair parted and swept to the side with a perfect swoop. The abundant freckles over his nose were the only thing that pulled him from the super handsome side of the metric to the super cute side. Thank goodness, because he would have girls hanging on him like fruit on a Fall apple tree without them.

She removed her finger, but her eyes lingered on his lips. After a full second, Todd's tongue darted out of his mouth to wet his lips, breaking her gaze. Her eyes flashed to his, and she saw everything she'd wanted to see when she was thirteen. Emotions, history, and admiration filled the wideness of this glance, the tilt of his head, and the soft smile on his mouth.

But was his love and admiration what she wanted? She stepped back, cleared her throat, and shook her head. She looked away. She wasn't wholly sure...

"Miriam," he whispered.

Her eyes flew back to his.

"There is something here. Please promise me you won't push it away before we explore it more."

She smiled at him. "Don't worry; until ten days ago, you were my dream guy, the only person I could ever see myself with, and it has been that way since before I can remember. I won't give up on us unless I have to." She blinked twice into the thousand-watt smile Todd gave her. Then she turned and moved through the gate.

When she got to Gerald, he smiled. "I really like that kid. He is hard-working, smart, funny, and has great taste because even though every other girl around here gives him time, he doesn't even look at them. He is completely crazy about you."

Miriam felt her cheeks flush. She put her arm around Gerald's waist, her head on his shoulder, as she did with her papa. "It's true. I was crazy about him as well."

He cranked his neck to look into Miriam's eyes, "Was?"

She closed her eyes, not wanting him to see her soul. Then she spoke. "My parents have decided I must get married as soon as possible."

"I understand that."

She moved away from him, "You do?"

"Yeah, but only because I heard them talking about it."

Miriam laughed and whacked him on the shoulder. "You're as bad as Peter."

Gerald nodded. "Li'l Boss reminds me of myself every day. That's why he's my favorite."

"What?" Miriam said with indignation in her voice.

"My favorite child. I'm certain I like both of you far more than my own spawn."

Miriam was about to ask him about his children when her papa and mama opened the door and moved onto the porch.

She smiled at them, and her pa said, "Will you sit, Miri? We want to talk to you."

Instead of answering, she sat.

Gerald excused himself, and her mama sat next to her. Pa stood still, but he leaned against the porch railing.

Her parents looked at one another, and then Pa spoke up. "I sent Todd to walk you home. How did that go?"

Miriam swallowed. "Good. Really good. I really care about Todd."

Her pa smiled. "I knew you did. You have since you were little."

Her mama squeezed her arm. The discerning woman looked into Miriam's eyes and said, "But. There is a big 'but' in the way." She turned in her seat. "What is it?"

Miriam exhaled and just said what she was thinking. "I do not think I need to get married anymore." Both her parents' eyes went wide, and she realized what she'd said. "I mean, not for the reasons we have discussed in the past. I mean, I want to get married, just not at sixteen."

She looked at her pa and stuttered through her thoughts and explanations. "My Nature is different now. I use it for the thing the Master wants. It makes me whole and useful." She clenched her hand. "I am in control of my Nature in a way I never was. I do not need a babysitter."

Her mama blinked at her. "Well, I wasn't expecting that."

"Me neither. I was expecting some tirade about Seth and wanting him to be in the running." Her pa's hands combed through his hair and scrubbed at his neck. "What a relief. I mean, I love the kid. I even respect him and understand him, but..." He looked meaningfully at Miriam's chest. "You should not feel so happy when your daughter slaps your potential son-in-law across the face. And let me tell you, I was so proud."

"Hirum." Her mother's voice held warning and somehow the *shut-up* sentiment.

Her papa looked at her face, and Miriam burst into tears.

"What?" He asked. "Was it something I said?"

Her mama rolled her eyes and pulled Miriam in for a hug. "I know. Those Johnson boys." She shook her head. "They are like smelly feet. Everywhere they walk, they leave behind something unsavory."

This made Miriam laugh through her tears. She pulled away from her mama and covered her mouth with laughs and cries.

Her pa came closer, looking at the two of them, "What is happening?"

Her mama took Miriam's face in her hands, and without looking at her, Papa said, "Go to bed, Hirum. You are obviously tired. I will explain later."

The man obeyed his wife, and once they were alone, her mother said, "Let me guess. You love him, and you hate him, with all of every cell in your body."

Miriam's eyes went wide at being understood. She wiped at her face and nodded. "That sums it up." She licked her lips and sniffed. "The crazy thing is, if I had to choose right now what boy I would marry, it would be Todd. I adore him. I can see myself with him. Like, as you said, there is a big *but* there too."

"*But* only if you did not ever have to see Seth again." She shook her head.

Miriam, again surprised, nodded to her mother.

"And the past repeats itself."

Miriam wiped at her face some more, her brow wrinkled with questions. "What do you mean?"

Her ma looked away, her hand gripping her neck and her other hand tugging at her long cornmeal braid. After a full minute of silence, she said, "If I tell you something, Miriam, you have to promise you will never tell another person."

Miriam nodded, "You have my word."

"Okay, well. Let me put it this way as someone who married the 'Todd' in her life. Understand, I love my life. I am happy and love your father with all of my heart and more every day. We have fun, and we still are passionate about each other. Obviously, we have eight children."

"Mama, I am sensing a big *but*. Please tell me there is not a *but* here."

"*But*," Her mother said, "I would never ever want to live in the same town with my 'Seth.' After twenty-plus years, just seeing him for a moment was enough to wreck my insides."

Miriam blinked rapidly and recalled ten days ago in Aunt Sarah's house. She was standing on a sewing stool, her mother grouchy and looking out the window toward the Edenia Road. Then the Johnsons were there. She remembered her mother's face. How crazy she was acting. She didn't go to the festivities to welcome the Johnsons that night. How she kept saying 'those Johnson men.'

Her mother understood her completely.

"Zeke?" Miriam asked.

Her mother looked away, picked invisible lint off her skirt, and nodded. Miriam opened her mouth to ask a million questions, but her mother raised her hand. "No, Miriam." She shook her head and licked her bottom lip. "I just cannot. I just never will get over what happened between us."

She thought this through and realized something. "It is because you never got closure. You two have never talked about it. Am I right?"

"You are right. And the terrible thing is, we can never talk about it. Never. I cannot be in the same room with him without feeling so much love and hate I want to explode." Then she looked straight at Miriam, "Besides, it would be a highly inappropriate conversation for us to have. I mean, can you imagine it? *Zeke, how could you leave me when I loved you so much.*" Her mother scoffed.

"He left you?"

She nodded. "In New York. He disappeared. No note. No explanation. I thought he was dead. Until he sent word to Hirum that he was not coming back. Miriam, we were married, Zeke and I, and he left me. I did not see him again until ten days ago." Her mother had fat tears in her eyes.

Something occurred to Miriam. After all these years, one of the reasons this hurt so much still was that her mother probably had no one to talk to about it. It was shameful. It was unacceptable behavior.

She thought of her papa. He must have loved her mama a lot to marry her after such a situation with his own brother.

Miriam pulled her mother to her and hugged her hard. "I am sorry that happened to you, Mama. But I am really glad you married Papa. You two are so perfect together. And I see how much you love one another."

Her mama sniffed. "It is true. I loved your papa first. Like I told you, he was my Todd. He was older than me and seemed unobtainable. Until one day, I grew out of my huge eyes, crazy hair, and penchant for beating up all the boys my own age."

They both laughed.

After they settled down, her mama grew serious. "I loved your father, but once Zeke grew up and started whipping me as many times as I whipped him, there was no contest. I fell into him so deep I did not have a single thought for any other human, let alone any other boy. I have never had a more passionate, fiery, all-consuming experience than that. But with fire and heat comes burns and scars." She placed her hand on Miriam's chest over her scars. "As you know all too well." Looking deeply into her eyes, she added, "Choose wisely, my love." And she patted her hand. Then she got up and moved to the door.

Miriam pulled her mother's words into her soul but also remembered the point of this conversation. "So, does that mean..."

"You are free," her mother said as she opened the front door. "We will not push the betrothal on you any longer. I will settle it with your father, never fear." She opened the inner door but paused again. "I love you, Miriam."

"I love you too, Mama."

CHAPTER 31

WEDNESDAY
Peter

Peter woke up with a head full of dreams and ribbon room stuff he needed to tell Seth and his pa, but all he could think about was how much he wanted to visit the twins and tell them everything he'd heard while eavesdropping on his mother and Miriam last night.

The picture of the two adults in Manhattan he'd shared with the twins made so much sense. He couldn't believe the story was so much more involved and shameful than he supposed, making him consider if he should tell the girls. The girls were barely on better terms with their father and mother, and he didn't want to do anything to cause more issues. The story didn't make their father look very good. It was just so juicy, and he hadn't gotten to see the girls much, and he hadn't gotten to have much fun or make any mischief, and darn it, he missed that.

After getting dressed, finger-combing his hair, and wiping his teeth, he left the house. As he walked, the nagging thought that he shouldn't tell them kept annoying him. He supposed he felt terrible, like he was shaming both his mother and their father. They had kept the story a secret from their families for twenty-plus years; who was he to let the cat out of the bag? But then again, it was Lilly and Abby. They knew how to keep things to themselves.

However, the closer he got to the Johnson house, the more he felt he shouldn't say a word about it and the more he wanted to. He opened the gate, and he would tell them. He knocked on the door, but he wouldn't tell them. And then he looked at the girls, together as usual, and beautiful to boot. Lillian's blue-green eyes made her look so different in such a good way. She was meant to have that color of eyes; it was just a fact.

They looked at him as he looked at Lillian.

Abby finally said, "Earth to Peter, what are you doing here?"

Peter snapped out of it and thought fast. "I thought we could hang out. I haven't talked to you guys much since..." He waved a finger at their obvious changes.

Abby said, "I was just about to jump in the tub. Since I can't take showers."

Peter cocked his head at her. "Why can't you take showers?"

"Because I don't like to be cold, duh."

"Cold?" Peter thought about what she was saying. "Why..." Then it occurred to him. "Oh my gosh, you don't know. Okay, so let me help you. Since your father lived here last, we put fifty-gallon holding tanks under every house. As a fire, your Nature can heat that water tank so you can wash dishes, take showers, and wash your hands with hot water. That is why all our faucets have two dials; one is straight from the well, so it's cold; the other is from the holding tank." He smiled at her slack-jawed expression. "So my mother heats the water in our tank to boiling in the morning and then again in the afternoon on cold days, and voilà, hot water all day...well, until dinner time."

"Oh, my heck! Yay!! I was just going to heat the bath water every time they took a bath."

Abby was really excited.

"Show me where it's at," Abby demanded.

"Yes, ma'am." He left the porch, entered the house, moved to the bathroom, and opened a little door behind the bathroom door. There, a metal tank sat with hoses coming out the top. "Pull your Nature to you," he said after the girls shuffled into the small space behind him.

He watched as Abby's golden eyes began to shudder.

"Now let go of your heat into this." He pointed at the tank. "You will hear when it starts boiling."

Her eyes flashed at him, and he scooted out of the way. "Be

careful. You are a weapon, Abby. You can't just look around now. Anything you focus on will burn, even humans. Or Guardians."

She narrowed her eyes at the tank and concentrated. After a few seconds, she asked, "Is it working?"

Peter pulled his Nature to him so he would be invisible and invincible, reaching out to touch the tank.

It did feel a tad warmer. It only took his mother one minute to boil the whole tank, but Abby was a beginner, so it would take her more time. He could feel it changing temperature as he held his hand there. He moved away and released his Nature.

"It is getting warmer." He stood. "If I were you, I would put my hand on it as you do it until you get used to what you are doing. Don't worry, your fire can't hurt you if you happen to concentrate on your own hand. But the tank can burn you if you get it too hot. The water will also burn you, so you should carefully adjust the temperature before entering the shower or using the boiling water anywhere else."

"Good to know," Abby said and knelt to touch the tank. "How long does it take?"

"It takes my mother about a minute. But it will take a little longer since you are new at it. Just make sure you stop when you hear..."

Peter was interrupted by the familiar sound of boiling water in the tank.

"...that. Stop, Abby. The tubing can only take temperatures up to boiling."

She blinked and looked away, shaking her head like Westley did when he was done with a foretelling.

"You have fifty gallons daily for everything, so you can't be frivolous with the hot water. Every morning the tank will refill, and no, you can't change it. It's on a timer for the whole town."

Abby smiled. "Got it! Now get out. I'm going to take my first shower in forever."

Peter looked at Lillian, and they filed out of the bathroom. Once Abby had closed the door, Peter turned to Lillian. "Do you wanna go for a walk or sit on your porch or something?"

She smiled and blushed. "Sure." She led him out to the front yard and around the house to a big tree. It had a substantial low branch, and Lillian went to it and leaned against it.

Her relaxed face and serene countenance made her even more beautiful.

"So, how are you doing? How is all this"—he waved to Edenia in general—"going for you? Have you explored with your Nature?"

She smiled at him. "A little. It's all going well. I seriously haven't felt this good in months, and having a Nature on top of health is just like a cherry on the most delicious ice cream." She looked down at her feet and then back up at him. "So, how do people who don't have a fire Nature in their house get hot water? Or do they go without as we did?"

"You only went without because we couldn't show you our Natures. Plus, it's a refining process newbies have to go through. You out in the world are so spoiled. Not having hot water really humbles you."

"I guess that's true. But what about the other question?"

"Well, the fire Natures are organized, and assign a Guardian to all the houses without…"

Peter paused as Lillian stood straight from the tree and approached him. She did so slowly, her eyes on him.

When he didn't go on, she said, "You are the most amazing people I've ever met. You are so giving and kind; you take care of one another and are so faithful and loyal. That really means a lot to me."

"Really?" Peter asked. Then he wondered why this act of service by the fire Natures inspired her so much.

"Did you know that we are not cousins? In fact, we don't share any genetics that my father knows of." She took a step closer, and it put her inside his bubble. He thought about stepping back, but this close, he could see exactly how flawless her skin was, which entranced him.

He replied in a monotone, "I did, in fact, know that."

She smiled at him. "Well, that is an important detail. That, and the fact that I will not die any time soon." She placed a hand on his chest.

He looked down at the hand and swallowed. "For what reason is it important?" he croaked.

"For this reason." She leaned toward him and kissed him. It was the lightest brush of lips. It felt like a butterfly wing.

Peter stopped breathing.

But then Lillian was speaking. "Because I love you, Peter Miller. I think you are the most attractive human I've ever seen in real life. I love your thinking and confidence, loyalty, and jokes. I just..." She looked away and shook her head. "I've never been...never felt this way before. It's a little overwhelming." Her eyes found him again, and her face turned serious. "I want to be your girlfriend. Can we do that here?"

Peter blinked at her. He had no idea what to say to that. Of course, he really cared for her. She was intelligent and beautiful, and that kiss zinged him right down to his toes. But...

He stepped back from her and looked at his feet, searching for the right words. He looked back up and noticed her face had gone red. So he put a hand up, "Listen, I really like you. I think you are beautiful, and that kiss...was completely awesome. I just..." He put his hands in his pockets and recalled what she had said a moment before. "You know how you said I was loyal, and that was one of the things you loved about me?" She nodded, her eyes as big as saucers and getting waterier by the second. "Well, that loyalty holds me back from everything that a regular boy my age would want. I..." He sniffed. "It's the end of the world, Lillian. The Master has work for me to do. I'm busy all the time. I can't be distracted..." He took his hands out of his pockets and took her hand in his. "Even if the distraction is as lovely as you are. I just...can we just hold on to how we feel until this is all over? And then we can talk about it."

She nodded and smiled at him.

"Do you understand?" He stepped closer to her and had a moment of temporary insanity as he glanced at her lips. The moment included visions of kissing her forever. Maybe he did love her. His hand moved to cup her cheek. "For all I know, I'm in love with you too. I just can't let myself think about it right now." And even to himself, his voice sounded hypnotized.

He shook his head, effectively pulling him out of the trance he found himself in. Stepping back, he took a deep breath and wiped his eyes. "We will talk about this later, Lillian. I promise you."

She took one step toward him. "What if there is no later?" She took one of his hands in hers. "You just said it was the end of the world. What does that even mean?" She shook her head. "It doesn't matter. I guess I just didn't want to die before I told you. I needed you to know. I've loved you since you showed up at my window in the middle of the night, and I will wait for you to finish your task, but know, Peter Miller, that you are claimed." She smiled at him possessively, and he couldn't help it. A thrill raced up his back.

Walking away, Peter figured he'd better keep his word and not be distracted. The morning was beautiful and fresh, so he found a quiet spot out of doors, and no sooner had he sat and moved into his ribbon room than he was pulled to see something that scared the living crap out of him.

He needed to talk to Seth.

CHAPTER 32

Yawning, Seth stretched in his bed. The sky was full of light, which meant it had to be at least seven a.m. He'd slept in a bit. Rolling to his back, he closed his eyes and began his new routine. *Master, what do you need of me today?* he thought toward the sky.

No sooner had he conjured the words than he was pulled into a vision. In that other sight, he stood so close to Miriam he could see her beautiful violet irises swirl as her Nature came to her. She was impressive and majestic in her magic. She was lovely and gentle, and oh, so stunningly beautiful. It made Seth want to weep with sorrow and rage in frustration at himself. Miriam placed her hands on the sides of someone's head. Seth looked away from her and saw that this person was just the first person in a long line of people coming before Miriam. They were all faceless in a creepy way. Still, Seth knew they were all Edenians. Seth's eyes turned back to the girl he dreamed about at night, Miriam; as her power raged inside, he saw her take a soul sliver from the Edenian. Once it was taken, she moved on to the next person in line. On and on it went until she was finished with everyone. By the end, Seth was practically holding her up. But they finished.

When the vision faded, the aftertaste of this was urgency. Today. This needed to be done now. Seth rose quickly, pulled his clothes on, and raced for the door.

CHAPTER 33

Peter

He raced toward his own house, knowing Seth wasn't at the Johnsons' house, having just left there.

Finally, he spotted Seth. "I've been looking for you," Peter said, a little out of breath. Seth looked in as much of a hurry as he was. "What is it? What did you see?"

"You tell me, first pip-squeak."

"What the heck is a pip-squeak? Never mind. What would you do if Willis came here?"

Seth exhaled loudly. "Like, what does that mean?"

"You know that I know who you are, right?" Peter nodded. "Willis is your uncle. You are Jones blood."

Seth's feet stumbled over that but only for a moment. He nodded, then gestured in a rolling motion with his hand as he said, "Get to your point, Peter."

"Yes, well, so, you actually do have relatives, and they are the Joneses. You get that, right? So, if a big fight is going down between the Joneses and the Guardians..." He raised his eyebrows at Seth but went on when the guy said nothing. "Conflicting interests, savvy?"

Seth looked at him like he was an idiot. "No, Peter. That is not how this works. I have no feelings toward the Joneses except hatred for betraying me. Have you forgotten what they did to Miriam?" he whispered fiercely, his face red with rage.

"Yes. I've seen it. It's gross." Peter took the opportunity to join the Jones bashing. "While we are on the subject, what kind of people would see Lillian, their niece and cousin, sick and demand a price or a trade to help her? They have more money than God. How did they justify not helping their own relatives freely?" Peter shook his head in disgust.

Seth nodded in agreement, but then he added, "Also, you may remember that I took an oath. I am a Guardian. No matter how much blood I share with them, the Joneses are my enemy. And we have a duty to stop them from getting into the Garden. And stop them I will, even if I have to kill them."

"Good, but hold up. We are not going to kill Willis or any of the Joneses. We will just trick them as per usual." He smiled. "I mean, killing them would defeat the point of saving their lives a thousand times, right?"

Seth bit his cheek.

"And you don't have to worry about the actual Garden. I mean, if Willis gets anywhere near the tree, the Master will kill him without even straining himself. We stop that, you know, every time we stop the Joneses from getting in. And we do it because we are awesome."

Seth shook his head. "You really love this, don't you?"

"Duh, why wouldn't I? And tomorrow, when the Joneses come, you will see exactly how cool being a Guardian can be."

Seth stopped in his tracks. "They're coming tomorrow?" He grabbed Peter by the arm, and his eyes went all still as they did when he was being taken by a vision.

"Oh no. Oh no!" Seth whispered.

"What. What, Seth?"

He grabbed Peter by the arm and started moving quickly. "Your house, now! Step on it."

⚜

PETER COULD TELL that his papa wanted to dismiss them. He had a house full of Edenians ranting about something, but just as he was about to do so, he looked at them for real and instantly sent everyone away. When the room was clear, he asked, "What did you see?"

Peter spoke up. "Willis is coming today."

"He will attack Edenia tonight, Hirum, and..." Seth paused, his face white.

"And what?"

"And it's not going to go well for us."

Hirum's face did a surprised shuttering expression. "It's what?"

Seth took a deep breath and shook his head. "I don't know exactly how to say this. I didn't see the details and don't want to say what I saw."

Hirum stepped toward Seth. "What did you see? Tell me instantly."

Seth's face paled even further, a strange look for a brown boy. "I saw death. Here. In Edenia. And I saw the Joneses do it."

"How?" Hirum exclaimed in an intense whisper.

Seth shook his head, eyes lowered.

"Well, maybe you were wrong. Maybe this is only a possibility. Let's get all three of you boys together. Let's see if that makes a difference." Hirum rushed out, his voice nervous.

"Fine, but, Hirum, that's not all I saw." He asked, "Where's Miriam?"

"Wait, wait." Peter moved closer. "Do you think we should tell her now? She might be freaked out all day if we do."

"Oh yes, because of Willis, here in Edenia." His father stated and shivered. He actually shivered. He pulled on his chin thoughtfully to cover it up.

Seth nodded. "We must consider her. She has been through hell the last few days."

"Your fault, by the way; just saying. If you would have stayed here..."

Seth glared over at Peter. "I know, Peter. And I will be paying for that mistake for a long time." He made a fist with his hand, jaw clenching, then his other hand slid down his face as if he were going to cry. Peter took a deep breath. How could he stay mad at Seth? When Seth looked at him again, his face had changed to resolve, and he said, "I'm really sorry, by the way." His eyes flitted to Peter's pa.

Papa touched his shoulder. "I can see that you are. You were in an impossible situation." He paused in a fatherly way and then added the stinging nettle. "That does not change the fact that you could have communicated. You could have trusted."

Peter didn't feel like Seth was saying sorry to him, but he butted into the moment, anyway. "I'll forgive you someday." He smiled, hoping to lighten the mood. "But that doesn't mean revenge is off the table." Peter grinned wickedly and dry-washed his hands like any good villain.

Seth shook his head. "Peter, I might end up really liking you if you're not careful."

This comment surprised Peter. "Really?"

"Yes, of course. I have two sisters I would do anything for. But I'm glad Miriam has a brother who cares enough about her to take revenge. So, bring it on. I deserve it. Once Willis knows what side I've chosen, I'm uncertain what he will do about it, but, frankly, I might be more scared of what you might do if I don't keep my word. And that's saying something because Willis will likely remove my skin with a pocketknife."

"Graphic." Peter shuddered, then asked, "Is that possible?"

Seth laughed out loud. "Are you serious? Well, if you don't already know, I'm not going to tell you. That would be like signing my own death warrant."

Papa had been silent for this little exchange, but once it was done, he said, "I believe Miriam should know now." And without preamble, his father yelled in his particular way, using his wind Nature, "Miriam!"

There were feet scrabbling, and then Miriam was there, her face surprised and concerned.

"Speak, Seth. She is here."

Seth took a deep breath and told them what he saw in his vision. "I saw Miriam take a soul sliver from every single person in Edenia. Man. Woman. Child. Today."

"She does this before Willis gets here?"

Miriam entered the conversation, her voice sounding stung. "What? Willis is coming?"

"Yes. Well, we don't know for sure," Papa said, and his face flushed as he looked at Seth. "We need to get Westley here. Speaking of which…" His papa opened the front door and faced in the direction of Westley's house. He then called the cowboy's name and followed it, saying, "Get your tail end here now."

Gerald entered from the back of the house. "Did I hear you correctly? Willis is coming today?"

"Tonight," Seth answered.

"And he's here to kill?" Gerald narrowed his eyes at Seth.

Seth looked at Miriam but then turned back to Gerald. "Yes."

"I will gather the men."

"No," Seth said to Gerald. "Gather the entire town. Round them up and tell them Miriam must take a memory from them. Tell them that every last one has to have it done."

Peter stood. "Well, if everyone has to do it, she might as well take mine now." He approached his sister and said, "Do your worst." Then he leaned away. "No, can you take the memory of that one time…"

"Peter, you know I can only take things within a certain time frame." She grimaced at him, but then she put her hands on his head. "But I'll tell you what, I'll take the memory of you making that stupid comment. You're welcome."

Peter shrugged and closed his eyes. Instantly he felt something—a tickle in the back of his head, then a slight slice of pain, and then it was over.

She moved away from him. Seth must have noticed something wrong because no sooner had Peter stepped away when a buzzing filling his head; Seth raced to Miriam's side, taking her in his arms, and asked. "Are you going to go down?"

Miriam did sway. "No," she said. "I'm okay. But that cost more than the soul slivers I take from the golden thread people. It wasn't bad, I just wasn't expecting it."

"I wonder why?" Seth asked, but he did not move away from Miriam, nor did she push him away.

"I suppose you should do me next," his pa said.

After it was done, Pa called everyone nearby to get the same treatment.

Miriam said, "How in the world am I going to hold so many souls?"

Peter responded, "You are the Vessel."

Miriam eyed him. "Really?"

"Hey, it's not my word."

She turned to Seth. "What do you think this is going to do?"

Seth's face became grave before saying, "I think it might save us all."

"And the other thing. The mission with the Travelers?"

"That is on hold for right now. I got the feeling that the Master knew Willis was planning this, but Willis hadn't decided on the day yet, so the Master just gave me a sense of urgency to get it done."

"But now it's too late."

"No, not for the outside souls."

Miriam's head whipped toward him. "Not the outside souls? But the inside ones are...what? Doomed?"

Seth looked into Miriam's eyes and did not blink. He did not say anything. But he did not look away for what felt like an eternity. Long enough for Miriam and Peter himself to get the point. A tear tumbled down his sister's cheek as a whole new wave of Guardians and their families moved through the front door, herded by Miriam's Warriors.

⚔

PETER LEFT the mayhem of the living room behind to find his parents. They were in the kitchen with Garren and the council. "We need to discuss their loyalties."

"Yes, who is to say they are why Seth sees bloodshed?"

"The Travelers are Guardians. They are dedicated to Miriam. There is no way they would betray us," his papa clapped back.

That silenced the room.

"How is this possible?"

"Yes, we all have given up all and served. How are we to die now?"

Peter watched his father's head droop. "I do not know."

His mother said, "What we do know is that Miriam is taking a piece of us all, as she was told to do. Perhaps that is the key to this. Perhaps we cannot die if she still has a part of our soul within her. Do not lose faith now. The Master has always watched after us. Have they not?"

The feel of the room changed with his mother's speech. His papa took advantage of it. "Now, all of you go to Miriam."

"Peter, what are you doing lurking about?" his mother demanded.

"I was just wondering what I should do to help."

"Go help the Travelers. I am sure it is a mess out there."

"Okay," Peter said, but he did not move.

His mother looked over at him, eyes narrowed. But once she looked at him, really looked at him, her face softened. "I forget that you are but thirteen sometimes." She moved to his side and wrapped her arms around him. "All will be well," she whispered in his ear. "The Master always has a plan. They will take care of us." She kissed him on the cheek. And Peter felt like he could move on.

He gave his mama a smile and said, "Thanks." He wanted to tell her he loved her, but that was weird.

She said it, though. "I love you, Peter Christopher Miller. You are the best and brightest of us all." She smiled, and he smiled back. "Now get to work!"

CHAPTER 34

Around noon, most of the town had gathered, and her father had moved the soul-taking event to the town square. Miriam stood in the shade of a tree, a line of Edenians before her in what seemed to stretch on for miles.

Though she had become much more stable after so much use of her Nature, Seth stayed close, steadying her when she felt tired, fetching her water, and generally being the most helpful human on the planet.

Perhaps some of the weak-kneed-ness had nothing to do with her task, and everything to do with the boy next to her.

The Travelers kept everyone in line, not that they needed to. Guardians knew what they were about.

Miriam talked to Seth while she worked, though it was a stunted conversation since she had to pause for each taking.

"So tomorrow, once we take care of this issue with Willis, we will resume collecting souls?"

"Yes," Seth answered. "I think." But then he went very still at her side. She looked over at him and saw his eyes glaze over. A moment later, he blinked, and he was back.

"What was that? A vision?"

His cheeks went pink. "Yes."

She took a memory from her teacher, Mr. Walsh. Then she looked back at Seth. "And?"

He smiled at her. "And nothing, it was just me having a planning session with Peter."

She nodded and took a memory from her aunt Betsy. The next

person in line was Todd. She blinked at him and smiled brightly. "Hi," she said, and felt her heart jump into her throat.

"Hey." He moved close. "I don't suppose I can choose what memory you take?"

She gazed at his handsome face and shook her head, "Nope, it's gotta be something within a day or so."

"Shoot. Because there was this thing that happened..."

"With the milk?" She giggled.

"Yes. I'm so happy you remember it." His voice was laced with sarcasm.

"Well, I am here as proof that you are not perfect; you're welcome." She curtsied.

"Let's just keep it between us."

She nodded and raised her hands. "I've just been taking people's sleep. Does that work?"

Todd pulled away, "Uhm, no, I would prefer you not take last night's sleep."

She cocked her head to the side, "Why?"

He blushed and glanced away. "I had a perfect dream last night. I don't want to chance it getting erased." He said this with his teeth showing like he was telling her a fantastic lie. But he wasn't. He was protecting himself. "And don't take yesterday evening either because this girl I'm crazy about told me I was the guy of her dreams. I would be distraught if I lost that memory."

Miriam blushed so hard she was sure the whole world could see it. "Fine, I'll take the last hour you've been in line."

"Nope. That won't do either. My vantage point was too beautiful. How about you take breakfast?"

Cheeks aflame, knowing if Todd had been in line the last hour, he'd had her as his vantage point. She nodded and placed her hands on his head. It only took a moment, and she had the memory. She breathed it into herself and pulled her hands out of Todd's incredibly soft hair.

He opened his eyes and looked at her. "Oh my gosh." He

blinked so much that she got a little dizzy watching it. "I can feel you." His eyebrows crunched together. "It's like I'm drawn to your position."

Then, Seth butted in. "We think it's your affinity for yourself. I mean the part of your soul that is inside of Miriam."

Todd glanced at him but only for a microsecond before his eyes were back on Miriam. "I understand now, wow."

"Don't let it make you crazy. I tend to flit around the world gathering souls," she said and felt really awkward.

He laughed. "This could never drive me crazy."

Then the man behind him said, "There's plenty of time for the two of you to flirt later. Can we get this over with?"

Miriam blushed, "Of course Uncle Myron." And she gave Todd a longing glance.

"Sorry," Todd said to her uncle and walked away. But he turned back like three times to smile at her.

"Don't let it make you crazy. I tend to flit around the world gathering souls?" Seth repeated her words, making them all sound like a question and ridiculous. "What was that about?" He laughed.

She grimaced. "Don't make fun of me. He's my childhood crush, and he makes me nervous."

"That is your childhood crush?" Seth asked, surprised. "He looks like a Ken Barbie doll."

"What's a Barbie doll? Is last night's sleep good to take?" she asked her Uncle Jai's mama. The woman nodded.

"I'll tell you when you're older. But really, Ken is your childhood crush? Why?"

Miriam closed her eyes, took the memory, and said, "Why not? Todd is an outstanding person. Besides being super handsome, he is good and smart and kind and..."

"Okay, okay, I get the point. It's just weird. I can't see you with him."

"Really?" She took another memory. "Well, you should work on that because I probably will marry him."

"What?" Seth exclaimed and moved from behind her to in front of her.

She shook her head at him, her eyes going big. "How is that a surprise? I told you my parents wanted to marry me off so I could have a babysitter." She pulled Seth by the front of the shirt to move him out of the line. But it only succeeded in pulling him closer to her. She looked into his black eyes and got stuck there for a hot second but realized the whole town was watching them. So she said, "You need to move out of the way."

He shook his head. "No. You can't marry him."

She pulled him over, stepped around him, and then addressed the next Edenian in line. "Is last night's sleep okay with you, Rillianna?"

The woman nodded, then eyed Seth with her mom-glare. Miriam took the memory.

"You're only sixteen," Seth exclaimed.

"Yeah, so? We do that here in Edenia. It's not a problem."

"You want to see the world!"

"I am seeing it. And I think it's the best I'm gonna get," Miriam replied and took another memory.

"It's the end of the world!"

"Maybe. But what does that mean for us? We live in Eden. For all we know, once all the outsiders kill themselves off, we could be the thing that starts the world over again. And I definitely will need a husband if we are going to repopulate the world."

Seth slapped a hand over his eyes. "Don't say things like that, Miriam!"

"Why?" she asked innocently.

"I can't even think about you..." His hand slid down his face and cradled his chin as he shook his head in disbelief or annoyance or confusion. She didn't know which. "It is really hard to argue with you. You are so distracting with your proper, serious answers and startling pronouncements. I need to access my logical brain. Give me a moment." He thought very hard for a long minute, and Miriam continued to take soul slivers.

Then his eyes got big, and he smiled. "You don't love him!" he said, triumphant.

Miriam finished taking the next memory and slowly turned to Seth. "Why would you say that?"

He shrugged. "You don't."

Miriam bit her lip, exhaled, and looked away for a moment. When she turned back, she spoke quietly. "Todd has been the man of my dreams since I was five. He is one of the best people I know. He's handsome and kind, and trustworthy. There really isn't anything unlovable about him." She finished and nodded with her lips swooped to the side as if to say *fight me on that*. However, the moment the attitude was out of her, she felt a slight panic grip her middle. What if Seth believed her? What if he thought that she loved Todd? She lowered her head and examined the ground. Did she want him to think that? She shook herself out of the ponderous questions and turned back toward the line of Edenians.

Seth was quiet as she took three more memories. His face getting stormier by the moment. Turning quickly, he moved behind her as if he were moving to the other side of the line-head. But instead he leaned in, his lips almost touching her ear, and whispered, "But you didn't say you loved him."

It made a full body shiver take her. And it made her mad that her body betrayed her that way. She wanted to hit him. She wanted to hit him so badly that she violently placed her hands on Willard's head.

"Ouch," he whispered.

"Oh, sorry. Is last night's sleep okay to take?"

He nodded.

Miriam really disliked Seth. She was breathing heavily now. Her mouth was tight. However, after taking the next memory, she seemed to cool off a bit. Then her brain betrayed her by rewinding to think about how Seth's breath felt in her ear as he whispered those words.

She thought about what her mama had said about fire. A chill ran up her back. Whether she loved Seth or hated him, could she live in the same town as he and be married to Todd?

She shook her head and took another memory. There was no way. She couldn't watch him marry someone else and repopulate the Earth with that other girl. It made her sick to her stomach just imagining it.

She took another memory, and when she was done, her mind told her to flip the concept.

What if she married Seth? Could she live in the same town as Todd? Watch him have babies with someone else? Her mind worked on this as she took a few more memories and concluded that the answer was a resounding yes. It probably wouldn't bother her in the slightest. She would actually be happy for him if he found a girl to love.

It struck her brain like lightning, painful and brilliant, that no other boy would even exist if she were married to Seth. They almost didn't exist now, and Seth had left her, betrayed her, humiliated her, and allowed her to be tortured.

What was with the hold he had over her? It was something to consider carefully.

CHAPTER 35

Westley

Noah took Westley by the shoulder and said, "I've received word. The rest of our people will be here in two days. All is prepared. With your help, we have food, space, the promise of medical help, and, after tonight's war, shelter."

Westley nodded and thought of the foretelling he'd had, the one he wasn't allowed to tell Hirum about but had to tell Noah about. "The Edenians' houses will be empty by tomorrow and ready for our people."

"What about the Armies of Babylon? Are we prepared for them? You say they will be on the heels of our people."

"Yes. Russia, China, and North Korea have sent upwards of a million sleeper agents into this country over the last ten years."

"The open borders have allowed that," Noah stated as fact.

"Yes, these sleeper agents have been trained and are ready to destroy and cause havoc wherever possible. By the end of this week, if things do not go as we hope, this country will be controlled by the communists."

"Have faith, brother."

"After all I have seen, how could I not?"

"Are the Edenians prepared?" the man asked him.

"I think so. The vessel has completed her second most important task. Miriam, Seth, Peter, and I have been working tirelessly on the primary task the Cherubim have given us. We have fifteen more memories to retrieve tomorrow."

"That will be a hard day for Miriam," Noah said, concern in his eyes.

"It will be. But she is made up of sturdy stuff."

Noah nodded. "We all must be. Those that are left." Taking Westley once again by the shoulder, he asked. "And you? What think you of the mission you will perform for those who come after us?"

Westley looked down at his feet. He clenched his hand into a fist. "I feel very strange about it. But the idea of being with Esther—now, that seems exactly right."

"Good, my man. Good."

"I also foretold that two of the prophets have been killed. Is that so? Is that where we are?"

"Yes, indeed. If it were not so, do you think they would be here? Do you think what will happen to the Guardians this very night would be happening?"

Westley nodded. "It is a marvelous and terrible plan, isn't it?"

"Yes. Yes, it is. I am just glad I'm on the winning side." Noah looked at the tent before them and pointed to the flap. "Well, are you ready to go in?"

"I will never be ready, but it's time," Westley stated, then took a deep breath.

Noah pulled back the flap, and Westley shielded his eyes from the Beings inside the tent, which glowed brighter than the noon-day sun.

CHAPTER 36

Miriam

The first golden thread took them to a town called Ashton in Idaho. According to Westley's foretelling, there would be no sun and death all around them, so the Travelers and Seth prepared for the worst. Miriam felt fear race up and down her spine the moment they stepped through the portal into an alleyway between two rows of houses (or at least that was where they planned to emerge). She felt like she was on an alien planet.

Miriam asked, as she looked at the several-inch thick grey coating that disguised everything around her, "Is this ash?" Her muffled voice had nothing to echo off.

"Yes," Gerald answered in a whisper.

Miriam bent to touch the stuff. It felt warm and soft and heavy. She brought the handful closer to her eyes to examine it more fully and noticed how muted the light was. Her eyes went to the sky in amazement. The air was utterly filled with feathery ash particles. Completely thick with it.

Seth was doing a great job preserving their air inside a bubble of wind Nature magic. If not, they would have breathed the ash in.

"How are we going to get into the house Seth saw?" Miriam dropped the ash in her hand, and it fluttered so slowly to the ground. "No one is going to open their door to us with this outside."

Gerald looked around. "Seth, which house is it?"

Seth's head was already turning around the small neighborhood of homes. They looked like covered lumps. Completely indistinguishable. He turned back to them, his face worried. "I'm not sure, actually. I can't tell the houses apart, and, in my vision, I was inside the house."

Seth had seen the father's name on a plaque and was able to Google the address from there. It was amazing the little ways the Master gave them just enough so they could always figure out where to go. And also, as someone obsessed with all things outside, computers were marvels of the modern world.

Remy spoke up. "What should we do, boys?"

"Should we brush off the mailboxes and check the addresses?" Ben asked. "You remember which number it was, right?"

Seth said, "I remember."

"Let's try this one." Gerald chinned a structure in front of them. "I tried to portal as close to the house as I could. So we have this choice or that one." He thumbed behind him. "Probably."

"Remember, men, stay close," Seth added. "Let's not have anyone die from ash inhalation today."

Miriam could not help it. She felt an acute admiration for Seth as he protected them all. It was similar to her feelings when she watched her papa do his thing with the wind, or her Travelers do their soldier thing.

Gerald nodded. "Keep it tight, boys, and on my mark, forward."

They moved as a skilled and practiced unit. Miriam watched how the ash moved with their steps. It was like clomping through thick snow, almost up to her knees, but this snow had sediment that rose with the movement of air.

"Seth, from below," Ben said with a cough.

"I'm working on it," Seth answered.

It took them twice as long as usual to get to the front of the house and wipe off the mailbox, which was sort of caved in from the foot of ash on top of it. "That stuff is heavy," Remy stated.

"This one isn't," Seth said.

Miriam followed the men. As they walked back the way they came, she noticed mounds on the ground that looked almost human-shaped. She blinked at them. Her eyes searched the lumps with horror. That was when she saw how carefully the Travelers avoided the mounds. They used their boots to slide body parts respectfully out of the way instead of treading on top of them.

She looked at the men who surrounded her. They were incredible humans. Whatever training and hardship they had gone through certainly prepared them for anything. And they were such a sophisticated mix of hard and soft. Her heart beat with gratitude for them.

Her eyes went to the landscape in front of her. Now that she knew what to look for, there was death everywhere. This place was nothing more than a graveyard.

Seth looked over at her. "Just as Westley foretold."

Miriam nodded. "I feel like I'm walking over a grave." She shivered.

Seth looked pale and sad and with vulnerability in his eyes, put his hand out for her to take.

She didn't hesitate. They both needed comfort. As she slipped her palm against his, a warmth traveled up her arm to her heart. Their eyes met, and Seth gave her a tight smile that spoke volumes about how cruel he found this situation.

They found the house, and once they knew which it was, Gerald opened a portal to the inside. He was past caring if people saw. The house was pitch black except for a lantern in the middle of the room. Everything was covered in a thin layer of ash. Sitting next to the lantern in a chair was a young girl with a handkerchief over her nose and mouth. Her eyes were closed, and her face had a bluish tent.

Instantly Remy moved into action. "She's hypoxic."

But Gerald pulled him back into formation. "Let's bring the circle to her."

They moved as one, and Seth shielded them as they encircled the chair and the girl. Remy instantly began working on her. He pulled the handkerchief down and checked her pulse. "She doesn't have a pulse but she's still warm. Help me."

The men worked on the girl. Seth kept hold of Miriam's hand as he watched. His black eyes flashed with colors as he used his Nature to help keep the oxygen circle clean. After a moment, he looked at Miriam and whispered, "I don't know what will happen here. Do you think you should get the memory? She might have just been holding on, waiting for you."

Miriam hadn't considered it.

Gerald turned to her. "I think we will get her breathing easier, but Seth is right. You better do it, just in case." And he moved away from her head so that Miriam could have access.

She let go of Seth's hand, her anxiety racing with the blood in her veins and knelt in front of the child. It only took a moment. This memory was of the volcano. Miriam saw it as if she were there. The loud sounds, the terrible smells, the dark cloud of ash rushing toward them, her hiding in the basement in a safe room, and the sorrow of death en masse. Miriam saw that as far as this child knew, she was the only survivor in the entire town.

She pulled away and found that she had tears in her eyes. The whole thing was terrifying. She stood and looked into Gerald's eyes. He instantly pulled her toward him. His large fatherly arms wrapped around her, and she cried into his shoulder.

The girl coughed and wheezed, and Miriam heard Remy laugh with happiness. "There you are. No, let's sit you up." She instantly started to wail, like an infant taking its first breath. Miriam didn't blame her one bit.

The circle reformed, with everyone trying to make their posture as comforting as possible. The poor child didn't need to be frightened anymore.

Remy was perfect. He cooed at her and told her she would be all right.

Miriam moved out of the way, and it caught the little girl's eye. Her eyes got big, and she put a finger in her mouth, comforting her instantly. After a few moments of intense staring at Miriam, she said, "Rapunzel?"

Miriam blinked at her. She had to be six or seven, but she had an innocence to her. Not knowing what she was talking about, Miriam smiled and squatted down. "Who is Rapunzel, darling?"

"You."

Seth whispered to her. "She thinks you are a princess from a fairytale."

Miriam looked up at him, a question on her brow.

"It's your long hair and eyes and"—he cleared his throat—"beauty."

She smiled and turned back to the irl. "Do you like Rapunzel?"

"She's my favorite. Are you her? You really look like her."

"Well, thank you. But no, I'm not. However, I am very good at making believe; we can play that if you want. I am Rapunzel. Would that make you feel good?"

She thought hard. "I want to play, but I'm hungry. Do you have any food?"

Miriam frowned. "I don't. I'm sorry."

Big huge tears welled up in her eyes.

Seth whispered, "We cannot leave her here to die."

Gerald and all the other Travelers agreed in one way or another. But Gerald said, "How would that go down at home, Miriam?"

Seth touched her arm, his eyes going dead for a moment.

"I guess we need to wait. He's doing his thing," Gerald added and watched Seth patiently.

When Seth came to, his still face morphed into a beautiful happy smile. "I absolutely love my job," he said, and practically glowed. "She's coming with us."

"Really?" Miriam asked, happy and surprised.

He nodded and expectantly raised his eyebrows. "Yes."

Gerald said, "Well, let's get going then." And he opened a portal.

After returning to Edenia, Seth took the child, Kaydra, to the tent city with the help of a Miriam and a Traveler. He informed them that the girl's aunt and uncle lived there.

Seth's story surprised them all.

"It was pretty bittersweet. I guess the wife, Maribelle, grew up in Ashton, and her entire family still lived there. They didn't want to leave and head to Missouri with the rest of the family."

"So, in the process of getting her niece, Maribelle learned her family is gone?" Gerald asked morosely.

"Yes, but according to her quote, they won't be dead for long. Jesus is coming, and at least now I know that they won't be tortured by the armies of the adversary." Seth delivered this with a bit of a smirk. "I swear I do not get where those people are coming from at all." And he shook his head.

Miriam looked around for Westley. He was one of those people, and she was glad he wasn't here while Seth poked fun at them.

"I'm sure we seem really strange as well." Peter looked at Seth flatly. "If you recall a few days ago, you thought we were Amish freaks."

Seth looked at the ground and blushed. "Touché, Peter. But they are so zealous, it creeps me out. They are way worse than you guys."

"How do you know?" Peter challenged. "Maybe they are exactly as weird as we are, just in a different way."

Seth nodded. "I get your point. I will try to not make fun of them."

Miriam smiled. The boy could take it, that was for sure. Even she hated when Peter, her younger brother, called her out on her foibles. Admiration again stung her heart as Seth took it like a champ.

Westley arrived back at the room through a portal with Richard and turned to find his counterparts. "Shall we do the next memory?"

Seth and Peter answered him with a resounding yes.

"THE TASK of the Vessel is vital and will commence before the cock crows thrice. The enemy tries to bind the plan with evil and treachery, making the work of the Lord for naught. Thus I give a warning; be mindful of the ground, and do not give up hope. Thou hast all the tools thou needest to find her."

Westley finished the strange foretelling as Seth and Peter broke free from their little vision circle.

Gerald looked at her, and she looked at him. "What does that mean?" he asked.

The hair rose on the back of her arms. "It sounds like I'm going to be lost."

"And what does being mindful of the ground mean?"

"What is going on?" Peter asked.

And Westley, who looked sheepish, repeated his foretelling. She saw all four men surrounding her go pale.

"If we were told to do this tonight, why would we have to fear? Why would the Master allow anything to happen to Miriam?" Seth asked.

"He just disallowed it by warning us. Now we have to take it from here." Peter responded.

Gerald said, "Let's decipher what it could mean, line by line."

Another mystery tugged at Miriam's mind as the men worked on that one. Her task was to commence before the dawn of tomorrow. Hadn't the golden thread-gathering already begun her task? What was her mission, if not gathering the soul slivers?

THE GROUND SEEMED to shift under her feet. Miriam stopped moving and looked past Gerald's shoulder to the gaping, massive hole in the ground at their new destination. Water filled the hole, but rooftops and building roofs broke the water's surface.

"There used to be a huge city here," Karl said. "I came for the Winter Olympics when I was a kid."

"This entire valley was full of people, buildings, and businesses," Ben stated.

"Where are they all?" Seth asked.

"I don't know," Gerald said. "I'm only interested in one of them. The one with the memories we need. Seth, which way?"

And that was when the ground rolled, ripped open, and swallowed Miriam up.

CHAPTER 37

Seth

He felt the ground slip and tilt. One moment he was upright; the next, he was sliding over the dirt and rocks as they tumbled toward the rim of the mammoth fissure. Seth raked his fingers over the ground, trying to catch hold of anything that might stop his tumble toward certain death, but there was nothing. He frantically dug bloody fingers into the rugged earth. He only had time to register the state of his fingers as he toppled over the edge.

The freefall was halted by a jagged piece of earth and rock jutting out of the side of the crevasse. Seth knew, just knew, this was his last chance to stop his descent. He could not do this with his power, so he asked for his Nature to come. He wasn't even specific. Instantly roots shot out of the wall and twisted their way around him. His knees froze to the rock. He stopped between the two forces so abruptly that it whipped his head backward. And that was when he got hit by a powerful force that happened to be Richard.

The man grasped onto Seth for dear life while simultaneously yelling out Sam's name, his eyes looking to Seth's left. Seth followed his eyes and saw several Travelers tumbling down the ravine. Instantly Seth flung a hand out to them, asking the earth to respond to their needs as it had to his.

He watched as roots, vines, and earth stopped and held the men.

Richard yelled, "This side, Seth."

Seth looked over and saw Boaz topple into the water. He must have struck his head on something, for the man was lifeless as he hit the surface and sank instantly. Seth asked the water to carry his friend to the nearest breaching housetop. It obeyed. Once there, he asked the water to come out of Boaz, but he couldn't see an answer to the request. It was too far away. Seth trusted that it was as it should be.

"Is that all of them?" Seth asked Richard.

"Yes, all that fell with us." Richards's eyes went up. "But Miriam. I saw the ground take her." Seth felt his eyes get huge. "She's still alive. I can feel her. But we need to get out of here, and fast."

At that, Seth used that sense he had inside of him to feel Miriam. Instantly he knew where she was. Up and in the ground from him. Asking the rock to hold Richard the way it had held him, Seth moved away from the man, "You okay?"

"Yes, yes. Get Miriam."

Seth asked the ground above him to provide a handhold for him. It complied, and Seth used it and the vines to pull himself up the face of the ravine. Step by step, up he went until he was level with Miriam. He considered. How should he go about this? He would have to get her up if he pulled her out toward himself.

Richard yelled up to him, "Get her up top. Don't pull her through this way. You'll have to get her up with you. It's just more danger."

Seth nodded. Feeling the connection between them, he pulled her with the earth opening the path before her as he simultaneously climbed. Finally, he got to the top. There he met four filthy, dirt-encrusted Travelers digging at the same exact spot Miriam would be coming through any moment. Marco was the most upset. He was yelling Miriam's name.

"Marco. I'm pulling her up," Seth yelled at the man, who looked at him with surprise.

Trent called, "She's here. I see her head."

All the men gathered as close as possible and dug faster. Between the earth moving at Seth's behest and the digging, it only took a few moments until Miriam's face was out of the dirt. He heard her spit, gasp, and yell, "Keep going, Gerald."

Seth looked at the faces before him. Karl, Ben, Marco, Trent but no Gerald. Seth felt helpless. He couldn't ask the earth to open and give Gerald up. The boys dug and dug, and Miriam looked over at him, "Seth, I'm assuming you were helping; I've stopped moving, though. What is happening? I'm hanging on to Gerald for dear life. Push us out!"

Miriam had him. If he helped her, he helped Gerald. Seth did as he was told. The men pushed the dirt away as Miriam came out. Shoulders, elbows, and then he saw Gerald's huge hand gripping Miriam's. At that point, Miriam moved, pushed with her free hand off the ground, and pulled her hips and butt out of the hole. He used the earth to move her feet, and out her legs popped; however, her arm stayed down. He told the ground to remain open and looked into the pit. He could see the big man's shoulder and told the earth to push him now that he knew where he was.

The men dug, using that opening combined with Seth's concentration. It only took a minute to get Gerald's head uncovered. The man was dirty. His nostrils and mouth seemed filled to the brim with dirt.

"Was he still gripping your hand, Miriam?" Marco asked.

"Yes, yes, he was," she whimpered, and spat dirt.

But Gerald showed no signs of life. Seth asked the dirt to leave the big man, and that was all it took. Dirt and spit dribbled out of Gerald's mouth. Ben slapped Gerald across the face and yelled, "Wake the hell up, Gerald."

Karl took his canteen and poured its contents down the big man's throat. Water that was from Edenia. They finally noticed movement. Swallowing.

The big man opened his eyes a moment later, and his very shallow, almost unnoticeable breaths came quicker. When Seth knew Gerald would be okay, he moved to the pit's edge. He saw Boaz. He had gotten onto his hands and knees. Good, that meant he would be okay. Of course he would be okay. They all would be okay. Not even the earth trying to swallow them up was enough for the Master and his power to overcome.

Seth palmed his face and turned away. His racing heart needed a minute. He cleared his vision of extra liquid before tears tumbled down his cheeks.

He looked behind him once more, and Miriam's eyes met his. She knew he had pulled her out. She gave him a tiny smile, which he really loved, but her eyes told him how she felt. She was grateful as well.

Seth spoke. "I need help over here. Gerald is going to be fine." He looked back to the men below. They were all attempting to make their own way up. However, the vines, water, and earth were not obliging them.

Karl and Trent moved into his periphery. "Any ideas on how to get Boaz out of this mess?" The water down below was filthy and putrid and malodorous. Seth did not want to stir it up by causing that water to follow his command. He did not want to make Boaz swim in it anymore if he could help it. It was too far away for the roots to reach.

"Can't you just have the water bring him to us?"

Seth nodded, "Yes, but that water is seriously gross. I don't want him getting in it again if we can help it."

The men examined the scene more closely. "Those are people parts, aren't they?" Ben asked from behind them.

"There are at least a hundred thousand dead people down there."

"That's probably a generous estimate."

Ben's voice came, "I don't think it's generous. I think it might be low."

"Unless they got out."

"I don't think they did. Look at that!" Ben pointed in the distance.

A ways around the rim, Seth saw a familiar sight. He'd seen it in his vision—a colossal crane whose long arm extended into the hole. At the end was a retractable platform. Seth could only assume it would be lowered to rescue people who survived this devastating sinkhole. But he saw a huge mound of human corpses next to the crane machinery and the carrion birds it drew.

"So, we are not going that way," Miriam stated firmly behind him and spat on the ground, still getting the dirt out of her mouth.

Seth thrilled at her voice. He'd known she wasn't in terrible trouble while buried, but it still scared him to think of her covered with all that earth like she'd been swallowed alive.

"Agreed," Seth stated just as seriously and pushed his thoughts to getting Boaz out of his predicament.

"How are you going to get them up?" she asked him and touched his elbow.

He looked behind at her, "My Nature will make pulling everyone but Boaz up simple." He closed his eyes so he could concentrate—Miriam's face was pretty distracting—and asked the roots and the earth to deliver the men to the rim of the ravine. "Be ready. They might need help getting over the ridge." Then he turned toward Boaz. "I just don't know how to get him up without forcing him back into this filthy water." Seth pointed to the man in the middle of the water on the rooftop. "Any ideas?"

"Are you all forgetting something?" Gerald's voice came from behind them through spitting and coughing. "Your brains must be seriously rattled."

"What are you nattering on about, Gerald?" Ben asked, annoyed.

"Are we Guardians, or what?" He looked at all of them and that was when Seth remembered that the Travelers could just wave their hand and make an escape for themselves. "Oh, never mind," Gerald said and waved his hand. Taking a step, he disappeared.

Seth turned to the rooftop and saw that Gerald, now on the rooftop below, approached Boaz. The man was pointing away from them to a different rooftop.

Seth followed the direction of his pointing and saw a thing strange to behold. It was a makeshift tent. A woman stepped out of it. She had several children with her. As soon as Seth saw her, he knew she was the one they needed to take the memory from.

Shaking his head, he grinned. How would they had found her if the earthquake had not knocked Boaz down there? The Master was so on top of this.

Gerald returned and approached Miriam, who was still digging dirt out of her hair and clothes. Gerald told her about the woman and the blood drained from her face. But she squared her shoulders and nodded. "Let's do it!"

The girl was braver than a lion tamer.

CHAPTER 38

Miriam

The outside lights were on, and the stars were out. Miriam found a quiet spot on her back porch to sit with her dinner. She had a lot to think about and wanted to be alone. Her mind pulled Seth's face to the forefront, and Miriam felt her heart tingle. She shook the image out of her mind and tried to be productive.

Not only had they collected ten more memories this evening, she had taken a memory from everyone in the entire town of Edenia today. She'd traveled all over the world, been buried alive—she shivered—yet the thing she needed and wanted to think about was Seth's shiny black hair and his vulnerable eyes. How he supported her the entire day. How he saved the Travelers and herself from the earth tremor that had almost killed them. Seth was so changed. He was incredible. Her heart thundered. She wanted to be with him. She wanted the freedom to touch and talk to him as if nothing but good had happened between them.

She realized that her anger stood between that possibility and the place they were now. She'd almost let it go, which was wholly incredible.

According to Westley and Seth, anticipating the ash from the volcano, which was supposed to arrive the next day, all the windows were open to bringing in as much fresh air as possible. Because of this, Miriam was distracted by the sound of people in the kitchen. Voices she recognized.

"...seen Miriam? I've hardly been able to talk to her." That was Todd's voice.

"I haven't, and you need to jump on that, Todd." It was Josie who answered.

"What do you think I am trying to do?"

"I'm afraid that Seth will put her under his spell again. He has some kind of power over her," Josie said.

"How she looks at him, and vice versa, does seem concerning."

"I didn't think she would be able to forgive him."

"She forgave us."

"She has always been far too forgiving," Josie replied.

"How can someone be too forgiving, Josie? She is the perfect amount of forgiving. I just wish she hadn't forgiven him so fast. I think I could have pulled her away from him if..."

"If we would have just been brave and not stupid, I am certain that you two would be betrothed by now."

"I'm not giving up," he said.

"You shouldn't but guard your heart, Todd. I think she really loves Seth, and though I want her to be happy, I don't want you to get your heart broken."

"She's been breaking my heart since we were kids. I'm used to it."

"But you're not giving up, right?"

"Not a chance. Now help me find her."

"I'll peek into her bedroom," Josie said.

"I'll check the back porch," Todd answered.

Miriam felt her heart jump into her throat. Did she want to be found? She had to make a decision quickly. She looked around the yard and soon knew there was nowhere to hide. But if he found her here, he would know she heard their entire conversation, and that would be embarrassing. What could she do? Her brain did not devise intriguing plans, so she did what she could: set her plate, which she hadn't touched, on the side table, leaned her head back, and closed her eyes as if sleeping.

The back door creaked open one second after she had relaxed her face. "Miriam," she heard him softly say, and then he realized she was 'asleep,' "Oh."

But her ruse had done its job, so she took a deep breath and stretched her back out. Then moved her head toward him and fluttered her eyelashes open. "Todd?" she asked and put her hand to her mouth for a totally real yawn. In fact, the whole thing felt real. She was exhausted.

"I'm sorry, I didn't mean to wake you. I didn't know you were out here."

She smiled at him. "It's totally fine. I've had a long day. I guess I didn't realize how tired I was." She patted the seat next to her and picked up her plate. "Come." She forked a potato and put it in her mouth. It wasn't hot any longer, but once the food was in her mouth, she took another quick bite, now realizing how hungry she was. Seth had filled her thoughts entirely, and at that moment, she understood something so real, so stark. She did not love Todd the way she loved Seth. Seth was like the Earth, and she, his moon. Todd was in the solar system too, as a distant planet perhaps, one she admired. Yes, Miriam thought as she looked into Todd's clear, beautiful eyes, he was definitely meant to be admired, but she was not pulled to Todd the way she was drawn to Seth.

Perhaps in another life...

But in this one, Seth was too big to be ignored. She and Todd were just not possible in a world where Seth existed.

She looked down at her plate, took a bite, and chewed. Perhaps it was time to tell Todd. "Can I talk to you about something?" She heard the tone of her own voice and knew that Todd would understand what she wanted to say before she even said it.

"I'm right, aren't I?" Todd asked.

"If you mean that Seth and I have something between us that I cannot ignore, and though I have obsessed over you for my entire youth, I can't..." She left it hanging.

"I understand," Todd said with a sad smile. "Can we still be friends?"

"Forever, Todd. Forever."

CHAPTER 39

Seth

Seth hadn't meant to go to sleep. The Joneses were coming, but the day had been long, and…he realized his room was pitch black and he'd heard a loud noise. As his brain woke more fully, he heard the unmistakable sounds of a struggle. He heard grunting and crashing and his mother's muffled screams. He was out of his bed and out the door of his room in a moment. But his other sight stopped him.

His vision of using his earth Nature to go invisible and get out of the house as fast as possible filled his mind; it was the only way he would get out of his home. And get out of his house he must. He saw Miriam's face. He saw death. But not for his family. It was imperative that he leave his family and the screaming behind.

Seth's stomach swirled as he pulled his Nature. Being invisible took a bit of getting used to. In the dark, he saw that his form was nothing, a sort of glowing, hazy outline. Though he couldn't feel himself, he could take the door handle and open it.

He was distracted by the sounds of fighting, and he adjusted to his invisibility as he did all his Natures.

Moving quickly to the living room, he saw three men attempting to hold his father down. At the same time, another circled the group, getting as many punches and kicks into his father as possible. But his father was not one to back down from a fight, even one so not in his favor. The man was thrashing and giving the four men almost as much as he was getting.

Seth wanted to sneak over and help take a few of these a-holes out, but he remembered what his vision had indicated. He had to leave his family behind. They were not in mortal danger. Gritting his teeth, he turned away from his father and stepped toward the open front door.

But that was when he saw his mother and sisters. They were huddled in the dining room, crying and calling for his father. A man with some kind of weapon guarded them.

Seth felt his heart sink. He couldn't leave them. He took a step toward them. he would not let whoever this was hurt them. His insides shrieked, and he took a step back.

One of the guys fighting his father said, "Just hold still, you crazy bastard. We just have to restrain you. You're Tally's son. We aren't going to kill you."

Clenching his jaw, Seth took another step toward the door, then another. Before he stepped onto the porch, he gave a longing look toward his sisters before descending the steps in two long strides. It was good that he was invisible because a man was circling the house, and he had a gun. Seth ran.

He noticed his feet were silent and was super impressed with himself. No wonder Peter loved his gift.

The moment this thought was done, he remembered his vision this morning. Peter and him in a bright forest, conferring.

And he knew his next step was to get Peter.

CHAPTER 40

Miriam woke with a jolt and realized she had drifted off. Her heart was thudding in her chest, and she smiled. The dream had been so real. Seth was so beautiful in it. Her mind reviewed the image of his strength the previous day. How he stayed with her. How he urged her on. Reminded her that she was saving her family and friends. She feared the rhythm of her heartbeat. It spoke of a change in the tide of their relationship. It hinted that her body had finally gotten the memo that she had forgiven him, and instead of reacting badly to him, she was excited by him.

Feeling uncomfortable by these revelations, she wanted to roll over, cover her head, and go back to sleep, but something was wrong. Her body only twitched at her desire. It did not respond. This roused something in Miriam's mind. Joneses, she recalled, and was instantly completely alert.

She tried to sit up and found she could do it, but she flopped back with so much effort. Her mind worked furiously. What was happening to her? It was as if she were drugged again. All the signs were there: her mind was slow, she was confused by how her brain and body felt disconnected, and her body did not obey.

Her heart went crazy with fear. What was this? How could she be drugged in her own room? In her own house?

She opened her mouth to speak, and only a moan escaped. She lay there, eyes wide, breath erratic, sweat dampening the bed beneath her. She told herself she would allow a five-second freakout, pull her crap together, and use her mind. Screaming inside, tears running down her cheeks, she did just that.

And then she stilled and listened and attempted to use her mind. The room was dark, and she was uncharacteristically silent. Eve did not breathe next to her. Then she remembered Eve was staying at Doc's. Papa thought it best if Seth's vision of injuries to Edenians were to happen. Gerald was right outside the door. He was guarding her. She would try to get his attention.

Her door opened as if she'd called to him somehow with only a thought, and an enormous shadow stepped in. She knew it was Gerald instantly, for his soul sliver rose to the surface.

She tried to speak to him, but it came out as a moan.

"Miriam, are you okay?" he whispered. "I'm going to turn on the light."

She heard the click of the button but no light.

"What the..." He clicked it several more times, but nothing. Moving to her side, he spoke quietly. "I can tell that you are not okay. What is happening? Why is there no electricity?"

Miriam found her voice, but it was difficult. "I feel drugged." Her eyes were used to the dark, and she watched the whites of Gerald's eyes flash there and gone as he blinked in the way he did while considering deeply.

A crash sounded in the hall, and she heard her father mumble, "Miriam?" His voice was more garbled than her own.

Gerald was up in a moment. She struggled, "Flash...light, drawer."

"I have one," the big man said.

She heard the rip of Velcro and then a click. There was light. Gerald cautiously went out into the hallway. Her father must have been there; he was the thing that crashed.

Gerald said, "Hirum, sir. What is wrong with you? Can I help you up?"

"Miriam."

"She is all right, except she says she feels drugged. You look drugged."

Her father said, "Yes. Willis."

At that moment, the front door banged open. And Miriam heard words that sent a chill down her spine.

"Frank, what are you doing?"

"What do you think? I'm here for the witch." It was a voice Miriam recognized in the recesses of her mind.

And then Gerald was bulldozed over. She saw them fly past her door. Gerald's flashlight rolled into Miriam's room as the sound of a full-on brawl filled the house.

Then a gigantic body filled her doorway. He was silent. He bent and picked up the flashlight. Miriam saw him for only a moment. He had white hair pulled back in a slick ponytail. Her heart jumped into her throat, and her instincts begged her to run. But the face was not the face in her nightmares. It was similar, though. He clicked the flashlight off and moved toward her.

She closed her eyes and turned her head—the only part of her still slightly mobile—away from the man. He said nothing to her as he pulled back her covers and picked her up.

Faster than she could process, she was outside in the midnight air. And in what felt like two seconds, she was crossing the Edenia bridge.

"Tally, is that you?" A high voice she would recognize anywhere spoke from the woods.

"Yes." A very deep, intimidating voice, a voice that rumbled her own chest via its closeness, responded.

"You got her?"

"Don't ask stupid questions."

"Well, hurry. We only have a few more minutes."

Miriam jerked. That was Willis.

"Shut up and get out of my way. I'm carrying a rather large teenage girl."

They walked a moment more before Willis spoke again. "He said ten steps in."

"Is Willis inside?"

Miriam was confused. The voice was not Willis? It sounded just like him. The high voice responded, "He is inside already, waiting for you and her."

"Is Von's team still in play?"

"Why are you so worried about your son? He can't beat six of our guys by himself."

"You don't know what you are talking about, Jeremiah. He's the most spectacular Jones we've ever had. He's taken down six guys with only a baseball bat."

"He was in his twenties. In his prime then."

Miriam felt the man, Tally, shake his head. "I won't stop worrying until Von returns with them in cuffs."

The walking paused, and despite her fear, she could feel the peace and closeness of Eden.

"Are you ready to do this thing?"

"What did I say about stupid questions?" Tally answered, and he moved forward into the light.

CHAPTER 41

The whole way to Peter's house, he half expected the boy to jump out of the shadows at him, having had the same vision. But he did not.

In fact, Edenia was almost creepy in its stillness. This started Seth's mind down the path of questions he hadn't considered while in his home, watching his family get detained.

This obviously was the attack he'd seen in his vision. But why were they only trying to kidnap his family? Sure, they were Joneses, but Tally and Willis had made it very clear in their treatment of him and his father that if you weren't with the Joneses, you were against them. So, what was happening here? Was Willis here? Was he harming Miriam? He had only seen that Willis was coming; that mixed with a vision of death worried him. He picked up the pace. And it did not take long for him to arrive. The door was open, and the house was dark. Seth did not worry about approaching carefully. He was invisible. He moved into the house and saw Hirum on the ground, trying to scoot toward the door. He wanted to bend down, but he decided to assess the place first.

He stepped over Hirum and opened Peter's door since it was the closest.

The boy lay in bed, his eyes wide, his body trembling. Seth did not even have to wish the invisible to go away. The moment he needed to speak, it was gone. "Peter," he whispered.

The boy's eyes found his. His voice came out halted and labored. "I...cannot...move. Garden...now."

Seth was startled aback. "What?"

"Miriam. Danger. Go." Even in this altered state, Seth could feel Peter's fierceness.

If Peter couldn't move, Seth would have to carry him, and as the thought came, a vision did as well. He needed to take Hirum as well. Seth took a deep breath and pulled strength Nature to him. A knowledge of his own physical capacity came with it. He knew that carrying the two bodies would be awkward but easy.

Seth took a breath and flung Peter's sheets back. He squared his shoulders, wiggled his arms under the boy, and lifted.

It was as if he were picking up a roll of carpet. Seth blinked and folded Peter over his left shoulder.

"Ouch" was Peter's response.

"Sorry." He adjusted the boy. "I have to take your papa too."

"I know," Peter said.

Seth maneuvered out into the hall. He touched Hirum with his foot. "Hirum?"

The man slowly moved his eyes up to Seth. It was totally creepy, like something out of a horror movie. "I'm going to pick you up now. We've got to get to the Garden."

Hirum, to his credit, nodded.

Again, picking up Hirum, one the biggest dudes in town, and throwing him over his shoulder was as easy and cumbersome as carrying a roll of carpet. Except it weighed less.

Seth had difficulty getting out the door, but he made it and moved quickly down the steps.

That was when he saw one of the Travelers, Boaz.

"What's happening? Where is Gerald? And what in the hell are you doing?"

"You mean heck, Boaz. What in the heck am I doing?"

The man, exacerbated, flung his hands in the air in a gesture that communicated clearly, at least to Seth it was clear—Whatever! Tell me what's happening here.

"Well, as per usual with my visions, I don't know. I know I must get these two into the Garden of Eden. Miriam is there also and in trouble."

"What? Where is Gerald?"

"I have no idea. But if all Guardians are in this condition, they need protection. They are sitting ducks. You had better get a few men and meet me in the Garden of Eden if Miriam needs more protection than just me. It's time to make good on your promise of loyalty, Boaz, because there will be blood tonight."

Boaz closed his eyes. "Yes, Miriam is that way. She's in the Garden, I am sure. I will do as you say." He turned and whistled like some kind of bird twice.

Within moments, four Travelers appeared before Seth. He hadn't stopped moving, though, so they were down the street from Miriam's house. The Travelers could get him where he needed to be much faster.

Boaz was talking. "Marco, gather up; something is wrong with the Guardians. They are sitting ducks in their homes. Take teams three, four, and five and protect and defend the Guardians. House to house. Bring weapons." Marco did not need more info than that and flashed away. "Remy, go see what the heck happened to Gerald. Last I saw him, he was checking out some noise on the inside." The man left. "Karl, Ben, you got Seth's six." The two men flanked him, and Boaz started scanning the perimeter.

"Wow," Seth commented. "That was super boss."

Karl did not respond, but he asked, "Do you think we really are going to have to go into the Garden again?" The man with one red eye and one brown eye seemed on edge about it.

"I really think we are going to."

The man fell silent.

"And honestly, we could get there more quickly if you did your thing. With the Traveling."

"Yes. Ben." The man nodded, waved a hand, and in one moment, Seth stepped through a portal and was on the other side of the Edenia bridge.

Seth took a deep breath as he moved into the Garden wood, but he was also excited. He had not gone into the Garden yet. He could feel the tension coming from Karl. Not five steps past the bridge, one of the other soldiers whistled, then whisper yelled, "Downed Guardian, over here."

And that other sight came over him. He saw as if from above, Edenia, he saw all the Guardians unresponsive like Peter and Hirum. He saw the Joneses, silent and meticulously moving from house to house, slitting throats and moving on. Seth felt his stomach whirl, and tears sprang to his eyes. This was how it happened? While they were somehow paralyzed en masse? Anguish in his voice, Seth said loud enough for all to hear, "They are killing them in their beds. GO! They are helpless. Hurry!"

Thanks to the military training these men had, they did not hesitate. Seth watched as each of them popped out of existence. "Karl, stay with me," Seth said. He wanted to ensure Miriam, Peter, and Hirum were not on the casualty list. "Make sure you are ready for a fight."

Three steps, two steps...

A bright light blinded him, and a feeling of peace, tranquility, and goodness radiated and reverberated through him and around him. And then he was blinking at the most beautiful, the most perfect, heavenly garden imaginable. Water, trees, flowers. It was breathtaking. Once the initial stunning awe settled, he could discern the situation.

He saw a dozen Joneses, including Willis and Tally. His grandfather was holding Miriam like a doll. She did not look harmed, but she was in the same condition as all the other Guardians, except the Travelers and his family.

The congregation was facing the most amazing tree Seth had ever beheld. It looked like gold and light and goodness and perfection. Swirls of golden-brown bark and wide, softly curving, forest-green leaves covered in golden veins of energy were the only similarities to a typical tree. There were also drooping, willowy, feather-like vines of gold, white, and light, which pillowed apple-sized orbs of purity that glowed a golden pink.

Seth was overwhelmed by the sense of power in the air and the electric pull this magical tree had.

Peter bit him, the little beast, and Seth remembered he was holding humans. Carefully and quietly, he propped Peter and Hirum against a nearby tree. He looked into Hirum's eyes, silently asking him what to do. But Hirum only had eyes for Miriam. "Protect... Miriam," he whispered.

Seth rose, and that was when he noticed, standing before Willis, a being. It was the strangest, most glorious being he could imagine. It was also the most difficult-to-comprehend thing he'd ever seen. It actually was four beings in one. It was like its head was a cube, each side containing a different face. One face spoke to Willis. But one face, the face of a woman, met his eyes. Seth shivered as she smiled at him. He smiled back, and he heard a voice in his mind.

"Hail Seth, Revelator. Are you ready?"

The voice scared him as it focused on him. He wondered, ready for what? as his mind was pulled into the future.

CHAPTER 42

Miriam stared with wide eyes at the conversation rolling out between Willis and the Cherubim. The voice of the Master was inside her head, but it was also strangely outside of her head, so all could hear.

Willis was so disrespectful. How the man dared to speak to the Master that way...did he not see the sword?

"My family has paid in blood and time for those," Willis interjected.

"You do not understand what you are saying."

"I think I do. I will not give up. I am here to collect what is mine."

"We will not allow you to touch the tree."

"Then it seems we are at an impasse." Talbert turned toward his brother, and Miriam watched them exchange a meaningful look.

It was then that she was unceremoniously dropped to the ground. Willis and Talbert, as a team, pulled several things from their belts, which she noticed had a dozen little compartments. They threw something toward the Cherubim, who had separated into a line of four connected and armed warriors in the time it took to blink.

Whatever they threw exploded when it hit the Cherubim's flaming sword. The explosion was strange, though. Instead of creating a half dome of agitated particles, the energy reverberated off the line of Cherubim. It doubled on its way back toward the Joneses. They and their men were truly and completely blown to the other side of the garden.

Then Seth was at her side. His face over hers, his breath in her face. "Miriam, are you hurt?"

"No." She was so relieved to see Seth. Tears filled her eyes, and she wished to embrace him with all her heart.

"I have to pick you up."

Miriam blinked at him but nodded, and she noticed her movement had a touch more vigor than it had just two minutes before.

Seth carefully slid his arms under Miriam, and her head rested against his shoulder. She smelled his skin, his hair tickling her face. She felt a sense of home more complete, more real than she'd ever felt, even here in Eden.

In the middle of this tumult, a tear of joy fell from her eye when she realized how tightly he held to her, how his cheek rested on the top of her head, as if he were carrying the thing he loved most in the world. Herself, her heart, her soul, whatever it was that could be lost to another person...that thing was lost to Seth.

"I will keep you safe," he whispered.

And she noticed where they were heading. Seth walked right up to the Master; they parted and allowed him to pass through their defensive line. Seth moved up an incline and, as easily as if he were setting down a doll, placed her under the Tree of Life.

She knotted her hand in his shirt and refused to let him go.

"Seth," she cried.

"I know you are scared. I know you do not want me to leave you. But I have a duty to perform. I must protect your family."

"Seth."

He reached toward her, brushed the hair out of her face, and tucked it behind her ear. "I know, Miriam. I..." he stopped, looked away, and bit down hard on his lips. When he found her eyes again, he smiled uncertainly. "I'll be back, okay?" He stood and took one step away before squatting before her again. He licked his lips and touched her cheek to wipe away some tears. "I love you." It was a whisper. And then he was gone.

CHAPTER 43

THURSDAY
Westley

Westley woke to the sound of the door crashing open. "Travelers up! They're here, and they are killing the Guardians. Up, you lazy dogs."

Westley's eyes were open, his mind engaging. He sat up and was surprised to see those Travelers not already on guard duty up and dressed. Clothes, boots, and weapons. He shook his head and blinked. How was that possible? Did they sleep in their clothes?

Sliding out of bed by habit, he went to his knees. But no sooner was he about to start his prayers did he recall what Gerald had yelled. The Joneses were killing Guardians. And no sooner had he realized that than the spirit of the Lord descended upon him, and he knew that today was the day for the other power he possessed—the power of the living God.

Blinking, he pulled his clothes on and scrambled to the door where Gerald appraised his mean of the situation.

"...every house. Root out those bastards and kill them on sight." The men nodded.

"Gerald. I have a task. I need one Traveler."

"What is the job?"

"Get me to the tent city and bring back some people."

"Great, I'm your guy. Frank, the psychopath, has hamstrung me, so I'm worthless in the fight these guys are about to get in."

Westley noticed the blood all over Gerald. "Did he get Miriam?"

Gerald tilted his head to the side and looked at Westley like he was daft. "Really? I look like this, and I'm the loser? This is Frank's blood, genius. He's food for the crows."

"Okay, great!" Westley looked around, "Is this a good spot?"

"I am not walking anywhere, so, yes." Gerald blinked at him. "Anywhere in particular, or just the tent city?"

"You know the hill just south…"

"Yes." Gerald waved his hand, and a portal opened.

"You will just keep it open until I…"

Noah stepped through the portal. It shocked the socks off of Westley and Gerald both.

"Westley. We've been waiting." Ten men followed Noah through the portal into the Divided Hall. Once they were all through, he said, "Let's move. We are needed; God's servants are being slaughtered."

CHAPTER 44

Seth

Seth moved away from Miriam, knowing he would do anything to save her. His heart beat for her so hard. However, not two paces from her, he stepped into a vision where he pulled a staff of plain wood from the Tree of Life. Running out into the city of Edenia, he charged the murdering Joneses. He did not understand how to do what needed doing, but he did it anyway, just as the Master showed him. Bracing himself, he stepped to the Tree of Life. The intricate brownish-gold bark felt almost soft and furry instead of rigid and scratchy. Because of that, he felt more confident. Slowly he pushed his fingers into the fabled, majestic tree. He pushed and pushed until his fingers touched something hard. This is what he needed. He pulled. When his fingers left the tree, they held a staff precisely as he saw in vision.

Seth ran like the wind. Like a wild river. He blurred through the trees, over the river, and into the town to the first house. He smelled the blood before he saw it. His eyes were still adjusting from the Garden's light to the world's deep night. He called fire to his hand and saw what no human should have to witness. It was a Guardian he had never spoken to and his family. Dead. Throat cut. Eyes blank.

Seth turned and heaved once, then he turned, and, using water Nature, raced to the next home and the next and the next. All were dead.

His vision had been accurate but far less graphic, which he was thankful for.

He left yet another house of the dead when he heard a noise.

Moaning. Seth raced toward the noise, calling earth Nature and invisibility to him.

He found them.

The Joneses.

Murdering a man in his bed.

They were going slow, enjoying the kill. Seth used the water Nature to spin his way around the Joneses, the staff spinning like a kung fu master. Some men were in the other room. They came at the sound of the noise. He brained Jones after Jones, moving faster than lightning. Once they were all down, he pulled the Joneses' bodies out of the way and moved to the man's side. His hand became a flame, and Seth saw it was the Doc. His throat was gushing blood. Seth recalled how the river helped. Without thinking more, Seth picked the man up and put as much pressure as he dared on the man's neck. Within three seconds, the Doc was in the water. Seth held him steady. "Come on! Work."

The Doc met his eyes, and Seth recalled the time he helped the Doc save Westley.

Seth's face went to the sky, "I do not know what I need to help him. Please, whatever it is, bring it to me." And he pulled on his healing Nature. In a single moment, vines and leaves snaked through the water toward him. They wrapped themselves around the Doc's neck. He would think they were strangling him if he didn't know better. But only moments later, the Doc was able to speak.

"Eve. My house."

Seth's eyes went wide, and he let the Doc go. "Are you..."

"Yes. Go," he whispered.

Seth had never run so hard in his entire life. It took him less than five heartbeats to get to Eve's side. She was naked and unconscious. The Jones men had assaulted her. At least they had not cut her throat. Seth's brain worked furiously, and he whispered, "They were saving her. They were going to come back." The horror of this scene made him feel like he was out of his own skin. Eve moaned. Pathetically. A mulling cry. And it snapped Seth out of shock. He grabbed a sheet from the floor and carefully maneuvered it around Eve's broken body. Tying it the best he could, he raced her to the river.

By the time he got there, tears of anger ran down his face. Doc was up and sitting on the bank of the river. He turned when he heard Seth splash in with Eve.

"Is she dead?"

"No. But she's injured, and they..." his face blushed, then blanched.

"Raped?" Doc asked and then cried out, "No. Not that!" And he was in the water as well.

"Seth, I got this. Tell the water to be calm for me and then find others. Bring them here."

Seth nodded, and with one sad look at Eve, he raced away.

He did not have to go far before he found another companionship of death. He brained them as quickly as the last, leaving them in their blood. After that, he found Boaz and Richard.

"Seth," Boaz gasped.

"Miriam is fine; the Master is protecting her."

Boaz nodded, but his face changed from worry to anger. "I think we got all of them."

"Did you find any living Guardians?"

Boaz nodded. "Yes, but their carotid arteries were sliced. That's a fifteen-second death, Seth."

"Not necessarily. These are Guardians. Get them. Bring them to the river. Now."

Boaz's eyes widened and blinked, and then he moved his hand and portaled out of sight.

Seth used his water Nature and his wind Nature together. Water to run, wind to yell as loud as would take for the whole town to hear. "Bring all the Guardians to the river. Whether you think they are dead or not. Bring them all now!" He proceeded to retrace his steps to the homes he'd visited.

He knew the word got out because several other Travelers were doing the same thing not five steps away from him. But the river swept the dead Guardians down its current.

Seth looked at the river, which was too swift for what he had in mind. He had to slow it. He felt a bit of disbelief. Could he slow the whole thing? There was only one way to find out.

He knelt and touched it. "Your children need your power. Please slow so they will not be swept away and lost." His water Nature swirled in his eyes as he said this, and instantly the entire river stilled. He could no longer hear the gurgling. He had another idea; it was too dark.

He looked at the trees of the Garden wood and pulled his fire Nature to him, "Your children need light. Will you burn but not consume?" And just like that, the trees were aflame. However, it was not a hot flame, only one made of light.

Doc, who was in the river beside a bloody Guardian, looked up and found Seth. The man smiled approvingly and shook his head in amazement as if Seth had just won a spelling bee.

Seth turned and went for more Guardians but found Tent City people led by Westley heading their way.

CHAPTER 45

His and his father's vantage point was great. He could see the Joneses at Tally and Willis' back. Peter watched as Tally dropped Miriam like she was a bale of hay, and there was a flurry of movement before an explosion. Peter saw all the Joneses fly through the air. His eyes sought the Master. They had spread out before the tree, swords at the ready, completely unharmed by the explosion. He smiled. The Joneses were complete idiots. Why did they not learn?

However, it did not take them very long to form a backup. The Master was not yet trying to kill them. They were only trying to stop them.

Karl, who had been crouched at Peter's side watching everything, suddenly stood. "Stay clear, Li'l Boss. I got you."

Peter looked over, which somehow felt more manageable than before, but he couldn't see what Karl apparently saw. "I can't move, Karl; how can I stay out of the way?" He was able to talk again. That was great.

Then Karl was right in front of them. A Jones approached with a deadly look in his eye.

"No, no, no, Sherman. You don't need to come over here. Go play with the Cherubim over there. He's what you're here for."

Peter watched as the man Sherman ignored Karl's warning and suggestion. Quicker than a jackrabbit, Karl had a knife in hand, waving it menacingly at the Jones. The man did not stop. And Karl was suddenly in combat. The man was lethal, and at that moment, it looked like there was no stopping Sherman from attacking. Karl didn't only use his body to fight; he used his mind.

He taunted, "Sherman, you know I'm toying with you; I don't want to kill you, you know I can, and I will if you try to hurt my buddy here."

Sherman's response was, "I got orders, man. You know how it is. I gotta do what I'm told."

"You do at that, I suppose. But can't we work something out? I don't wanna kill you." Karl moved forward and the other man took a swipe with his knife. It was a close thing, but Karl dodged just in time.

He went back to distracting. "Tell me, Sher, what did Willis do to the Edenians? Why can't they move?"

The man concentrated on the parries and feints Karl threw his way.

"I suppose it wouldn't hurt to tell you. But first, what happened to your eye?"

Karl shrugged, "I'm only half good enough to live here." This was his only answer. "So, what were we talking about?"

Sherman shook his head and looked at Karl like he was a total loser. "Willis perfected a primary motor cortex blocker last year." Sherman clocked Karl in the shoulder, throwing the man back a few steps. Karl rolled in response and bounced on his feet like a boxer.

"Come again?" he asked.

"Willis has had us dumping nanobots in the freak's water system for over a year, just waiting for today."

"Nanobots? Is that what we were doing..." Karl went for a kick to the other man's leg but missed and effectively spun himself around. Sherman took advantage of the gaffe and tightened the space between them, landing a few good punches to Karl's middle.

Peter worried as the man grunted and shoved Sherman off of him. This wisely made some room between Peter and the Jones.

"Tell me about the nanobots. Are they the type of bots that, once inside, can dump a payload, like paralysis drugs?"

"Ding, ding, ding, you got it. You did it to them just like I did. Every time you went on a dump mission," Sherman said, employing some mental tactics himself. He lunged at Karl. The man moved to the side at the last moment and shoved Sherman in the neck just so. It spun the guy, and he almost lost his balance. Peter realized Karl could have killed Sherman just then, but he didn't. He was toying with Sherman.

He kept talking, confirming Peter's suspicions. "But those sorts of things need a jolt to do their job."

"An EMP."

"You used that shielding thing Tally brought back from Russia, didn't you?"

"Yes and no. Willis improved it and made our motherboards incorruptible."

"You EMPed the EMPers."

"Yep."

Karl attacked. He got in a good jaw swipe, which started a flurry of fighting moves that made Peter's brain swirl. Sherman was bleeding from his upper arm when it calmed, and he was out of breath.

"But how did you get it in?" Karl asked, as relaxed as a napping puppy.

"Dropped it," Sherman answered, holding a hand to his bleeding arm.

Karl shook his head. "Impressive."

"Yes, and now Les and Frank have a bunch of paralyzed Edenians to play with." Karl's face went stony. But he kept his cool. "What is he doing with them all?" Karl asked.

"What do you think?" There was a pregnant pause.

"No." Karl shook his head and narrowed his eyes. "These are innocent and good people, Sher. They are unarmed and helpless."

"Your brain is muddled. The witch screwed around in your head."

"Don't you talk about her that way."

"Shut up and fight then; may the best man win."

It took about three seconds for Peter to understand that Karl had been holding out big time. Five seconds after that, Sherman was down. Karl removed his knife from the other man's eye socket and wiped it on his victim's pants. "What a waste."

Peter wanted to look at his father and was surprised when his neck turned. His father watched him and attempted to move his hand. It did not work well, but he was able to shake his head at Peter. "Do not look, Peter. You do not want to see that."

That was not at all that Peter thought; he was glad Karl was on his team right now when he was vulnerable. That throw was perfection.

Karl griped, "Blood spilled in the Garden of Eden."

It surprised Peter to hear the sentiment out of the warrior's mouth. "It wouldn't be the first time."

Karl nodded, a look of understanding between them. "Looks like history is repeating itself. Evil men are coming in the dead of night. Murdering innocents. All for an apple."

"It'll end the same way; just you watch," Peter answered back.

Then Karl approached his pa, squatted down, and whispered that Peter could hear because he just could. "Sir, something Sherman said gave me pause."

"I know. But I am lying here helpless, Karl; what can I do?" his father asked, and he did look highly agitated.

What had Sherman said?

"It would kill two birds with one stone, sir, and that is how Willis does things."

"History repeating," his papa whispered, and Peter put all the terrifying pieces together.

Karl looked over at the Joneses. They were throwing things at the Master, attempting to hurt them. "What do you want me to do? I do not want to leave you here unguarded, but if there is a massacre going on in Edenia..."

Instantly Peter pulled his head out of the mud and utilized the skills he and Seth had practiced. A moment later, he was inside his ribbon room. He moved to the bright grouping that was Edenia, and he saw his worst nightmare. Severed threads. Hundreds of them.

"Father," he screamed. "They are! They are killing everyone."

At that moment, he heard yelling from behind him and running feet. Seth and the Travelers finally made it back to Eden. Richard joined Karl, who veered off the attack to check on them.

Richard asked if they were okay, and Peter nodded and told both of them to go to join the fight. They raced over the turf of the Garden floor toward the Joneses.

The Travelers versus the Joneses. The two forces met and engaged in a way Peter did not know how to describe. It was fists and movement and violence. They both had the many Edenia-savvy weapons, and their hand-to-hand skills were the best he'd ever seen, but the Travelers had perfected the art of ripping open a portal and ending up behind their combatant.

From there, it was easy. The Travelers cleaned their clocks, and Peter couldn't help but be impressed and excited by the fight.

CHAPTER 46

Westley

The carnage was in every home. Many Guardians were dead, hours dead, and Noah said they were not to help those. But the ones that were still warm and bleeding could be saved. The twelve of them went as a group from house to house, laying hands on the barely dead and not dead yet, and through the power of God, commanded them to be healed.

By the time Westley and the elders found the doctor in the river, they had healed ten Guardians. And once they saw what the Travelers were doing with the bodies of the Guardians, they too gathered in the water of the river Eden and commenced healing.

Doc yelled to them, "What is happening in the rest of the town? Have you seen any more Joneses?"

Westley called back, "No."

"Where are they?" His forehead creased with worry.

"How do you know there are more?"

"I don't, but I what to make sure." The Doc looked around him and pointed to the tent people. "What are they doing?"

"Using the power of God to heal."

The man's eyes went wide, his eyebrows went up, and his mouth formed a frown. "Really? Great."

"Where is Miriam?" Westley had to know that the girl was safe. No one knew, but Westley had smuggled Esther off to the tent city for the night; he knew the Joneses would not go there, so she was safe.

Doc shrugged. "I don't know. But she has many people watching out for her. I wouldn't worry."

Westley nodded and moved to search for more people. As he

crossed a yard, he found something odd. It was the size of a banana box, the kind he'd seen in grocery stores. It was black and metal and smashed in on one side, which oozed battery fluid. He squatted down and saw how the Joneses had connected the batteries to each other with some kind of shielding on the outside. Also, there were wires coiled around conductor junctions and some other technology he did not recognize that looked like the insides of a computer.

"What in the world?" he said out loud and looked around for something to pick the things up with. Finding nothing, he went inside the house before him, grabbed a spindled chair, and placed it carefully over the black metal. Then he looked around to memorize his location and set out to find more semi-alive Guardians.

CHAPTER 47

Miriam

She saw him when he reentered the Garden. She was almost able to move again. At least her thoughts were clearing. Seth and several Travelers charged the Joneses lingering and helping Willis, Tally, and Jeremiah attack the Cherubim.

Watching Seth use all of his Natures as if he were born to be a Guardian to fight men twice his size, strength, and skill stirred something so primal in her that she could not think about anything but Seth. In the middle of a war, all she saw was this boy.

It made her think again about what her mama had said, and she knew that she had the same feeling toward Seth. Instant attraction. Quick love. Obsession on the border of madness. But also understanding. And a willingness to give of oneself.

She looked behind her at the boy of her thoughts. It was all there —all the parts.

Gifts such as instant love and understanding were NOT for every relationship, but for special ones. She looked at the tree above her, and the image of Adam and Eve filled her, and Miriam let an idea play out in her mind. Those two were made for one another. They were married without even speaking to one another. They just were love.

But Eve betrayed Adam. She allowed the situation and the serpent to beguile her. Big time. Without consulting her husband, she moved from the Garden to the mortal world. She, in a way, let the serpent kidnap her and drag her away from Adam. But what did Adam do? He said where you go, I go.

Perhaps that was not exactly what she and Seth were, but it

certainly had similarities. Close enough that if their love story one day became mythology, it could be told in a very similar way. Seth was her match. Her equal. Her Adam.

She realized this was entirely out of their hands. It didn't matter that they were young, and it didn't matter that they only knew one another for a few days, and it didn't matter that they came from different worlds. This feeling was a gift from God. It was magic. And she found that she was so grateful for it.

Pulled back to the present, she watched the Master protect the tree of life without moving a muscle. This filled her over-excited brain with awe.

Wishing she could be useful, she pled to the Master, who stood not ten feet from her, "Please deliver me from this." They did not even acknowledge her pleas.

She watched as the Jones brothers pulled out glowing staffs of green and blue. They held them like a sword, though they looked like light. They charged the Cherubim, throwing something from their belt right before they sliced.

Whatever they threw and whatever they meant to slice did nothing to the Cherubim, who stood undaunted, using as little movement as possible to combat the attacks.

Miriam heard a voice inside and outside of her body. "The mortals have done all they can."

Another part of the voice answered and spoke, "How many?"

"Half."

And just like that, two of the Cherubim moved forward from the line; they disappeared and reappeared directly before the Jones brothers, towering over them like gods. The brothers were surprised but still managed to issue a flurry of attacks like loud shots fired, sword strikes, and thrusts. To no avail.

The two Cherubim spoke in unison, "You have shed the innocent blood of our children again." At that exact moment, their flaming swords flashed, taking the Jones brothers' heads off their bodies. "Death is justice."

The Cherub in front of Miriam looked directly at her. "Vessel, be healed and rise to deliver your gift." And at that moment, blood and life flowed to Miriam's limbs and her mind. "Quickly now. Before the spirits leave this world, you must touch the fruit." And her eyes, made of light, looked up into the branches of the tree of life.

Miriam followed her gaze. The orbs of light pulsated, and Miriam stood and reached her finger toward them.

As she touched the fruit, several slivers of souls rose inside her. As soon as she acknowledged who each piece belonged to, they left her. The tree pulled them out. The apple-like fruit morphed as it sucked the memories out, from golden orbs to red heart-shaped chrysalises.

"That one is done. Move to the next. You must be quick," the Cherub stated in her mind.

Miriam did. She used both hands independently and touched the orbs as quickly as possible. As she got used to it, they filled faster and faster, and she moved to the next and the next more quickly than she believed possible. Orb after orb pulsed, colored and crystallized into a cocoon. Her arms got tired, holding them above her head, and no sooner had she thought this than there were arms around her holding her up.

Those arms were brown and strong and beautiful. Seth.

She leaned against him, and they worked together silently to get the souls out.

What felt like an eternity later but was only a few minutes, Miriam felt the weight of so many souls inside her diminish almost entirely, and the Tree of Life was full of red fruit.

"It is finished," the Cherub said. "Now you wait. Be patient. All is done for thy good." The words echoed around the empty insides of her being. After what felt like an hour later but could have been five minutes, the Being spoke again. "Go mourn for your dead, for tomorrow brings a new fight. Tomorrow comes the fire."

Her words were ominous, but Miriam was too confused to worry about it. She felt light, and with Seth holding her, she felt almost perfectly happy.

And then the female Cherub and the other parts of the Master were gone.

Miriam wondered what the Cherub meant.

CHAPTER 48

There was an explosion, and the feeling in the Garden shifted. Peter looked to the Master. They separated. Two of them appeared before the Jones leaders, and Peter watched as they finally attacked. It was an epic take-down. One slice of Their fiery sword and both heads of the Jones brothers hit the ground. The Travelers, spurred on by the Master, attacked with enthusiasm the remnant of the Jones men who had teamed up to cover their backs.

Willis and Tally and so many others were dead. As they watched the vestiges of the Joneses' elite team squaring off with the Cherubim, Peter knew how it would end. More of his attention was on Karl and Richard, who reported the state of things outside the Garden to his papa.

"I'm sorry, sir, but I saw her, Luanne was gone."

His papa was glassy-eyed.

Karl asked, "Who else?"

"Garren had his throat slit in his sleep. Jai, it was a headshot. Sarah's throat was cut. Hannah and her two little children are dead. Dorothea was strangled in her crib. Those are the ones I saw personally." The man listed Peter's family members like they were strangers.

Peter could only blink his eyes and rage inside himself. His father stared in pale silence.

Karl said, "When will the others be here? I keep watching the Master deflect the Phantom Hunters, but They do not attack. They are just letting us take them down. Why do They not do more? I am sure there is a reason."

"I don't want to wait; I want to kill them all now. They murdered helpless people in their beds," Richard stated, and the hatred in his voice was palpable.

His papa spoke in a monotone. "If you want them dead, you might have to go over there and do it. The Master will not kill any who do not intend to take the fruit and follow that intention with action."

"Oh, that makes sense," Richard answered.

"It doesn't matter; Miriam is changing all the fruit, the clever girl. They can't have it even if they could get to it," Karl commented.

Peter could not take the conversation. Not when his heart was breaking. Not believing it could be real, Peter closed his tear-filled eyes and pushed himself into his ribbon room. The moment he saw it, he felt sick. The typical cluster of bright Edenians looked dull and small. The threads at the weave, rising into the future, looked like a comb that had lost half its teeth. More than half.

Taking what felt like a shuddering breath, Peter pulled himself in tight and started tallying the names.

Simeon, Joseph, Aunt Betsy, Foster, the whole Oliver family, Mrs. Brandy and her son Ian, Todd, Josie and their parents, his grandparents, Sherman Walker, Obadiah Collins, Olivia Angelolo, Charity Bartlet, Henri Fraz, Parley...

The list went on and on.

The enormity of the loss crushed him.

In the place of darkness and light. Of life and knowledge, Peter felt hopelessness crowd into his being. He closed out the images of his ribbon room but did not leave it. He allowed himself to drift.

The agony of spirit filled him, and he needed the nothingness of this place before he had to face the eyes of his father and the death of his mother.

Uncertain of how long he'd been in the state of limbo, an awareness came to him. A pulling of some sort. He was moving. He brought his vision back and found himself looking away from the ribbon.

Beyond that, in the sea of nothingness and black was something he'd never noticed before. Stars.

Or what looked like stars. Tiny, distant balls of pale light. He stared at them, his spirit head tilting as he tried to understand what they were and what he saw.

And then he saw it. The stars were in the shape of a tree. A large tree. There were bigger stars and smaller stars, some that acted as an outline and some that hung from the branches of the tree just like…

Just like fruit.

He moved, almost without deciding to.

In no time, he approached one of the now enormous fruits. And saw with his eyes and his mind exactly what it was. Inside was the soul of his mother, Garren, Dorothea, Simeon, and Joseph. Somehow, they were individuals, but they were also together.

Just like the Cherubim.

He moved to the next apple. It was Hannah and her family. Together but individually. He moved to the next. Aunt Sarah, Uncle Jai.

Peter pulled away and felt a confused sort of elation mixed with absolute terror.

He turned away from the tree of stars and saw the ribbon in the distance. From somewhere, something made of light and power appeared like a vast cosmic sword and began to slice great swaths of thread from the weave. So many lives were shorn by death in a moment. As Peter watched, a million threads curled, folded, and blended into the weave, which cared not for the loss, but only kept weaving. It seemed he was watching the first volley of a massive war with uncountable casualties. He got an overwhelming sense that it was time for the tapestry to cut all the threads, to weave its edge, to be finished.

He watched, for he knew not how long the sword of God sliced, and the weave bent and did just as he thought. It stopped weaving.

Overwhelmed and needing to process everything, he pulled himself from the weave. Again, he saw the face of his father. He wanted to tell him all he'd seen, but he could not explain it because he did not understand it. Peter bit his lip and looked around the Garden. Karl and Richard had left and were now in combat with the rest of the Jones men. Other Joneses, bloody and dead, filled the floor of the Garden, defiling the beauty and peace and sanctity of the place. Hate filled his heart. Before the feeling overtook him, a Being of light and awesomeness appeared before him.

The Master.

"Vengeance is mine," They spoke. "You, small seer, must look harder at the creation. Do not lose heart. All is done for thy good." Then the Being reached a hand down to Peter, and out of instinct, Peter reached back. Only after he stood did he realize that he could grab the hand. He was somehow healed from his paralysis.

"Watch," the Master said.

Peter first noticed the bodies of all the Joneses sinking into the earth. Within moments, the Garden was clear and pure again. Not a trace of defilement or death remained.

"Not that. That." They pointed to Miriam at the tree. With Seth's help, his sister changed the fruit from balls of light to red heart-shaped objects. "All things are done for thy good."

Peter knew now what his vision meant. Miriam was placing the memories she had taken (or the pieces of souls she'd collected) into the tree of life's fruit. Instantly, Peter knew that this meant that his loved ones were not gone. They were not dead, but transformed. "Thank you." And his eyes once again filled with tears, but these were tears of joy.

They nodded and held out a hand to Peter's father. "Rise, wise one." His father rose. They both turned to the Cherubim. "Like your ancestors did on such a night of loss and sorrow, you will hold a vigil to comfort those who have lost and honor those who have died. However, because the Vessel has been preserved, you have patience and do not lose faith. With the dawn comes a new battle, and you must be prepared."

CHAPTER 49

Seth wished he could take Miriam into his arms as her papa told her about all the death. Instead, she found her way into her father's arms. It was as it should be, but it also made Seth feel helpless. He looked around the Garden. It had gone back to looking completely normal. All the bodies were gone. All the Joneses were dead. His mind returned to his own family.

He caught Hirum's eye and said, "I'm going to check on my family."

The sad man nodded and mouthed the word "Thank you."

With a longing look at a crying Miriam, he moved to leave.

Once in the darkness of the Garden wood, he pulled his water Nature to him and began running toward the still-burning trees.

He glanced at the river as he crossed the bridge and sped away. Many were on the bank and still in the water, crying and helping. There were bodies everywhere. He closed his eyes in sorrow. This was a night of death for Edenia.

He wondered what Miriam had done to the fruit of the Tree of Life and hoped it would help the death toll somehow.

Though he stood with her and helped her, he had no idea what she had done because he hadn't asked and hadn't seen a vision about it. Perhaps it was none of his business.

It only took him a few moments to get to his house. He burst through the gate, hoping beyond hope that his family was still there. A charred body, gruesome and smoking, was on the front porch. He paused and saw that it was a Jones, not a Johnson. Opening the door, he considered the disheveled appearance of the living room and the second and third Jones bodies that lay there. He turned toward the dining room to find a fourth Jones body.

He was glad to see all the men who had been holding his family captive were now dead, but he couldn't help the tingle of fear that ran up his spine. "Mom!" Seth yelled into the emptiness. He waited. No answer. "Dad! Lilly, Abby!"

Silence. No one was here.

He moved back onto the porch and scanned the darkness. "Mom, Dad!" He yelled out into the night. He was confused why there were no lights on anywhere. Edenia was darker than he'd ever seen it, and silent. And he felt alone in the darkness. Where was his family?

He wished he could have a vision of where they were so the fear building up inside him would calm, but no vision came. Folding his arms, he crumpled to the porch. Were they dead, just like everyone else? The smelly remains of the Joneses on his porch pulled his attention.

No, they had gotten away from the Jones men. Wiping his hand down his face, Seth forced himself not to crumple on the inside. They had gotten away. He took a deep breath and centered himself.

After they got away from the bad guys, what would they do? The moment his mind calmed enough to really ponder this question, he knew the answer. His family was one of action; they would be where they were needed. They would be at the river helping out.

He stood, and pulling his Nature to him again, raced for the river Eden.

He found them close to the mill house. They were all in the water trying to save an Edenian Seth did not recognize. Lillian was there, pulling this and that from the bank of the river, attempting to heal the Guardian, who was so obviously dead.

Finally, his father said, "He's gone, Lillian, and I can't find anyone else that needs our help."

Lillian collapsed in sadness, and Seth's mother put an arm around his sister and told her, "You did well. You healed a few. It was incredible."

"We can't heal them all, Lillian," Abby added.

Seth walked up behind Abby, who was watching the scene from the bank of the river. He put an arm around her, and she turned toward him, her amber eyes flashing with fire.

"It's me!" he said and held his hands up.

"Seth!" Abby cried out and wrapped her arms around him.

And within a moment, his family surrounded and embraced him.

His mother found his eyes and said, "We didn't know what happened to you!"

Lilly added, "We were so scared."

"I wasn't," Abby said. "I knew you were on some mission and that the Master wouldn't let his favorite Revelator get killed."

"What have you been doing?"

He smiled at her. "No, THEY wouldn't."

"They?"

"Yes, they are four beasts that sort of live in the same space, so they are one but four," Seth said and raised his eyebrows up and down mysteriously. His family was impressed and had a million questions, so he told them everything. The girls and even their mother oohed and awed. His father looked at him as proud as can be.

"You actually went into the Garden?" Lillian asked.

"And saw the Cherubim? And fought Joneses?" Abby added.

"Yes!"

"Do you know why everyone but us was paralyzed?" his father asked.

"I have no idea. I can't wait to figure that out. What happened to you guys?" Seth asked, not sure he wanted to know.

His father looked at him very seriously and told the story. "I did feel groggy, almost drugged."

"Yeah, he did, or he would have had those Joneses down in a heartbeat. He was amazing," Lillian said.

"And fierce," Abby added.

His father did not look pleased, though, as he looked down at the Guardians all around them. "The way they were drugged, it was bizarre." His face hardened, his jaw ticked. "And merciless. This was cold-blooded murder."

"Yes," Seth said, leaning into his father's solemn mood.

"We all feel it. The waste. The heinousness. I'm so angry and upset," his mother said and wiped away tears that were running down her face.

"I can't stop replaying it in my mind," Abby said, shivering. "It was so strange, like we were drunk, almost. Then I saw these guys; they were completely paralyzed." She motioned to the bodies.

Silence filled the air. Seth's family grieved for their new friends.

Lillian added with wide eyes, "But if that's how it feels to be drunk... You can count on me never doing it. I could never like feeling that out of control of myself."

"Yes, well, you only got a mild taste," their father added. "I wouldn't recommend it." He gave all three of his children a look that was as good as a warning, and it made Seth smile, and, as usual, Abby stole Seth's exact sentiment out of his brain and voiced it.

"Yes, Father, we will have plenty of opportunities to go on a bender here in Edenia."

This comment, which would have typically brought a chuckle, only brought tight, sad grins. Everyone felt how terrible this situation was, but Seth was sure they were still in the 'is this real' stage of grief.

Seth wanted to change the subject and the scenery. "Hey, can we head home? While we do, Dad, tell me more about the fight."

Out of respect, his father waited until they were down the road a ways before he said, "Well, with the dizziness, I just couldn't get the upper hand. I was too slow. There were too many of them. I wasn't thinking properly. And then I remembered where I was. It has been so long since my mind reverted to using Nature that I hadn't added it to the equation. And just like that, my mind cleared. I devised a plan, put my back into executing it, and then used my Nature on the boys. They were not expecting that for sure."

Seth smiled and nodded, excited and impressed with his father's story. But of course, his father glossed over all the essential things, so he looked at his sisters and mother. "Details, please."

Abby was totally willing to oblige him. "Dad became the demon we've always known was inside him. He put up such a fight that the guy that was guarding us came to assist the three fighting Dad. As soon as we were safe, Dad pulled his Nature to him and was able to move so quickly they didn't have a chance. He had them knocked out and disarmed in less than a minute.

"It was totally epic," Lilly added.

"What we could see of it," his mother said. "Still, it was rather... entrancing. Your dad is a serious force to be reckoned with," his mom said with a bit of extra spice in her tone. She traced a hand up Seth's father's back and pulled him to her. The girls groaned and looked away, but Seth watched as his father leaned down with a happy grin and kissed his mom.

"I am just so glad you are all okay," Seth said to them all. "So many aren't." He looked at the road. "Three of Miriam's brothers, two of her sisters, and her mother are dead..."

Seth's father interrupted the rest of his report with a shock. "What?" He left his wife's side and took Seth by the shoulders. "Luanne is dead?"

Surprised by his father's passion, he nodded and added, "They were not nice to her, either. They raped her first." He shook his head. "Probably because she was so pretty." His eyes found his sisters. "They raped Eve, too, and were keeping her for later."

His mother took his sisters by the arms and pulled them close to her. "What beasts."

"Seth, take me to Hirum; take me to my brother; I need to be with him."

Seth nodded, broke off from the rest of his family, and led the way.

CHAPTER 50

Miriam

Miriam wiped her nose and eyes for the hundredth time as the sun rose. She looked out at the sea of dead bodies before her: friends, family, Guardians. There were so many that the entire grounds of the Garden wood were covered. Only the tree trunks halted the endless blanket of death.

Directly in front of her lay her mother. She had a gaping gash at her throat, and now dried blood soaked her night dress. Her eyes had been closed, her face pale, her body unmoving. It was this that disturbed Miriam the most. Not a twitch or a breath, no pink flush on the skin. Nothing. The body before her was not her mother. It was a husk. She knew to the depths of her core that her mother, or the thing that made her mother her mother, was not gone, but only somewhere separate from this husk of a body. She also knew something else. Her mother's memory was no longer inside her. It had been one that she put into the Tree of Life, as she had with all who had died. She did not know what that meant, but she did know that the Master had said it was vital for her to do what she had done. So there was a glimmer of hope that somehow her work in the Garden meant something.

Someone approached her from behind. It was Peter. She took him into her arms and held him for a long moment. When she pulled away, Peter stared at the body that was once their mother. He pulled in a strangled breath before blinking and sucking his lip into his mouth. His face turned away, and he looked at all their lost relatives.

"Why did this happen?" he whispered.

"I don't know," she answered and then pulled him to her again. She would tell him her secret, and maybe it would bring him the comfort it brought her. "But Peter," she whispered in his ear, "you know how I took memories from everyone in Edenia?"

He nodded against her cheek.

"Well, every single memory pulled out of me by the Tree of Life was from someone who died."

He pulled away from her. "I know. They are going to be turned into Cherubim."

Miriam took a step back from him. "What?"

"I don't know what they can do in that form that they couldn't do as Guardians, but the Master and the Gods have turned them into Cherubim. I saw them in my ribbon room."

Miriam blinked at this. Her mind whirled a million miles an hour.

Peter spoke up. "You say that Foster and Todd both died?"

Shock after shock. Miriam found his eyes. "Yes." Her hand covered her mouth as a tear tumbled down her cheek.

"Yeah, so I guess you won't have to fight your feelings for Seth any longer. He's the only one left willing to marry you."

It was callous. It was morose. It was terrible. It was such a Peter thing to say at this moment. How could he be so...

She growled at him. "Peter Christopher Miller! You are the worst!" She slapped him on the shoulder and stomped away as carefully as possible to avoid the many bodies on the ground.

Rounding a tree, she found her papa. He was straightening the vest on the body of her grandfather. Tears poured from the man, wetting the dead man who had raised him.

She went to him. "Papa!" she said, and a fresh gush of tears streamed down her cheeks. Papa, Gabe, Peter, and Eve were all that were left of her entire family. Both sides. And the only reason so many had lived from her family was Gerald. The Traveler had fought like a dragon and saved half of her family. She owed that man so much.

Unbridled, her mind went back to Seth. What would have happened this night? The night of Willis' big plan to kill all the

Edenians and get into the Garden if Seth hadn't done what he'd done.

There in her papa's arms, a flash of understanding hit her brain like an avalanche. Gerald would have come into Edenia as a soldier for Willis. He and the other Travelers would have moved directly to her, being drawn by the power of their bond, and then they would have had to make a choice. That choice was a bigger gamble. That choice was not certain.

A feeling filled her that things had worked out as they should, and the well of tears within her dried up. This was all as it should be. And now it was time to tell her papa that.

"Pa," she said as she pulled away from him. "I put Grandpa and Grandma, Garren, Dorothea, Simeon, Joseph, Uncle Brian, Hannah, Aunt Sarah, Mama, and everyone else here; I put their memories into the Tree of Life. The Master told me to do it. And Peter. Peter saw them in his ribbon room. He says that they are becoming Cherubim."

Her papa looked at her as about a dozen emotions crossed his face.

"There is a reason. Papa. A reason. Don't lose faith," she said, and smiled at him with a face full of tears and hope.

He put a hand on her shoulder and nodded. "Thank you for telling me." He looked away and seemed to compose himself. Turning back to her, he wiped his eyes dry and said, "I think we should start the vigil. Don't you?"

She nodded and smiled tightly.

CHAPTER 51

Westley

With the vigil over, the Garden wood ground embracing the dead's bodies, the Edenians retreated to their homes. They needed time to process and be with their remaining loved ones.

Westley found himself moving out of Edenia and up the hill to the east. Today was the day he and Noah had been planning and preparing for.

His mind flitted over what he knew would occur over the next twenty-four hours. The Being millions had worshiped for millennia, the Savior, the man who had descended below all things and then rose above all, would arrive.

The last of those faithful who had been watching for this event were almost here, where it would all go down. Westley was wise enough to be one of them.

But before that, war.

On the heels of those faithful he expected to arrive any moment were the armies of the world. A war like none other would commence right here on this very spot.

And the Lord of Hosts, God of all, would show forth his power in protecting those who had chosen him and destroying those who had chosen sin and the machinations of the world.

A thrill like none he'd ever felt before overtook him, and his body trembled.

Rubbing the goosebumps on his arms, he reached the top of the hill. Looking up to the sky, he saw a vast, dark cloud to the west. It was massive and moving his way. It must be the cloud of ash from the Yellowstone super-volcano eruption.

His eyes fell to the earth and the space between himself and the ash cloud, and he had to calm the goosebumps again.

The crowd of walking people filled the entire horizon like a wave from the sea. Huge, overwhelming, incredible. He looked over the mass of bodies and felt so grateful to his great God that there were so many of them. He did not want any to suffer in the battle ahead, so the more who were on the Lord's side, the less would have to die.

He considered the massive group. The ash cloud followed the people as the pillar of fire followed Moses' people when Pharaoh's armies were chasing them.

The ash was a protection, a separation between the people of God and the armies of the world that followed them.

Again, he felt the chills and had to calm the gooseflesh. This was so exciting, and his Nature took him at that moment. He spoke, "After all the death and devastation are over, then comes the peace and the understanding. In one day, the Lord of all will claim his prize, and it will be these people. Zion, the pure in heart, those who have been brought through trial, hardship, and refinement. And the wicked shall be trodden under the foot of Cherubim. And he will destroy the unfaithful who doubted the promises of the most high to his people."

He heard his foretelling and couldn't help it. He smiled and whooped. It was time. The blessed day was almost here.

CHAPTER 52

Peter sat in their living room across from his papa, Miriam, Esther, Gabe, and Eve. It occurred to him that this was all that was left of his family. Papa and Gabe looked wistfully heartbroken. Miriam was hurt and confused and uncertain. It was Eve's haunted look, though, that he was apprehensive about. Not only had she lost her family, but Gregory had also died, and Eve had been violated while paralyzed and unable to defend herself.

Peter felt terrible. He wished for healing of some sort that would help. His papa had thought telling everyone what he and Miriam had seen would help, and it seemed to help some members of his family, but not Eve.

He found himself shaking his head no as Westley let himself into their house. Esther rose immediately and went to him. "Are they here?"

He nodded and smiled down at her, then his eyes moved to Peter's papa. "I know that this is a tender time, Hirum, but I have to tell you that my people will be here in less than an hour, the ash cloud about an hour behind that, and the army within twenty-four hours."

Hirum shook his head as if to shake off all he could not control, and all he wanted to leave behind. He focused on Westley.

"All right." He sniffed and rubbed his forehead. "We have everything in place, except now…" His voice cracked. "I have no idea how many wind Natures we have left." He began to pace.

Westley took Peter's father by the arm. "Hirum. We have time. I will find out…"

Westley was interrupted by the door opening again and slapping hard behind Seth. He spoke. "There are fifteen wind users left. Including my father, who is a newbie."

Peter grumbled, "Of course, the Revelator shows up right when we need him." He gave Seth a begrudging smile and couldn't help but envy how useful having ALL the Natures was. Plus, everyone was a little jealous that the Johnson family had no losses. Not every family had lost someone. But then it occurred to him as, in his mind's eye, he saw Tally and Willis' heads falling to the garden floor. He supposed the Johnsons had lost family, and they also had the knowledge that their family members were the ones who had killed every Guardian that was dead.

Peter thought about what Sherman had admitted while he was fighting with Karl. The Joneses had drugged them all like what they had done to Miriam. It was devious, and technology had come far in order for this to happen. A huge sense of loss rose in his throat, and he only just barely stopped himself from bursting into tears.

Seth spoke. "I know this is terrible timing, but I just had an urgent vision. The rest of the tent people are coming, and Westley will be completely consumed with helping those people, so we need to join together and get the rest of the golden memories. Miriam, the Travelers, and I must finish gathering them before this day is out. We must. It is the most important thing the Master oversees. Which means..."

"...as his Guardians, it is the most important thing we are in charge of," Hirum finished.

Seth nodded. "Yes."

Peter and Miriam stood simultaneously and moved toward Westley and Seth. The men gathered around with Miriam in the center and joined hands with no more discussion.

Peter was pulled into the ribbon room he was now thinking of as the shearing room. So much cutting of threads. So much death. It occurred to Peter that Edenia was not the only place in the world to see death. The whole world had.

He moved involuntarily toward the first golden thread, and as he absorbed it, he was instantly pulled to a second, which was not typical. Then he was pulled to the third, and by the fourth, he realized the urgency that Seth had mentioned. The whole world was in commotion, and if their job was to be done, it needed to be done quickly.

CHAPTER 53

Miriam

Existence felt like a whirlwind. The Travelers gathered. Seth told them what would happen. They formed up, and off they went.

Miriam, in the space of a few hours, visited Canada, Finland, China, Russia, an island called Tristan da Cunha, another Island called Maui, and Italy, Monaco, Nigeria, Argentina, and Mexico.

Everywhere she saw death, destruction, and war. It affected the beauty of all the new places.

Seth, at one point, leaned over to her and said, "You are by far the most traveled girl I know." He constantly reminded her to enjoy what they saw and pointed out cool and unusual things so she would not miss them.

It was a great distraction.

As they neared the end of the list of memories to take, a feeling built inside Miriam. An urgent anxiety flitted in her stomach. She touched Seth. The second their skin met, something like what happened inside the circle of three, something like when she took memories, happened to her. In her mind's eye, she saw the Garden of Eden; however, instead of her sight being drawn to the beautiful Tree of Life or the Master, she kept seeing the other tree. The shriveled black and silver tree. The Tree of Knowledge of Good and Evil.

It zinged into her mind over and over again, and she knew the moment this memory-gathering thing was done. She also knew she now needed to go to that tree.

Seth looked at her askance. "Are you seeing that too?"

"The tree?" she whispered.

He nodded at her.
She nodded back.
"I think we are supposed to go."
"I agree."
"Right after we are done with this?" he asked.
She nodded.

CHAPTER 54

Peter

About thirty minutes after Miriam, Seth, and the Travelers left, a group of tent people entered Edenia. Westley smiled and approached them. "Porter, Mason, what the heck are you doing here?" He pulled the two front men into a bear hug. They clapped him on his back, just as happy to see him.

"Noah sent us to be your seconds. He has to stay on the city's east side to welcome the other group," the man with the close-cropped brown hair and thick beard said to Westley.

"An army is also chasing them," the short stalky man with sandy blond hair and grey eyes added.

"Dude, your eyes are super creepy!" the bearded man said and punched Westley in the shoulder. "What in the heck has happened to you here?"

Westley turned and pulled Esther to his side. "This is what happened to me," he answered, and looked down at Esther with the grossest, lovey-dovey glance. "Esther, these are my two best friends in the world: Porter and Mason." He pointed to the bearded man, then touched the stocky man.

"It's nice to meet you," Esther said with a smile and a shake of both their hands. "Mason, are you from the Canadian Isles?"

"I am at that," Mason said, his face surprised and confused.

"I just noticed your accent and how you put things."

"Esther is amazing with dialects and languages," Westley put it in by way of explanation.

"Really!" Mason answered. "How did you come to be good at those things? Don't you stay here for your whole life?"

Esther smiled. "No, actually..."

A cry came up from the crowd of Edenians and tent people. Off in the distance, in the field and wilderness beyond the entrance to Edenia, a few travelers stepped from the trees onto the road. And after that initial few, the woods teemed with human activity. And almost as one, hundreds of men, women, and children moved from the brush to the road.

They looked worse for wear. They looked threadbare and tired. They looked skinny and hungry.

Peter's Pa moved to the front of the group, a bushel of apples on his shoulder. A dozen Guardians holding similar bushel baskets waited with him. They were preceded by the blue-green-eyed healers. "By the light of the saints," his papa whispered. "There are so many of them."

Westley approached. "Saints is what we call ourselves, so that's a good exclamation. What will come from this side is only half. And all of them are tried and chosen, godly people." He took Peter's papa by the shoulder. "Thank you, Hirum. We would not have room for so many in the valley."

"I'm not sure we will have room for them here," his pa stated with awe in his tone.

"They will make do."

Peter's group stood in silence for the full ten minutes it took for the tent people—or the Saints, whatever they wanted to be called—to get to the border.

Once inside, Papa and the healers walked out to meet them. Peter joined them. Westley and his friends did as well, and he outpaced those carrying food.

"Ho there, brethren," Westley called. "We are happy to see you. Welcome to Zion!" He said this louder than the rest, and the group of Saints whooped and hollered their joy. Energized by the news, they moved more quickly. Westley did not stop them once the groups joined. He turned and walked with them. "I'm Westley, Noah's second."

The man in front had a shaggy beard of salt and pepper and startlingly clear blue eyes. "Greetings, Westley; I'm Moses, the leader of this rag-tag group of Saints."

Westley smiled. "What an appropriate name for such a job as this!"

"You have no idea," the man answered with a twinkle in his eye.

Peter's papa met them, then offered all that passed him an apple. "Hello, I am Hirum Miller. This is my town, Edenia. We are fellow servants of the Highest and will provide you Saints shelter and hospitality."

"Hello, Hirum Miller, Guardian of Eden. I am pleased to meet you, finally."

At this point, Peter stopped in his tracks and pulled over to the side of the road. What was going on here? How did this man know who his father was? Peter pulled apples from a basket and handed one to a small, dirty child with holes in his shoes.

Who were these people that called themselves Saints?

⁂

AT IMPORTANT MEETINGS in the past, Peter had to eavesdrop; this time, his papa invited him to join the adults. There was a lot of boring stuff like this: where everyone would stay, how meals would be handled, and so many tedious but important things. Especially for these poor people who'd been on the road for what Peter learned had been eighteen months.

Moses—or as his people called him, Bro Mo—explained the travel as a gathering. He went from town to town, asking people to join him on his travels. Those who agreed went through a pretty brutal experience. He spoke of several terrible viruses—they called it a desolating plague—that afflicted them and were healed by their God's power. He spoke of riots and mobs and evil men trying to kill them. According to the stories, as long as they laid down their weapons and did not fight back, the bad men left them alone after just a little bit of terror. There was starvation. People ran the group out of town. The police thought they were an invasion. So many dangerous and trying things happened. The rumors of all the death and war also reached the ears of the Saints. Many got scared and left the group. Then when the armies from the foreign nations arrived on both the east and west coasts, that was a sign that they had to speed their travel. Then the volcano. It changed everything about their last-ditch gathering efforts. They had to hurry the last few days to stay ahead of the ash.

There were hours of stories, and Peter's papa sat and gave the man his full attention the entire time. And then Noah was there with another man, a man stricken in age, or so it seemed from his shoulder-length hair of white and gnarled hands. But he surprised Peter with his energy, straight back, creaseless brown skin, and bright eyes that seemed wise beyond comprehension. Noah introduced him as Abraham or Brother Abe.

At this point, his pa looked at the men in front of him, his eyes narrowed. "I'm having a bit of..." He didn't finish his sentence. Instead, he started another one. "So, Noah, Abraham, Moses? These are names we all know well. Are we... Is this it, then?" Peter failed to understand the question.

However, the men in the room nodded, eyes twinkling as if they understood all.

His father turned to Noah. "Thank you so much for telling me this was what we were doing here. Who you are?" Fire tinged the sarcasm.

"Would it have made a difference?"

His pa took a deep breath and bit his lip. "I suppose not. Still, I have secrets of my own that were shared."

"Yes, but they were not secrets to me." Noah smiled. "If you recall, I grew up here." He gestured down at the floor of the first house where they stood. "Before the whole flood thing."

Peter's eyes went huge as he looked at the men before him, realization dawning on him. These were the men from the Torah and the Christian Bible. His jaw fell slack, and then he saw it. The light.

It wasn't that these men had bright eyes or energy. It was that they *were* bright and light. They *were* energy.

There was a silent pause as everyone looked at the man the way he was.

It was Westley who spoke first, though. "Noah? Is this true?" He stepped toward his friend and looked at him. "I mean, I can see that it is, but..."

Noah put his hand on Westley's shoulder. "Dear friend, we will all have time to show who and what we are. You understand that better than most."

Westley was stunned into silence.

Abraham, the Abraham in some sort of more-than-mortal body, moved toward the men and said, "Can we focus? That ash will be here in about twenty minutes, and I need to know that the people I have just spent the last two years gathering aren't going to suffocate."

His father nodded and blinked and swallowed. "Yes, sir. I have about a dozen men and women who can use the wind as I can." Hirum Miller pulled his Nature to him and, with a twist of his wrist, made a tiny twister on the palm of his other hand.

Abraham smiled. "That's a neat trick. So you use the same keys of power bestowed on the Cherubim, not directly the Father's power."

"Yes, we are under the Master's authority."

Abraham and Moses nodded in interest. "It makes perfect sense."

"As do all God's works, once you have eyes to see," Noah quipped.

"So, this wind power you have will allow the ash to pass without harm."

"We have a twofold plan that is already in the works. We have been asking the wind from the north to blow the ash south for days. So, what ash makes it past that crosswind will find a gradient barrier that will enclose the ash high enough that the next wind from the north or south will move it off. We recently lost many of our people, including wind Natures, so as long as they do not pass out from exhaustion, we will be perfectly fine. It will be as if nothing is happening."

"Well, there is a place we can help you. We will fast and pray that your wind Nature, as you call it, will be strengthened and given endurance," Noah said and looked to his brethren for confirmation. They both nodded their agreement.

"Well, that takes care of the report and the immediate problems. We will need to talk about the armies that will be here on the morrow."

"Yes, but for now, let us eat. I feel like it has been a year since I've had a decent meal."

"It has been."

Noah answered, "I guess it depends on what you call a decent meal. The Edenians are excellent in all ways, but they do not eat meat."

The two other men smiled and nodded. Abraham added, "Good for you. I myself have stopped the practice as well. Each to their own." Then he said to the side for Hirum's ears only, "It's going to be a rude awakening for them when the Lord doesn't allow us to kill animals in his paradise." And the man elbowed his papa.

Abraham elbowed him in the ribs and made a joke. Peter shook his head and blinked. Was this really happening?

Abraham's sparkling brown eyes found Peter's, and he winked.

Yep. This was really happening.

CHAPTER 55

The Garden looked the same as it had twenty hours earlier when she lay paralyzed under the Tree of Life while her mother and most of her family were murdered. The night history repeated itself—the night of death.

Miriam swallowed as she thought and ambled through the beautiful bushes and flowers toward the Being who had been her Master her whole life. Seth stood beside her, and she desperately wished she could reach out and take his hand in hers. But she couldn't, not yet.

When she approached, she heard them inside her mind. "You are here."

She nodded. "I am here to do the thing I need to do."

The Cherubim smiled. "It is good. This is almost the end, and the last of our tasks."

"I don't know what to do," Miriam admitted quietly.

"Do as you have done before, Vessel." The Master pointed to the Tree of Life and its golden, glowing fruit. "Except only put the souls you've collected with the prophet, seer, and revelator. Keep the Travelers' souls and Seth's within you."

Nodding her agreement, Miriam walked over to the Tree of Life. It had morphed from a tree brimming with golden fruit to one with a mixture of golden fruit and red chrysalises. She pulled down a branch holding a golden fruit and closed her eyes; she allowed one of the golden soul slivers inside her to rise.

Her Nature took her, and suddenly, she was performing the pulling but in reverse order. Pushing the piece of soul into the fruit before her, her Nature acted like it had a mind of its own. The soul sliver rolled and pulsed as it swirled inside the fruit. But Miriam could not pause to watch. Another soul silver rose, and the same process happened. She felt like she was on a swing; her stomach lurched and spun. She closed her eyes and just held on for dear life as the golden memories, one by one, left her and went into the fruit.

About halfway through the souls, the fruit she held onto came unexpectantly off the branch. It surprised her, and she stepped back as she opened her eyes. Before her, the once beautiful golden fruit shriveled, shrunk, and lost every radiant bit of glowing golden inner light. It was still yellow, but it now resembled a normal everyday apple.

She looked from the apple to the Master and then to Seth. "What happened to it?"

Seth moved toward her and cupped the hand that held the strange fruit in his hand. "I think you put the knowledge of good and evil into it." He took a deep breath and looked at her. "Now it's my turn."

Her eyebrows wrinkled at him, but she watched as he took the apple from her hand and walked over to the tree. Miriam followed him, and so she saw when he pulled his green plant Nature to him.

He held the fruit up to a silver and black branch and watched as the branches animated themselves and grabbed the apple. The stem and the branch formed a new bond with the fruit and cradled it as if it was always meant to be there.

Seth looked at Miriam, his eyes still an electric green. She smiled at how different and beautiful he was. He smiled back.

"Shall we do it again?" he asked and looked at the Master.

"Do this three more times." The Being stated firmly.

"So, a total of four?" Seth asked, confused. "I thought it was only two fruits on this tree."

The Master raised a hand with four fingers raised but said, "Unless you are uncertain."

Seth and Miriam looked at one another, both clearly very uncertain of anything, including what They meant by their question.

"Are you certain?"

Seth answered, "We trust you. If you say four, we will do four."

The Cherubim nodded their head with a slight smile on the face before them.

CHAPTER 56

FRIDAY
Miriam

By the time they left the Garden, it was a deep night on the outside. Miriam looked toward the sky, wanting to discern the time by the placement of the stars.

However, Seth interrupted her quest by saying, "That was incredible" into the quiet of the darkness. Then he took her hand in his.

Miriam felt exactly the same about what they had just done in the Garden, but she couldn't comment because her heart was in her throat. She looked down at their hands and knew in every part of her soul that it was time to do what she'd wanted to do the other night when they were interrupted on the bridge by Todd.

She whispered to herself something her grandfather had said to her once that had been rattling around in her head all day. "Forgiveness is to abandon all hope of a better past." Miriam stopped in her tracks and looked away from Seth. She bit her lip. Did she let go of the past she'd imagined? Could she put it well and truly behind her?

He let go of her hand and said, "I'm sorry, I..."

And that was all it took. The second they were not touching any longer, she knew. She would do anything, forgive anything, just to hold Seth's hand. She loved him. She had to let the past go.

"No!" she said to him with vigor. "No! You are right. This is where we are." She took his hand back and slowly threaded her fingers through his. Then she looked into his dark eyes in the dark of the night. She could barely see his face, so she reached up and touched his cheek.

She swallowed hard, then said, "Come with me. I am ready, and we need to take care of this, or we will be damned, and it's the end of the world, and I have no intention of being damned at the end of the world for such a stupid thing as a grudge." She'd rattled this off in one breath.

"Okay," Seth answered, sounding as if he had no idea what she was talking about.

They made it to the river near the bridge. Instead of crossing it and leaving the Garden wood, she moved to her left and down the bank of the river about thirty paces. When she stopped, she asked Seth, "Have you made fire yet?"

Seth frowned. "Yes."

She moved to a tree and pointed at a lantern left here from the old days when there was no electricity in Edenia. She reached inside the thing, and sure enough, there was still a candle. "Can you light this, please?" she said, and opened up the door of the lantern so that the wick would be exposed.

"I will try." Seth concentrated on the wick, and two seconds later, it was alive with fire. He smiled and looked over at her. She smiled back.

"Come over close to me so you can see me in the light," she said, and he obeyed her.

She lifted shaky hands to the buttons on her shirt. It only took her a moment to get two buttons undone and for Seth's eyes to leave her eyes and go to her hands.

An eyebrow rose, and his glance found her again. "What are..."

She interrupted him. "Seth, I have to do something, and I need you to see it. I think it will be healing for both of us. But you have to promise you won't freak out."

Seth looked down at her shirt, which was halfway unbuttoned, then back up at her eyes. "Uhm. I'm not sure I can promise that. I don't know what's happening."

Miriam didn't want to say the words. She didn't want to explain. She just wanted to get this over with, so she opened her shirt and revealed the brands on her chest.

Seth looked at the burns, and the blood drained from his face. "Oh my Lord, Miriam..."

She shushed him. "These are the scars of your betrayal, but they are also scars that the Master told me would be for my good, and I can honestly say they were worth it."

Seth looked at her, amazed.

She went on. "You do not get to see what I see when I make memories. When I took your memory, I saw how much you cared for me, how you wanted to come clean about your phone and your deal with the Joneses."

He looked confused.

"You saw the aftermath of Peter's accident. You saw all of us using our Natures. You looked scared and disgusted, and I was scared it was too much. My father was scared it was too much. My father commanded me to take your memories so you wouldn't run away and tell the Joneses all our secrets."

"And you obeyed."

"Yes. But in that, I saw how you felt about me. About the betrayal. And how you didn't want to do it anymore. You knew that this place was magical and it would fix your problems. The problem was, I misread you. We all did. And once I started taking, I couldn't stop until I'd taken what I'd decided to take. That's how it works."

He nodded at her and blinked, thinking back on his own version of what had happened. "I found out you were the memory thief because of that, and the rest is history."

"Not quite." Miriam smiled. "In the Garden, the Master told me that all had been done for my good. ALL. And I saw it then—without all that happened between us, the Travelers would never have come to me, to us. Them coming literally saved their lives. They would be fertilizing the ground in the Garden right now if you had not happened. And you saw how they moved together today, how they saved me from that guy in Belize, and how they are perfectly skilled for getting these memories. I could not have done this without them. All of this, it was mercy. It only felt like pain."

"And Westley said this is the most important thing the Master is doing right now."

"Yes, you see. Without all that has happened in our past, this present would not exist. We are actors doing the will of higher Beings, so how can I hold you accountable for their plan? How can I ignore the good that has come from my trials? And I never condemned you for your choices regarding Lillian. Well, not after I understood your reasons. You were in an impossible situation."

Seth shook his head and exhaled heavily.

"And so, I think it is time I get rid of these." Miriam's chin gestured down to the scars on her chest.

"Okay," Seth responded, wiping a tear from his eye before it could fall.

"But I need your help."

"Anything."

"Will you calm the water and warm it a bit?" she asked.

Seth looked at the river Eden, his face still in concentration. Then he looked at her. "Done."

She took his hand, and they walked into the water together.

On most banks of the Eden, the river bed dropped off rather steeply, but right at this spot, there was a small shelf to stand on so that only their shoulders, necks, and heads were out of the water. Miriam kept Seth's hand in hers. She looked at the gorgeous black chasms that were his eyes and said, "I forgive you, Seth." Those words settled into her soul, the water, the world, and Seth. When they had done their job, she used her free hand to splash water onto the scars, and the water carried them away.

"Whoa! They're gone," Seth exclaimed in a whisper, and took her shoulders into his hands, moving her shirt out of the way and turning her toward the lamplight just to make certain. "They're gone. Like really gone. How..."

She smiled and giggled a little. His awe and happiness were so adorable. His eyes moved to her mouth and the smile she wore.

His face softened, and he said, "I love your smile."

She went still and waited for his eyes to meet hers. When they did, she whispered, "I love you, Seth. So much it fills me and simultaneously devastates me."

It was his turn to go still. He studied her face intently and saw the truth of her feelings there; she was certain, for she allowed them to be displayed fully.

"You mean that, don't you?"

She nodded and smiled and whispered, "Yes."

Ever so slowly, a smile and tears filled Seth's face. They were the smile and tears of a seemingly condemned man who'd just been acquitted.

His wet hand came out of the water and moved to her cheek. It slid back until his palm lay flat against the curve of her jaw. The tension between her eyes and his, between her breaths and his, between her heart and his, built quickly.

Miriam felt impatience rip through her; her hand rose out of the water and snaked up Seth's chest, over his collarbone, and around the back of his neck. Her eyes dropped to his lips as she moved toward him.

But he still did not bend the little inch so their lips would meet.

Miriam took her eyes away from his mouth to assess what the issue was.

When he did not move, he only took deep breaths through his nose; Miriam realized he was attempting to control himself. So she said, "Seth, if you don't kiss me right now..."

His eyes blazed. "But your family. You told me. Don't we need to have some sort of proper discussion?" His teeth clenched, and he rested his forehead against hers.

"Seth," she said sternly. "You're mine, and I'm yours, and there is nothing anyone can do about that ever again."

Seth lifted his head from hers. His eyes were alight with fire, and within the space of a heartbeat, his other hand had captured her face, and his lips crashed into hers.

It was not a soft kiss, or an organized kiss, like she'd seen her parents share. It was frantic. Seth possessed her face between his palms, and he used his leverage to move his soft, defined lips against hers again and again in fiercely passionate pecks.

However, the pent-up frenzy only lasted a few moments before Seth's hand slipped from Miriam's face to her waist and then her back, where he crushed her against him. With this transfer of power and possession, the meeting of lips lingered and blossomed. Breath and mouths and emotions mingled, then slowed, then simmered.

Miriam's mind tried to keep up with the process and thus innocently allowed Seth to take the lead in it all, content and too overwhelmed to do anything but react to him. The sensations Miriam experienced were nothing like she imagined they would be. They were fuller and deeper. She didn't just feel kissing on her lips; it was an explosion in her brain, a tingling in her whole body, a sensation of floating in a cloud of joy and pleasure, and a carnal craving for more.

Just as that need for more grew, Seth surprised her by putting a bit of space between them. His kisses turned into small brushes of lip separated by him looking at her. After a single slow, incredibly soft, lingering kiss, Seth pulled away, breathing like he'd just hiked a mountain. And that was when Miriam realized she was breathing hard, too, and that was not the only thing she noticed. Other parts of her body felt more alive than they ever had, and a desire deep in her gut called her to explore those feelings.

She took a deep breath and shoved those feelings down.

Finally, her eyes met Seth's for more than a moment. She saw the sparkle of something extra there and knew if he felt half of what she did, they needed to get out of this water and get around other people for strict self-preservation reasons.

She moved a step away from him. But Seth was not having that. He took her wet hair in his hand and used it to pull her back to him. He planted another smoldering kiss on her lips. It curled her toes and made her lightheaded. When he finished, he said, "Let's get out of the water."

Miriam bit her lip and grinned. "You might have to carry me. It seems my legs have turned to jelly."

Laughing, he lifted her easily and made his way through the water. As he did so, Miriam felt strangely emotional. "Seth," she said as he moved onto the bank. He didn't respond immediately, and her water-drenched skirt dried as Seth used his water Nature to ask the water to leave their clothes.

She shivered as he said, "Hmmm." But instead of looking at her face, he reached over to her now-dry blouse and buttoned it. Her eyes were full of tears.

Once his eyes did find hers, he was concerned. "What is it?" His hand was instantly on her face, thumb brushing away a tear that had splashed down her cheek.

"I just feel..." She paused and reached up to tangle her hand in his dry shirt. "...overwhelmed."

He smiled. "Tell me about it." He leaned back and, gathering her hair—which was flying all over the place as the wind came up—pulled her in for a hug.

As he held her, Seth whispered into her hair, "Miriam, I know this is overwhelming and crazy, but I have never felt this way, ever." He tightened his hold on her, his face going deeper into her hair. Then he moved to look into her eyes. "I remember eating lunch with you that very first day; what was that...ten days ago?" She smiled at him and nodded at his calculation. "I saw you smile and listened to your excellent way of expressing yourself, and I knew, then, that if I allowed myself, I could be crazy about you. I think it only took two more conversations, and I *was* crazy about you. Like lost. I knew the whole time it was impossible to feel the way I felt so quickly. But I did. And with that came the inkling that if we could manage to not screw it up, what existed between us would be completely epic. Like no one gets to feel this way about another person."

"We definitely tried to mess it up."

He laughed. "We sure did, didn't we?" He took a step back. Looked at her, then leaned forward and kissed her mouth softly. "But we fixed it through your understanding, your goodness, and my repentance and dedication. Who does that? No one. They just say goodbye."

"But I couldn't."

"Me neither." He took her face in his hands. "I never could." He kissed her lips. "I love you so much. I want to be with you, always."

"You think we can manage that?"

He smiled, "Well, your parents are pretty eager to marry you off." His tone was flippant, a smile in his eyes, but then his countenance became serious. "I didn't come here thinking I would have a life partner before I was old enough to graduate from high school, but if that is what needs to happen, I'm in."

Miriam wrinkled her forehead at him. "Are you serious?"

Seth looked up at the stars, and then, after a deep breath, he found her eyes, "As serious as a brain tumor."

Miriam smiled sadly at him and looked down at the ground so she could consider his words.

Her parents wouldn't make her marry anymore, but Seth didn't know that. So she would love to enjoy this courtship and take a breather from all the pressure to get married. She wouldn't take too much time; it was the end of the world.

On the other hand, she wanted to explore all aspects of this new relationship, which wouldn't be possible, not in Edenia, until they were married. They probably would never be able to even kiss again until they were married. She thought of her father's face and what he would think if he knew they had kissed.

And then there was the fact that she really loved him.

She looked at him, and he analyzed her face. He must not have liked what he saw there because he said, "Did I screw everything up? I put my foot in my mouth on the regular..."

She put a finger over his lips, looked into his eyes, and smiled. "I am on board; let's just take it one step at a time. I don't want you to ask me to marry you, especially when your culture is totally against that sort of thing, just because my parents have tried to marry me off. It should be a natural conclusion to our feelings."

"I agree. And I sort of thought that was what was happening here."

"It is..." She put her head on his shoulder, tears again coming. She used the time to sort through what was happening inside her. It was everything, from the kissing for the first time, and this hug—Edenian teenagers never were this free with their physicality—to the enormous display of letting go she just underwent from traveling the world during the end of the world, to using her Nature in a way that actually felt right, precisely right. It was all so big.

And then these feelings between Seth and herself. He'd loved her the whole time. It was a dream, and all she'd ever hoped for, yet she felt caught in a tornado not of her own making. Her feelings for him were as real as any love could be, but they were big and intense, and so rushed.

It was as if something pushed them, a force bigger than a tidal wave putting pressure on them to be something they weren't yet, to feel things they hadn't earned. It was just a bit overwhelming.

Seth's arms tightened around her, and he said a thing that astonished her. "I do feel"—he paused and swallowed—"urgency. Like everything between us is in a hurry, and I must be far braver than I normally would be. We just don't have the time I wish we had."

Miriam pulled away from him, her eyes wide. "I feel that exact way. That is what I was just thinking about. It's like we are being pushed from behind by a gale-force wind."

Seth smiled at her. "You always have a way of taking my tangled words and thoughts and putting them into a comprehensible sentence." His face softened the way it always did when he admired her. "I feel it. All the pieces are there. The admiration. The love. The self-sacrifice. The desire. The chemistry. And I choose you. I want to be with you. So, all the puzzle pieces of epic love are there. Plus, we have been through some pretty hard things."

"It's like all the ingredients are on the counter; they are measured out and ready, but instead of mixing them slowly and in the proper order, a force bigger than us is dumping them in a bowl and using a whirlwind to mix them before tossing everything in the oven," Miriam surmised as she examined all her thoughts over the last few minutes.

"Yes! Exactly!"

"So, what are we going to do about it?" she asked and scrunched her eyebrows at him.

"I don't know."

"Well, there seem to be only two options when facing a tidal wave; fall to your knees and embrace what is coming, or run. Either way, you're dead."

Seth laughed. "Morbid," he said, and caressed her with his glance. He was doing that a lot. But then his face turned sly. "I feel like we did a little embracing just now." And his eyes danced with the double entendre.

"Yes," she said and smiled at his wit. "I love embracing."

"I wouldn't mind doing a little more embracing," Seth said, brushing the softest, most delicious kiss over her lips.

"Umm," she hummed, her eyes still closed. "I love that kiss."

He chuckled. "Me too. But I pretty much love every kiss you are involved in." He pulled her into his arms and placed his cheek on hers. His mouth was right next to her ear. "So, if we embrace the tidal wave, if we don't stop the Master from making us into a batch of rushed cookies, if we don't let the gale-force wind cartwheel us down the road, what does that look like?" he whispered.

The breath of his whisper on her neck tingled her spine and made her feel weak in the knees. She cleared her throat. "I think it looks like a lot of kissing—my personal favorite part—and dealing with the whole end of the world thing, and..."

"And?"

"...and some pretty intense conversations with our parents."

"Ugh," Seth said as he pulled away from her. "I've seen how your father is with Esther and Westley. I don't want that."

"Yes, but you will take what you can get, won't you?" she challenged. "Because after that comes together forever."

Seth swished his lips to the side. "That sounds about right, because I seriously love you, Miriam Miller."

Miriam leaned forward, took him by the front of his shirt, and for the first time in her life, she initiated a kiss. He surrendered to her wants this time, and she embarked on a slow experiment of moving her mouth in ways that felt good.

It did not take long for her clinical mind to abandon technique and yield to the more innate desires inside her. However, this set off a physical chain reaction that began tension of a different kind. She stepped back. Her hands flew to her lips like they were a viper in the grass, tempting her to do all she could not.

Seth was breathing hard. His eyes were smoldering flames of black. "I don't think taking things one step at a time will work for us, Miriam. We have always been ahead of schedule, and if we don't embrace that fact, there is a third option in our little tidal wave scenario. We run toward the wave, but that death would be suicide."

She understood what he meant. At this moment, in their present state of single-ness, running toward the wave was just what they did with that kiss. Somehow in that foggy haze of hormones, a thought occurred to her. What were they racing toward? What were they being pushed toward? What was the point of their feelings being so intense? What death were they fleeing from, embracing, or racing toward, really? Was it so important that they love each other so intensely? So quickly? Why?

At these thoughts, the woods around them filled with light. A resounding word rattled into Miriam's brain as she turned toward the light, toward the Cherubim.

"Finally," They said and moved to stand in front of Seth and

Miriam. Seth took her hand but did not take his eyes off the Being in front of him.

Miriam said, "Finally, what?"

"Finally, the two of you are right with each other and asking the right questions at the same time. Know that you have been brought together for a purpose. You have been made for one another as Adam was made for Eve and Eve for Adam. Your covenants to one another are essential. Now that you are certain, go to the Elders in the tent city. They will bind you together so that you may complete the next part of your task. Do not hesitate. Do not delay. This is a warning; you must do this now."

The Cherubim turned to leave but paused. "One more warning: do not act as man and wife until you have been changed."

A chill as big as a monsoon shivered up Miriam's back, and she looked at Seth. His black eyes were as wide as the Grand Canyon, and his face drained of blood.

The voice interrupted her thoughts again. "Go now. Time is short. Take Westley and Esther with you. Have them do the same."

CHAPTER 57

As they passed through the Quad, Seth felt the silence between them. He wished she'd say something because his brain rattled around the words man and wife. He kept trying to shake it, but it echoed in his head.

Logistically a certain amount of familiarity had to occur first, and they just weren't there yet. He had barely touched and kissed her for the first time, and he wanted that to keep progressing at the natural(ish) pace.

He shook his head.

What in the world was happening right now?

He had just been wondering how he was feeling so much so fast for this girl. He'd just said he wanted to spend all the time he had left on this earth figuring that out when he was told Miriam was made for him, the way Eve was made for Adam. What in the world could that mean?

It almost insinuated the feelings between them were not real.

His mind twisted and turned and freaked out over the idea.

Miriam spoke, and he could not believe how she mirrored his own thoughts. "Does that mean that the power we just spoke of, 'the cookie maker,' is forcing us to feel this way, and if He were not pushing the matter, we would regard one another differently?"

Seth tightened his grip on Miriam's hand but did not answer. He did not have an answer. He did look up at the dark night sky and let the thoughts of his heart out of his chest, pushing them toward something bigger and wiser than himself.

That faith, that openness, was all it took.

Between one step and the next, Seth was pulled into a vision unlike any he had seen before. It was the colors and the breeze and the feel of it. He was still holding Miriam's hand. He knew he was because he could feel her, but he did not look at her because his surroundings stole his breath.

They stood on top of a huge stone pillar, which shot a thousand feet into the sky. All around them was a massive ocean of the most cerulean blue water he had ever seen. The air smelled of salt, and sea, and fresh dirt. Not a hint of human in the soft wind. His eyes could easily see all the way to the bottom of the pillar into the water, which his mind registered as not usual. There he found the most frightening creature he'd ever seen in his life. Enormous and black and scaled. It looked like a dragon out of a movie. He watched it thrash and roll in the water and would have continued staring for much longer except for a squeeze of the hand he held.

He turned toward the touch. Miriam was there. His eyes went to her, and he instantly saw subtle changes in her. Her blonde hair was more intense, and it shimmered like a chandelier in the sun. He looked closer to see actual gold strands of hair coming from her head. Not all, but enough that she looked otherworldly.

If it were possible for her to be even more beautiful, she was. Her skin also had gold in it, just under the surface. Tiny flecks of... something...lay there, warming her face and making her look like something out of a comic book. He must have been giving her an awed expression, for a moment later, her cheeks pinked, and Seth saw the golden flakes shimmer and glow. The gold was not random; it was in an intricate swirling pattern so perfectly matched to her skin that it only showed with the coloration of her blush.

She smiled, her eyes watching her hands as they intimately swept up and over his chest and around to his back, then up and around his neck, effectively pulling him into her embrace. Her fingers twisted into his hair, and she met his eyes.

Seth smiled back at her, and wanting more connection between them, he moved to touch his lips to hers. The kiss had only begun when a loud screaming came from above them. They looked skyward, and Seth was entranced by a massive, colorful animal flying in the air. It was so close that Seth only saw its abdomen as it soared over them. It actually blocked out the sun for a moment.

He stepped out of Miriam's arms and turned completely around, his gaze following the colorful mixture of scales and feathers. That was when he saw where he was. His eyes fell on the Tree of Life. The gold-hued tree with orbs of light and whiteness was unmistakable. He noticed a difference; the orbs were all very small, like unripe fruit. Still, its magical, peaceful aura and wispy branches of bark and energy and power reached out and touched his soul. His wonder turned to awe.

Seth approached it, his mind speculating how it could be in the strange place with him and Miriam. He put a hand on the brownish-gold bark and felt the strength of the ancient behemoth.

Then Seth heard a musical laugh. Peeling his eyes off the tree, he looked for the source.

Around the greened top of the hill and past the small black and silver and red Tree of Knowledge of Good and Evil—which had four bumpy yellow fruits upon its short branches—Seth saw what he thought was Esther and Westley, except they were changed.

Their faces were the same, but somehow more delicate in features and far more pale in color. Their ears were the first strange thing Seth noticed. They were long, pointed, and stood up like all the elf cartoons he'd seen. Also, their bodies seemed stretched. All slight and long and thin in form. Their hair was blondish white and completely straight down their backs. Their laughs were joy, and music and happiness rolled into one enchanting sound. They were wrestling and playing together, many kisses and caresses intermingled.

Seth smiled at them and wondered at this change in rigidity. However, his breath caught in his chest when Seth looked past the lovebirds rolling in the grass.

There, just like something out of a book, sat Neverland. Or what he had imagined Neverland to look like as a child. An island, far more extensive than he could actually take in completely, floated on the water. It was dotted with mountains that leaked waterfalls in a magical rainbow of sparkles, glistening rivers winding back and forth as they made their way to the sea, and valleys swathed in plants, trees, and flowers so colorful they looked like splatters of paint on a background of green. It was utterly mesmerizing.

Seth felt something inside him leap with intense joy. He knew this place. It was not the place he had come from, but it was his home. He had always been meant to be here with Miriam.

He turned and found his wife; she had stayed close by. He took her hand, pulled her to his side, and then turned back to enjoy the view.

It surprised him when his eyes filled with happy tears. It had all been worth it. Everything that had happened before, in the other place they had lived.

She spoke. "We are home, at last." And she reached up to wipe his tear. "And every human that fills this Earth will be connected to you and me. You will never be alone again."

Her words had the intended effect on his heart.

She pulled him close and whispered in his ear. "With that in mind..."

He pulled away from her. Her cheeks were again pink with an intricate gold pattern underneath. And this helped him understand what she meant. A thrill raced up his spine, and he pulled her in and placed his lips on hers.

His passion for Miriam poured into her through this connection of lips, breath, and soul. And a moment later, he had laid her down on the soft grass, his form next to hers.

"Seth." She called to him and placed her hand over her heart. "Do you remember when we were on Earth the day we made our covenants?"

He smiled, though his mind did not know this story because it hadn't happened yet.

"Do you remember what you told me about our hearts? How you and I, we are like the halves of a heart. And our love is based on the idea that a heart needs all the chambers to work?"

He didn't know how to answer this question. So, he smiled at her and hoped she would go on.

"I've thought about that a lot, and you are right. I don't think the Master forced us to love one another; we were made in such a way that our souls were two parts of one whole, the way a heart is two halves of one whole. Though we are complex and have our own processes and functions, we must have one another to be complete. And that was why we were so drawn together, and why we feel so strongly."

Seth's mind rolled this over, and the further he thought about it, the better of an analogy it was. "I guess us being here, in this place, starting a whole new race of people proves my theory was right."

"What kind of trials do you think we will have in this place? And without our Natures, as they were, do you think we will need to use the source the Mother told us about?"

Seth sighed and looked around. "I don't know." Seth was confused about this Mother business and the source. What was the source? He said, "But I am glad we have Esther and Westley with us."

"Yes, although I wouldn't complain if they jumped off that cliff for a few hours." He laughed as she reached toward him and pulled him to her lips. His hands went to her face and slid along her silky cheek until his fingers found the start of her soft hair. Breaching the barrier of her hairline, he deepened the kiss.

After a while, he pulled away to take a breath. Their eyes met, and he said, "I can't believe I got this second chance with you. I can't believe we get to begin this world together. I can't believe we get forever."

"Forever," she whispered, and put two warm fingertips to his chin. She looked at his mouth, then back up to his eyes, her gaze lowering shyly. She bit her lip and whispered, "I think it's time."

"Time?" Seth questioned.

"Yes, time. We have been here a while now. I think it's time we obey Mother's command," she answered, her face very serious indeed.

"Yes?"

"Yes," she whispered, rose, and took his hand. She moved toward the small silver tree they had put the memories into. "Shall we do it together?" Her hand reached for the fruit.

SETH CAME out of the vision with a huge pull of air, as if he had been holding his breath the entire time.

Miriam stood before him, concern in her eyes. "What was that? You were gone forever."

"Forever," Seth said between deep inhales.

"Yes, for like five minutes. I've never seen you gone that long. Not even with the golden thread people."

"Sorry."

"No. I'm not mad. I was nervous," she said, and slipped her hand up his arm.

He pulled her to him and hugged her tight. "I'm sorry I worried you," he said, and his mind raced over the new information he just received.

They had been on a different planet!

That itself was enough to ponder for a month, but their bodies had changed, their task had changed, and they were the only humans around.

Oh my gosh! he thought. Esther and Westley were there as well. They were not even humans; they were elves. Now that he thought about it, there were dragons and so much color, like a totally different spectrum of color.

He held Miriam even tighter, his mind excited at the future prospects of this new life.

Miriam pulled away from him, "What did you see?"

Seth smiled. "A heart."

She tilted her head to the side. "A heart?"

"It actually was a vision for you, in answer to the question you asked me about if our feelings were real or forced."

"Wait! Like an actual heart? Whose was it? And how does that answer my..."

"No, no. Let me explain." He stopped her guessing. "But let's walk while I do. We've got places to go and people to see."

She looked up at him as they started out. "You seem different. More calm. More okay with what we are about to do. If you figured something out that makes this"—she motioned between them and the road ahead—"less provocative, please tell me instantly."

He smiled but kept his eyes forward, knowing if he looked at her beautiful face, he'd just end up making out with her again, and he had forever to do that. Right now, he had to marry her.

"I can tell you the answer I got; I hope that will help." As they walked, Seth told her what her future self had told him in the vision about the heart. Miriam took it all in and spent the rest of the walk to Seth's house in silent consideration.

Once they reached his house, he slowed, and they determinedly walked up the steps. Standing before the door, Seth allowed himself to look into Miriam's amazing violet eyes. She felt calmer to him.

"We are different ventricles of the same heart," she whispered to him. "I guess I've known that from the day I saw you walking up the Edenia road. My stomach went haywire; my body sort of freaked out."

"That doesn't sound like a positive thing."

"It wasn't, but then you were not living your best life, were you? And you had not decided what you wanted. Agency is always a part of these things. Since at the moment you were planning to choose the hard path, that sick stomach was a forewarning."

"And now?"

"Now, I can't even describe the differences. If you could see yourself or the self you've displayed since you chose this life from my perspective... Seth, I'm in awe of you, and my stomach feels the same."

He grinned. "I'm really glad. It has been a challenging road for us both."

"The dark side wanted you bad, and I can see why. Look how much of a difference you have made here. We needed you so much and didn't even know it." She touched his face and stepped closer. Her eyes examined every inch of him. "It's like this. What if there was an awesome soccer team lacked a star player? Then it got its star player, you, but the other team persuaded you to never show up to the game."

"It wouldn't be very sportsman-like."

"No, but when has the opposition ever played fair?"

"So, in that scenario, I'm the best player?"

She poked him in the stomach. "Yes, but you are also the guy who got convinced to play for the wrong team."

"I was."

"An interesting thought is how this all would have turned out, as far as us, if my dad hadn't put off coming here." He thought about it for a moment and thought of all the ways he could have screwed things up with Miriam if he had two or three years of living in Edenia. "I'm just going to let that go."

"Probably best. I'm just so glad you're the guy who came back in the last inning." That incredible smile of hers brightened up his heart.

He would also let go that soccer did not have innings. Squeezing her hand he pulled it to his chest.

"And honestly, I can't wait to be your wife," she whispered.

That was it. He couldn't help himself. He pulled her to him and kissed her slowly on that amazing mouth. She smelled of nothing and everything. Fresh and windy and skin, her skin. It was so good being with her this way. But...

He pushed more, the kiss deepening, and it was then that Seth realized he was chasing the feelings from that other existence.

Somehow this same interaction, there, felt...more, everything. Intense, sweet, connected. And he remembered something Miriam had said in his vision; she'd said they were connected to the source, whatever that meant, but it perhaps meant that this source made them more alive somehow.

Distracted by the kissing and the thoughts rolling around in his head, he was startled when he heard his front door open and his father's voice say, "Seth. Uhm, what is going on here?"

Seth pulled away quickly from Miriam, but she did not let him get far. They stayed together, sides touching as he met his father's eyes.

Seth glanced at Miriam just long enough to see her smile encouragingly before turning back to his father to say, "We've come to invite you to our wedding."

CHAPTER 58

Miriam

They didn't sit in the front room as Seth delivered the information to his gathered family. They all stood silently as everyone eyed Seth, her, and each other. His father didn't even look at them since they had broken the news to him first. His eyes were glued to the staircase like it was the most exciting thing in the world.

Abby was the first to speak. "I feel like this is rushing things."

And Lillian chimed in, "Why would the Master want you guys to get married tonight?"

Miriam spoke up, "They didn't say tonight; they said Now."

His father turned toward them, "Well, that is not a statement allowing analysis, is it?" He stood to his full height. "You best go change your clothes, son, and manage your hair. Quickly."

Seth looked at Miriam, smiled, and then released her hand. "I'll be right back."

Miriam blinked at him and felt the corners of her mouth lift. Then he was moving toward the back of the house.

As soon as he was gone, Jenna approached her. "Miriam, are you certain about this?"

Zeke was not far behind. "Considering everything, we would not blame you one bit if..."

She interrupted them, "I thank you for your concern, but I am extremely happy about this turn of events." She put her hand to her mouth, covering the huge smile she had on her lips. "I love Seth. I have been pulled toward him since the moment you all arrived. I have forgiven him everything. Indeed, there was not much to forgive."

All in the room began to complain about this statement, but

Miriam silenced them with a word. "Please. Please let me finish." They quieted. "I know you all have your own perspective on this, and I held the same one for a while, but the Master has given me a new perspective, one I cannot ignore. And I can no sooner hold Seth accountable for what had to be than I can hold Eve accountable for eating the fruit in the Garden. It had to be. And once the hurt was healed, all that is left is..."

Tears came to her eyes. "...is an absolute admiration, complete devotion, and a raging love for your son that I do not fully understand. Would I like to flesh our relationship out a little more before jumping into such a commitment? Perhaps, but..."

She shook her head in wonderment. "...but that is not the Master's plan. And frankly, I'm relieved to have our feelings for one another out in the open. We can be brave about them instead of hiding them and cautiously hurting one another repeatedly. We can talk about this extra energy, this unique force pulling us together. I would say I have no choice in the matter, that this was thrust on me, except it doesn't feel that way. It feels so perfectly right." She licked her lips and looked down at the floor.

"You don't need to convince us anymore, my dear," Zeke said, putting a hand on her shoulder and giving her a half smile. "I understand you perfectly." She met his eye and saw something there. A knowing. A deep recognition.

It made Miriam remember that this man was her mother's first husband. Her one true love. She remembered how her mama had talked about him. She remembered that Zeke was the original Revelator, and she knew, down to her bones, that Zeke and her mother were made for one another first. Had they stayed together and chosen differently, Miriam and Seth never would have existed, let alone meeting as they did.

Peter's ribbon room came to her mind. The threads being woven. How time and the Gods had backup plan after backup plan for the important things. How the weave willed and wove every choice into the tapestry of life without missing a single knot.

If she had not just proclaimed her love for Seth publicly, she might have needed a moment to reevaluate her future and discover if this was actually her choice, or fate. But then she had Zeke in front of her. He had chosen to NOT do what the Master wished, and his life was happy and healthy.

At that moment, a quiet presence brought a picture and a feeling to her mind. The image was of Westley and Esther. The feeling was, "Fear not. I will have these instead if you choose to let this go."

The idea startled Miriam. What were they going to do? Why did the Master need them? Her eyes must have told Zeke what was happening inside her. He hugged her and whispered into her ear, "I did not choose it, and though I love my life, it has been my biggest regret. That is all I can tell you."

His whisper was so quiet. So soft, she was certain only she heard him. Her mind went back to her mother and her tears. They both regretted it.

He pulled away from her. And she nodded at him and smiled a small smile.

"Miriam, are you ready?" Seth said, and when she turned, she saw her love.

That was all it took. Fears, trepidation, and doubts were erased. She went to him. He was so handsome in his black slacks and white tunic, his hair pulled back into a smooth ponytail at the base of his neck.

She folded into his arms and kissed where his jaw met his ear, then whispered, "I can't wait."

CHAPTER 59

Seth

When he, Miriam, and his family arrived at the Miller house, he saw the surprise and relief on their faces.

"We've been waiting forever for you," Esther complained.

He squeezed the hand of his wife-to-be and smiled. They already knew. But Miriam looked uncertainly at her father.

Hirum was in his Sunday best, waiting in his living room with those who had survived the Jones attack. He said, "What, did you expect it to be a surprise? We have two people who can tell the future in this house." The man looked affectionately at him but then gave his fourteen-year-old son a raised eyebrow.

Esther spoke up. "Go, Miriam, put on your dress." She instantly had tears in her eyes. "Mama and Aunt Sarah would have loved to see you in it, but they will love that you will use it to get married in."

Miriam looked at Seth, squeezed his hand, and left the room.

Seth smiled at everyone and said, "Well, that was about as easy as I could have hoped."

Hirum Miller approached Seth and cleared his throat. "I only have three daughters left." His eyes welled up with tears, "And tonight, I lose two of them."

Seth took the man by the upper arm. "I am so sorry for your loss, Hirum. If I could have..."

"It is not your fault. But this has made me think a lot about all those memories Miriam took, and how she put them into the tree." He wiped at his eyes and nose. "Have you seen anything about that?"

Seth shook his head. "I haven't. But I am sure I will. It can't have happened for no reason."

"So, did you do what you needed to in the Garden?" Hirum asked.

"Yes, and you will never believe it. Miriam used all those memories we've gathered to make four very interesting fruits that I attached to the other tree in the Garden."

Peter piped up. "Yep, that makes sense. They were the consummate knowledge of good and evil. I felt every single one of them."

Hirum nodded. "But why would the tree need new fruit?" He rubbed at his jaw. "Does that mean we are going to be starting over?" His eyes went wide as he said his thoughts out loud. "Who will be the new Adam and Eve, and what will the Master do with the rest of us?"

Westley spoke up in the way he did. "And then when the end comes, the Lord of Hosts will destroy all the wicked of the Earth, and the righteous will be translated, and then will they live in peace for a thousand years with none to molest or make afraid."

Seth smiled and turned to Hirum. "Well, I guess that answers that." He nodded, then asked, "What is happening with the wind users? How is the ash interference going? I can help as soon as we are done here."

"Won't you be busy once you're done getting married?" Peter asked with a wicked grin, but then must have realized the full implication of what he'd said and dry-heaved. "Never mind. I don't want to know, but can I add 'ew, gross.'"

Hirum's eye fell upon Seth in a narrowed, fatherly manner that scared the socks off Seth.

He shook his head. "No, no, no, that is not what this is about. It is about making covenants. I don't know why, but that is what the Master said. He gave strict instruction that THAT was not to take place." He found he was holding his hands placatingly and relaxed them back at his sides.

Hirum's forehead wrinkled in a concerted manner, but Westley spoke up. "The covenants are incredibly important, yes, and we need to have them in place, but I have not gotten that instruction. Does it hold for Esther and me as well?" And Seth gave the man credit because there was no disappointment in his face or tone. It was only a need, a primal desire to do what was right and good. He was fortunate to have such a man as a partner to start a new world.

"Honestly, I have no idea. But if you haven't received direct instruction on the matter, I would assume you're good."

Now Hirum's fatherly narrowing of eyes was directed at Westley. The man smiled and said, "I leave all that in your daughter's hands, sir. I have no expectations."

The man grunted and crossed his arms.

Seth decided to change the subject. "So, how are all the new tent people settling in?"

Westley gave him a relieved smile. "They are doing well. Getting rested up for the big day tomorrow."

Hirum looked at him. "The big day? Do you really think the army is going to attack us? Why would they do that?"

"It is that time in history, Hirum. I think the Guardians will be just as involved in the fight as we are."

Seth felt himself get taken away in a vision. Before him, he saw the armies of the world, a conglomerate of every country. Millions of men and women. He saw them approach the tent city. Those inside the tent city stood in a line, hand in hand, unified. He saw a glowing sort of power binding their hearts together. Then the army fired its first volley. And out of the mist surrounding the field before them, a hundred Cherubim rose, their swords of fire, of water, and of earth cut the bullets out of the air. More came, and they all were stopped. Then at a signal, the mighty warriors called Cherubim moved as one toward the armies of the world. The ground shook, the earth opened, fire rained from the sky, lightning crashed, and the armies of the world disappeared in a ball of fire and Cherubim swords.

Seth once again had the feeling of having his breath stolen from him. Hirum was before him. He met the man's eyes, but something else had happened. Westley and Peter were both touching him.

His eyes went from one to the next. "Did you see that?"

They both said in unison, "In the way we see things."

Hirum blinked at Westley and then at Seth. "Well, I think Westley's foretelling made it pretty clear. Your God will do what he said he would always do, Westley, and fight your battle for you."

"Except he is going to use our dead mothers and siblings. He's turned them into Cherubim to do it." Peter added.

A silence filled the room as each man considered what they now understood would happen tomorrow.

It was incredible. Seth shook his head and looked at Westley. Finally, he broke the silence. "What great faith your people have."

"Yes!" Westley stated flatly and smiled.

At that point, a door down the hall opened, and Esther appeared. She had changed her hair; a circle of flowers was in it now. She looked lovely and so much like a mixture of Luanne and Miriam; Seth could not help but admire her for the absolute beauty she was.

Then Miriam appeared. She wore an incredible dress, bright aqua. It accentuated her pale peach skin and white-blonde hair, now intricately braided over her shoulder. She, too, had a wreath of flowers around her head. She looked stunning. Breathtaking.

Seth went to her. He couldn't help it. He pulled her to him and looked into her eyes. He whispered, "Oh my gosh, you are gorgeous."

She laughed and gave him a very chaste peck on the lips. "Can we please go get married? I've waited forever for this."

He smiled at her and turned to face the room, where he noticed that all eyes were on him and Miriam.

Her father moved to his daughter. "Are you finished?" he asked with a raised brow at Seth.

Seth had enough sense to look embarrassed and move out of the way. It was time for his mother, sisters, and father to gush over how pretty she looked. He admitted he'd forgotten his family was even in the room since they had stayed so silent. When he looked over at his dad, there were tears in his eyes. Seth went to him. "What is it?"

The man sniffed and wiped at his face. "I'm sorry. This is not me." He took a deep breath and patted Seth on the shoulder. "I am just really proud of you, son. I've really tried hard to stay out of the way, and so I haven't really seen you in action, and let me tell you, that was impressive."

"Thanks, Dad," Seth answered awkwardly. "I don't really have much to do with it. It's all the Master."

"I can see that, but you are a willing vessel, which is just as important as the magic itself. Believe me, I know."

Seth nodded.

IT WAS NEARLY DAWN. The sun crept above the horizon, wispy clouds refracting light and color. Seth peered out a second-story window in the first house. The place had changed. It was completely set up now with beds and dressers. Many of the tent city leadership were stationed there. Seth had Miriam's hand in his and felt a little jittery as they and their families entered the building. It was surreal since this was the first building he'd entered when arriving in Edenia. If he'd only known then what he knew now.

They were met by Noah, who smiled broadly at them. "We have been waiting for you." His deep voice rumbled. "We are all gathered in this room." He motioned to Seth's left.

Seth's mind caught the words 'we are all,' and he wondered who all was. In the room, gathered in a circle, were a few faces he recognized: Mo and Abe and four others he'd never met before. All of them were prominent men with strong jaws and clean-shaven faces, piercing eyes, and shoulders like oxen. They smiled as one, and while everyone piled in the door, Seth couldn't help but feel dazed by the men before him. There was a feeling they gave off. They had presence.

Miriam leaned over and whispered, "This room feels like the Garden."

And she was right. The feeling here was the same as in the presence of the Master. A peaceful excitement.

She whispered again, "Who do you suppose they are?"

"I have no idea," Seth whispered back. "But I'm getting the chills just standing here."

Once his and Miriam's families were settled in their seats, Noah came forward. "Welcome. We are so glad you are here. If the two of you will sit there." He pointed to the middle of the room and two chairs.

Miriam led the way. Once they were seated, the seven men gathered around them.

"Seth, Miriam, we are gathered to individually give you a gift before you are covenanted one to another. Gifts that shall play a special role in your future and the future of your Earth. We will do so quickly."

A man with green eyes, as green as Esther's, and fabulously thick chestnut brown hair stepped forward. "I will place my hands on you during the blessing," he said in a deep baritone, and raised his eyebrows in question.

Miriam answered, "Yes, Father, please proceed."

He did smile at her in a fatherly way, and she bowed her head submissively. Seth examined the man before him and wondered at the word Father. He speculated as the man placed one hand on Miriam's head and one hand on Seth's.

Those in the circle tightened around them, and Seth saw them all touch the man touching him. The words he spoke were not in a language Seth understood, so it felt strange for these words to be a gift of some sort.

The pattern was repeated. Each man in the circle stepped forth and placed hands on heads, then spoke in a way they did not understand.

When all was finished. They silently stood back. Seth looked up at the men and noticed they were all looking toward the closed door, waiting in silence, and there was a hole in their circle. A spot for another person.

Seth had about a million questions as the room filled with light.

Between one blink and the next, a man and a woman appeared standing in front of the closed doors. Both beings made the light and countenance of the Cherubim look dull and fragile.

They wore light, flowing robes of no particular color, perhaps white. They had skin akin to the robes, light and undistinguishable. The room was filled with energy and tremendous peace.

The beautiful woman who had appeared out of nowhere stepped forward and spoke, her face filled with a smile. "Miriam, Seth, I am so happy to be with you. I am the Mother of All Living, and this is my Son, Manuel. We will be the ones to marry you if that is all right."

Seth did not know who these people were or if they were people, but he knew it was an honor to have them marry him. Miriam squeezed his hand, but he did not look at her. He could not take his eyes off the glowing beings before him. He nodded to them almost as an afterthought.

They both smiled and came forward through the hole in the circle, which closed after them.

They took Miriam and Seth by the hands and held hands themselves, forming a circle within a circle.

"Repeat the words of the covenant after me." The man said in a voice that sounded like the rushing of rivers.

They did. Each and every word, they repeated. Finally, he said, "You are now sealed up unto each other and to the Mother and to Me with all the gifts and covenants to begin the plan of life once more."

"Do you know what we mean by this?" the man who did not have a solid form asked.

Seth knew. He knew Miriam and he were destined for a new world, but Miriam did not know, so he kept silent and waited for Miriam.

"No. I'm afraid I do not," Miriam stated politely.

The woman of light took her hand and looked into her eyes. Her eyes were like the swirling of the universe, the agelessness of a black hole. "Vessel, I will tell you what must be known. Soon this Earth will have done its part. Soon the Father God and the Creator God, my other son Jehovah, will come and finish the journey of the mortals here on Earth. Those mortals who have proven worthy will move on to their next estate. This is how the Father has set up his test. But with its conclusion, the cycle must start again, for this is the work of the Gods. Only this time, it will be my turn to determine the rules and create the world. Mine and this son, this Creator God, Manuel. The Father and I have organized spirits of a most elegant nature, and we have created a world for them to live out the new cycle. There the spirits of God will take on flesh and be tested. Just as you see done here."

Miriam looked struck, and though Seth had seen this all in his vision, listening to it explained out of the mouth of this Goddess, well, it rocked his world.

All Miriam said in her awed state was "Another world? Like this one?"

Manuel laughed a lovely sound of pure joy. "No, it is not exactly like this world, for the Mother and I have made a world far more magical than the Father would ever permit here. Her worlds are full of color and enchantment and oddities while the Father's creations consist of order and symmetry and science."

Seth knew exactly what this meant. The world had dragons, skin filled with gold, elves, and scenery akin to wonderland.

Miriam swallowed. "That sounds very interesting and enticing. But, if you don't mind me asking, what does it have to do with me?"

The Goddess took Miriam by the chin in a gentle but earnest way. "Miriam, you and your husband have been chosen to act in a sacred role as the mortal father and mother of my new world. I will remake your bodies only the slightest bit so you will be compatible with the magic there, and I will also give you the ability to procreate. However, there is a cost; by consuming the fruit you and your husband formed on the Tree of Knowledge of Good and Evil, you will forget all that has happened on this planet. In exchange, that fruit will give you the specific knowledge needed to live on my new planet. And then..." But the Goddess cut off as she kept her eyes on Miriam.

Miriam's hand squeezed him, and he turned to see the blood drain from her face. Seth was startled by this revelation, but Miriam looked like she was about to pass out.

She spoke. "I won't remember anything?" Miriam shook her head at this idea, and her eyebrows knotted with sadness and confusion.

The Mother spoke, and her words surprised him. "I have made a provision, an alternate plan if you choose not to go, but you and Seth are the exact right spirits needed for this task. I value passion and chaos, and drama. The two of you have that in abundance."

"Passion, chaos, drama?" Miriam questioned. "That sounds like the opposite of me."

"I also appreciate obedience, diligence, and loyalty. It probably is a world more tailored to those with a Seth-like disposition, but as he was a chaotic force for you here, you will be a force of peace for him there. Trust me. It works out."

Miriam turned to him after a long look at her papa, who sat with his eyes wide and his mouth agape. "Seth, what do you think of all this?"

Seth licked his lips and smiled at her. "I don't want to answer," he said slowly, and her hand on his tightened. Her eyes pleaded with him to advise her. "I mean, I have an unfair advantage and don't want to sway you."

She cocked her head at him and said, "You saw a vision, didn't you?"

He rubbed his nose and looked at the mother before turning back to her. "I did."

The wheels in her head turned quickly. He saw the emotions of each choice flit across her face.

Finally, Miriam's eyes met the Mother. "Trust you," she repeated. "All right. I will trust you."

The Goddess smiled. "So you freely choose to go and do as I have explained?"

"I will," they both said in unison, and Seth felt the words bind him.

The Mother spoke again. "Glory be." And she smiled to all in the room. Turning back to them, she finished. "Go to the Tree. Wait there, and all will be accomplished, as I have said. Heed me, though, once you have been changed, stay in the Garden until you feel confident with your new body. Then, and only then, must you eat of the fruit of the Tree of Knowledge, for once you do, you will become mortal, without magic, until you can find the source and submit to its dictates." Her voice rose with joy and strength. "Then you will go forth, be fruitful, multiply, and fill the world with sons and daughters. Love one another, serve one another, and have peace between you. This is my commandment and my blessing." The woman of light, the Mother, gave them both a smile so penetrating Seth felt it to his ankles.

In the next moment, they were gone. The light, the warmth, and the utter exuberance of being in their presence left Seth feeling tired and groggy. They all stayed silent for several minutes, taking in the feelings there were left behind.

Soon though, Noah broke the silence. "Westley, Esther, you are next."

⸸

WHEN THE MOTHER returned to issue the same invitation and give the same instruction to Esther and Westley (with a few caveats about how they wouldn't be human but elven), Miriam squeezed his hand. When he looked at her, she mouthed *I love you* to him, and Seth felt as if his heart were about to burst open. He reached his other hand over to cup her cheek, then brought their clasped hands to his lips. "I love you too," he whispered after kissing her knuckles.

CHAPTER 60

When they left the first house, they headed straight to the Garden in obedience to the command of the Mother. However, they knew everyone around them was preparing for the arrival of the armies of the world. Miriam had given each of her family members the tightest hug. She whispered her love before she allowed Seth to pull her away.

Seth, Westley, Esther, and Miriam quickly traversed the Garden wood and entered Eden. What they found there was nothing short of miraculous.

The Tree of Life was ablaze, and it looked like firecrackers were going off inside its branches. But that was not all. The Garden was full of Cherubim pairs made from Guardian families.

Seth said, "Find your mother before she has to go. She is here." Miriam's eyes flew to his, her face asking the question her mouth could not. But as she turned, she saw them. The Being composed of five separated and raced to Miriam and Esther with joy and excitement on their ageless Cherubim faces.

Miriam felt her heart burst with love for her beautiful mother, sister, and brother. Her Aunt Sarah and Uncle Jai. Hannah and her brood. Grandpa and Grandma. The whole Miller clan that had been so harshly separated gathered around Esther and Miriam, who both laughed and cried.

"Mother, I miss you. I love you."

"I'm so proud of you," said her mother and aunt and grandmother.

Miriam felt a tug on her arm, and Josie and Todd were there.

They, too, got hugs and fond farewells. Miriam felt as if her whole body were on fire. The love and the completeness of having everyone here, for her to say goodbye, was a precious gift.

So when a sudden change happened among the Cherubim and a tremendous horn blew, Miriam did not begrudge the separation that had to happen. With a final touch to her mother and a whispered "I will miss you," the Cherubim were gone.

Miriam melted and cried before Seth on the garden floor as her family left, but they were mostly happy tears.

CHAPTER 61

Peter stood with his father and his sister Eve. They held one another's hands. The hilltop between Edenia and the tent city was bright as noonday, the ash having been swept away for now by a blustering, blizzard-like northern wind. The tiny particles floating in the air far above the shield the wind users had created did nothing to stop the sun.

Peter turned a 360-degree circle as he saw the Saints standing triple-deep in a line surrounding this hill, the tent city, and Edenia. Not a hole, not a hiccup.

The armies of the world were no more than fifty feet before them. They, too, surrounded the area; however, the ranks they made were many, many more than three deep. Ash fell on the armies, hindering their view.

The colorful armies were masked with great bug-like things that covered their mouths, noses, and eyes, and were armed to the teeth. Peter could tell they were disturbed, still, by what lay before them.

Weaponless men, women, and children all held hands—just as Seth had told them to do. The fact that they had light radiating from their chests stopped the armies in their tracks.

The two sides stood there, facing one another, waiting.

Peter saw the signal to attack first because he was so high up. The men at the front of the line pulled their long-range weapons from their backs and held them at the ready.

A colossal roar sounded when the bullets were let loose, and Peter grabbed at his father's hand, excited to see what he knew would happen next.

Peter waited. Then out of the mist, Peter watched the most epic, most incredible thing he'd ever seen. Like angels of vengeance, Cherubim rose from out of the fog and ground and stood between the armies and the tent people. With barely a movement of their great swords, they cut the bullets from the air. The Beings then separated, quadrupling their numbers, and paused for the men to counter.

There was a cry from the other side, and several cowardly men threw their weapons down and ran. Those men got shot in the back by their own commanders.

Then the earth shook. It opened, swallowing whole groups of soldiers. Fire fell from heaven, and lightning rained down on the armies of the world. The wind rose (at least outside the barrier) and spread the fire, feeding it and helping it expand. And through it all, the Cherubim, with their mighty swords, swished in and out of the ranks of men, taking heads from shoulders with the speed of a wind Nature, the strength of an earth Nature and the power of a rock Nature.

Peter wished it would have lasted longer. It was seriously the most extraordinary thing he'd ever seen; however, within thirty minutes, the armies with their millions were soundly beaten. All were dead or dying. Not one stood to fight.

Then the fire really rained down from the swords, from the Cherubim, and from heaven. Within moments, all the land surrounding Edenia was aflame—a rushing, consuming, unstoppable wall of heat and destruction.

Peter smiled to himself; fire Nature always got the last word.

As the world burned, he saw the Cherubim. Finished with their duty, they approached the line of tent people. Peter didn't know how he saw her, but he did.

With a cry, the cry of a child, Peter yelled, "Mama!"

Her head whipped toward him, and within the space of a heartbeat, she stood on the hill. Garren, Joseph, Simeon, and Dorothea were with her. The younger children completely surprised him with how they looked like adults. But he could still see them for who they were.

They fell together in a pile of hugs and kisses, freer with their affection than they had ever dared to be in real life.

But that was when Peter had to revive his idea of seeing the most remarkable thing in the world during that fight because as he looked up, he saw a man in the clouds.

A man made of light. A man in a red robe. A man so beautifully awesome, Peter felt down to his toes the power of him, even from a great distance. Peter fell to his knees, his eyes upward. Though this world and its inhabitants—many of them—had ended this day, Peter knew completely that this Earth would also get a new beginning on this day.

CHAPTER 62

Seth

After Miriam cried her eyes out, Seth took her into his arms and held her. They sat under the Tree of Life, Seth mentioned, which now looked relatively barren.

Miriam looked up and answered, "Yes, it is. That is so strange. I have never seen it empty. Do you think the fruit will grow back?"

"I'm sure it will. That is what trees do, isn't it?"

She smiled. "I suppose so." A thought must have occurred to her because her eyebrows rose, wrinkling her forehead. "What of the Travelers soul slivers? I still have them inside me. And what of yours?" She sat up.

Seth pondered on it, but nothing came.

Suddenly the Cherubim gathered and formed. They spoke, "It is time."

Miriam rose quickly, "But Master, what of the Travelers' soul slivers? I should not take them with me. And what of Seth's?"

"We have spoken to the Travelers. They are here; they will tell you."

Miriam looked up as all twenty-two of her Travelers entered the Garden. They approached her and Seth, Gerald at the front.

"Well, little lady, I hear you are off on a grand adventure."

Seth watched as the men smiled at Miriam. They loved her. They protected her well.

"Yes, I guess I am. I think I know how to give your soul slivers back. When I made that fruit"—she pointed to the yellow apple-shaped fruit on the Tree of Knowledge—"I did it differently. So, I think I can do it."

"Look, Miriam, the Master explained it all to us, and we all agreed we want you to take the soul pieces with you as a gift. With the new magic there, you will be able to use them as a shield and a protection."

The Cherubim grunted at him.

Gerald turned to him. "Calm down. I'm not going to say anything else."

Seth asked, "Won't that be agony for you? Feeling and knowing which direction she is but never being able to find her?"

The Cherubim spoke, "You will be so far away the connection will be completely undetectable."

"We want you to have them. Even if we can't feel it, you will know we are with you, protecting you," Gerald said, and took her hand.

She looked around at the faces before her with Seth. He saw both sadness and hope.

Gerald hugged her and said, "You are like my own daughter. I love ya, kid. Be careful."

After every last one of the Travelers hugged Miriam and patted Seth on the back, they filed out of Eden.

It was just the four of them now with the Cherubim. "It is time to go, humans. Are you ready?"

But they did not wait for their response. The ground beneath them shook. Miriam grabbed Seth, and he steadied her by holding onto the ground with his earth Nature.

And then, as suddenly as a blink, they were in the air. They and the entire Garden of Eden.

As they rose up and up, the ground beneath them became translucent. Seth gaped as he watched the earth sink, and the space between himself and the earth widened.

Esther shrieked and buried her face in Westley's chest. Miriam looked on, her reaction clearly amazed fascination.

He put his arms around her waist and leaned over her shoulder to watch the ascent together.

However, the Cherubim were suddenly in their heads again. "We did not take this route so that you can enjoy the ride only. Look." And they pointed.

Seth turned his head and saw a man of glory in the clouds, descending as they ascended. He wore a red robe and smiled at them as they crossed paths in the air.

Westley ran to the edge of the Garden, fell to his knees, and cried out something inaudible to the man Seth now knew was Jehovah, the son the Mother Goddess had spoken of. He and Miriam's knees hit the ground simultaneously, and Seth felt tears of joy and gratitude in his eyes. This God was the sacrifice and savior of this world Seth was leaving behind.

The moment was short, but it was profound.

CHAPTER 63

Miriam

After seeing Jehovah, her Master's Master, they breached the Earth's atmosphere, which seemed like a perfect place for the silence and reverence that fell upon the group. But also there was a distant giddiness floating in her middle. How was this happening to her?

All she'd seen overwhelmed her, including the savior of her birth world, a Goddess, a creator God, and now space. But the darkness of space and the light from the sun were so much in contrast that her soul tingled with awe, and she found herself relaxing against Seth's chest, just existing in deep silence.

The Cherubim's voice entered their minds again. "If you are uninterested in moving between the stars, I will get us to our destination immediately."

Seth spoke. "I think we are all interested; however, we just saw a God. And not just any God, the one that created the only Earth we've ever known, the one who facilitated our test on that Earth, and the one who paid for our sins while there. So, maybe give us a moment to take that in."

The Cherubim nodded, but they also smiled as if, with Seth's statement, all was right in the universe.

Seth and Miriam stood together as they passed the moon, Mars, and other planets. Each was massive and colorful and simply unreal.

As they entered the great expanse of space, she spoke. "Are we really going to a new planet?" She huffed an excited sort of laugh. "I mean, I'm not stupid. Seriously, in the space of an hour, think of all we've done. I'm feeling like perhaps my brain is just now catching up."

Seth nodded, "No, I get it." He wrapped his arms around her, warm and soft and perfect. "It has been a very crazy two weeks. But of all of it, not including seeing Gods, of course, because that was just...wow." He laughed and shook his head in amazement. "Besides that, I am most happy that we will be together forever."

Miriam pulled her hand off his chest and smoothed down a lock of his hair. "I certainly am interested in forever, but at this point, I will take five minutes to ourselves."

Seth sighed. "We haven't gotten very much alone time, have we?"

"No. But I get the feeling that is about to be remedied." She smiled and slid her hand around his neck. The contact gave her chills up and down her body. She gave him a half grin and brushed a kiss on his lips. "You are so beautiful, Seth; I..." She licked her lips and looked at him through her eyelashes. "I am seriously the luckiest girl alive."

"You're about to be the only girl alive." Seth laughed.

"No. What about Esther?"

"She won't be a girl anymore. She will be an elf, apparently."

"That is so weird. Though I guess we won't think it's weird for long," she said, thinking of what possible changes could happen to her sister. After taking a rather long look at Esther, she remembered that she couldn't keep this memory. Soon, she would not know their kinship ever existed, and perhaps it wouldn't exist anymore. Literally, if Esther was going to be a different species. The shock of that befuddled her.

She turned her gaze back to her husband. "How much do you know about where we are going? And how long have you known?"

He pulled her tight and pressed three kisses to her cheek before answering. "Do you remember when I had that really long vision after you forgave me?"

She nodded.

"Well, I've known since then. And I've only seen it. I don't really know about the things we will face there."

"I thought you said you saw a heart."

Seth smiled. "I did. That is what we talked about in the vision. You told me what I needed to say to make you comfortable."

"Really?" she said, a surprised smile on her face.

"Yes, really."

"That twists my brain in knots. Like the chicken and the egg. Which is first?"

Seth nodded and looked down at Jupiter as it got smaller and smaller.

"We have forever," she whispered, repeating it to him.

"Yes. Forever."

"This isn't going to be easy. Starting a new world, living like savages, forgetting everything we've ever known."

"No, it's not, but as the old saying goes, nothing worth having comes easy."

She turned to him and tucked herself into his embrace. The hug was tight, and he rubbed her back, feeling every mountain and valley of her spine. When he pulled away what seemed like a millennium later, it was only because he couldn't stand to have her so close for so long without kissing her. So, he leaned down. Her soft lips brushed and molded against his own, and every nerve in his body became happier and happier by the second. Forever, he thought, and smiled.

EPILOGUE

Peter stood in front of the mirror of his bathroom. He straightened the robe covering his shoulders and ran a hand through his hair. Sighing. He ducked through the bathroom door. He couldn't wait to move into his own house, where the doorways were taller.

Ducking again to make it through the front door, he almost managed to get his foot crunched by Butch. No more Butch after today, except for when he came home for Sunday brunch.

He made his way down the porch, out onto the road, and quickly continued toward the new, huge white structure that was now the center of Edenia. The marble on the outside sparkled, and the spires seemed to reach into the clouds.

Several people exited their homes and walked with him, including Gerald, his wife, Mazie, and their two children. Gerald greeted him with a nod. "Li'l Boss, you are looking quite dapper today."

"It's a good day," Peter answered. And he scooped up Giselle in an arm and tickled her under her chin.

"It's funny Daddy calls you Li'l Boss; you are as big as him," the cherubic little girl said in her serious way.

"That is funny, isn't it?" Peter answered and gave her a kiss on her plump little cheek. "Your daddy does a lot of funny things, though, so we shouldn't be surprised."

Gerald shook his head and reached for his daughter. "Come here, munchkin. Your shoes will muss Peter's robes." He cuddled her in close. "Plus, we can't have Li'l Boss tainting your ideas of my charm with his foul tongue."

"What's a foul tongue mean?" she asked and pulled on Gerald's beard.

Peter laughed. "Now that is an appropriate question for your pa if ever I heard one."

Gerald rolled his eyes.

They walked in silence for a few steps.

Then Peter asked, "Any word?"

Gerald shook his head disappointedly. "I am about to give up."

"Why don't you just ask Him?"

"He wants us to do things on our own."

"Yes, but there is a limit, Gerald. Five years of searching for your kids is long enough; you won't even recognize them if you find them. Just ask. He will be here today. I know He will tell you."

Gerald nodded that he would ask as they turned onto the Edenia Road.

There was a crowd waiting outside the building. His eyes saw his mother and father and all his family, except Miriam and Esther, but there was one particular person he was searching for.

Then his eyes found her. A girl of surpassing beauty and purity, of goodness and faithfulness. Her bright blue-green eyes found him simultaneously, and her luscious mouth curved into a smile. The action brightened her entire face. She was all in white, just as he was, but with a crown of spring petals adorning her head. A twin sister—of almost equal beauty but also a fierceness Peter admired—stood next to his bride. Abigail wore pink robes, her own husband at her side, yet she clung to her sister in a way that displayed her love and relinquishing on this day of new covenants.

Peter approached and took his bride by the hand. "Lillian," he whispered into the space between them. He gave her a soft kiss on the mouth. "You look devastating."

She smiled at him. "I like you in white as well."

Her eyes captured him, and he did not answer.

Someone cleared their throat. It was his father. "Would you like to go in, son?" The man's eyebrows rose, his pale blue eyes all the more startling now that his physical form was made out of light and immortality.

His mother, who was also a Being of light, touched his cheek. "Peter, you look so handsome. Just exactly like your Papa thirty-five years ago."

"Thank you, Mother," Peter said, taking her hand and bringing it to his lips. He looked back to his bride and said, "Well, why are you all standing around? Let's get inside. It's time I make this woman mine."

⁂

AND THEY LIVED HAPPILY FOREVER after.

ABOUT THE AUTHOR

Theresa has been writing for fifteen years and has more story ideas than she could possibly write and still have a life. She is an avid audible 'reader', boardgame lover, Zelda player, book collector, adventure chaser, and history 'studier', besides being a mother of three, a musician and a homeschooler. Also in her life are, a white schmorkie named Percy Jackson, a hot husband named Andy and many many supportive and amazing friends. She lives on the Olympic Peninsula but is an Idaho girl at heart.

This has been an
Immortal Production